૰

KIM BALDWIN

"Her...crisply written action scenes, juxtaposition of plotlines, and smart dialogue make this a story the reader will absolutely enjoy and long remember." – **Arlene Germain**, book reviewer for the *Lambda Book Report* and the *Midwest Book Review*

૰

ROSE BEECHAM

"...a mystery writer with a delightful sense of humor, as well as an eye for an interesting array of characters..." – *MegaScene*

"...her characters seem fully capable of walking away from the particulars of whodunit and engaging the reader in other aspects of their lives." – *Lambda Book Report*

"...creates believable characters in compelling situations, with enough humor to provide effective counterpoint to the work of detecting." – *Bay Area Reporter*

૰

JANE FLETCHER

"...a natural gift for rich storytelling and world-building...one of the best fantasy writers at work today." – **Jean Stewart**, author of the *Isis* series

૰

RADCLYfFE

"Powerful characters, engrossing plot, and intelligent writing..." – **Cameron Abbott,** author of *To the Edge* and *An Inexpressible State of Grace*

"...well-honed storytelling skills...solid prose and sure-handedness of the narrative..." – **Elizabeth Flynn**, *Lambda Book Report*

"...well-plotted...lovely romance...I couldn't turn the pages fast enough!" – **Ann Bannon**, author of *The Beebo Brinker Chronicles.*

"...a consummate artist in crafting classic romance fiction...her numerous best selling works exemplify the splendor and power of Sapphic passion..." – **Yvette Murray, PhD**, *Reader's Raves*

HONOR GUARDS

by
RADCLYffE

2005

HONOR GUARDS

ISBN 1-933110-01-5

THIS TRADE PAPERBACK ORIGINAL IS PUBLISHED BY
BOLD STROKES BOOKS, INC.,
PHILADELPHIA, PA, USA

FIRST EDITION: SEPTEMBER 2004
SECOND PRINTING: MARCH 2005

CREDITS
EXECUTIVE EDITOR: STACIA SEAMAN
PRODUCTION DESIGN: J. BARRE GREYSTONE
COVER PHOTOS: SHERI AND LINDA CALLAGHAN
COVER DESIGN BY SHERI (GRAPHICARTIST2020@HOTMAIL.COM)

By the Author

<u>Romances</u>

<u>Honor Series</u>

<u>Justice Series</u>

INTRODUCTION

I wrote *Above All, Honor* as an action/romance novel, and as the series has evolved, it has developed into the story of relationships in a world that is dangerous and often deadly. Because much of the story is set in Manhattan and one of the main characters is the daughter of the president of the United States, it seemed integral to the continuing saga to deal with the events of September 11, 2001.

I agonized over the appropriate time to write about this topic in a work of fiction. Certainly, there will never be a time when the horrific events of that day are forgotten or when the anguish of all who lived through it is assuaged. At some point, the events that occur during our lives become part of the history of the world. Whether we experience those events firsthand or via images and other records, the tragedy never lessens, nor do the memories dim. This book is meant to be neither an explanation nor a resolution of events that are beyond comprehension.

The timeline of 9/11 contained in the book is accurate and based upon *Report From Ground Zero* by Dennis Smith (Viking Press, 2002); *Last Man Down* by Richard Piccioto and Daniel Paisner (Berklely Publishing Group, 2002); *Inside 9-11: What Really Happened,* by the reporters, writers, and editors of *Der Spiegel* magazine (St. Martin's Press, 2002); and *One Nation: America Remembers September 11, 2001* by *Life* magazine (Little, Brown, 2001).

This was a difficult book to write, to beta read, and to edit due to the intersecting plotlines and the oftentimes difficult subject matter. I am indebted to a superb group of readers and proofreaders: Athos, Denise, Diane, Eva, JB, Laney, Paula, Robyn, Sue, and Tomboy, and to Stacia Seaman, my excellent editor, for their outstanding work and tireless support.

Sheri's covers always speak for themselves far more eloquently than I can, but once again she has found the perfect visual representation of the story. Thanks also to Linda Callaghan for donating the image of the White House.

Somehow Lee finds a way to be supportive, cheerful, and patient even when I am not (which is especially true at the beginning, middle, and end of a new work). For that and all the possibilities she brings to my life, I am beyond grateful. *Amo te.*

Radclyffe, 2004

Dedication

To the Victims of 9/11

CHAPTER ONE

16 August 2001

The hotelier at the small *pensione* on Rue Seguier looked up from her newspaper as the door opened to admit two strangers. It was well after midnight—not a usual time for new guests to arrive—but she was used to the unusual in St-Germain, the *arrondissement* of Paris long known for its artists, philosophers, trendsetters, and, in recent years, for its tourists. The customs and proclivities of that latter group were often unfathomable, but she had grown used to hiding her rare feelings of surprise or dismay regarding the habits of guests. Nevertheless, this evening, her curiosity was immediately piqued.

Two women in formal evening clothes approached across the expanse of thick carpet. Two far from ordinary women, even for the Left Bank. One was an astonishingly beautiful blond in a shoulder-baring, midnight blue evening dress and matching sequined wrap—very *haute couture*. Her thick, golden hair was caught back at the nape of her neck and her makeup, subtly and expertly applied, merely enhanced the natural beauty of her large, deep blue eyes and upswept cheekbones. Her mouth was full and lush, as if meant for kissing, or laughter. She was laughing at the moment, the fingers of her right hand curled possessively around the arm of her escort.

That woman, too, was captivating, but in an entirely different way. Slightly taller than her blond companion, she wore a fitted evening jacket and black tuxedo trousers. She was dark where the other was light—not just in coloring, but in the undeniable aura of intensity she projected. Jet-black hair curled just over the edge of her collar in the back, while in the front a wild, unruly wave apparently defied taming as it slashed across her forehead. Her eyes, even from across the room, were dark and penetrating. Whereas the blond carried herself with the agility and grace of a dancer, this sharper, leaner woman glided with the muscular ease of a jungle predator. Each, in fact, projected an air of animal vitality and strength, and together, they were an astonishingly attractive couple.

And a couple they most certainly are. The way they move with one rhythm, the way their bodies just barely touch but are so clearly united—oh yes, they're together.

"*Bonsoir.* May I help you?"

"We'd like a room, if you please," United States Secret Service agent Cameron Roberts said in perfect French. She glanced at her companion and smiled. "Something private, with a view."

"I believe I have something for you," the clerk replied with a wisp of a smile. She turned and collected a key from a series of wooden pigeonholes behind her. The service in this small hotel, whose decor spoke of more genteel times, was still handled personally as opposed to by computer. There was an air of intimacy in the small foyer, which was replete with ornate wood furnishings and muted chandeliers. "You will be able to see Notre Dame from your balcony. We can also have breakfast sent up if you ring the front desk in the morning."

Cam glanced at her lover with a raised eyebrow as she withdrew her wallet. "Okay?"

Blair Powell shifted until her hip gently rested against Cam's thigh and placed a palm on her lower back. Although they spent nearly all of their waking hours together, they were rarely free to touch. Now she relished each small contact. "Perfect."

They had never spent the night alone together before—not *truly* alone, when there had been no one outside the door or someone, somewhere, on duty monitoring their location. They had been lovers for more than half a year and had awakened with each other less than half a dozen times. This night, in this tiny *pensione* in this city of lovers, they were for the first time able to simply be lovers.

"Here you are." The clerk handed a key across the counter to Cam, who filled out the short information card that accompanied it. "The second floor."

"Thank you," Cam and Blair said simultaneously before turning away, hand in hand.

Renee Savard was asleep when the knock sounded on her hotel room door. Rolling over carefully, anxious not to injure her still-healing left shoulder, she peered at the bedside clock. 2:12 a.m.

Coming almost instantly awake after years of having been trained to jump from deep sleep into immediate action, the FBI agent rose rapidly and reached for her robe from a nearby chair. She pulled it on carefully. The gunshot wound to her left shoulder was healing well, and although she had been advised to keep the joint at rest as much as possible, she had eschewed the confining support of the immobilizer after the minimum allowable time. Not only was it difficult to dress while wearing it, she felt helpless and vulnerable with only one functioning arm. A little pain was worth being able to defend herself if the need arose.

A few seconds later, she peered through the security view-hole and then, smiling broadly, quickly released the lock and opened the door. "What are you doing here? I thought you had the duty tonight."

Paula Stark stood in the hotel hallway, flushing faintly but unable to hide her pleasure. She was still in the dark jacket and pants she had worn while on duty as the lead Secret Service agent on Blair Powell's team. Her weapon was secured in the hip holster clipped on the right side of her waistband. Shrugging, she extended her hand, offering a small bouquet of red roses and white baby's breath.

"I just happened to be in the neighborhood."

Charmed, Renee leaned a shoulder against the doorjamb and slowly surveyed the dark-haired, muscular young agent, appreciating as always her clear-eyed, wholesome appearance. "I didn't expect to see you for a while. After all, *I'm* on leave, but you're here on assignment."

"Is it okay? I mean...I know it's la—"

"Mmm. It's great." Renee held out her hand for the flowers, which she lifted to her nose, smiling once again. Then she turned aside and gestured to her room. "Come in."

Stark stepped inside the hotel room, her heart fluttering madly. Courtship was something new to her, as was any kind of relationship—and a relationship with a woman hadn't even been on the horizon for her a year ago. But the day that Renee Savard had been assigned to temporary duty on Blair Powell's security team, all that had changed.

In the midst of the manhunt for a deadly stalker who had threatened Blair's life and nearly cost the commander hers, Stark had discovered how very much she wanted this one particular woman. They had come very close to consummating their relationship little more than a week before.

"I can't believe you just volunteered to work another night. What is that—three in a row?" Renee definitely had a threatening look in her eyes as she crossed the living room to stand in front of Stark.

"Two—well, two and a half, I guess, but I didn't volunteer for last night," Stark said quickly in self-defense.

"Getting stood up two nights straight could seriously bruise my ego, you know."

"Well, it's kind of a tricky situation since the commander and Egr—uh, Blair—are trying not to be too obvious about spending time alone together," Stark began seriously. "It's easier if I—"

"Paula, shut up." Then Renee effectively implemented the order by pressing her mouth to Stark's.

Stark's small cry of surprise gave way to a soft moan as Renee's tongue moved gently over her lips, then into her mouth. In surrender, she just closed her eyes and let the warmth and softness of the caress move through her until every cell tingled. When the kiss ended, Stark opened her eyes, amazed to find she couldn't focus. Her head was spinning too much.

"That was awfully nice," she managed, her voice slightly unsteady. The apartment suddenly felt extremely warm, too.

Renee rested her palm against Stark's cheek, then gently swept the dark hair back from her temple with trembling fingers. "Yes, it was. And there's a lot more where that came from."

"There's no quota or anything, is there?" Stark brushed her

lips over the fingertips stroking her face.

"None at all." Renee's voice was husky and low. "In fact, I believe there's an endless supply."

"That's good, because I'm going to want a lot."

"Starting now?"

"What about your sister?" Stark rested both hands on Renee's waist and stepped closer until their thighs touched. She was happy to find that Renee was a bit unsteady, too.

"She's a cop—seven to seven. And she won't bother us if we're...asleep...when she comes in."

"Yeah—now would be good, then." Stark was a little worried that her legs weren't going to move if they waited much longer, because they were beginning to shake all on their own.

"Sure?" There was nothing teasing in Renee's tone now, only a gentle question, full of patience and tenderness and sweet longing.

"I want to make love with you so much," Stark confessed, her body vibrating with urgency. "I've wanted to touch you for what feels like forever."

Renee drew in a sharp breath. "I can't wait."

Stark slipped one arm around her waist. Just before she kissed her, she whispered, "Then let's not."

In the bedroom, Renee reached down to unbuckle the strap securing her arm across her chest. Her hand was shaking.

"Need help?" Stark's throat was dry, her voice husky.

Smiling shyly, Renee nodded. "I think so."

Stark stepped closer and carefully began to remove the restraining support. "Is this safe to do?"

"Which part?"

There was something in Renee's tone that brought Stark's head up sharply. She searched the depths of Renee's blue eyes. "Is there something wrong?"

"I'm nervous," Renee confessed. "I...I don't know why."

"Second thoughts?" Stark tried to keep her voice steady. Nervous? Try terrified.

"You're special," Renee whispered, her fingers feather-light on Stark's face. "I want...oh God...this will sound silly. I almost want to wait until we know where this is going."

"You mean besides bed?"

Renee nodded wordlessly once more.

"It doesn't sound silly." Touched, and in some ways relieved, Stark lightly clasped Renee's waist. Her body was ready, and she thought her heart was, too. But there would only ever be one first time for them. "It sounds...really nice." She took a shuddering breath. "I don't mind waiting."

"You don't?"

Stark grinned weakly. "Well, yeah...I mind*...but I don't mind. You know?"*

"Mmm." Renee kissed her lingeringly. "Yeah. I know."

Even though they'd *both* pulled back, Stark worried that Renee would change her mind altogether about being with her. Still, she wanted their lovemaking to be about more than just the physical pleasure of it. She'd experienced that wild thrill for a few frantic hours one night with Blair Powell, and as wonderful and memorable as that encounter had been, she hoped for much more with Renee Savard. Although she didn't know exactly what kind of sign she was waiting for, she sensed that waiting was the right thing to do. And for Paula Stark, doing the right thing was everything. So—she'd take it slow even if it meant they never got past the kissing stage. *And I die from lack of oxygen and terminally swollen body parts.*

"You still haven't told me what you're doing here," Renee said as she picked up one of the plastic hotel glasses and started toward the bathroom for water.

"The commander gave us the rest of the shift off," Stark replied as she followed into the adjoining room. "I know it's late, but it's so beautiful outside, and I thought...maybe you'd like to go for a walk."

"A walk?" Renee turned, tilting her head, an odd expression on her face. "You show up in the middle of the night and ask me if I want to take a *walk?*"

Uncertain, but determined to push ahead, Stark nodded solemnly. "I guess I probably should have called—"

Quickly, Renee closed the distance between them and put her arms around Stark's neck, stopping her next words with a kiss.

After she'd indulged herself in the softness of Stark's mouth and assuaged some of the hunger that always rose when she imagined how Stark's powerful body would feel against hers, she lifted her mouth away and laughed softly. "I think it's wonderful. Let me get dressed."

"How's your arm?" Stark inquired when she could catch her breath. It always took her off guard when Renee kissed her—or touched her in any way, for that matter. She spent a large part of every day thinking about touching her and being touched in return.

"Better."

"Need any help?" Stark asked, disingenuously.

Renee raised a brow. "Are you trustworthy?"

"Ah..." Stark shrugged and grinned. "On my better days. Sort of."

"Are you all right?" Renee asked softly, watching Paula's expression turn inward. She stroked her fingers down the broad cheek to the sturdy jaw and then across the surprisingly full lower lip. "You're so beautiful."

Stark blushed hotly and ducked her head. "No," she said, her voice husky, "you're beautiful. I'm just...serviceable."

"Serviceable, hmm?" Renee laughed, drawing her hand down the center of Stark's chest, indulging herself in the urge to touch her. "We'll see about that eventually, won't we?"

Stark lifted her eyes to Renee's and saw the same wanting there that she knew must be in her own. "I guess we will. Eventually."

Renee backed away, because to do anything else would have meant going forward. There'd been other women, but nothing serious for a long time, and the recent flings had rarely been anything other than brief mutual diversions. First the FBI Academy and then the demands of building a career within the competitive, old-boy network of the Bureau had consumed not only all her time, but also all her energy. She hadn't realized how deeply she had longed for some human connection, beyond just the physical, until Paula had come along with her unvarnished honesty and tender compassion. Now, as much as she ached to have Paula in her arms, in her bed, she wanted to wait until she was sure it would be more than another momentary respite from loneliness. For as tortuous as delaying sometimes was, she treasured the sweet anticipation.

"Sit down," Renee said softly. "I'll be ready in five minutes."

Obediently, Stark pulled out one of the small chairs by the tiny table that occupied the space in front of the windows.

"So Egret is all tucked in for the night then?" Renee asked casually as she pulled jeans and a clean blouse from her closet. Egret was Blair Powell's code name and the one most of the agents used when referring to her.

"Uh-huh." Stark hesitated, still reluctant to discuss her protectee, even with the woman who was as much a part of the team as any of the Secret Service agents who guarded Blair on a daily basis. Renee had nearly been killed thwarting a plan to kill the president's daughter. Stark's silence wasn't a matter of distrust, merely one of long habit.

"Paula?" Renee glanced up as she carefully worked a sleeve up her injured arm. "Something wrong?"

Stark averted her gaze from the expanse of skin revealed as Renee leaned over to slip into her jeans. Renee had left her blouse unbuttoned and her breasts were barely covered. Her coffee-colored skin, smooth and tight, invited a caress. "Uh..."

Head down, her voice curious, Renee repeated, "Problem?"

"No. No problem." Shaking the fog from her brain, Stark hurried on. "The commander is with her. They're just...taking some personal time."

Renee buttoned her blouse and tucked it into her jeans, still favoring her left arm. "Really? That's something of a breach in protocol, isn't it?"

Uncomfortable, Stark shrugged. "Yes and no. We escorted them most of the way to their destination, and the commander is with her."

"Sounds like they're playing hooky to me." Renee stepped into her loafers. "And I say good for them. They've both been through hell the last six months, and they certainly deserve some time alone just to enjoy each other."

She crossed the room to Paula and held out her hand. "And so do we. Come on, let's go for a walk in this gorgeous city."

In one motion, Stark stood and slid an arm around Renee's waist. Leaning close, she kissed her softly. The kiss didn't end until she had traced the inner surface of Renee's lips not once, but several times. Drawing back, breathless, Stark nodded. "Yes. Let's do that."

As if by design, both Cam and Blair stopped outside the door to 213 and turned to each other. Cam lifted a hand and stroked the backs of her fingers over Blair's cheek.

"I love you."

Blair tilted her head and kissed Cam lingeringly before tightening her hold on her lover's hand. "I love you."

Cam unlocked the door and together they crossed the threshold. Blair turned and slid the security chain home, then glided forward into the moonlit room and threaded her arms around her lover's neck, resting her cheek against Cam's chest. In a voice filled with wonder, she murmured, "I can't believe we're really here. If you only knew how many times I've dreamed of this."

"I know." With her arms around Blair's waist, Cam drew her gently closer and rested her cheek against the top of Blair's head. "Me too."

"I wish..." Blair sighed, knowing that wishing would only bring disappointment. She was who she was, and that would follow her for the rest of her days. She was the only child of the president of the United States. Even after her father left office, the privilege and burden of that reality would remain. Eventually her notoriety, she knew, would fade, but that was a long time in the future. It was her father's first term in office and there would very likely be a second. She was going to be in the public eye—or in the eye of the hurricane—for years to come. "Sorry. I promised myself I'd work on not tilting at windmills."

"You did?" Cam's voice rose with a combination of incredulity and laughter.

"Cut it out." Blair jokingly slapped a palm against Cam's chest, then rested her head on Cam's shoulder. "Well, since we had that talk with my father and he's been so great about our relationship, it seemed that the least I could do was stop being so angry at him for something he can't help."

"I'm glad." If Blair was less angry at the restrictions her

high-profile existence demanded, it would make Cam's job as her security chief much easier. Much more importantly, though, it would make Blair's life a happier—and far safer—one. Ultimately, that was all Cam cared about. "Does that mean that you're going to stop trying to lose your security detail on a regular basis?"

"I've never tried to lose you," Blair murmured as she pressed her lips to the undersurface of Cam's jaw. She rocked her hips suggestively against the lean form as she kissed her way to the corner of Cam's mouth. "I just never seem to be able to get you all to myself."

"You've got me now," Cam whispered, her lips to Blair's forehead. She reached with one hand to release the clasp at Blair's nape and pocketed the heavy gold jewelry. Slipping the same hand beneath Blair's hair, she threaded her fingers through the thick wild tresses, loving the way their heavy softness filled her palm. She loved everything about the way Blair felt. "I love you."

Blair didn't think she would ever grow tired of hearing those words. It wasn't something she had ever anticipated or even consciously desired. She had spent most of her adult life avoiding commitments and entanglements, preferring to preserve her anonymity in the only sphere in which she could—her private life. She managed that by routinely misdirecting her security team and slipping away to engage in anonymous liaisons that left her emotionally untouched. Although she hadn't consciously sought to put herself at risk, her actions had placed her in danger more than once. Nevertheless, she'd thought herself independent and content, if not particularly happy. All that had changed the morning Commander Cameron Roberts had walked into her penthouse and informed her that the game had new rules. Cam's rules.

"I still can't believe what you've done to me." *Made me want you so much, need you so much. When I never thought I would.* Shaking her head, Blair leaned back in the circle of her lover's arms and searched the dark eyes that held her own. "I don't know how you managed to get me at such a disadvantage, Commander."

"Oh?" Cam slid the zipper down the back of Blair's dress and inched her hand inside to caress smooth, warm flesh. Her fingers drifted over the hollow at the base of Blair's spine and then lower, over the gentle swell of firm muscle. Her stomach tightened as it always did when she touched Blair. Arousal followed fast on wonder, and need coiled in her depths. "God, I want you."

"Cam," Blair murmured, unfastening the studs on Cam's dress shirt and carefully placing each small, silver-encased pearl in Cam's pocket. She tugged the starched white shirt free of the waistband of the tailored silk trousers and parted the fabric to expose flesh. With a sigh, she pressed her palm to the center of her lover's chest, then drew her nails down the middle of her body, smiling in satisfaction as she felt Cam twitch. "I love to make you want me."

"You don't have to try." Cam's voice was hoarse with desire. With trembling hands, she carefully drew the gown from Blair's sculpted shoulders and released it to pool in midnight folds around their feet. Blair's breasts were bare, her only remaining garments a black satin thong and the thin lace garter belt that held the silk against her thighs. Cam's head reeled as blood rushed into the pit of her stomach and surged between her thighs. Groaning, she ran both hands down Blair's back to cup her buttocks and pull her close. "I've missed you."

"Three days of smiling at strangers and making polite conversation while all I wanted was to be alone with you..." Blair pushed her hands beneath Cam's shirt and claimed her breasts, hot skin against hot skin, "just about killed me."

"How do you think I felt?" Cam's breath came in quick gasps as her nipples tensed beneath Blair's teasing fingers. With trembling hands, she released the garter belt and brushed silk down silken skin. "Watching everyone watching you. All the men and more than a few of the women."

And as hands stroked fevered flesh, their lips met for the first time since they'd entered the room. While they explored and reclaimed each other with deep hungry kisses, they opened buttons and slid zippers and whisked the last barriers of clothing to the floor, kicking off shoes until they both stood naked, cleaving to each other.

"Take me to bed," Blair urged, her hips thrusting insistently.

"Yes. Yes." The room was small and the bed only a few feet away. Without even thinking about it, Cam curved her arm behind Blair's legs, lifted, and carried her to the bed. In the next instant she lowered herself upon Blair's body, groaning at the first full contact.

"Oh, yes—I've missed you."

Blair arched to meet the weight of her lover descending, and their legs entwined, bringing heat to heat.

"Oh God."

"You feel so good."

"I want you so much."

"I love you."

While the moonlight silvered around them and the world faded, they lingered and teased and demanded and took until they shivered on the edge of abandon.

"Cam," Blair breathed as the passion rose up from her depths at last, seizing her soul as it obliterated reason. "Oh, Cam."

"I love you," Cam whispered when she felt the orgasm take her lover, felt the blood surge and the muscles clench around her fingers, and felt the frantic beat of their two hearts joining. She closed her eyes and slowly stroked, deeper each time, drawing forth the last drop of her lover's desire. With Blair crying out and then crying softly in her arms, Cam surrendered to her own release with a sigh of gratitude and wonder.

For the first time, for a few stolen hours, they were free to be only two women in love.

CHAPTER TWO

```
0313 16Aug01
Query RedDog: Do you read?
RedDog: roger team leader
Do you have target in range?
RedDog: negative...target off radar
FIND HER. Operation Hydra is active.
    Awaiting strike date
RedDog: roger. Will advise when target
    secured
```

"I'd ask you to come up," Renee said as she and Stark stood on the sidewalk outside her hotel. "But it's four thirty in the morning and at this point, our choices for what comes next don't include much beyond going to bed."

"That's okay," Stark said softly, reaching out to touch Renee's fingers. "I had a great time. There's something about walking around in a city while it sleeps, especially one as beautiful as this, that makes me feel as if I'm in the middle of a wonderful dream. Being with you tonight was like having that dream come true."

Renee's lips parted in surprise as she caught her breath. Her voice was husky when she spoke. "How come all the training to make you such a tough Secret Service agent hasn't beaten that tenderness out of you?"

Stark shrugged, a wry grin lifting one corner of her mouth. "They tried pretty hard, but it just seems to be something I can't get rid of."

"Thank God."

"I'm not sure it's a good thing," Stark amended, her voice

troubled. "I'm supposed to be able to put my feelings aside to do the job right."

"Oh, no, honey," Renee protested gently. "I know that's the party line—no emotional attachment with the protectees. No personal investment. But *I* say that when you stop caring is when you'll get careless." Boldly, Renee took Stark's hand and pulled her from beneath the small awning into the deep shadows of the building. She framed Stark's face and kissed her tenderly. "You're just right, on *and* off the job. I hope you never change."

Swallowing audibly, Stark lightly clasped Renee's waist. "I can safely say nothing's going to change the way I feel about you."

Renee rested her forehead against Stark's, savoring the simple pleasure of the moment before kissing her again. "Promise?"

"Promise." Stark sighed. "And you don't have to worry about whether to ask me up or not, because I'd say no anyway."

"You would? Just like that?" Renee's tone was a mixture of surprise and consternation. As much as she was enjoying their slow courtship, part of her hoped that the waiting was at least a little bit as uncomfortable for Stark as it was for her. "I'm not sure I like the sound of that."

"Oh, believe me, I'm suffering greatly." Stark laughed and caught Renee's hand, swinging their joined arms gently. "But that's not what I meant. There's something I...uh...need to do."

"At this hour?" Renee tilted her head, narrowing her gaze as she studied Stark astutely. "Let me guess. Secret Service Agent Stark is still on duty."

"Yeah." Sheepishly, Stark nodded. "Something like that."

God, it would be so easy to fall totally head over heels in love with you. I really do need to slow down. Renee reluctantly released Stark's hand and gave her a playful shove. "All right then, go. Go. Call me tomorrow when you get a break."

"Okay. Thanks." Stark started to turn away, and then—as if in afterthought—swiveled swiftly back, pulled Renee to her, and kissed her resoundingly. When she lifted her mouth away, she had to struggle for enough air to speak. "Sleep...well."

Renee, her lips tingling and her heart racing, stared after Stark as she strode purposefully away. *Oh, I will. If I can ever get my body to quiet down.*

Half an hour later, Stark slowly approached a nondescript black sedan parked at the intersection of Rue Seguier and Rue de Savoie. A lone figure, cast in shadow, occupied the front seat of the vehicle. Before Stark could reach out to tap on the door, the window rolled soundlessly down. Leaning an arm against the top of the car, Stark peered inside. "Hey. Want some coffee?"

The face of the striking African American woman who regarded her with a raised brow could easily have graced the cover of any fashion magazine. Felicia Davis nodded, smiling a Mona Lisa smile. "Now why aren't I surprised to see you?"

"I could say the same thing." Stark grinned. "How long have you been here?"

"Since about 0230."

"Do they know?"

"No, and I'd prefer that they don't." Davis lifted a shoulder gracefully. Even the shapeless windbreaker she wore couldn't detract from her natural elegance. "I think it was the commander's intention for them to be alone."

"There's a café open around the corner. Espresso?"

"Make it a double. And bless you." Felicia rolled the window back up as Stark turned to head down the street. Throughout the conversation, she'd kept one eye on the entrance to the *pensione* where Commander Cameron Roberts and Blair Powell were spending the night. She understood why they wanted to be alone, and she had no desire to dispel that illusion of privacy. On the other hand, it was her responsibility to see that no harm came to the first daughter. She'd do what she could to see that that happened while respecting both her commander's and Egret's wishes.

A moment later, Stark returned, and Felicia unlocked the doors. Stark slid into the passenger seat, closed the door, and handed the thimble-sized cardboard container of coffee to the other agent. "Does Mac know you're here?"

Felicia sipped her espresso silently and then, after a moment, turned her head and regarded Stark thoughtfully. "No."

"I just thought...you know...that maybe you had checked in with him," Stark stumbled. *Jesus, Paula, could you be any less smooth*. She knew, or at least she *assumed*—as did most of the rest of the team—that Felicia Davis and Mac Phillips, the team's communication coordinator and second in command, were romantically involved. The two agents were both very private, but they *had* been known to date. "I figured he sent you."

"I was in the command center when Fielding checked in after the commander dismissed the night shift. He said that you and he had escorted them to this location. He seemed only too happy to get the rest of the night off." Her tone suggested that she did not approve of his approach to his duty, but she didn't comment further. She was a relatively new member of the team, and she'd been brought in from the technical division for her computer skills. Not being a regular member of the protective branch made her a bit of an outsider. To some.

Stark flushed. "I probably should've stayed here."

"I wasn't being critical." Felicia's quiet tone supported her words. "I trust the commander's judgment, and I don't think she would have done anything to put Egret at risk. I'm here because that's what makes me comfortable."

"Me too, I guess. Look, is it okay if I keep you company?"

"Fine. I expect that the commander will check in with the comm center first thing in the morning. We should probably be off-site before an official team arrives."

"Yeah," Stark mused, sipping her coffee. "What time do you figure?"

"Knowing the commander? She'll call Mac at 0700."

"So estimating half an hour for Mac to put the first shift on-site, we should leave here at 0715." Stark contemplated going back for more coffee and baguettes. "I don't feel like starting the day with the commander pissed at me."

Felicia sighed and stretched her long legs beneath the cramped dash. "I don't think she would be. But I'd like them to think that their night was exactly what they wanted it to be."

Surprised, Stark studied the woman beside her. Felicia was a difficult person to figure. She rarely mentioned anything personal, and she often appeared aloof and distant. Like so many high-powered computer experts, she seemed to be more comfortable with data and machines. Clearly, however, she understood the critical matters of the human heart.

"Yeah," Stark murmured, thinking of her recent stroll hand in hand with Renee on the Champs Elysées and how precious those moments had been. "Now and then it's good to dream."

The combination of a warm breeze carrying the scents of freshly baked bread and coffee, the distant hum of traffic, and voices wafting up from the street below woke Cam. She turned on her side toward the open French doors and opened her eyes to the pink-purple haze of dawn. It wasn't the otherworldly burst of color that made her heart race, however. Blair, wearing only Cam's tuxedo shirt, stood framed on the threshold to the tiny balcony with its ornate wrought-iron railing. Her expression was pensive as she gazed toward the Seine.

Lying still, Cam took advantage of the very rare opportunity to study Blair in repose. So often, their time together was spent at briefings, traveling to or from the first daughter's many official or private functions, or in the company of other members of the team. Being alone with Blair, especially in quietude, was a rare treasure. As was so often the case, the gift was fleeting.

Blair turned her head and looked back into the room, a soft smile curving her lips as her eyes met Cam's. "I thought I felt you wake up."

"I'm surprised *I* didn't feel you leave the bed," Cam said quietly, stretching beneath the rumpled sheets. Her body felt unusually relaxed, almost loose. That was another rare occurrence, and Cam recognized the lassitude as the aftereffect of their lovemaking and the pleasure of sleeping with Blair in her arms. "I think you might just have worn me out."

"Really?" Blair's smile widened and she arched one blond brow. "I'm not sure that bodes well for our future, Commander. I tend to be a more than a once-a-week kind of girl."

"I shouldn't worry, Ms. Powell." Throwing back the light coverings and swinging her legs to the floor, Cam chuckled. She glanced around and spied her trousers. "I have remarkable powers of recovery."

"I know," Blair murmured, watching appreciatively as Cam

stepped into her pants. Naked from the waist up, she was beautiful—all tight muscles beneath smooth skin and seething with sensuality. Feeling the familiar urgency that just the sight of her lover instilled, Blair's eyes traveled to the irregular scar above Cam's left breast and the long incision that extended from just below her breast around her side to her back. The once bright red ridges were pale pink now, but no matter how faint they might eventually become, Blair would always see them. Just as she would always see Cam lying on the sidewalk in front of her apartment building, bleeding to death from the bullet meant for Blair. *Thank God you're so strong. What would I do...*

Wondering at the odd tone in Blair's voice, Cam zipped her trousers and met her lover's eyes. Quickly, she crossed to her, slid both arms around Blair's waist from behind, and pressed her chest to Blair's back. She nuzzled her face in Blair's hair and kissed the edge of her ear. "Don't."

Resting her weight against Cam's body, Blair folded her arms over Cam's to hold her closer. "Don't what?"

"Don't remember. It's over." Cam kissed the sensitive spot just below Blair's ear. "Let it go, baby."

It should have bothered Blair, that subtle command, but it didn't. The tenderness ablated any edge the words might have carried. Indolently, she stretched back an arm and thrust her fingers into Cam's hair. "No one has ever been able to read my mind before."

"No one has ever loved you the way I do."

"I don't want to live without you."

Cam drew a swift breath, shocked by the statement. It wasn't that she doubted Blair's feelings for her, but she had never expected to occupy a place of such pivotal importance in this particular woman's life. Blair was nothing if not strong and independent—so much so that sometimes she drove Cam to distraction. Theirs had been a stormy beginning, and even now they locked horns on practically a daily basis, usually disagreeing over how much security Blair required. Professionally they had *begun* to learn to compromise. Personally, they had barely defined their present, let alone their future.

"I want to spend the rest of my life with you," Cam murmured, her mouth against Blair's neck. "I'll do anything possible to make that happen."

"I wish we could live together."

Cam closed her eyes and held Blair closer. She had trained herself from childhood not to want things she couldn't have. Blair had been the first woman to make her break that rule, and still, she tried not to want more than what they had. The wistful tone in Blair's voice washed that resolve away in a heartbeat. "We will."

"You know that's not possible."

"Not today," Cam turned Blair to face her, but kept her within the circle of her arms, "and not tomorrow. But it will happen, I promise."

"Is that what you want?" Blair's blue eyes searched gray.

Cam's gaze never faltered. "With all my heart."

"I'm sorry. God." Blair sighed and shook her head. "I don't know what has gotten hold of me. Maybe it's being here with you. I went to school here..." She shrugged and smiled wryly. "It wasn't a great time."

"How so?"

I was lonely. I was lost. I wanted what we have now, but I was afraid it would never happen.

Blair pushed aside the melancholy with a shrug. "My father was the vice president then, and I was a bit of a handful for all concerned, I guess."

"I can just imagine." Cam kissed her lightly on the lips. "I don't envy your security chief."

"Which one?" Blair laughed. "The position was practically a revolving door. They'd do anything to get out of it."

"I thought that's the way I would feel too," Cam confessed. "I *did* feel that way when I first got the assignment. I don't feel that way now. Even if I weren't in love with you, I would want this job."

Curious and surprised, Blair cocked her head. "Why?"

"Because it's essential to the security of the country."

Blair's eyes widened. "You really believe that?"

"Absolutely. And so does every member of my team." Cam leaned her shoulders back against the door frame, cradling Blair in her arms, as they both looked toward the Cathedral of Notre

Dame. "The currency of power today isn't arms, it's terror—and that is much subtler and much more difficult to defend against. If something were to happen to you..."

"Nothing will," Blair stated emphatically, hearing the worry in Cam's voice. She caught Cam's hand and slid it inside the shirt, pressing her lover's fingers to her breast.

Softly, Cam groaned. "You don't honestly expect me to think now, do you?"

"Mmm," Blair sighed. "I just love to have your hands on me."

Cam rested her cheek against Blair's hair and breathed in her scent. "If you were used as a political marker against your father, there's no way he would be able to resist the influence. He'd either have to submit to whatever demands were made or step down. Either way, we would all lose."

"I didn't really appreciate that before—not the way I do now," Blair admitted. "I'll try, darling. I really will."

"I know." Cam cradled the softness of Blair's breast in her palm, lightly brushing the tender skin and the taut nipple. This woman was critically important to a nation constantly at war, even if those struggles were not acknowledged in the media. But even more, she was beyond precious to Cam—to her heart, to her very life. "I promised you once, that first day, that I would try to make this situation tolerable for you. I still will, as much as I can. I love you."

Blair shifted until her mouth met Cam's. Against her lover's lips, she murmured, "God, I love you too."

"We have an hour or so before I need to call Mac," Cam whispered.

"They offered us breakfast in bed." Blair pushed Cam back into the room and shrugged out of the shirt. "Hungry?"

Cam ran a hand slowly down the center of her abdomen, watching Blair follow her movements. She flicked open the button on her pants and drew the zipper down. "Yes."

CHAPTER THREE

Eyes closed, Cam was alive with sensation—with the rich tangle of Blair's hair sifting between her fingers, with the warmth of Blair's mouth firing her already heated skin, and with the tenderness of Blair's lips drawing her ever closer to the edge of surrender. Rising from her distant reaches, the first whisper of orgasm curled in the pit of her stomach and danced like tendrils of flame along her spine. Her skin tingled, the muscles in her thighs trembled, and her hips lifted in silent supplication, entreating her lover to take more.

"It's so good," Cam whispered in wonder.

Moaning softly, Blair stroked a hand down the center of Cam's stomach, feeling the muscles tighten in preparation for the final thrust toward completion. It was always at this moment, when the pure and simple beauty was about to blossom beneath her hands and flower against her lips, that the breath stilled in her chest and the blood thundered in her ears.

Cam's cell phone rang.

Cam groaned, the pleasure transformed to agony. Blair lifted her mouth.

"*Don't* answer it."

But Cam was already rolling onto her side and reaching for her phone on the bedside table. Desperately, she fought back the urgency clamoring for escape like a wild thing in her depths and struggled to clear her head. Hoarsely, she rasped, "Roberts."

Breathing heavily, Blair pushed away, flopped onto her back, and stared at the ceiling. She fisted one hand in the sheet and drew it over them both. *All we wanted was a few goddamned hours!*

She'd allowed herself to forget everything except being with Cam for those few hours, and now their idyll was over. She pushed her hand through her hair and wrestled with the fury. *It's no one's fault. Not Cam's. Not whoever's on the other end of that line. No one's. It just is.*

At another time, in another place, she would already have been out of bed and pulling on her clothes. If she'd cared at all about the woman she'd been about to pleasure, she would have vented her rage on whoever was close by—herself, her temporary lover, or, on occasion, her friends. But now, she was alone with the woman she loved, and there was nowhere for the anger to go except inward. If she allowed *that*, it would destroy even the memory of the few hours of peace she'd found in Cam's arms.

Cam closed the phone, set it down, and turned back to Blair. "I'm sorry—"

"No," Blair quickly rejoined, shifting to face her lover. "No, it's all right." Drawing Cam near with one hand behind her head, she put her mouth to Cam's and gently kissed her while sliding the other hand between Cam's thighs. She smiled against her lover's lips as she heard the deep groan. "You're still throbbing."

"I'm still ready to...God, don't stop..." Cam's vision blurred as Blair stroked her.

"Never," Blair whispered, watching Cam's eyes glaze. When Cam threw back her head, neck arched and body quivering, Blair pushed her onto her back and thrust into her in one long, deep stroke, taking her over, taking her. "I'll never stop...never, never..."

"Ahh…God." Cam sighed when she could catch her breath. She wrapped limp arms around Blair's shoulders and pressed her lips to her lover's damp temple. "Great timing."

"Me or the phone?" Blair asked lazily.

"What phone?"

Blair dipped her head and kissed the base of Cam's throat. "I love you, but what have you done with the commander?"

Cam stroked Blair's back and sighed. "That was Mac."

"I figured. He's the only one with balls big enough to call us when you've taken us off-line." Blair mentally steeled herself. "What is it?"

"Eric Mitchell didn't give us the two weeks he promised."

"He filed the story." Blair's voice rang hollow. It had been almost a week since she and Cam had met with the reporter, but she remembered every word of their half-hour interview.

Cam answered the intercom, listened for a moment, and said, "Send him up." She settled the phone carefully back into its cradle and turned to Blair. "Ready?"

Blair nodded. Silently, she extended her hand and immediately felt anchored when Cam's fingers clasped hers. She leaned forward and kissed Cam fleetingly. "I'm fine."

While Cam went to open the door for their visitor, Blair walked to the wide windows on the opposite side of Cam's living room and looked out over DC. They'd chosen to meet with the reporter in Cam's apartment rather than at the White House. This was not an official meeting; this was intensely personal. A clandestine photo of her and Cam had appeared in newspapers across the country not long before. The image was just blurry enough to obscure Cam's identity, but the fact that they had been captured in an intimate moment was abundantly clear.

Speculation was rampant within the media as to the specifics of Blair's "love affair," and various "confidential sources" put her in the arms of mafia kingpins, movie stars, and even members of her father's cabinet. Ordinarily, she would have brushed it off and allowed the rumors to die away, eclipsed by the next natural disaster or national emergency. But her relationship with Cam was not going to go away; in fact, she hoped that it would become even more central to her life. And if that was the case, they could not live in secrecy any longer.

In an attempt to forestall rumors and to control the dissemination of misinformation, she had decided, with her father's blessing, to reveal the nature of her sexual identity as well as her romantic relationship with Cam. She had chosen a reporter who was also the husband of a college friend, hoping that old loyalties would translate into some degree of discretion. At the sound of Cam's deep voice at the door, Blair turned, determined and resolute.

"Ms. Powell," Eric Mitchell, a tall, thin, balding thirty-year-old, said as he approached with an outstretched hand. "I'm honored to be of service."

Blair shook his hand, finding his unwavering pale blue gaze

somewhat comforting. She indicated a nearby chair and then took Cam's hand and sat with her on the facing sofa.

"I'd like to make a statement," Blair said calmly. "I'm happy for you to include any of my comments in your article, but I would ask that you discuss the timing with both the White House chief of staff, Lucinda Washburn, and the White House press secretary so that they can be prepared with a response."

Mitchell removed a slim notebook and a ballpoint pen from his inside jacket pocket. He flipped open the cover and smoothed down a blank page. Looking up, he regarded the first daughter. "I don't need the White House's permission to file a story, Ms. Powell."

Cam made a soft noise that verged on a growl.

Blair squeezed her lover's hand and smiled coolly. "I'm well aware of that, Mr. Mitchell. I was only asking as a courtesy. Considering the circumstances."

"I understand, and I'll do my best."

"Ms. Powell is scheduled to perform state duties, including meeting with the president of France and the ministers of health of several European nations in Paris next week," Cam said pointedly. "While she's out of the country, it's imperative that we not be faced with the heightened media attention this story is likely to generate."

"I appreciate the burden of public scrutiny, Ms. Powell." Again, Mitchell nodded, looking expectantly from Cam to Blair. "I'll do my best to work with my editors and the White House on a mutually acceptable release date."

"Thank you," Blair replied, believing in his sincerity while at the same time knowing only too well how difficult it was to control anything in the bright glare of Washington's spotlights. She looked once at Cam, who returned her gaze with a smile and a squeeze of her fingers. The steady assurance in Cam's eyes and the solid comfort of her shoulder pressed to Blair's were all she needed.

Turning her attention back to the reporter, who waited silently, she said clearly and quietly, "I wish to make a public statement regarding my private life. Due to the unique circumstances of my family's visibility, I felt it important that I clarify certain issues raised by the recent photo of myself and my lover, who happens to be another woman."

The reporter's expression did not change. He held Blair's gaze comfortably. "Does your father know?"

"Yes."

"Does he approve?"

Blair's expression was glacial, but entirely composed. "That's a question best presented to my father, although I should think there are matters of much greater importance for you and the rest of the news media to focus on."

"That may be, but it's a question that everyone will want to have answered."

Blair hesitated, wondering where to draw the line between the personal and the public, especially where her father was concerned. "My father is aware of my sexual orientation and is supportive."

"And the woman in the photograph is your current lover?"

"Yes."

Cam leaned forward. "I'm the other person in the photograph."

For the first time, Mitchell's composure faltered and his eyebrows rose in surprise. "You are the head of Ms. Powell's security team, are you not, Agent Roberts?"

"That's correct." Cam eyed him flatly. "But I'm here today as Ms. Powell's lover."

"Are your superiors aware of your relationship?" He kept his eyes on them, but he was writing furiously.

"Not yet. But I expect to advise them within the next twenty-four hours."

"Do you expect to be dismissed?"

Blair stiffened.

"I don't know," Cam answered calmly.

Mitchell turned his attention back to Blair. "Does your father know about Agent Roberts as well?"

"Yes."

"How long has he known?"

"That is of no relevance," Cam interjected swiftly. There was a definite edge to her tone now.

"Do you expect to continue your relationship after this public announcement, especially in light of your unusual professional relationship?"

"Yes," both women said emphatically.

From that point, the interview had proceeded much as Blair had expected, with the usual questions about when she had first become aware of her sexual orientation, the details of previous liaisons, and suppositions as to the effect of the announcement on her father's reelection campaign. Most of the questions she refused to answer because there were some things no one had the right to know. She also refused to speculate on the position of the White House. It had not been a pleasant discussion, but it wasn't nearly as difficult as she imagined it would have been had Cam not been with her.

After much debate and chest thumping from the West Wing in the days after the interview, a consensus had been reached as to when to release the story. Mitchell and his editors argued that there was a strong likelihood of a leak from the Hill and that some other newspaper might break the story. They wanted to file immediately. Lucinda Washburn claimed that would put Blair at undue risk while abroad. Eventually, all parties had compromised on a delay of two weeks, which would enable Blair and her security team to be back in the U.S. when the news came out.

"God." Blair sighed. Going public about something so very personal had been a difficult decision—one that she'd avoided making all of her adult life. If she hadn't fallen in love with Cam, she might never have willingly disclosed the information. "That's not good news."

"I'm sorry, baby." Cam pushed up in the bed, her back against the headboard, Blair still in her arms. "We need to get back to base so Mac can bring me up to speed. I have to get a sense of where this is headed."

"We won't have to cut the trip short, will we?"

Cam was silent.

"Damn it, Cam! I will not allow public opinion to dictate my life." Blair *did* get out of bed then and paced angrily, unmindful of her nakedness, around the small room.

"Blair," Cam said softly. When her lover failed to acknowledge her, she tried again, slightly louder. "Blair."

Blair stopped at the foot of the bed long enough to fix Cam

with a steely glare before she resumed stalking the ten feet between the door and window.

"It's not public opinion that I care about," Cam went on in a level voice. She hadn't moved, but remained propped up against the pillows, the sheet drawn to her waist. "We don't really have enough people of our own for any kind of crowd control, but I can draft extra security from the French if necessary."

"I know that tone of voice, Roberts," Blair said sharply, halting abruptly and turning to face Cam, hands on her hips and eyes flashing. "You've got your *command* voice on, which means that my lover just left. I hate it when you do that."

"I know." Sighing, Cam pushed the sheets aside and climbed from the bed in search of her pants for the second time that morning. She pulled them on and then stuffed her hands into her pockets while edging a hip against the small night table to give Blair more room to continue her pacing. "There's been a resurgence of right-wing dissidence throughout Europe in the last five years, and France is one center of activity."

"You think someone's going to try to shoot me because I'm a lesbian?"

Every minute of every day, Cam lived with the knowledge that someone, somewhere, might try to harm the woman she loved for reasons that would be unfathomable to any sane individual. But assassins were not sane, and fanatics needed very little rational motive to carry out acts of terrorism. "I have to consider that a possibility, yes. And that means that I have to reassess our vulnerability in light of this new development. It's part of what I do."

Blair walked to the table and picked up Cam's cell phone.

Cam regarded her quizzically.

"I have to call Felicia."

"Any particular reason?"

"I need clothes." Blair punched in the number to command central and snapped, "Get me Davis at this number." Then she sat down on the edge of the bed and put the phone beside her.

Curious, Cam asked, "Why Felicia? Stark's your lead agent."

Smiling despite herself, Blair shook her head. "It's a girl thing. You wouldn't understand."

"Probably not." Grinning, Cam sat down beside her and reached for her hand. With the other, she pulled the sheet across the bed and wrapped it around Blair's body. "The view is spectacular, but you're going to get cold."

"Not while I'm this pissed off," Blair muttered, but she allowed Cam to cover her.

"Do you understand my concerns?"

"Yes." Blair entwined her fingers with Cam's. "But I don't like it. I'm scheduled for a tour of the breast cancer center at Institut Gustave-Roussy this afternoon. I was hoping that I would have a few hours to myself in the morning to sketch in the Tuileries gardens."

"All of that may still be possible. Let me just get the updates on recent cell activity in the Paris environs and a look at what's breaking on the newswires." Cam lifted Blair's hand to her lips and kissed her fingers. "Just give me an hour or so to brief with the team and then we'll discuss the day's itinerary."

Blair turned her head and studied her lover's face. Cam's dark eyes were tender and warm. "You never used to ask."

"I know." Cam brushed the backs of Blair's fingers against her own cheek, needing the contact. "But that was before I fell in love with you."

"Do you think the longer we're together, the more rope I'll be able to get from you?"

"I don't think so," Cam said musingly, her eyes dancing. "I think you've gotten just about as much as I intend to give."

Blair shifted closer, threaded an arm around Cam's waist, and rested her head on Cam's shoulder. "I'm very persuasive."

Wrapping her in an embrace, Cam pressed her lips to Blair's forehead. "Mmm. Believe me, I *know.*"

At that moment, the phone rang and Blair snatched it up. "Blair Powell...Felicia?...I need an emergency makeup kit and something to wear. Yeah...slacks and a shirt will do. Can you raid my room and pack a bag?...Sure, half an hour's fine." At Cam's raised eyebrows, Blair pointedly ignored her. "Let me give you the address where we are." After giving Felicia the details, Blair closed the phone once more and set it aside. Regarding her lover seriously, she asked, "Shall we call down for breakfast or is there something else you'd rather do for half an hour?"

Cam framed Blair's face with both hands and leaned in to kiss her lingeringly, enjoying the softness of her lips and the heat that rose beneath her palms. When she drew her mouth away, her voice was husky. "There's *always* something I'd rather do with you, Ms. Powell. But considering the circumstances, I think breakfast might be the safest choice."

Blair ran her fingers down the center of Cam's bare chest. "I know you're not the type to play it safe."

"You have severely tested my limits." Laughing, Cam caught Blair's hand and stilled her teasing movements. "So I'll have to decline the offer of other pleasures for the time being."

"Oh yeah?" Blair planted both hands on Cam's chest and pushed her backward onto the bed, climbing astride her hips as she fell. Leaning over with her arms braced on either side of Cam's shoulders, she slowly lowered her head, her eyes fixed on Cam's. "We'll see about that, Commander."

```
0635 16Aug01
Query team leader: Do you read?
Team Leader: Roger, RedDog
Target located. Awaiting green light.
Team Leader: Observe at the ready
Roger. Strike team out.
```

CHAPTER FOUR

Twenty-nine minutes later, a knock sounded at the hotel room door. When Blair started to rise, Cam caught her arm and stood quickly. "I'll get it."

After pulling on her pants and shirt, Cam reached for her weapon, which was lying in its holster on the bedside table. She slid it out with practiced ease on her way to the door. There was no peephole in the heavy wooden door, and she glanced over her shoulder to ensure that Blair was not in the sightline of anyone outside in the hall. Then, her hand on the knob, she asked, "Who is it?"

"Davis, Commander."

Automatic held down at her side, Cam inched open the door for identity verification, then stepped aside and allowed Davis to enter.

Felicia stopped at the foot of the bed, her eyes face front, appearing to take no note of the rumpled solitary bed or the fact that the first daughter sat in the middle of it with nothing on but a bedsheet.

Blair held out a hand for the overnight bag. "Thanks."

"You're quite welcome, Ms. Powell." Turning away, Felicia returned to the door. "I'll take the hall, Commander."

"Very well." Once again, Cam blocked the sightline to Blair as her agent opened the door and slipped out.

"Do you do that on purpose, just to make me crazy?"

Cam turned, returning her automatic to the holster and securing it to the waistband of her pants at the small of her back. Ordinarily, she wore a shoulder holster but had found it difficult to camouflage in the evening jacket she'd worn the night before. "What?"

Blair blew out an exasperated breath and stood up. "Never

mind."

Cam fingered the studs from her pocket one at a time and began to fit them into her shirt. "What?"

"Put yourself between me and even the remotest possibility of danger."

Frowning, Cam looked up. "You mean just now?"

"Yes," Blair said slowly, cocking her head and giving Cam a look. "I mean just now."

Cam opened her fly, tucked in her shirt, and zipped up. "That's just SOP. I don't even think about it."

Blair regarded her lover contemplatively, not angry, but curious. "How do they teach you to do that?"

"What?" Cam slid both arms around Blair's waist and kissed her softly. "What?"

"You're being unusually dense this morning." Blair rested her forearms on Cam's shoulders, watching the colors swirl in Cam's eyes.

Cam grinned. "Too much sex."

Despite herself, Blair smiled. Then her expression grew serious. "How do they teach someone to be willing to die for a paycheck?"

"It's not about that," Cam murmured. "You know that."

"I don't understand why you do it."

Cam rested her forehead against Blair's and took a long breath. "It's an honor."

Blair made a small sound and pressed her face to Cam's neck. "Oh God. I do love you."

"I'm so glad." Cam kissed her once more, still softly, but this time she allowed herself the luxury of lingering. She traced her tongue over the soft surface of Blair's lips and into the warm welcome of her mouth, knowing that it could be hours or even days before she might do so again. Then, resolutely, she released her hold and stepped away. "I love you, too."

"I'll be ready in just a second." Blair was subdued as she turned away to sort through the clothes Felicia had packed for her. Even though she would be with Cam for almost the entire day and probably most of the evening, it would not be the same. She would not be free to touch her without thinking, or to smile or laugh or cry with her without restraint. Even though their relationship was no longer a secret, her behavior was still under scrutiny, and the personal was about to become very public.

"Blair," Cam said softly.

Blair looked up, a question in her eyes.

"I miss you, too."

Oddly, the admission lifted Blair's heart. Knowing that she was not alone in her longing gave her the strength to banish the loneliness. "Thank you."

Nodding solemnly, Cam shrugged into her jacket and checked to be sure that she could access her weapon without interference. Satisfied, she said quietly, "I'll wait outside with Felicia."

"Of course. I'll be out shortly, Commander."

The short ride in the Peugeot, one of the regulation French security vehicles, passed in silence. Felicia drove while Cynthia Parker, the newest member of Blair's detail, rode shotgun in the front passenger seat. Parker was on temporary loan from the White House security division, replacing Ellen Grant, who was recovering from an injury sustained while thwarting an attack on Blair. Parker, in addition to having ten years in the protective division, had worked in counterterrorism, and Cam had requested her specifically for the Paris detail.

In the backseat, Blair and Cam sat wordlessly side by side. As the car turned into the wide driveway fronting the Hotel Marigny, Cam murmured, "I'll call you as soon as we're done briefing."

Blair reached out and rested her hand on Cam's thigh. "I need to shower and change. Just come when you're done."

Covering Blair's fingers with her own, Cam squeezed lightly. "Fine." Then she released her lover's hand and checked the activity streetside before opening the car door. Two agents, Hernandez and Michaels, approached and, once they flanked the rear door, Cam stepped out. She looked up and down the plaza, then to the hotel entrance, and finally up the building's exterior, checking every window. Most modern hotel windows did not open, but it was a simple matter to cut out a square of glass through which to extend a rifle barrel. With luck, the glint of sunlight on steel would give an early warning, but many weapons had a matte black finish that prevented precisely that kind of reflection. She saw nothing amiss and turned to lean into the vehicle. "We're ready for you, Ms. Powell."

As soon as Blair stepped out, the two agents immediately closed in on either side. Cam walked slightly ahead, and Blair knew without looking that Felicia was right behind her. The phalanx of guards escorted her inside the building, across the lobby, and into the elevator. They rode to the top floor and into the east wing where two penthouse suites had been reserved for Blair and her security team. The second suite had become the command base while she was in Paris, and the agents, including Cam, slept in rooms one floor down. In the hall outside Blair's room, Cam murmured, "I'll see you soon."

Blair watched her lover disappear into the room opposite hers, and then she opened her own door and stepped inside. Felicia took up a post in the hallway outside. Alone, Blair wearily stripped and headed toward the bathroom. She didn't regret the loss of a night's sleep, because the hours with Cam had more than made up for it. Her weariness now was not from fatigue, but rather from the long years of the restricting routine. Nevertheless, reaching in to turn on the shower, she felt a surge of happiness. She remembered falling asleep, and much more importantly, awakening, in Cam's arms.

Cam shed the evening jacket as soon as she walked into the temporary comm center. Laptops were open and running on every available surface, and an entire bank of monitors displayed images of the hallway outside and the interior of all the elevators that serviced Blair's floor. A youthful-appearing blond man in his early thirties, wearing dark chinos and a blue button-down shirt with the sleeves rolled to his mid-forearms, sat in the center of the U-shaped array of electronics. He had a healthy complexion and cornflower blue eyes and might have passed for Brad Pitt on one of Pitt's less scruffy days.

"What have we got, Mac?" Cam asked as she walked over and dropped into an adjacent chair.

"Good morning, Commander," Mac Phillips said with a

friendly smile. If he took note of the fact that his commander was still wearing the clothes she had worn to the embassy gala the night before, he showed no sign of it. "The data information service from the NSA gave us early warning that the...news release regarding Ms. Powell was due to hit the streets this morning." He glanced at his watch. "In approximately four hours now."

As soon as Blair had given Mitchell the interview, Cam had advised her team of it, leaving out most of the details but warning them to prepare for increased media attention at any moment.

"Let's get the team together so we can review the adjustments we need to make in the rest of the itinerary." Cam glanced at her watch. "Give me fifteen minutes. I'll be in my room if you need me."

"Very well, Commander."

Cam left to shower and change, wondering just how much she was going to have to disappoint her lover. When she returned to the comm center, dressed now in her usual work attire—dark suit, white shirt, black tasseled dress shoes—all of her agents except those currently detailed to Blair were present. Most she had worked with since she had assumed command of Egret's personal security detail nine months earlier. There were a number of new faces—several agents who had been assigned temporary duty due to the increased security required when Egret traveled abroad and one replacement for a core team member absent due to injury.

Cam accepted all of them at face value because she fundamentally believed in the integrity of the Secret Service. On the other hand, she trusted fewer than a handful implicitly. Those agents had been tested under fire with her—more than once—and those select individuals she trusted without reservation. Those were the only people she would entrust with Blair's life, and she counted on them to take command in the event that anything were to happen to her. She had given the responsibility of shift rotation to Mac, with the understanding that at least two of these unofficial "core" agents would be present on every detail.

"Commander," a number of voices called as she entered.

Nodding to her team, Cam walked to the corner credenza. She poured herself a cup of coffee from a pot that sat brewing twenty-four hours a day and carried it to the center of the room where two aluminum catering tables placed end to end served as their conference table. She set her cup down and surveyed the waiting agents. Felicia and Reynolds—one of the newbies—were absent. Both were stationed outside Blair's room. After the morning briefing, those who were just coming off the abbreviated night shift would be off duty until their next rotation. The exception was Paula Stark, who as Egret's lead agent worked swing shifts—part of the day and part of the evening shifts—when Egret was most active.

"Good morning, all. Let's have the routine updates first." Cam slipped her PDA from her inside pocket, opened it, and powered up. She glanced briefly at Blair's itinerary for the next two days, although she knew it by heart.

Mac shifted printouts, then succinctly and efficiently reviewed the timetable for the day's scheduled events along with the personnel assignments. He opened a window on his laptop and a sectional map of Paris came up on a 42-inch plasma screen monitor at the end of the table.

"This is the planned motor route to the hospital. Two cars will be placed here," he highlighted an intersection, "and here, for backup and evacuation."

He tapped the keyboard, and an image of the front entrance of the massive hospital appeared. "Egret's ETA is 1600 hours. The advance team will vet the lobby and do a walk-through of her tour at 1300 and again at 1500, then detail here," he highlighted a point just outside the main doors, "to escort her inside with the primary team."

"What do we have on the surrounding topography?" Cam asked.

"Three structures within critical range and with sightlines to the entrance," Phil Rogers, the advance team coordinator, interjected. "All are commercial buildings, all open for business today."

Internally, Cam winced, because that meant dozens, perhaps hundreds, of people could potentially access a point from which to see, photograph, or fire upon the first daughter. Her face remained composed. "Anything turn up on the occupants?"

"No, ma'am," Rogers replied. "The French ran the leases and corporate ownership records when they got the advance itinerary from us last month. Nothing popped."

If the preliminary checks had revealed anything the least bit suspicious—a lessee with a criminal history or a business with strong ties to anti-American interests—deeper checks, including surveillance, would have been requested from "friendly" intelligence operatives in the region, most often CIA or their French counterparts.

"Employees?"

Rogers frowned. "Harder to evaluate. The French aren't so much uncooperative as lousy record keepers...their computer archives are even less capable of interfacing than ours back home."

Cam sighed. It was common knowledge within the intelligence community that the dozen or so U.S. agencies involved in information gathering and analysis often didn't talk to one another—and even when they wanted to, their data storage and retrieval systems were often antiquated and/or incompatible. As a result, interagency intel exchange was often impossible. Internationally, where diplomatic relationships with the host countries were often volatile at best, the situation was even worse. The upshot was that safeguarding political figures on foreign soil was more often than not a nightmare. "How many people are we talking about?"

"Fifty."

"Do you have teams on-site?"

"Yes, ma'am." Rogers glanced at his own PDA. "The *Service de protection des hautes personnalités* will deploy operatives to all three locations at 1200."

"Interior and exterior?" Cam asked sharply. She hated relying on any security forces other than her own, but it was neither practical nor possible to travel with the numbers of personnel truly required to protect an individual from all potential avenues of harm. A car containing explosive devices could careen through a roadblock and ram Blair's car; a suicide bomber could walk up to her on the street and self-detonate; a shooter could rent a room across from her favorite restaurant or salon and just wait. Eventually they would get a clear shot. Protection service relied on meticulous, exhaustive planning for any and all contingencies, but the save often came down to instincts and intuition.

"Yes, Commander."

"Risk assessment?"

"Low," Mac said. "Friendly government, economically stable, little in the way of recent unrest. Egret is popular, plus she has ties to a number of well-positioned people—diplomatically and socially—from the time she lived here." He smiled. "The French love her, Commander."

Some of the French a little too much. Cam considered the obvious attentions of the French ambassador's wife, whom she knew to be a former lover of Blair's, toward Blair at the gala the previous night. Cam's mouth quirked but she did not smile. "Very well—the hospital tour is a go."

As people made notes and shuffled papers, Cam set her PDA down beside her coffee cup and placed both palms flat on the table. She leaned forward slightly, and when she said, "New developments," everyone immediately sat slightly forward in their folding chairs and gave her their complete attention.

"At approximately 0500 stateside—1100 hours local time— a news article will be released containing a personal statement from Egret that states she is romantically involved with another woman."

Cam surveyed every individual in the room. No one moved. Not a single eyebrow flickered. Satisfied, she sipped her coffee and collected her thoughts.

"The effect on our current situation is uncertain at this time. I expect that by the end of the day the news will have been disseminated internationally. It will definitely be a topic for discussion, but my concern is whether it will be a catalyst for any kind of action involving Egret." She looked at her new political analyst. "Parker?"

Cynthia Parker, early thirties, solidly built and confident, took her time replying. Her dark brown eyes, a shade richer than her hair, were focused and calculating. "I wouldn't expect an *organized* protest for at least twelve hours after the peak of the media exposure. In Paris in particular, sexual orientation and activity is not a hot button. I don't think we're likely to see much fallout." She shrugged. "The previous administration's sex scandal was a joke over here. Hell, most of Europe was laughing at us for even noticing who the president screwed."

"Agreed." Cam looked to Mac. "We'll need to increase our crowd control response."

"Roger that."

"It's also possible she'll be confronted by individuals at some of her upcoming venues," Cynthia continued, her gaze holding Cam's. "Possibly even socially."

"That's a personal matter which I'm sure that Ms. Powell will handle as she sees fit." Cam's voice was even and controlled, but she felt a surge of anger that Blair might be faced with even further invasion of her privacy. She knew without a doubt that Blair could handle any comments or questions, but she hated that her lover would need to. It was just another instance where Blair's personal life was on display and where others felt that because she was a public figure it was appropriate to question her about private matters. Cam drew a breath and pushed aside the anger. She needed to focus on her job.

"What about fundamentalist group reaction—religious opposition, right-wing cells?" Cam was not worried about picketers. While she did not want Blair harassed or embarrassed or accosted in any way, protestors were usually more of a nuisance than a threat. Usually. She *was* concerned about the groups with paramilitary or terrorist affiliations. A direct assault was not going to come from the established right-wing political parties, regardless of their doctrine. These groups were infiltrating the political structure through mainstream bureaucratic channels, helped by their increasing popularity in recent elections. Of much greater concern were the underground extremist groups, especially in light of increasing intelligence that these groups were forming loose coalitions across racial and religious lines.

Cynthia replied immediately. "Reports show no increased activity over baseline for the last six months within the major cells operating in Western Europe. The Austrian Freedom Party, Sweden's White Aryan Resistance, the Flemish Bloc in Belgium— all of them are fairly visible and their communications are constantly monitored. There's nothing coming over the wire to suggest any focus on Egret." She appeared to consider her next words. "But that intel is only as good as our sources."

"Mac?" Cam asked. "What do we have from the Central Security Service on extremist activity in this area?"

"I can't be certain that we're as up to date as we might be, because channels from that direction tend to run slowly," Mac stated. A momentary flicker of displeasure crossed his smooth features and was gone. The intelligence community was a huge network of interfacing agencies, each of which dealt with a portion of national and international intelligence. Many functioned under the umbrella of the National Security Agency, but every agency from the CIA to the FBI and individual military intelligence branches gathered information through their own networks. Theoretically, that information was pooled, distilled, and then disbursed to those who needed to know, including the Secret Service. Mac received bulletins directly from the NSA and CSS around the clock. "But I haven't gotten any alerts."

Nodding, Cam turned her attention to their steganographer, Barry Wright. "Anything locally of concern?"

"Nothing specific, just a worrisome increase in traffic in general." Barry was a new breed of cryptographer. He spent the bulk of his time monitoring the Internet, analyzing sites known or suspected to be shields for communication between individuals, radical groups, and even governments involved in right-wing or terrorist activities. The most common way to transmit "hidden" messages was to insert them bit by bit into jpeg image files, called "cover" images. The recipient then deconstructed the image code and put together the camouflaged message. It was a sophisticated and time-consuming encoding and decoding process, but very difficult for intelligence agencies to detect. "There's been a buildup in chatter over the last six months, but nothing that's come together as a coherent picture. No hits on Egret other than the usual notices of her travel plans."

A muscle in Cam's jaw bunched. Blair's schedule—hell, even the president's schedule—was posted on the official White House Web site for anyone to read. The Secret Service protested the practice vigorously, but the media consultants had won the point.

"Okay then," Cam said briskly, closing her handheld and putting it away. "First team—I'll advise when I've checked with Egret regarding her morning schedule. Have the cars ready and a backup team available."

"Yes, ma'am," Stark replied sharply.

As the agents stood to disperse, Cam said quietly, "Stark—wait a minute, please."

Surprised, Stark stiffened. "Yes, Commander."

Once they were alone, Cam refilled her coffee and raised an eyebrow at Stark, who shook her head. Sipping hers, Cam leaned back against the sideboard. "You're off duty until 1500."

"But—"

"You'll be in the lead car, first team for her hospital tour. I want you fresh."

Stark knew better than to protest again. "Yes, Commander."

"Tell Felicia the same thing."

"Uh..." Stark's pulse shot into the stratosphere.

"The coffee cups steamed up the windshield," Cam remarked blandly. "Next time you're doing street surveillance, drink it cold."

Stark's face went from red to white in less than a heartbeat.

Cam placed her cup carefully on the stack of dirty dishes next to the coffeemaker. On her way to the door, she added, "You can tell Felicia thanks, too."

CHAPTER FIVE

```
0930 16Aug01
Query RedDog: Do you read?
RedDog: Roger, team leader
You have green light 1600 IGR Confirm
RedDog: 1600 IGR Green light
Good hunting Godspeed Team leader out
```

Outside in the hallway, Cam nodded to Felicia and Reynolds. "You're relieved, Agent Davis. Check in with Stark."

"Yes, ma'am."

Cam knocked on Blair's door and a moment later, it opened. "Good morning, Ms. Powell. May I have a moment?"

Blair smiled. "Of course, Commander. Please come in."

Once Cam was inside, Blair closed the door and locked and chained it. Then she turned to where Cam waited only a few feet away and stepped into her waiting arms. With one hand clasping the back of Cam's neck, Blair leaned into her and kissed her. Then she drew away and lightly ran her fingers along Cam's jaw. "You're tense. Difficult meeting?"

"*You're* frightening." Cam made a conscious effort to relax her shoulders. No one except Blair would know by looking at her, or very probably even by touching her, what she felt. Blair, however, could read her body and her mind with alarming accuracy. "Just the usual briefing."

"Uh-huh." Blair walked a few feet away, sat on the broad arm of the sofa, and leaned against the back. She wore a blue silk robe, belted at the waist, and her hair was still damp from the shower, finger-combed and falling freely around her face. "I'd like to sit in on one of those morning chats some time."

No, you wouldn't. Cam considered her answer, and then decided to go with the simple truth. "It's your prerogative, but I'd rather you didn't."

"I'm not surprised." Blair tilted her head and studied her lover, who looked drawn, as she often did when a public outing was scheduled. Blair knew the risks, and she knew the additional pressure it put on Cam to ensure her safety. "I think I know why you're tied up in knots, but I'd rather not guess. Want to tell?"

Sighing in surrender, Cam crossed the room to sit on the sofa by Blair's side. On the way down, she grabbed Blair and tumbled her into her lap. With an arm around her lover's shoulders and one at her waist, Cam nuzzled her neck. "I really like you in this robe. You look exactly like you did the first morning we met, except I couldn't touch you then. But God, I wanted to."

"You're trying to distract me," Blair murmured as Cam leaned over until they were nearly reclining face to face. She slid her hand inside Cam's jacket and ran her hand down Cam's side. "I'm beginning to recognize that tactic, Commander Roberts."

"Busted. I'm in trouble for so many reasons." Cam kissed her then because she was beautiful, and she was vital, and she was everything that made Cam's life worth living. "I love you so much."

Blair's heart skipped a beat. "Amazing. You have no idea what hearing that does to me."

"I know what feeling it does to me." Cam rested her forehead against Blair's and closed her eyes. There were moments when she wished they were anywhere else, *anyone* else. She wished that they never needed to walk out the door, and if they did, that she would never need to look over her shoulder for some dark force that might sweep into her life and in the space between two breaths destroy everything that mattered to her. Most of the time she could separate herself from those fears. She was trained to deal with reality and not to dwell on possibility. But there were times, when Blair was in her arms and she felt nothing but total completion, that she couldn't keep the dread at bay.

"Cam?" Blair's voice held a concerned note. "You're shaking."

Cam took a long slow breath and pushed up on the sofa as Blair swung her legs around until she was sitting beside her. "Sorry."

"Want to tell me what that was about?" Blair took Cam's hand, folded it between her own, and rested their joined hands on her thigh. She loved Cam's hands. They were bold and strong and incredibly tender, just like the woman herself. "Sweetheart?"

"I'd rather not. It was just one of those...passing things," Cam said gently. *You'll feel responsible, and you don't need to be burdened by something else you can't change.*

Understanding privacy, Blair simply nodded, but she'd seen the pain. "All right. Then back to the initial question. Why don't you want me at the briefings?"

Cam eyed Blair with obvious exasperation. "You are the most single-minded, relentless, and all too frequently annoying individual I have ever met."

Blair smiled sweetly. "That's another stall tactic. You're not going to goad me into an argument."

"We talk about you." The words came out with a combination of apology and anger. "I don't want you to hear that."

Surprise showed in Blair's eyes. "Cam, I *know* that you talk about me."

"*I* talk about you," Cam said quietly. "You think you don't like my command voice when we're together? You'd really hate it in there."

"And you think...what? If I heard you discuss Egret with your team that I'd feel like I meant less to you?"

Cam looked away briefly, then brought her eyes back to Blair's. When she did, there was uncertainty and unease in their dark depths. "I don't know. Maybe. I don't want to risk it."

Shaking her head, Blair turned and drew her legs up onto the couch until she was kneeling by Cam's side. She took Cam's face gently in both hands and tilted her head until their faces were inches apart. Her gaze bored into Cam's. "Listen to me. I know what you do. *And* I know what they don't know, Cameron—what they'll never know. I know your fear, and I know that you can't let them see it." She kissed her, tenderly at first and then with fierce possession. She felt Cam's hands on her back, pulling her down until she was once again in Cam's lap, her arms around Cam's neck. When she drew her mouth away, she murmured, "I know that you have to go away from me to do what you need to do."

"No," Cam said swiftly, her voice strained. She took Blair's hand and placed it over her own heart, cradling it there. "I'll never go away from you. Not ever."

"That's good," Blair sighed, resting her cheek against Cam's shoulder. "Because I'm starting to count on you being around."

"Good thing." Cam rested her chin against the top of Blair's head, feeling the melancholy drift away. Blair brought her not just peace, but the joy of being known. "Because I pretty much plan on sticking around."

"You want to take a walk with me?"

"I'd love to."

Outside, Cam and Blair walked together ten feet ahead of the three agents who accompanied them. Blair carried a small portfolio in one hand. Her hair was down and she had changed into blue jeans, a navy polo shirt, and sneakers. Had they not exited from the Hotel Marigny, the residence reserved for state visitors, Blair could easily have passed for any other tourist. Cam carried nothing, needing to keep her hands free to access her weapon. Despite the fact that her jacket concealed a wrist mic, a radio pager, a cell phone, and her automatic in a shoulder harness, she appeared so casual that she might have been a tourist as well.

"Do you mind if we don't take the main avenue, but stay on the side streets on the way to the gardens?" Cam asked, her gaze traveling over both sides of the thoroughfare ahead.

Blair hooked her left hand through the crook of Cam's arm. "Not at all. I'm not in the mood to fight with the crowds on Champs Elysées at the moment." She took a deep breath of the warm summer air and sighed with contentment. "It's beautiful this morning, and I just wanted to be outside for a while."

"They're still renovating a large part of the Tuileries Gardens, apparently," Cam remarked. "It's not likely to be as crowded as some of the other areas because of that."

"I know. It doesn't really matter where I am, as long as I have a few hours just to relax."

"If you want to be alone—"

"No," Blair said quickly, squeezing Cam's arm. "Not from you. From...all the rest of it."

"Then I'll keep you company while you sketch." Cam smiled. "I think I told you that I used to spend hours with my mother and her friends when they were working. She always had a studio in the house, and she often had students who spent weeks—sometimes months—with her. I modeled now and then."

"Did you?" Blair gave Cam an appraising glance. "Commander Roberts, you are full of surprises. Would you pose for me?"

"Of course."

"Nude?"

Cam's right eyebrow rose. "If you wish."

"On second thought," Blair mused, "I'm not sure I'd be able to concentrate." She gave Cam another look. "Would it excite you, to pose for me nude?"

"Yes."

"I think..." Blair's face took on a contemplative expression, "that I'd like to tell you which part of you I'm touching as I draw. Would you be able to feel my hands on you?"

"Yes." Cam's voice was deep and heavy, echoing the pulse of excitement in the pit of her stomach. "You'd know—you'd see the flush on my skin and my nippl—"

"Stop!" Blair gave a small groan. "God, I really shouldn't be thinking about that out here. But I'm not going to forget the offer."

"You needn't worry. I won't renege."

From the Rue de Rivoli, they turned onto a path that led into the huge expanse of the once-gracious gardens of Catherine de Médicis. Many of the formal plantings and trees had been destroyed by blight over the ensuing five centuries, but an intensive replanting had been underway for close to a decade, and much of the beauty had been restored. Near one of the large octagonal fountains, Blair found a bench that was free and relatively secluded.

"Okay?"

"Looks good," Cam agreed, and with a subtle murmur into her mic, she deployed her agents before sitting down beside Blair on the bench. The air was warm and she would have removed her jacket, but couldn't because of her weapon. She was used to that inconvenience and quickly forgot it.

"I think this is one of my favorite things to do," Blair commented as she withdrew a sketch pad and pencils from her portfolio.

"Sketch outdoors?"

"Mmm." Blair was already bent over her sketch pad, making swift, sure lines across the paper. "Especially with you nearby. You really don't mind?"

"No, it's one of the most enjoyable things that I've ever experienced. I'm reminded—"

"What?" Blair looked up, concerned by Cam's pensive tone. "What, sweetheart?"

Cam shook her head. "Sorry. I didn't mean to disturb you. I was just thinking that it reminded me of my childhood in Italy. It was..." She shrugged. "I guess like most people's childhoods, it was sometimes idyllic and other times unbearable."

Blair reached across the space between them and ran her hand down Cam's arm until she reached her fingers, which she lightly clasped. "I love you."

Cam smiled, squeezed Blair's hand, and then let it go. "Draw, Ms. Powell."

Blair smiled. "As you wish, Commander."

At 1150, a thin, dark-complected man with short brown hair, wearing gray coveralls and carrying a small toolbox, walked down the narrow alley behind a fifteen-story office building. His stride was confident, his carriage comfortable, as he walked up to the service door. A keypad was set into the door frame, and he unhesitatingly punched in a series of seven numbers. Then he reached down, grasped the knob, which turned easily in his hand, and slipped inside.

"Blair," Cam said quietly.

"Hmm?"

"It's almost noon."

Blair did not look up, but continued drawing for another few moments. Then she set the pencil down beside her and eased her cramped shoulders. Running a hand through her hair, she looked out over the gardens. Here and there groups of tourists or families strolled about with cameras, expressions of excitement on their faces. She turned to her lover, who sat with her long legs stretched out in front of her, ankles crossed, arms down by her sides, her hands loosely curled around the edge of the bench. If Blair didn't know better, she'd think Cam was completely relaxed. She would also bet any amount of money that Cam knew the exact placement of every individual within her sight range, how long each had been there, and exactly how long it would take any of the three invisible agents to reach Blair's side. "Are you able to enjoy any of this?"

Slowly, Cam slid her left hand over until her fingers met Blair's. "I see you, Blair. Even when I'm working. I always see you."

"I'm sorry." Blair smiled wryly. "God, I can't believe I'm jealous of your job now."

"I think being together takes a little getting used to."

Blair laughed. "You think?" She slid her sketch pad into her portfolio and secured her drawing pencils. "I am completely new at this. I don't have a clue as to what I'm doing." She glanced at her lover, who regarded her seriously. "The only thing of which I'm entirely certain is that I want us to be together."

"Then we are in complete agreement." Cam stood, lifted her left hand, and advised her agents of their departure.

The service entrance opened into a warren of storage rooms, with a bank of elevators at the end of a long hallway. Next to the elevators, a sign marked the stairwell. The man in the electrician's uniform pushed the bar handle, and the stairwell door opened soundlessly. With steady steps, he began the climb to the roof.

In the main lobby of the building, two bored French security officers lounged behind the information desk, conversing with the receptionist who relayed calls to the various offices and provided directions to those visitors who might need them.

Francois Remy glanced at his watch. "Do you want to do the first walk-through or do you want me to take it?"

Henri Bouchard shrugged. "I'll take this one, and you can have the next."

"Good enough."

Henri set out to take the elevator to the fifteenth floor to commence the inspection of the building. His route would wend from one end of each hallway to the other and down the stairwell between floors. Most of the offices were occupied, and he would spot-check those, particularly the ones facing the Institut Gustave-Roussy. He sighed as he watched the numbers above the elevator doors count down to one. *Such a lot of fuss for one woman. If she weren't an American...*

When the man with the toolbox reached the fifteenth-floor landing, he found a door to his left that led to the corridor and offices. To his right, a narrow staircase led up to a single gray steel door at roof level. He made his way up and paused a few steps below the door. A red sign warned that any attempt to open it would trigger a central alarm.

Unhurriedly, he set down his toolbox, opened it, and removed a set of screwdrivers, a wire stripper, and fine needle-nose pliers. Working quickly but coolly, he removed the faceplate from the alarm box, inspected the simplistic design to ensure that no backup alarms had been added, and rerouted the signal around the door connection. Then he replaced the faceplate, secured his tools, and pushed open the door. It had taken him exactly six minutes to reach the roof from the street.


```
1200 16Aug01
RedDog in position
```

CHAPTER SIX

At precisely 1200, Bouchard stepped off the elevator at the east end of the fifteenth floor and headed down the corridor at a steady pace. From behind partially open doors came the low murmur of voices and the insistent hum of myriad electronic devices. He paid particular attention to the offices on the north side of the building, the ones that faced the wide boulevard below and the medical complex opposite. At that morning's briefing, he had been given a list of locations on each floor that posed particular security concerns, but a thorough check suggested nothing out of the ordinary. When he reached the west end of the hallway, he pushed open the fire door and stepped out onto the six-by-six-foot landing. To his left a steep, narrow staircase led upward, and he climbed several stairs to get a clear look at the door to the roof. As he knew from the building specs provided to his team by the captain, the door was alarmed. If the circuit was disrupted, a switch on the main board in the reception area in the lobby signaled an alert. His partner was at that moment watching those monitors. Satisfied that nothing was amiss, he started down the stairwell to the fourteenth floor. He checked his watch as he reached the next level and nodded, pleased to note that he was right on schedule.

"We depart at 1530," Cam said as she walked Blair to the door of her suite. It was hard to leave her again so soon, but they both had jobs to do. "I'll be in the comm center until then if you require anything."

"That's fine," Blair replied softly, mindful of the other agents close behind. "I want to change and make some phone calls." Lowering her voice even further, she met Cam's eyes. "Thank you for last night, and for these last few hours."

Cam nodded. Briefly, she touched Blair's hand and then turned toward the room across the hall. By the time she reached the door, Blair had disappeared.

Inside, Cam walked directly to Mac, who was in his usual place in the center of the electronic activity. She pulled over a stool and sat beside him, ignoring the flickering monitors with their dizzying kaleidoscopes of shifting images. Her only interest was the stack of computer printouts by his left hand. "What do we hear from the media?"

"Well," Mac answered, leaning back in his swivel chair, "it's not above the fold, but the article made the front page in most major cities stateside."

"As expected," Cam noted grimly. "Have you heard anything from the White House?"

"Lucinda Washburn called and left a message for Egret to call her ASAP." Mac gave Cam a sideways glance. "I didn't think it was necessary to interrupt you in the field."

"Thanks. I think she needed a bit of a break." Cam gave him an appreciative smile. "I'll pass on the chief of staff's request."

Mac merely grunted. He had nothing against Lucinda Washburn, arguably the second most powerful person in the country, but his sole allegiance was to the team. And to Blair Powell. "I expect that the White House press secretary will make some kind of statement at the afternoon briefing."

"I suppose once Aaron has officially addressed Blair's announcement, every major news outlet will pick it up." Cam sighed. "I don't expect we'll see much media response at the hospital today, but she has the meeting with the minister of health and the representatives from the WHO in the morning. That's going to get some coverage."

"You know," Mac commented, "Egret's status in the administration is closer to first lady than first daughter, since she fulfills so many of the obligations that would have been her mother's responsibility."

"Yes. And because of that, she is much more visible to the world at large." *And much more vulnerable,* both thought, but neither said. Cam's gaze hardened. "We have to consider her at high-alert status at all times."

"Roger that, Commander."

"Our advance teams are on-site?"

"Yes, ma'am. I should have the first reports soon."

"Good. Keep me advised. As soon as the lead team arrives, we'll brief."

"Yes, ma'am."

"Anything out of the ordinary, anything at all, from any source—I want to know."

"Yes, Commander."

Paula Stark jerked awake and blinked furiously. Her first thought was *bright. Very bright.* She closed her eyes. She next recorded an unusual sensation beneath her cheek. *Soft. Warm.* She drew a breath. *Smells good. Cinnamon?* She opened one eye a slit. An image of a long-necked giraffe filled her vision. Closing that eye again, she rolled onto her back, registering that she was indeed lying supine and that her head was propped on something yielding, but firm. Warily, she peered upward, finally focusing on the blue eyes a couple of feet above her own that regarded her with gentle amusement.

Stark blinked. "Renee?"

"You were expecting perhaps someone else?"

Stark blinked again. The last thing she could clearly remember was the commander telling her to stand down until the afternoon briefing. Then she had called Renee, told her she had a few hours free, and they had agreed to have breakfast together. "Uh-oh. Breakfast?"

Renee shifted slightly and deposited the newspaper she'd been reading onto the coffee table beside her feet, which were propped on its tiled surface. "You fell asleep in the middle of toast."

Stark groaned. She curled on her side and pressed her face to the curve of Renee's abdomen, hoping to hide her acute humiliation. She registered at that point that the material beneath her cheek was soft, brushed cotton and that a multitude of tiny animals danced on the edges of her field of vision. "You have a jungle on your boxers," she mumbled, her mind a mass of confused embarrassment and awakening arousal.

Chuckling, Renee insinuated her fingers through Stark's dark hair and massaged her neck softly. "You should see what I've got inside."

Stark's blood pressure shot through the roof, her stomach flipped, and her heart came to a complete standstill. Her breath whooshed out on a reflexive moan.

"However," Renee continued, her stomach tightening as she felt Stark tremble, "since it's 1300 hours and you're due at a briefing in an hour, I don't think you're going to get a chance to find out today."

I fell asleep on her. Literally on *her. Jesus!* Thoroughly mortified, Stark rolled back once again and looked up with imploring eyes. "I'm so sorry. I'm such a dud."

"A dud?" The corner of Renee's mouth lifted in a smile at once tender and seductive. "Let's see—you worked all day yesterday, you were up all night, and then you were ordered to take a few hours' downtime. The first thing you did at that point was call me." She curled downward and kissed Stark's forehead, then her mouth. "Believe me, sweetie, you have nothing to apologize for. But if you don't get your tail in gear, you'll be late for one of Roberts's briefings. Then we won't have to worry about the condition of your ass, because she will have chewed it off."

Sweetie. She called me sweetie. Stark curled one arm back, found the hand stroking her hair, and threaded her fingers through Renee's. "A week ago when we were back in New York, we were half a second away from tearing each other's clothes off. I want you just as much right now." She took a breath, took the plunge. "More. A lot more."

Renee's blue eyes widened, and her full lips parted in surprise. "One of the things I lo—find so enchanting about you is your absolute lack of pretense. You say what you mean." *At least I hope you do, because that's why I'm falling in love with you.*

"Why did you stop? Back then." Stark's question was soft, gentle.

Renee sighed and looked across the room, but her mind looked back over the last ten years of her life. Pensively, she replied, "I haven't had many relationships of consequence in my life, and none to speak of in the last few years. Most of them couldn't stand up to the demands of the training and then the work that we do." She shrugged and sighed again. "You know what I mean—the hours are terrible, we can't talk very much about the specifics, and even when we do, most people won't understand it. It was just easier not to get serious about anyone." She felt Stark grow still against her side, and she looked back down, finding dark, understanding eyes as she brushed her fingers through the hair on Stark's forehead. "You and I—we had something in common, right from the beginning, even if at first we didn't see eye to eye."

"The job," Stark replied, knowing that Renee knew what *she* knew—that the job defined who they *were* as much as, or more than, what they did.

"Mmm. Yeah...but it's not just the job. You're special." Shyly, Renee added, "You make me *feel* special."

"I hope so," Stark murmured fervently. "I think you're the most wonderful woman I've ever met. I *hope* I make you feel that way." She flushed. "Except I don't know exactly how to do that."

"Maybe thinking about me first before anything else, even after twenty-four hours with no sleep doing one of the most stressful jobs in the world, is a good start."

"You didn't quite answer the question," Stark pressed carefully. *Tell me if there's something wrong—if there's something you need that I can give you.*

"No, I didn't." Renee smiled wanly. "I want you today just as much...more...than I did that night. I think about it; I dream about it. I'm just...afraid."

That wasn't what Stark expected. Her brows furrowed in concern. "Why? Is it something I've done? Something I've said?"

"No, just the opposite. You're a little bit too good to be true." Renee blushed and twirled a lock of Stark's hair around her fingertips. "I'm afraid if I sleep with you, and it doesn't work out, it's really going to hurt."

Stark pushed up on the sofa until she was sitting beside Renee. She slid an arm around her shoulders and pulled the other woman close. With her lips lightly brushing Renee's hair, she whispered, "I think you're special, too. I don't know how to tell when the time is right, but that's what I want. For it to be right."

Sighing with contentment and not a small degree of frustration, Renee threaded her arm around Stark's waist. "Thank you."

"For what?"

"For being patient."

Laughing, Stark dipped her head and captured Renee's mouth. She slipped her tongue between Renee's lips, danced over the surface of her tongue, and slid out again. "I'm not patient. In fact, I'm pretty sure something's going to explode before long. But I'm not taking any chances on messing this up."

With a small cry, Renee pushed her hands into Stark's hair and shifted until she was lying half in her lap. Her mouth on Stark's was hungry, needy, demanding. In another second they were lying stretched out on the sofa, Renee's thigh tight between Stark's, Stark's hands beneath Renee's blouse, their hips moving in perfect synchrony, thrusting hard. Someone groaned.

Stark wrenched her mouth away. "Oh man. Man...I want you so bad."

"Oh yeah." Gasping, Renee pressed her forehead to Stark's chest. "Oh yeah. I think maybe I'm done waiting."

"You gotta wait..." Stark's voice was a desperate plea. "Just a little longer. I gotta go."

Groaning, Renee could only nod.

"I'm gonna think about you all—"

"Shh," Renee murmured, pressing tightly to her. "Once you walk out of here, I don't want you to think about anything except the job. I want you totally focused on Egret, just like you always are. Then, when you're off shift, I want you to come back to me. Safe and sound."

"I don't know how I got so lucky," Stark whispered, tilting Renee's chin up and kissing her with a series of tender, gentle caresses.

"*We* got lucky," Renee sighed against her mouth.

The thin man knelt by the three-foot wall that rimmed the flat expanse of the rooftop, shielded from view by the oversized air-conditioning units and heating ducts. If anyone opened the rooftop door, he would hear them, and he had the advantage of surprise.

He did not, however, expect visitors. The first security check was over, and the second was likely to be cursory. After assessing the sightline to the hospital entrance, he once again opened the toolbox, this time lifting out the upper compartment. Beneath that lay the barrel of a Heckler and Koch G36 assault rifle. From various pockets in his gray coveralls, he removed the remaining components of the weapon, which he had fieldstripped just that morning before departing the rooming house he had inhabited for the last fourteen months. Quickly and efficiently, he assembled the 3.6 kilogram weapon and loaded it with a standard magazine carrying thirty rounds. In the lower compartment of the tool chest were additional magazines. The German assault rifle was capable of firing 750 rounds of 5.56 x 45mm bullets per minute.

He did not expect to need more than one.

Seated on the sofa in the high-ceilinged palatial suite, Blair drew out her sketch pad and opened it on her lap. Critically, she appraised that morning's work, thinking about the upcoming show scheduled in Manhattan in three weeks. It wasn't her first gallery exhibition, but it was her first solo showing. She was nervous and excited and just a little resentful that she couldn't concentrate completely on the work that mattered the most to her. Her other responsibilities—her official duties—so often interfered. Although she was proud to represent her country and happy to assist her father in any way possible, his dream had never been her dream. Nevertheless, she had embraced it as much as she possibly could. She flipped through the pages until she came to the last drawing she had done. Cam had not been aware of Blair sketching her, or if she had been, she had not shown any sign of it.

Cam was Blair's favorite subject. Not only was she beautiful, with the coloring and bone structure that any artist loves to draw, but Blair reveled in the opportunity to study her. Even knowing it was impossible, she still tried to capture the essence of Cam's unique nobility and strength through her art. Lightly, she traced her fingers over the drawing, feeling Cam's flesh beneath her own.

I love you.

Carefully, she closed the pad and secured it away. Then she

leaned over and drew the phone from the table beside the sofa and punched in a series of numbers from memory. After less than a moment, her call was answered.

"Johnny? It's Blair. I don't suppose there's any chance... You're sure?...Of course." A minute passed, and then she sat up straighter. "Dad?"

"Blair. Everything all right?"

"Yes, fine."

"Still in Paris?"

"For another two days. Everything is going well on that front."

"Have you been to the hospital yet?"

The question startled her. She hadn't realized he had any idea of her itinerary. She swallowed and kept her voice even. "Just about to go in an hour or so."

"Doing okay?"

"Yes. Fine." She took a deep breath. "I guess you've seen the newspapers?"

A dry chuckle came through the line. "I haven't actually read any of the articles, since I already know from you what the interview entailed. But I gather someone jumped the gun."

"Looks like. I just wanted to make sure that...I'm not *sure* what, exactly," she confessed.

"It's okay, honey. There's nothing you need to be concerned about. Just concentrate on the trip, and try to enjoy it as much as you can."

"What does Lucinda have to say?" Blair pressed. Lucinda often had a better sense of the undercurrents of public opinion than her father did.

"Lucinda worries a little too much sometimes."

"You should listen to her. I'm sorry if I caus—"

"Blair," her father's voice was at once firm and gentle, "I can't think of anything you've ever done that you need to apologize to me for. I am nothing but proud of you."

She heard a muffled conversation and knew that he had covered the phone.

"Look, Dad, I know you're busy. I can—"

"Sorry, I *am* running late. How's Cam?"

Blair's heart skipped a beat. "She's...she's fine. Traveling is difficult, and she's preoccupied."

"She should be. But she's okay...with this other?"

Blair's throat tightened. She wasn't certain, but she *thought* her father might be asking her if everything was all right with her relationship. "She's great. I'm...happy."

"That's the best news I could get. I'm sorry, honey. I'm going to have to go. Call me again soon."

"Okay. Yes. I will."

"Be careful. Bye, honey."

"Bye, Dad." Blair set the phone down gently. They'd never had a conversation anywhere near like this one. It was terrifyingly strange and strangely wonderful.

Intentionally or not, she had kept a barrier between herself and her father all her life, just as she had shielded her private self from the prying eyes of the public and hidden the true longings of her heart from the women she had touched. Until Cam. Loving Cam had changed everything, and as frightening as that sometimes was—to be vulnerable and exposed, not just to heartbreak, but to the unmerciful scrutiny of strangers—she had never felt so free.

CHAPTER SEVEN

Felicia was the first of the lead team agents to arrive for the briefing. When she entered the comm center, Mac was the only other person present. A murmur of conversation emanated from the adjoining room where Cynthia and Barry spent most of their time, hunched over their consoles searching for intel hidden in cyberspace. She walked to the sideboard, poured a cup of coffee, and crossed the room to the conference table.

At the sound of the quiet movement behind him, Mac swiveled away from the monitors and silently observed Felicia. She was dressed in the same two-piece suit, tailored shirt, and functional shoes that all the agents, male or female, wore. On her long, svelte frame, however, the outfit managed to appear elegant. Her slender neck, high-arched cheeks, and fine-boned jaw gave her the look of an ancient priestess or warrior. She was painfully beautiful, as well as being intimidatingly intelligent and inestimably competent. They'd had two dates before she'd told him in firm gentle tones that it had been a mistake.

Mac cleared his throat. "Good afternoon."

Felicia looked up from the most recent field reports related to the afternoon's engagement and turned her head with a smile. "Hello."

Nothing in her eyes to suggest familiarity. The same pleasant yet cool inflection she used with everyone. He swallowed his disappointment and tried to tell himself that it didn't matter. "Did you get a chance to see anything of the city during your downtime?"

"A little," Felicia replied carefully. It was not her habit to discuss her personal life with colleagues. Mac was different, and that difference concerned her. Ever since they had spent sixty or so stress-filled hours in each other's company, monitoring an operation that ultimately might have cost the president's daughter her life, she had felt more for him than for any man she had ever worked with. Any man, she acknowledged, with whom she had been involved in *any* way for a long time. Eventually, she'd succumbed to the uniqueness of that unusual connection and had broken one of her own rules. She had dinner with him. Twice. He was precisely as she had expected him to be. Charming, intelligent, gentle. After the second evening, when he'd walked her to the door of her East Village apartment building, he'd kissed her briefly on the mouth. The kiss had been slightly more than friendly, but not intrusive or demanding. It had been a very nice kiss. It had been a kiss she wouldn't have minded repeating. And that's when she'd told him that there would be no more dinners.

"The Secret Service isn't exactly the way to see the world," Mac commented wryly.

Felicia grinned. "No more than the navy. Or any other branch of service."

"Still, a posting in Paris does beat spending a week in a lot of other places I could think of."

"Agreed."

"Felicia—"

Stark walked in and abruptly stumbled to a halt. She took one look around the room with the sense that she had just walked in on something personal. Coloring, she desperately sought a way out.

"Paula," Felicia said smoothly, indicating the seat across from her with a graceful hand. "Get some coffee and have a seat. We can go over the deployment positions before the commander arrives." She glanced at her watch. "Which I estimate will be in two minutes."

"Uh...okay. Sure. Fine."

Disappointed, but not entirely certain he knew what he'd been about to say anyhow, Mac turned back to his ever-present companions—the flickering images on the dozen monitors where shadow figures moved in and out of focus with jerky, robotic movements. As he gathered his papers, he thought that there were times when he was no more tangible to others than those disembodied people captured on his screens. He recognized the sensation as loneliness and quickly pushed it aside.

On the rooftop, the thin man glanced down when he felt a faint vibration emanating from his belt. He removed the two-way pager and glanced at the text.

```
1358 16Aug01
Query RedDog: in position?
```

He thumbed the small keyboard with practiced efficiency, doing it by feel just as he assembled and disassembled his weapons in total blackness.

```
Roger.
Green light. 1600. Team leader out.
```

With another flick of his thumb, he deleted the message. Though the sun blazed down on his back and unprotected head and he wore far too many layers of clothing for the August weather, he had no conscious sense of discomfort. Snipers—men and women who could lie for hours in uncomfortable positions, in snow or mud or tropical heat, without moving a single muscle—were known to have markedly quiescent autonomic nervous systems. When studied, their heart rates were found to be exceptionally slow, their blood pressure reflected little response to adrenergic stimulation, and their galvanic skin reactivity was abnormally low. Assassins, theory had it, were not created, but born. The challenge was in the selection process.

He returned his cheek to the stock of the assault rifle and sighted through the laser scope to the sidewalk in front of the hospital at the precise point where the lead car would pull up and Blair Powell and her entourage would disembark. He anticipated a clear shot. However, it wasn't absolutely required. His ammunition was capable of traversing the human body with almost no deceleration and minimal alteration in trajectory. A body shot, assuming that the individual between him and his target wore body armor, *could* be problematic because, although his ammunition would penetrate the armor, the exit velocity and direction would be skewed to an unpredictable degree by the impact. He might miss the primary target. But if anyone did stand between him and his target, a shot to the head would take out both. He had established the necessary kill-shot angle via computer simulations using the height of every agent assigned to Blair Powell's team.

He hoped that the Secret Service followed their usual quadrant-based protection pattern, because that would put someone directly behind the target. And *that* challenge would make the mission more enjoyable.

"Updates, please." Cam crossed the room and took her usual seat at the head of the table. Those agents not yet seated hurried to find places.

Mac began immediately. "No reports of problems from the advance team. The first walk-through at 1300 was all clear."

"Any sign of interest from the press yet?" Cam had taken half an hour to shower and change and now wore a summer-weight charcoal silk suit with a shirt in a slightly lighter shade of gray.

"Not at the site as of this time," Mac advised.

"What do we have coming over the wires?" Even though almost all of their intelligence was received by computer or electronic transmission, the idiom remained.

"Television stations are carrying the story now, and there was a brief mention of the article and its 'shocking' revelations on one of the British news channels."

Cam's eyes darkened to black. "Every news station and paper in Europe will follow suit. That means a much higher rate of individual contact attempts. I don't want our perimeter breached. Keep her in a tight ring whenever she's on the ground."

Murmurs of assent rang in the air.

Cam turned her attention to Barry Wright. "Anything suggesting an organized response from the underground groups?"

Shaking his head, he frowned slightly. "Still the same dense chatter, but nothing any of us can pin down. No names, no locations, no specifics. If there's something planned, I can't find the details."

"Keep looking," Cam said succinctly. She trusted him to find the hidden messages more than she trusted the NSA.

"Yes, ma'am."

"Everyone knows the drill. This visit will be well publicized because the Institut Gustave-Roussy is the largest cancer center in Europe, and the administrators are hoping this will prompt contributions. They've had a major media campaign running all week, so expect TV cameras and reporters. What with the personal angle thrown in, probably a bigger-than-average crowd. *No one* comes within six feet of her outside that building. Once inside, make sure everyone has a press pass or a visible hospital ID." She turned to Mac. "You have photos of the PR people from the hospital as well as the doctors and nurses on the floor she'll be touring?"

Mac passed out several stapled sheets of paper to each agent. "All here. Obviously, there will be others we didn't anticipate, but these are the individuals likely to have personal contact with her."

"Take a good look, people. If you don't recognize someone or they don't have clear identification, pull them aside and verify. I don't care about ruffling feathers or bruising egos. If it looks wrong, assume it is." She rolled her shoulders to ease the tension she always felt when Blair was making a public appearance. It was nearly impossible to keep her completely safeguarded at any time, but prepublicized public events were the most dangerous. Assassins, kidnappers, or anyone else with an agenda would have plenty of advance notice to fine-tune their plans.

Plus, it didn't help that Egret chafed under the restrictions of the close coverage and tended to disregard it. Cam understood her lover's aversion to tight security, but she couldn't relax the protocols. Her job, as well as her instinctive need, was to keep Blair safe. Sometimes that meant making her angry as well. She stood. "Bring the vehicles to the entrance at 1500. Davis and Stark— you're in the lead car with me. Mac, Fielding, and Reynolds— you're backup in the follow car. Stark will brief you on positions once we're streetside."

A chorus of *Yes, Commander*s followed.

"I'll be with Egret until departure."

The thin man observed the path of an ambulance as it approached along the Rue Camille Desmoulins. To the casual observer, it looked like any other of the dozens of ambulances that came and went from the country's largest public cancer hospital twenty-four hours a day. Even a trained professional would have had difficulty telling this vehicle from any other while it was moving. It was unlikely that its low carriage or slightly overwide transverse dimension would be obvious. This particular vehicle was easily hundreds of pounds heavier than its functional counterparts. In the interior, where emergency equipment and drugs were ordinarily stored in shelves and bins bolted to the walls, there were ammunition racks. The patient stretchers had been removed and replaced with narrow benches along either sidewall, each large enough to accommodate five men in full body armor sitting shoulder to shoulder. Post production, the vehicle had been armored to the National Institute of Justice specifications for Level V protection. Armormax Pac 500 overlapping shields reinforced the roof, lateral walls, floor, and the gas tank. The transparent areas were polycarbonate/glass laminate, capable of withstanding 17.2 foot-pounds per inch of impact. Nothing short of an antitank short-range missile would disable it, and even that would require a shot directly into the driver's compartment.

Moving slowly but drawing no attention, the ambulance coasted into the emergency loading area a hundred yards from the main entrance. Far enough away not to be of concern but close enough that the assault team could reach the target in the first minute of chaos following his shot. *Cut off the head and the snake dies.*

He showed no reaction, not even a blink, when the radio pager on his belt vibrated again. With his eye still fixed to his scope, he reached down, slipped the small square of plastic from his belt, and held it up at eye level.

1430 16Aug01
Avenger on site

Cheek still resting on the abbreviated stock of his weapon, he returned the pager to his belt. Unless he received a directive from the team leader countermanding his orders, his actions and his fate were sealed. God Bless America.

Blair had changed into a cream-colored jacket, matching knee-length skirt, and a deep rose silk blouse. Her medium heels were a slightly deeper hue than her suit. She answered the knock at her door, kissed Cam briefly on the lips as she entered, and locked the door.

"How are you doing?" Cam asked, sensitive to the pensive expression on her lover's face.

"Okay." Blair's voice was quiet and her expression solemn. She forced a smile and ran her fingers along Cam's jaw before leaning close to kiss her again. This time she lingered, playing her tongue over Cam's and biting teasingly at her lower lip.

Cam sighed, a mixture of regret and contentment. She rested both palms loosely on Blair's hips beneath her jacket, holding her close but leaving her room to move away if she needed to. "Lucinda call?"

It was Blair's turn to sigh. She nodded. "Just a few minutes ago."

As Cam expected she would, Blair broke their contact and walked to the windows on the far side of the enormous room. She leaned a shoulder against the centuries-old woodwork and gazed out.

"Trouble?" Cam kept her voice even but she was furious. Furious that her lover should have to answer to anyone regarding something so very private; because Blair was such a private woman, the intrusion was an even greater violation. That Blair should also need to answer to the White House chief of staff—the woman who had guided Blair's father's campaign and who was critical to his reelection—was more pressure than anyone should have to bear. Cam crossed the room, stopped just behind Blair, and placed her hands very gently on her shoulders. "Baby?"

"Trouble? No. Not really." Blair crossed her arms beneath her breasts and settled back against Cam's solid presence. "For Lucinda, she was exceptionally calm."

Slowly, Cam massaged Blair's tight shoulders, working her thumbs into the firm muscles on either side of her spine. As Blair always did when making a public appearance, she had caught back her thick wavy blond hair with the gold clasp that Cam had placed in her pocket just hours before. Brushing the beautiful hair aside with a fingertip, Cam dipped her head and kissed the back of Blair's neck.

"Mmm," Blair moaned softly. "That could almost make me forget everything."

With her lips still skimming Blair's skin, Cam murmured, "It's supposed to." Feeling Blair relax, Cam slipped her hands around Blair's waist, embracing her fully but still allowing her the freedom to escape. Blair was still vibrating with tension, and when she hurt, she was very much a wounded animal. "What did she say?"

"Lucinda made all the politically correct remarks. You know... it doesn't matter who you love, as long as you love. It's no one's business but mine. She even reiterated that the White House and *the party* supported freedom of choice and gay and lesbian issues."

"But?"

"She suggested that we curtail public displays of affection."

Cam forced herself not to react, either physically or verbally. She could do that, because she was trained to do it. She could stand in a room and listen to the president of the United States make plans for war without blinking or just as easily ignore an illicit tryst being consummated within earshot, or even right in front of her eyes. She was not only paid to turn a blind eye, she was indoctrinated with the ability to observe without reaction. But this was her lover, and pretending she didn't want to curse was a struggle. "I suppose I'll have to stop fucking you in the Suburban, then."

Laughing, Blair felt some of the tension melt from her bones. She let her head fall back against Cam's shoulder. "And you can't feel me up at state dinners anymore."

"Damn." Cam kissed Blair's ear. "Does that mean you won't be slipping your hand down my pants at the president's dinner dance tomorrow night?"

Blair turned and wrapped her arms around Cam's neck. Her eyes sparkled and this time her mouth lifted in a genuine smile. "Guess not, Commander. Want to rethink this whole affair?"

Cam kissed her lightly. "That depends."

"Really?" Blair tilted her head and narrowed her eyes dangerously. "On what?"

"On how good you are when I get you alone."

Blair leaned in and nipped Cam's chin. "Better than you can

possibly imagine."

Cam groaned, the sudden heat in her belly making her legs weak. "Okay. That's it—no more teasing. I need all of my blood going to my brain for the next few hours."

Pleased, Blair brushed her fingers through Cam's hair and stepped away. "I know. But thanks."

"For what?"

"Making me laugh when I wanted to—ah, God."

"What?" Cam asked gently.

"I don't know. Throw something? Cry maybe. It doesn't seem to make much difference." Blair shrugged off the melancholy. "I have to keep reminding myself that Lucinda has only one goal in mind, and that's keeping my father in the White House. That's not a bad agenda. I like her. I always have. It's not her fault that she's so single-minded."

"No. Nor is it yours how you choose to live your life, or whom you choose to love."

Blair leaned once again against the magnificent window casing. "I didn't choose to love you, Cameron. I just couldn't help myself."

"Same here." Cam tucked her hands into her front pockets and edged a shoulder against the opposite side of the leaded-glass windows. She regarded her lover contemplatively. "Are you ready for this afternoon?"

"Which part?" Blair laughed humorlessly as she thought about the media attention to come.

"The hospital."

Blair gave a small start. "God, it scares me to realize how well you know me already."

Cam lifted a shoulder. "Not nearly as well as I want to. Not nearly as well as I *intend* to."

"Hospitals." Without being aware of it, Blair shivered. "It doesn't matter what they look like or how hard everyone tries to make them feel welcoming. There's something about the air...or maybe it's the light. Or maybe it's just the way everyone walks around with that horrible mixture of hope and despair warring in their eyes." Blair lifted a hand and let it fall helplessly. "All of a sudden I'm twelve again. It all happened so fast, and then she was gone."

Cam nodded, understanding all too well how life could change in the blink of an eye. Her father had been killed in a car bombing, and in the space of time it had taken for her to run back to the house for her book bag and return to the sidewalk to find his car engulfed in flames, her world had been altered forever. Blair had never talked to her about this before, and Cam chose her words carefully. "How fast?"

"Less than a year. The tumor was aggressive, and despite everything she did...and she did everything right...it didn't make any difference." Blair turned her head to look out the window, seeing nothing as she waited for the brimming tears to subside. "*Everyone* did everything they could have or should have. It just didn't help. They even did a bone marrow transplant, which was experimental back then for breast cancer. Some women *do* go into remission after that, but not as many as with leukemia or the other blood malignancies. She didn't."

Cam made a small noise of comfort. Blair was lost in memory, and Cam just let her talk.

"The last few months she was more often in the hospital than out. My father was a newly seated governor and tremendously busy. Still, he was there as much as he could be." She glanced back at Cam. "But a lot of the time I was there by myself."

Wanting nothing more in the world than to take Blair into her arms and make every hurt she had ever suffered disappear, Cam railed inwardly at her impotence. She yearned to reach into the past and rewrite history, so that the child Blair had been would never have felt frightened or lonely or in pain. The inability to do that was one of the most frustrating things Cam had ever experienced. Never before had she realized just how terribly helpless love could make one feel. Throat tight, she asked gently, "Was it hard?"

Blair smiled wistfully. "Sometimes. But it was wonderful, too. We talked so much. Probably more than we ever would have if things had turned out differently." She laughed quietly, more freely this time. "Girls do tend to spend decades at odds with their mothers."

"I'm sure Marcea would agree," Cam remarked, referring to her own mother.

Blair closed the distance be.ween them and put her arms around Cam's waist. "Marcea adores you, and you know it." She rested her head lightly on her lover's shoulder. "I'll be fine."

Cam kissed her temple and stroked her back. "Of course you will."

"You'll be nearby, won't you?"

"Every single minute."

CHAPTER EIGHT

1505 16Aug01

Slowly, the thin man raised his head and squinted infinitesimally against the bright August sun. The boulevard below had suddenly come alive with activity. Within the span of five minutes, six television news vans and at least as many cars, most bearing the logos of news agencies, crowded into the street directly in front of the Institut Gustave-Roussy. For a relatively low-profile humanitarian visit of little international import, this degree of coverage seemed unusual. He had anticipated and considered media presence in planning his position, the deployment of the ambulance, and the exit strategies, but the current situation could prove to be problematic. Even as he observed the beehive of commotion below, two more vans, the printing on the side panels indicating German and Italian networks, jockeyed for position with the others. The boulevard was rapidly becoming congested. Vehicles were angled into no-parking zones and fire lanes, some were left double- or triple-parked on the shoulder, and swelling crowds of reporters, photographers, and television crews jostled in an ever-increasing shifting mass on the sidewalks.

If the motorcade arrived as planned, he could still make his shot. There would be a momentary hiatus when the target would be exposed just before the swarm of media hounds and paparazzi descended, and that was all the time he required.

Extraction and evacuation through the maze of vehicles, however, might not be so straightforward. His finger lightly depressed the trigger, just short of the pressure required for discharge. What happened after he fired was not his concern.

"All set?" Cam had shed her jacket and weapon harness and sat on the broad plush sofa, her arm loosely draped around Blair's shoulders. Blair had kicked off her shoes and sat curled against Cam's side, her feet drawn up onto the sofa. For the last twenty minutes, she'd been leafing through a French magazine, but Cam had the sense she wasn't really reading anything.

"Mmm, I guess." Blair tossed the magazine onto the coffee table and rested her left hand on Cam's thigh. "What do you want me to say if they ask me about you? About...us."

"What would you say if I weren't your security chief?"

"I'd tell them to stuff it."

Cam smiled and stroked Blair's arm. "Let's pretend that's not an option."

"The last thing I would do is give the press an entrée to my lover and expose her to the kind of scrutiny I've been subjected to all these years."

"Might I suggest 'no comment' then?"

"Yes." Blair's tone held a trace of scorn. "Putting it diplomatically, as ever, Commander."

"Works for me." Cam lifted a shoulder. "No need for you to fight unnecessary battles."

Blair shifted so that she could see Cam's face. "They already *know* it's you because we told them."

"True. We acknowledged that the newspaper photograph was of us and, in the process, dispelled some unseemly rumors about you. That was worth the exposure."

"Maybe. And maybe it wasn't so smart," Blair said quietly. "Mitchell practically drooled when he found out you were my lover. The press—hell, the public—loves that kind of story. It could still come back on you professionally."

"It won't." *And if it does, I'll deal with it.* She studied the storm brewing in her lover's eyes and couldn't decide if it was anger at the invasion of privacy or worry over her. "Hell, your *father* even supports me staying on as your security chief."

"Yes—that means a lot." Blair smiled, thinking just how *much* that meant now. "He asked about you today."

Cam's eyes darkened, and she straightened automatically.

"Oh? Does he have any concerns? I can report—"

Blair laughed. "Relax, lover. He wanted to know if you were okay about the press thing."

"What about the press?" Cam's confusion was clear.

"Oh God—you really don't think about yourself in the equation." She brushed her fingers over Cam's cheek. "He wanted to know if *we* were okay—if the media attention was bothering you."

"What? Does he think I'd walk away because of it? Walk out on you?" Cam's voice held an edge, and a muscle bunched along her jaw. "Maybe he and I should have a talk."

"Sweetheart?" Blair forced back another laugh even as her heart swelled with wonder and delight. "You can't take him on—he's the president."

"He's your father, too, and if he doesn't understand how much I love you, then he needs to."

"You mean it, don't you?" Blair's throat grew tight with the swift rush of emotion. "Oh, Cam. I can't quite get used to it, but I love how you love me."

Cam framed Blair's face gently with both hands. "I want you to feel it every day, everywhere, forever."

Blair turned her face and kissed Cam's palm. "I've never felt so special."

"Good," Cam whispered. "Now forget about the press. You're not required to provide any further information."

"They'll be hungry for more."

"They're always hungry." Cam leaned forward and kissed Blair, savoring the softness of her lips and the heat of her mouth. "Let them starve."

When they separated, Blair's voice was steady and sure. "It's time to go, Commander." She rose and held out a hand. "I have some ribbons to cut and a speech to make. After that, I'm hoping that my lover will take me out to dinner somewhere quiet and private."

The corner of Cam's mouth lifted as she took Blair's hand. "I'll be sure that she gets the message, Ms. Powell."

"See that you do."

Before they reached the elevators, Cam's mic vibrated. She

lifted her wrist. "Roberts."

Advance team reporting. We've got unusually high media traffic on the main approach route, Commander.

"Numbers?"

Two dozen vehicles. Head count's a hundred and rising.

Cam's expression hardened. Crowd control and close-range security outside the hospital were now the critical issues. She could draft the hospital security force as backup, but they weren't trained for this kind of maneuver and would likely prove to be more hindrance than help. The last thing she needed was an overeager hospital guard manhandling a reporter. She wanted to prevent an incident, not precipitate one.

The official French security personnel were already posted as perimeter protection, and she would not leave her borders exposed by pulling them off that detail. The elevator doors opened, and she and Blair stepped on.

"Roger that." She keyed her mic to a different frequency. "Mac."

Go ahead, Commander.

"Your vehicle will take the lead. Egret's will follow."

Roger that.

"Trouble?" Blair asked quietly.

"Nothing to worry about," Cam replied smoothly.

"Don't try that with me, Cameron."

Cam sighed. As they exited into the main lobby, Stark and Felicia moved in on either side, falling into step as Blair walked toward the front doors. "The media are out in force. We may need to adjust."

"Just get me through them."

"Absolutely."

Mac, Reynolds, and Fielding waited under the canopy on the sidewalk. As soon as Blair appeared, they turned and moved ahead of her so that she was ringed by agents.

Blair glanced at Cam. "What's with the close-range coverage?" She spoke quietly, so that Felicia and Stark did not hear.

"I forget," Cam murmured as the men fanned out by the side of the second Peugeot and she reached for the rear door handle, "that you know so much about what we do."

"You're stalling," Blair observed as Cam held the door and she slid with practiced ease into the vehicle.

Cam settled next to her while Stark got behind the wheel and Felicia took the front passenger seat. A pane of Plexiglas with a built-in speaker separated the passenger compartments. "The news release this morning introduces an unknown factor into our usual security protocol. Being out of the country amplifies that. I'm being cautious."

"You're always cautious." Blair smiled fondly and rested her hand once again on Cam's thigh. "I've come to expect that. One thing I've always felt with you is safe."

"Thank you." Briefly, Cam covered Blair's hand with her own and squeezed. "Of all the things I hope you feel because of me, that's one of the most important."

"I know. It isn't something I was looking for, and certainly not something I expected to find with another person."

"Then I'm truly honored." Cam gave an apologetic shrug. "I need to ignore you for a bit while I work."

Blair settled back, her face composed and her eyes distant. "I know. You go ahead. I'll see you later."

1549 16Aug01

The view through the high-powered scope was a few inches of sidewalk directly in front of the main entrance to the Institut. At the moment nothing showed between the crosshairs other than concrete. But in eleven minutes, a vehicle would slide to the curb and the first agent would step out. In the span of ten seconds, she would look first straight ahead and then left and right before finally swiveling to look back over the top of the vehicle to the buildings across the street. Unlike his predecessor, he would not allow a glint of sunlight on steel or twitch of nerves to give his position away. He would see her, but she would not see him. At that point, he would have a clear shot directly between her eyes.

By eleven seconds after arrival, the front doors would open, and the agent in the passenger seat would step to the end of the open rear door while the driver circled the vehicle to flank the lead agent.

At fifteen seconds, the primary target would emerge. Within twenty seconds, the tightly positioned group would begin moving, making his shot more difficult. That five-second span between her exit from the vehicle and her first step was his window of opportunity.

More than enough time.

Cam opened a channel to the advance team. "Advance team—report."

It's a mess, Commander. You'll need to slow to under 10 kph just to get down the street to the entrance.

"What's the situation streetside?"

We've cordoned off the sidewalk, but it's a long approach. Time to full cover four minutes.

The original estimate had been two.

"Assessment?" She didn't like the fact that the motorcade would need to slow to a crawl for the length of the boulevard in front of the Institut. They'd make very good targets at that speed. She especially did not like that it would take twice as long as expected to get Egret into the building. Even with no specific intelligence indicating an elevated threat level, anything that forced her into a defensive position raised her suspicions. Ten seconds passed with no response. "Rogers—are we clear on current course or not?"

His hesitation only added to Cam's reservations. Phil Rogers had done advance work for the team before, and she found him thorough and astute. His eye-level read of the situation was critical, but ultimately only her assessment mattered.

I would categorize the situation as suboptimal but secure, Commander.

"Very well, Agent Rogers. Stand by."

Cam leaned forward and activated the global positioning system on the computer built into the partition between the front and rear seats. She worked the keyboard rapidly, zooming in on the Paris street map until she brought up the six square blocks surrounding their destination. When she entered a series of coordinates, three alternate routes outlined in red, yellow, and green appeared on the grid.

"If we sneak around the reporters," Blair said quietly, "it will look as if I'm afraid to confront the issue."

"You've already confronted the issue," Cam pointed out, her eyes still on the screen.

"I want to go in the front door as planned. I won't have it seem that I'm ashamed."

Cam opened another channel. "Mac, divert to Alt Route Yellow."

Roger that.

After repeating the same instructions to Stark, she contacted the advance team again. "ETA nine minutes—switching to ARY. We'll use the emergency entrance on the south side."

Roger that.

"Cam—"

"I can't be concerned with appearances." Cam met Blair's irritated gaze unwaveringly. "I'm sorry."

"My father was right not to remove you from this post," Blair observed flatly. "Your involvement with me doesn't affect the way you do the job. I should've remembered that."

Cam wasn't certain if that was a criticism or not, but she didn't have time to consider it.

ETA five minutes.

The faint vibration at his hip produced no physical response. His heart rate did not accelerate, his blood pressure did not elevate, his finger did not move even a fraction of a millimeter on the trigger. Once again, without moving his face from its resting place against the rifle stock, he lifted the pager to eye level.

1556 16Aug01
Abort sequence two

He inched his head upward and watched emotionlessly as the armored ambulance rolled slowly down the lane toward the main street and wended through the haphazardly parked news vans until it disappeared from sight around the corner. Then he rested back on his heels and dispassionately disassembled his weapon. With careful precision, he repacked the main assembly into the bottom of his toolbox and stowed the various smaller mechanisms in his pockets in exactly the same order in which he had withdrawn them almost four hours earlier. Task completed, he turned his back to the wall and sat down on the roof, his legs stretched out in front of him.

He would wait three hours before making his way down the stairwell and out of the building. Then he would return to his two-room apartment, resume his unassuming life, and await further instructions. His orders might come that night or the next day or the next week. He could only hope that he would be given another critical role in the complex plan to send notice to the world that even the mightiest of superpowers was vulnerable to those with a clear and certain calling, and that the righteous would ultimately prevail. The sweat running into his eyes brought tears swimming to their surface, but he did not blink.

God Bless America.

CHAPTER NINE

"One in every eight women will develop breast cancer." Blair stood at the front of a large, well-appointed auditorium. It was designed to accommodate several hundred people in individual plush fabric chairs arranged in traditional tiered, semicircular rows, and it was full. Her audience consisted primarily of potential benefactors, with a smattering of hospital personnel. After touring the research and clinical wings, she'd spent the last twenty-five minutes discussing the disease that had killed her mother. "One woman dies of breast cancer every twelve minutes."

Cam stood eight feet away, slightly behind and to Blair's right. Stark occupied a similar post on the opposite side of the raised stage, near the entrance from the rear hallway. Mac and Felicia were at the back of the lecture hall flanking the main entrance. Two more agents stood guard in the lobby and others were posted outside at the hospital entrance and with the motorcade.

"We can do better with those numbers," Blair said with certainty, speaking without notes as she leaned toward the audience, her forearms stretched out on either side of the streamlined lectern, her fingers curled loosely over the forward edge. "With better diagnostic tools and more tumor-specific treatments, fewer women will die and more will live longer and more productively."

She stepped out from behind the podium and strode confidently to the center of the stage. Seeing this, Cam subtly shifted her position, concerned about Blair's exposure in the densely crowded room. Although everyone had been prescreened and IDs had been scrupulously checked, there had been no reasonable way to scan for weapons. That level of security, requiring portable metal detectors and handheld wands and a hell of a lot more people than she had at her disposal, was usually only feasible for the president and vice president. Blair was always vulnerable when in public, and that was the simple reality that Cam lived with and was forced to deal with. The only true protection for the first daughter was ensuring that those who guarded her were able to physically shield her in the event of an attack. That demanded that her security agents be close enough to position themselves between her and danger.

"The researchers here at the Institut Gustave-Roussy and those at similar institutions worldwide need our support—our *financial* support." Blair's voice was steady and strong as her eyes swept the room, pausing briefly on different individuals, making fleeting but powerful contact. "My mother was thirty-two years old when she was diagnosed with breast cancer. She was thirty-three when she died. It's heartbreaking that one so young should die, but death at any age from a disease that we might prevent is the true tragedy. Please, let's work together to eliminate breast cancer from the list of killers. Thank you."

Amidst applause and murmurs of assent, the president of the Institut approached with his hand extended and a deep smile. Blair turned to him with a gracious smile of her own. Her head throbbed and her throat was dry, but she needed to keep up the public façade just a few minutes longer.

"Thank you, Ms. Powell," he said as he shook her hand warmly. "We are honored by your presence here today and appreciate your support on behalf of our endeavors."

Cam listened with half a mind as the final speeches wound down. The greater part of her attention, however, was occupied with the details of her exit strategy. Blair had been extremely unhappy with the earlier diversion to the side entrance of the hospital. Cam knew her lover well enough to know that she would not consent to leave that way.

As the audience began to disperse and a crowd of attendees surged toward the stage for a private word with Blair, Cam moved closer still until she was only a few feet away. Stark mirrored her movements. Only someone watching very closely would have appreciated their actions. Blair spoke with members of the staff and potential donors for an additional twenty minutes, her smile never wavering, her words warm and engaging.

Cam had seen her at many public functions and knew her to be supremely adept at the social and political nuances required when interacting with everyone from heads of state to inner-city residents. Despite Blair's reluctance to engage in the politics of the White House, when called upon to represent her father's administration she was not only good at it, but she excelled. Cam also knew that these functions took a toll on Blair, particularly when they involved talking about something as personal and difficult as her mother's illness and death.

At 1730, Cam leaned near and murmured, "It's time, Ms. Powell."

Without turning in Cam's direction, Blair nodded and cordially greeted another smiling individual. Five minutes later, she thanked the president of the Institut and started up the aisle toward the exit.

"It would be less complicated if we used the side exit," Cam advised as they walked.

Eyes straight ahead, Blair's smile never wavered. "I'm sure. But I'm going out the front door."

Cam sighed. In the time since their arrival on-site, she'd had time to adjust for the greater-than-anticipated crowds in front of the hospital and reposition the team. In all likelihood, some of the eager reporters would have left for other assignments in the interim, diminishing the problem further. Although she wasn't happy about Blair's unanticipated exposure under less than ideal circumstances, she allowed that the margin of safety had been augmented to the point that objecting would only anger Blair for little gain.

"As you wish."

"Thank you, Commander."

They stepped into the lobby and four more Secret Service agents converged on them. Seemingly oblivious to the close proximity of the bodies keeping time with her, Blair moved steadily toward the large double doors and the sunlit sidewalk beyond. Cam advised the outside team of their approach with a few terse orders issued into her wrist mic. Then they were outside and the questions began.

"Is it true you're sleeping with several of the women on your detail?" a sharp female voice called out immediately.

"How do you feel about having your lover take a bullet for

you?"

Blair stiffened perceptibly but her step did not falter, nor did her expression change.

"How do you think your announcement will affect your upcoming gallery exhibit in New York?"

"Is this just a publicity stunt to promote your artwork?"

When Blair slowed, Cam slid a hand behind her right elbow. "Please keep walking."

"What do you think this will do to your father's reelection possibilities?"

"Does the White House approve of your affair?"

"Ms. Powell," a burly redhead in a short-sleeved white shirt and creased trousers called, leaning far over the rope barricade with a microphone extended. "Why didn't your father run on a gay rights platform, considering that you're a lesbian? Was he hoping to keep that a secret?"

"My father demands equal rights for everyone," Blair answered sharply as she glanced in his direction.

Stark opened the rear door of the Peugeot when Blair was five feet away.

"I want to make a statement," Blair said urgently as she attempted to withdraw her arm from Cam's grip.

"I'm sorry," Cam replied, continuing to move forward while firmly directing Blair toward the interior of the vehicle. "Not here."

And then Blair was inside and Cam was sliding in next to her, blocking her view of the crowd outside. Still, the sound of cameras clicking and shouted questions rang in her ears even after they pulled away from the curb.

With a sigh, Blair closed her eyes. "Well, that was fun."

Cam didn't answer. She checked in with the lead vehicle and follow car to ascertain that the exit route was clear. She didn't intend to have a high-speed chase through the streets of Paris with a pack of overeager paparazzi hoping for another shot at Blair. When she was satisfied that everything was in order, she turned to her lover. "Are you okay?"

"I suppose so." Blair's tone was weary, but when she glanced at Cam, she smiled. "It was about what I expected. I'm just a little tired."

Cam reached across the space between them and took Blair's hand, squeezing gently. "I love to hear you speak. I know it's hard for you, but I can tell that you reached the audience. You accomplished something important this afternoon, Blair."

Surprised and touched, Blair whispered huskily, "Thank you. Thank you for reminding me of what matters."

"I'm sorry about the abrupt change in plans earlier—"

"Are you?" Blair asked, more curious than critical.

"Well—yes and no." Cam shrugged. "I'm sorry to have upset you, but I would do the same thing again under similar circumstances."

"Of course you would." Blair's mouth lifted into a half-smile as she shook her head in fond resignation. "I don't know why I'm surprised every time you behave exactly as I should expect you to. I've never met a woman whom I have so consistently failed to influence."

Cam's brows rose in shocked amazement. "Then you haven't been paying attention, Ms. Powell. Because you've changed my life."

"You shouldn't say things like that under the circumstances. It makes me want to kiss you...among other things."

"See what I mean?" Cam grinned. "My judgment is clearly impaired."

"Hardly that," Blair murmured, thinking about how effortlessly Cam slipped from her role of lover into that of security chief. That transition both frustrated her and made her feel incredibly loved. Both emotions gave her pause. "That was just the opening bell with the reporters, you know."

"I know," Cam acknowledged grimly. *And I hate what that does to you.*

"It would probably be better if I gave some kind of press conference and just got the questions out of the way."

Cam shook her head. "I'm not so certain about that. It would simply put you at their mercy and there's no guarantee that the questions would stop. You're the news of the hour and will be until something else comes along with a higher popularity rating. Until then, I think you should continue with business as usual and try not to engage the subject."

Blair rubbed her temples and sighed. "I'll have to think about it. God help me, I suppose I'll have to talk to Lucinda as well."

"All right. If that's what you feel you must do." Cam moved closer on the seat and slid her arm around Blair's waist. "But not tonight, okay? Let it go for tonight."

For just a second, Blair allowed herself to rest her head against Cam's shoulder before straightening up and inching away. "With pleasure."

"Do you have plans for tonight?"

Blair regarded her quizzically. "I had hoped to spend the evening with you."

"I need to make some calls when we get back to the hotel, and then I'll come by and we can discuss it."

Intrigued by the ambiguity in her usually straightforward lover's voice, Blair only nodded as the vehicle pulled to a stop in front of the hotel. "That sounds fine. I'm going to take a couple of aspirin and lie down for a few minutes."

"Good." Cam touched Blair's cheek briefly. "I'll see you in an hour or so."

It was closer to two hours later when Blair answered the knock on her door. Cam waited on the threshold in casual dark chinos and polo shirt under a light blue blazer. Blair motioned her inside and cocked her head, studying her lover appreciatively.

"I like you when you're relaxed."

Cam grinned and took in Blair's soft cotton slacks and scoop-necked silk tee. "You look pretty relaxed yourself." She caught Blair around the waist and kissed her. "Mmm. Smell really good, too."

"That's what a power nap and a hot bath will do for you." Blair leaned back, her hands on Cam's shoulders. "What's on your mind, Commander?"

"This." Cam nuzzled Blair's neck and kissed the base of her throat.

"*Besides* that."

Cam laughed. "Grab your jacket and let's take a ride."

"Where are we going?" Blair asked.

"Out."

"Like on a date?"

They were both painfully aware that dating was not a real possibility for them.

"Something like that."

"Tell."

Slowly, Cam shook her head, a mischievous glint in her eyes. "Nope."

Blair narrowed her eyes. "I am not fond of power plays, Cameron."

"Really?" Cam pulled her close again and nipped at her earlobe, prompting a sound halfway between a moan and a snarl. "I never noticed that."

"And I thought you were so observant." As she spoke, Blair slid a hand between Cam's thighs and squeezed.

Cam gasped, her legs suddenly weak. "Christ."

"I'm sorry—what was that?"

"If you don't stop that," Cam managed through gritted teeth, "I won't be able to walk, and *you* won't find out where we're going."

"Hmm," Blair mused, stroking her fingers softly over Cam's crotch. "Tough choice."

"Please. I want to take you out." Cam kissed her lover's ear. "Later you can torture me as much as you want."

Laughing, Blair removed her hand. "Now that's a deal."

One of the things Stark found so appealing about Paris was that it stayed light later into the evening than she was used to, even when compared to summer evenings back home. When she entered the lobby of Renee's hotel shortly after 8:00 p.m., the sky was bathed in the warm golden glow that preceded the purple dusk. The team had been in Paris a little more than four days, but Egret's schedule had been so full that there'd been little downtime other than the rest periods between shifts. This was the first full evening that she'd had off, and even that had come as a surprise when the Commander had unexpectedly taken her aside and told her she was free until the next afternoon. When she'd started to protest that she was due on rotation again at 0700, the Commander had merely repeated, "Take a break, Stark. Tomorrow night I want you on point."

She'd had the good sense not to argue any further, but had hurried back to the room she shared with Felicia Davis.

"Where's the fire?" Felicia asked as Stark hurried into the two-room suite.

"There's been a change in assignments, and I've got the night off."

Felicia arched her brow. "Really? Good for you. I was just about to go out for a stroll. Want to join me?"

"Uh..."

Laughing, Felicia shook her head. "Never mind. I take it you have plans."

Discussing her personal life was a new experience, primarily because she'd never had much of one to speak of before. She liked Felicia, a lot. Still, added to her natural reticence was a small degree of uncertainty about discussing her relationship with Renee. It was one thing to admit her own involvement with another woman when it could conceivably have professional repercussions, but quite another to make that statement for Renee.

"I'm sorry," Felicia said quietly. "I didn't mean to put you on the spot."

"No, I'm sorry." Stark reminded herself of how critical Felicia had been to the successful completion of their last operation, and more importantly, how personally supportive she'd been when Renee was in the hospital and Stark was pretty much a basket case. "I'm going to spend the evening with Renee."

"Of course, I should have realized that. I hope you have a great night."

"I don't have much experience with friendships or relationships," Stark said quietly. "It's not personal...my not talking about it."

Felicia settled onto the sofa and crossed her legs, one long elegant arm resting across her bent knee. "I don't think this work is particularly conducive to friendship. There are so many secrets we must keep that we forget how to open up to other people."

Nodding, Stark pulled out the desk chair and sat, regarding with new interest the woman she spent numerous hours with every day. "I've never thought about that very much, but you're right. We spend all day with a handful of people, week in and week out. But we never really talk about anything other than the job. It gets kind of...lonely."

"Yes. It does." Felicia sighed. "I think Renee is a wonderful woman. I hope you two have a chance for something together, if that's what you want."

Stark blushed even as she grinned. "That's what I want...more than anything."

"You're a sweetheart. I can see why it would be easy to fall for you."

Stark's brows shot through the roof and her mouth dropped open. "Uh—"

"Oh, you're perfectly safe," Felicia pronounced, laughing. "I'm not in the market for a relationship, and if I were, although you're terribly cute, I'm afraid my tastes run to men."

"I sort of thought you and Mac..." Stark lifted a shoulder. "Is that off-limits?"

Felicia's dark eyes grew somber. "No, not off-limits. It's just not in the realm of possibility. For me, workplace relationships just aren't a very good idea."

"It gets complicated."

"Yes, and, as you know, when you're a woman trying to advance in this hierarchical business, it doesn't help to be sleeping with a man who's your superior."

"So it's not that you don't like him?"

"Quite the contrary," Felicia said softly, almost as if speaking to herself. "I like him quite a lot."

"You know, I haven't called Renee yet—to tell her I'm free. We don't have any specific plans...so you're welcome to join us for dinner or something."

"Oh no, I don't think so." Felicia gave Stark a fond smile. "Go see your girlfriend and have a great evening."

Riding up in the elevator, Stark was a mass of nerves thinking about what the evening held in store. *A great evening. How could it be anything else? I'm going to see Renee.*

True to her word, she hadn't thought about that morning or their kiss or the possibility of more while she'd been working. But the minute she'd gone off duty, all she'd been able to think about was the way Renee had felt lying against her—the softness of her mouth, the heat of her skin, the weight of her body. The wonder and excitement had swirled through her depths and settled in the pit of her stomach, surging upward to take her by surprise at unexpected moments. By the time she rapped on the hotel room door, she was shivering with anticipation.

Renee opened the door, took one look at Stark, and gave a small groan. "God, you look so good." Then she reached out, took Stark's hand, and drew her gently into the room. Pushing the door closed with her foot, she settled both arms on Stark's shoulders and leaned forward to kiss her. She kept an inch of space between them, fearing that if their bodies touched, she wouldn't be able to let her go until she had her in bed.

As if sensing Renee's hesitation, Stark rested both hands lightly on her hips but did not step any closer. Instead, she allowed her mouth to convey the depths of her longing. She caressed Renee's lips, sucking and stroking and probing until they were both moaning. When it became impossible to go on without taking a breath, she lifted her lips away a fraction and murmured, "It's so great to see you."

"Yes," Renee breathed.

"Would you like to...go out for dinner or something?"

Renee rested her forehead against Stark's, playing with the hair at the back of her neck, caressing her softly. "There *is* something I would like to do before the *other* thing that I'd like to do."

Stark stared at her questioningly. "Translation?"

"I want to see Paris."

"All of it?"

Renee nodded.

"That might take us all night, maybe even longer."

Renee laughed. "Are you tired?"

"I don't think so." Stark brushed her fingers over Renee's cheek and along her jaw. "I don't feel much of anything when I'm with you except you."

Renee's lips parted in surprised pleasure. "You're not allowed to speak until we leave this room. Because every time you say something like that, all I want is to get naked with you."

Stark opened her mouth but Renee swiftly put her fingers against her lips. "Shush. I mean it." Renee's lids grew heavy when she felt Stark's mouth move against her fingers in a soft kiss. "Bad idea." With tremendous effort, she moved away until a foot of neutral ground separated them. "I'm going to get my jacket, and we're going to see Paris."

"Anything you want." *Anything at all.*

CHAPTER TEN

The Peugeot idled at the curb in front of the entrance to the hotel, Hernandez at the wheel and Reynolds beside him. Blair glanced from them to Cam. "Double-dating?"

Laughing, Cam held the rear door for her. "Just for the vehicular portion of the evening. They're staying outside once we arrive."

"Good." Blair watched out the window as they crossed the Seine and moved slowly through the crowded streets of the Left Bank. "Where's Stark? I thought she was on tonight."

"I rearranged the shifts and gave her some downtime. I want her as lead for the finale tomorrow night."

"Ah yes—the presidential ball." Blair grimaced. "The farewell performance."

Cam reached for her hand and squeezed gently. "Tired?"

"Just the usual travel frazzle." Blair kept her tone and expression light. She'd heard the concern in her lover's voice.

"Will you be glad to go home?"

"Oh God, yes." Blair watched the nightlife pass by outside the window, thinking of how many times she had wished she could lose herself on just such a crowded street, to slip away unnoticed and awaken somewhere else—to *be* someone else. With the exception of her clandestine forays into the dark bars and darker hours of so many lost nights, she'd never managed to escape her history or her destiny. Glancing at Cam, she realized that she no longer had any desire to be anyone other than who she was, or to be anywhere else—not as long as she had this one woman's love. "It will be good to get back to New York. I miss painting, and I'm anxious to finish up the last canvases for my show." She smiled and her face was free of worry or regret. "But, despite the circumstances, this has been one of the best trips I've ever had...because you're here."

"There's nothing that I would change about anything," Cam replied seriously, unconsciously echoing Blair's thoughts, "except to give you your freedom."

"Knowing that you understand why it's hard for me sometimes is just as good." Blair gave Cam's hand a small shake. "So will you tell me *now* where we're going?"

Cam's grin flashed. "Nope."

"There are things I could do to punish you for this, you know."

"I live in hope."

Blair laughed and glanced out the window, raising a brow when she saw the street sign. "Rue Christine. Stein and Toklas's street. Are we going sightseeing?"

"Not exactly."

Hernandez pulled the vehicle to the curb and Cam activated the speaker. "Keep comm channel four open. Parker and Davis are your backup."

"Yes, Commander."

And then Cam opened the door, gestured for Blair to follow, and they were on the street. Alone.

Blair glanced back in surprise when neither of the two agents stepped out to join them. Rarely had Cam acquiesced to fewer than three agents being with her when she was out in public. Perplexed, she glanced at her lover. "Cam?"

Shaking her head, Cam grasped Blair's hand and quickly drew her down the narrow, crowded street to 7 Rue Christine, one of a series of small houses with a tiny landing and stained-glass windows flanking its red painted door. Cam knocked, and a moment later, a petite dark-haired woman wearing a flowing green silk tunic and wide-legged sienna trousers opened the door.

"Cameron!" the beautiful woman exclaimed as she stood on tiptoe and kissed Cam's cheek. The deep brown eyes she turned to Blair were alive with quick intelligence and warm welcome. "Hello."

"Bonita," Cam said with obvious affection, "may I present Blair Powell." Cam smiled at Blair's look of stunned surprise.

"Blair, Bonita Ponte."

"Oh," Blair exclaimed, too taken aback to formulate anything close to a sentence. Then, at the sound of the woman's rich melodious laughter, she came to her senses and extended her hand. "I am so honored, Ms. Ponte, to meet you. I so love your work."

"Please, call me Bonita." She took both Blair's and Cam's hands and drew them into the house, closing the door behind them and leading the way into a luxuriously appointed sitting room. Two sofas of burgundy brocade with hand-carved mahogany frames faced each other in front of a marble fireplace. Thick carpets layered the floor in a riot of color. Above the fireplace hung a painting which Blair recognized as one of Marcea Casells's, Cam's mother and—as was her unexpected hostess—a hero of Blair's.

"Please, make yourselves comfortable." Bonita motioned toward the sitting area. "I'll be right back. I imagine that you are hungry."

"I'll give you a hand," Cam said quickly.

Bonita shook her head with an indulgent smile. "No, you relax. I'm sure you've both had a long day." With that, she swiftly disappeared in a billow of silk.

"Bonita Ponte. God, Cam. How do you know her?" Blair still couldn't quite believe they were in the home of one of the world's foremost Expressionist painters. She loved Ponte's work and had studied her style and technique while an art student in Paris.

"I've known her since I was a child. She and my mother are best friends." Cam lifted a shoulder. "I wasn't sure she would be home while we were here, but I took a chance and called her. Luckily, she just arrived back yesterday from a series of shows in Italy." Blair's expression was hard for Cam to decipher. She'd rarely seen her so subdued. "Is this okay?"

Still adjusting, Blair could barely speak. She wasn't certain which was the greater gift, the opportunity to meet one of her idols or the fact that Cam understood how much it would mean to her. Throat tight, she murmured, "It's wonderful. Thank you so much."

Bonita returned with a small serving cart that held a bottle of champagne on ice, glasses, and assorted hors d'oeuvres.

"I spoke to your mother just recently, Cameron," Bonita said conversationally as she handed them flutes of champagne. "She mentioned that you were able to attend one of her shows not long ago. She was very pleased."

"I'm afraid I've missed far too many, but I'm trying to make up for that."

Bonita gave an insouciant shrug. "She understands that your work is important and demanding." She appraised Cam gently. "You look well. You're...recovered?"

Cam blushed, uncomfortable with any reference to her near-fatal gunshot wound less than a year earlier. "Absolutely fine."

"Good," Bonita stated briskly. Then, she turned to Blair. "And you have a show soon, I understand."

Blair nodded self-consciously. "Just a small exhibit."

"Tell me about it."

Cam leaned back, one ankle crossed over a knee as she sipped champagne and listened to the two artists talk. Even though she was soon lost when the topic turned to narrative rhythm, tonality, variations in scale, and dimensional perspective, the flow of conversation was relaxing. The theory and even the practice of painting were not foreign to her, but the passion that the other two women shared was something only an artist could truly experience. Seeing Blair's unbridled delight, however, was enough to make Cam feel more than satisfied.

Shortly before eleven, Bonita stretched with a sigh of pleasure. "I can't remember having such an enjoyable evening in some time. I'm losing my taste for travel," she said as she looked from Cam to Blair, "but not for good company. I'm so glad you both could come."

"It's been wonderful," Blair agreed.

"Would you like to see the studio?" Bonita asked.

Blair's eyes grew large. "Oh, yes."

Pleased, Bonita rose and extended her hand. "Come with me. You too, of course, Cameron."

After a brief tour and further animated discussion, Bonita said, "I would be so pleased if the two of you could spend the night. It's impossible to really show some of these canvases without daylight." She glanced at Blair. "There are several I think you would enjoy seeing."

"If it isn't an imposition," Blair glanced at Cam, who nodded her assent, "I'd love to."

"Wonderful!" Bonita slid an arm around each woman's waist and drew them down the hall to a guest room at the far end. "Here you are. Everything you need is in the cabinets in the bath." She withdrew toward the door. "And if you'll excuse me, I'm going to retire. I still haven't quite recovered from my latest sojourn."

"Thanks, Bonita."

"Yes," Blair echoed. "Thank you so much."

"Oh, you don't need to thank me. I'll see you in the morning." She gave them one last smile. "There's no need to rise early. I don't intend to, but if you do, I trust you'll find the coffee on your own."

When they were alone, Blair gazed at Cam with an expression that Cam had rarely seen before. Contemplative, questioning, almost uncertain.

"What is it?" Cam asked, worried. "Didn't you have a good time?"

"Oh no, I had a fantastic time." Blair leaned against the doorway to the bathroom, regarding her lover with fierce concentration. "I don't understand what's in it for you."

"What?"

Blair frowned, searching for words to describe what baffled her. "Me. Us."

Cam blinked. "You don't know?"

Blair shook her head. "No," she said slowly, softly. "There's so little I can really give you. You brought me here tonight because you knew it would make me happy. And it did...wildly. That you would know that, *do* that, makes me feel so...loved." She sighed, shook her head again. "I don't even know how to begin to give you that."

"Blair," Cam whispered, her voice deep, her eyes tender. "You don't have to do anything. It's you...just you. For me, the joy is in loving you."

Blair's eyes brimmed with tears and before she could stop them, they spilled over. Cam gave a small cry and quickly took Blair into her arms.

"No," Cam murmured, her lips pressed to Blair's forehead,

her fingers gently catching the falling tears. "I wanted tonight to be special. To make you happy, not to make you sad."

"I never thought it would be possible," Blair confessed, her face to Cam's neck, "but I'm actually crying because I'm happy."

Softly, Cam laughed. "Don't scare me, then."

Blair smiled and brushed her palm over Cam's chest. "Did you know that Bonita was going to ask us to stay here tonight?"

"No. But I wouldn't be surprised if she and my mother discussed it."

"I'm not certain if I should be embarrassed or not that your mother is arranging trysts for us." Blair laughed shakily, unused to having so many people care for her.

"I think the tryst is just a side benefit." Cam teased Blair's blouse from her slacks and slipped her hand beneath, massaging her fingertips in the hollow at the base of Blair's spine. "Bonita obviously had a great time talking to you this evening."

"Mmm." The gentle kneading was lulling her mind even as it awakened her flesh. "I hope so. It was amazing for me."

"Are you okay with staying here tonight?" Cam brought her free hand between them and began to work open the buttons on Blair's blouse.

Blair unbuttoned Cam's chinos and slid her fingertips beneath the polo shirt to circle Cam's navel. "I'll stay anywhere with you if we can be alone. Staying *here* is a dream come true."

"That's good," Cam's voice was husky as she made her way up to unclasp Blair's bra, "because I have a terrible need to spend the night with you."

"Then let's get started." With her eyes locked on Cam's, Blair drew her lover to the bed.

Paula Stark craned her neck and scanned the enormous structure. Spotlighted against the night sky, the Eiffel Tower looked majestic—and really, really tall. "I read somewhere that there are 1665 steps to the top level."

"That's true," Renee agreed reasonably. "But you can't walk to the top level any longer. Only to the second level and then you take an elevator to the final floor. So there aren't really that many steps."

"Oh, I see. 1625 steps. That's much better." There was an edge of sheer terror in Stark's voice. "If we walk all the way up, I'm going to need an ambulance to take me back to the hotel."

Renee laughed. "Oh, come on. You're a Secret Service agent. Besides, I've seen your body. I know you're in great shape."

Even in the dark, Stark had a feeling Renee could see her blush. "When?"

"When, what?"

"Have you ever seen my body?"

"I've seen you in the gym." Renee edged closer in the line to the admissions booth, letting her thigh rub against Stark's. "And besides that, I've had my hands on you. I know just how well built you are."

Stark's step faltered as her legs turned to jelly. She gulped, audibly, she was certain. "You can't say things like that if you want me to climb up hundreds of stairs."

"We can see all of Paris from up there," Renee whispered. She slipped her hand into Stark's, and their fingers entwined as naturally as if they'd touched a thousand times. "I want to remember two things about tonight—seeing Paris from the top of the Eiffel Tower, and making love with you."

"Oh, jeez," Stark whispered in an agony of arousal and wonder. "I'll climb it twice, if you want."

"I believe you would." Renee swallowed around the lump in her throat. "And that's exactly why I'm crazy about you."

"If you want my legs to work long enough for me to get up to the top of that thing," Stark complained breathlessly, "then you have to stop saying things like that."

Renee laughed and rubbed her cheek against Stark's shoulder. "I can't make you any promises."

Smiling at Renee in the glow of the lights from the monument, Stark swung their joined arms in a slow, easy arc. "That's okay. None are required."

"We can go back to the hotel now," Renee said quietly. "I'm finding it pretty hard to keep my hands off you, and I've made you wait when I'm not even sure why."

"No." Stark realized that there was no hurry, not when every second they spent together—talking, walking, gently touching—was magic. "Let's go to the top and see Paris first. Let's have it all."

"Oh, yes." Renee let caution slip away on the promise in Paula's eyes. "Let's have it all."

2345 16Aug01

The brown-haired, blue-eyed American joined three men and one woman in a third-floor apartment on the outskirts of Paris. The other men, like himself, were dressed casually in open-collared shirts and rumpled trousers. His service weapon was secured at the small of his back beneath his lightweight linen jacket. The thin, sharp-faced blond woman, in dark jeans and a blue work shirt, carried her Vector Mini Uzi automatic pistol in a hip holster on the right side of her wide leather belt. Two Olympic Arms PCR-5 assault rifles lay on the coffee table in front of a frayed, stained sofa.

The room smelled of stale takeout and too many cigarettes. Through an open door on the right that led into what was meant to be a bedroom, he could see the pale glow of computer monitors and assorted communication devices. Before speaking, he removed a small black box the size of a deck of cards from his jacket pocket. When he pushed the power button, a blinking red light appeared.

"We're secure," the woman said impatiently. "Do you think we are amateurs?"

Silently, the American quickly and efficiently swept the room with the surveillance scanner. As he dropped it back into his pocket, he addressed the tall, dark, bearded man who sat on the sofa regarding him impassively. "There was no choice but to abort the mission this afternoon. The premature press release created an unexpected obstacle due to the number of press vehicles and reporters on-site."

"We could have lost our people," the man said flatly. "Why was the order given so late?"

The question was posed with little inflection but the implied criticism was apparent.

The American flushed, but kept his voice even. "The alteration in the motorcade's route was made by the security chief only minutes before arrival."

"That woman is a problem and should be eliminated," the woman pronounced acerbically. "This is the second time she has interfered with our plans."

"No," one of the other men objected. "Any move against her would only alert others of our primary target."

"I agree," the American said. "I recommend—"

The man on the sofa stood abruptly, and the room fell silent. "I have just received orders from Hydra command. The strike is on schedule, and we have been directed to take her at the same time. By executing both plans simultaneously, we will demonstrate our power to the world just as we expose the soft underbelly of the decaying American pretenders."

"When—"

"You'll receive your orders from our allies in your country when the time is near. You must be prepared to act at any moment, because the wait will not be long. Our people are already in place. It has begun."

The American felt a thrill of excitement. For years he'd been nothing more than a silent player, providing information while others planned and executed missions. At last, he would have the opportunity to act—to take back his country and deliver it into the hands of those who understood its true power and destiny. "I am ready."

God Bless America.

CHAPTER ELEVEN

"Ooh." Blair sighed with a sensual moan. She stretched, naked, rejoicing in the warmth of Cam's body beside her and the cool cotton covering them both. "How can crisp, clean sheets feel so incredibly wonderful?"

"Happy?" Cam leaned up on an elbow, resting her head on her hand as she drew her fingertips along the edge of Blair's jaw. She marveled at the beauty of Blair's face in the moonlight. Being with her like this, alone in the middle of the night, was a rare occurrence, but one that she knew would never cease to thrill her, no matter how many times she experienced it. Blair was so many things she loved—intelligent, strong, vital, and passionate. She was also very beautiful. And Cam loved to look at her.

"Mmm." Blair started to shift onto her side to see Cam better, but Cam's hand on her shoulder restrained her.

"No," Cam murmured, drawing her fingertips back and forth in the valley between Blair's breasts. "Stay like that. I want to look at you."

The low heavy beat in Cam's voice settled in the pit of Blair's stomach, and her heartbeat quickened. "Just look?"

The corner of her mouth lifted in a grin, and Cam nodded. "For now."

"You've been playing with me quite a lot this evening, Commander," Blair chided just a bit breathlessly. Cam's fingers had shifted onto her breast, although they lay motionless just below her nipple. Even the promise of a touch from those strong, sensitive fingers made her breasts ache and the nipples tighten into hard knots of desire.

"Not nearly as much as I intend to." Cam brushed the sheet down Blair's abdomen with the edge of her hand until it angled across Blair's hips, white and sharp in the moonlight. Cam traced a finger beneath the edge of the cotton, lingering for an instant over the swell of flesh between Blair's thighs.

Involuntarily, Blair raised her hips, but the tantalizing touch was already gone. "What if I told you I'm too tired?"

Cam dipped her head and brushed her lips over the hollow at the base of Blair's throat. With her mouth against the racing pulse, she murmured, "Are you?"

The heat in the pit of Blair's stomach flared, searing her blood. Fighting to keep her voice even, she replied, "I asked you first."

Chuckling as she kissed a spot between Blair's breasts, Cam reached down and pushed the sheet away completely. She trailed her fingers back up the length of Blair's thigh and smoothed her hand along the curve of Blair's hipbone. Then she rested her cheek against the firm rise of Blair's breast and watched the muscles flicker in her lover's abdomen as she walked her fingers along the inside of the arched prominence, over her belly, and up to her navel. She flicked at the gold ring piercing the skin there. Then she caught it between thumb and forefinger and tugged.

Blair gasped, her legs twisting restlessly on the bed as she gripped Cam's shoulder hard.

"If you're tired..." Cam tugged again. "Then I'll just have to put you to sleep."

"How?" Blair's throat was tight with urgency. Patience in bed was not her usual fare. She liked Cam to take her hard and fast, especially the first time—or she liked to have Cam the same way. Perhaps it was because they rarely had the luxury of time on their side; more likely it was due to her relentless hunger for Cam, like an ache in her bones. Whenever she touched Cam, the need to be close to her, to be inside her, to take *her* inside, obliterated all restraint. But tonight, after all that Cam had given her, she wanted Cam to have exactly what she desired. She would let Cam take her, and she would rejoice in the giving. "Tell me how you'll put me to sleep."

Still toying with the gold ring, Cam flicked her tongue over Blair's nipple. "With my mouth."

"God, I love your mouth on me." Blair couldn't help herself. She was burning from the inside out. Moaning softly, she drove her fingers into Cam's thick hair and pressed her lover's face more firmly to her breast. Still, she went no further, even though she ached for Cam to fill her.

"I know." Cam shifted lower, capturing Blair's leg between her own. She pressed against Blair's firm thigh, knowing that her lover would feel the evidence of her arousal, slick and hot and hard. "And I'm going to kiss you, everywhere, until you come."

"Oh, yes," Blair whispered, pushing up on her elbows to watch Cam suck her nipples, one then the other. Seeing Cam's lips caressing her throbbing flesh and feeling the electric shocks of pleasure at the same time made her shudder and twitch. Watching Cam's hips thrust indolently against her thigh, feeling her lover's passion coat her skin, made her stomach convulse. "I need you to touch me so much. Don't make me wait too long."

"I'm going to make us *both* wait." Cam eased her hips away a fraction, relieving the exquisite pressure against her screaming nerve endings. She was in danger of climaxing just from the thrill of exciting Blair. "I'm going to touch you everywhere." She danced her fingers down Blair's abdomen, brushed tantalizingly over the heat between Blair's legs, then skimmed lower, stroking the soft skin of her inner thighs. "I *need* to touch you everywhere."

Strength failing, Blair surrendered, falling back against the pillows with a low whimper. "God, I don't care...do anything... everything. Just don't stop."

The surface of Blair's skin sang. Cam's fingertips painted images of moonlit glades and sun-drenched valleys on the canvas of her mind. Her heart thundered with the joy of loving and being loved. Carried on the inexorable tide of her lover's devotions, she was unaware of the lips caressing her turgid flesh or the mouth that drew her passion forth on a sea of desire. All she knew—in her body, in her soul, in the deepest reaches of her heart—was the woman who claimed her, and freed her, with the power of this love. *Cam. Cam.*

Her orgasm rose slowly, gathering force from some place far, far beyond her fragile body. Only when the fist of need in her depths opened and pleasure flooded her thighs did she become aware of the relentless joy of Cam's mouth driving her to climax. Panting, she pushed herself up, forced her eyes open, and clenched a hand in

Cam's hair. "I want...to watch...you...make me come."

Then the sharp edge of pleasure verged on pain, the muscles shredded from her bones, and her soul soared on the sweet ache of fulfillment. Bent nearly double, she clutched Cam's shoulder as she shuddered and moaned. When the wracking spasms released her, she collapsed onto her side, her fingers still tangled in her lover's hair.

Cam rolled with her, gathering her close and pressing Blair's face to her chest. "I love you. I love you so much."

Blair couldn't speak. She could barely breathe. It wasn't the exquisite orgasm that had stolen her control but the overwhelming emotion that she was unable to contain when Cam touched her. *Not just when she touches me. When she looks at me. When she's anywhere near me.*

"Baby," Cam murmured tenderly, her cheek resting gently against the top of Blair's head. "We need to get under the covers. You're going to get chilled."

"In a minute," Blair mumbled, wrapping her arms around Cam's waist and burrowing closer. "I feel so good. *You* feel so good."

Cam laughed and fumbled the sheet partway over Blair's body. "Yeah. I feel pretty terrific."

Blair's head lolled back on Cam's shoulder and she regarded her through heavy eyelids. "Pretty pleased with yourself, aren't you?"

"Pretty much." Cam kissed Blair's nose lightly. "I've been thinking about doing that all night."

"Really." Blair chuckled weakly. "You have remarkable powers of restraint, Commander."

"Not really." Softly, Cam kissed Blair's mouth, tracing her tongue over the full curve of Blair's lower lip. "I came just now— all it took was feeling you let go."

Blair groaned. "Cameron Roberts, you are the sexiest woman I've ever known. If I weren't completely wasted, I would throw you down this moment and ravish you."

Laughing, Cam eased back against the pillows, drawing Blair with her. As she went, she pulled the covers after them until they were cocooned in each other's arms. "There's always the morning."

"Yes," Blair whispered drowsily. Although she knew that wasn't necessarily true, that it might be years before she could go to sleep in her lover's arms and count on awakening with her, she refused to allow anything to dispel her happiness. That, too, was a new sensation—the willingness to accept joy, however fleeting, as the gift it was. "Loving you is the best thing that ever happened to me."

"Blair," Cam breathed, softly stroking the blond head resting against her shoulder. "You can't know how much that means to me."

"I do know." Blair reached out, found Cam's hand, and entwined their fingers. She drew their joined hands between her breasts, held them against her heart. "I feel it in here. I feel you inside me, loving me. Loving *you* has made me whole."

"I never intend to stop."

Promise? Blair didn't dare ask.

Cam moved their joined hands to her chest and pressed them to the spot above her heart, unmindful of the scar that marked it. "I promise."

There were two levels at the top of the monument, one inside and one outside, offering a 360-degree panoramic view of Paris and its environs for 80 kilometers in every direction. The night was clear, and although it was summer, at 280 meters above ground level, the air was cool. It was also nearly midnight, and there were very few visitors on the outside observation deck. Below them the city sparkled, lights blazing like fiery jewels. The wind ruffled Stark's hair as she leaned forward to capture as much of the view as possible. She held Renee's hand, grateful for the contact, needing to feel grounded as the dizzying heights left her disoriented.

"It's really incredible, isn't it?" Stark raised her voice above the wind, her eyes bright with a shimmer of tears. She could write that off to the effects of the wind, but the tightness in her chest wasn't due to the weather or the elevation. All she could think as she stood on the edge of Wonderland were the quiet words of the woman beside her. *I want to remember two things about tonight:*

seeing Paris from the top of the Eiffel Tower and making love with you.

Renee wasn't looking at the view. Stark's face glowed with youthful enthusiasm as her dark hair whipped about her face. Her fingers gripped Renee's tightly, and her voice had been husky with emotion. *I hope you never learn to hide your feelings.*

"Beautiful." Renee moved closer and threaded her arm around Stark's waist beneath her jacket and leaned her head against the sturdy shoulder. *You're so beautiful.*

Stark slid her arm around Renee. "I'm really glad you let me ride the elevator. If you hadn't, I probably would have had to lie down when we got up here, and then I would have missed the view."

"I'm sure you could have made it," Renee assured her, "but I really didn't want to tire you out so soon. I have other plans for doing that."

Stark gave a slight jerk, then turned her face from the view and met Renee's eyes. "You know, I'm constantly excited when I'm near you. Actually, I'm constantly excited most of the time just thinking about you. So it would be good if you didn't remind me of it too often, because I think I'm starting to get tissue damage."

Renee cupped her hand behind Stark's head and drew her close. She kissed her, unmindful of the occasional person passing by. Part of the reason she had been able to wait as long as she had before dragging Stark into bed was that kissing Paula Stark was an experience in itself. Stark's lips were full and warm and incredibly inquisitive, coursing over Renee's in a continuous wave of soft caresses and tender sucks. Every now and then, she'd feel a tiny pinpoint of pain that was quickly soothed by the gentle stroke of a warm tongue, and she'd realize that she'd been bitten. The surprise, the pleasure, the shifting sensations, first gentle then demanding, settled deep in her core and made her ache with wanting. But the hunger was so enjoyable that she was happy to let it rage unanswered. At least she had been. Now with every passing second it was becoming more and more difficult to hold her need at bay. She pulled her head back, gasping. "I want you. God."

Stark rested both arms gently around Renee's waist, their thighs lightly touching. They were alone again in their small section of the monument, with all of Paris at their feet. She couldn't quite believe that this incredible woman wanted her. If Renee only knew that she hadn't a clue as to how to please her, or even how to begin to show her how much she wanted to be with her. Other than a few less-than-memorable forays into relationships with men, which she had been more than willing to set aside when she entered the training academy, she'd had one night of true passion. And that night had been with a woman she did not love and who did not love her. It had been unforgettable—an epiphany, both physical and emotional—and she couldn't honestly say now that she regretted it. It had been an important part of her self-awakening, but the fevered lust had been an inferno, leaving nothing in its wake but ashes. And in those few heated hours, she'd done little more than allow herself to be consumed. "There's something I have to tell you."

Hearing something close to self-recrimination in Stark's voice, Renee tilted her head, then shook it slowly. "No, there isn't. Unless there's someone else, right now, there isn't a thing you need to tell me."

"There isn't anyone. That's what I wanted to say. There never *has* been anyone. A few hours, once, but—"

"Are you trying to tell me that you're inexperienced?"

Mutely, Stark nodded, glad for the darkness to hide her humiliation. "I want...I want tonight to be everything you hope it will be. And I—"

"Oh God," Renee murmured. She framed Stark's face in her hands. "Sweetheart, it already *is* what I hoped for. More, even." In the moonlight, she saw the fleeting look of consternation cross Stark's face. "You don't know, do you?"

Feeling more inept every second, Stark shook her head again.

"When I'm with you," Renee said gently, stroking the bold, strong angle of Stark's jaw, "*everything* is new. Because of you... because of your kindness and your tenderness and your honesty. Nothing before tonight matters, because tonight—with you—will be the first time it's ever been right for me."

Stark's heart fluttered, and she was glad for the hold she had on the woman in her arms, because, for an instant, she felt as if she could fly. "Would you mind if we left now? I just don't think I'll be good for anything else until I can hold you with nothing between us."

"That sounds just exactly like what I need."

Arms around each other's waists, they cast one last glance at the City of Light, then headed for the elevator and the promise of the night.

CHAPTER TWELVE

Stark stared at the numbers on the rectangular panel to the right of the elevator doors as they slowly ascended. Renee stood silently beside her, the fingers of her right hand lightly wrapped around Stark's forearm. She could feel the heat even through the brushed cotton of her blazer. 12...13...14...With each passing floor, her heart rate accelerated and the roiling in her stomach ratcheted up a notch.

I'm going to blow it. I don't even know what she likes. I'm not even sure I'd know how to do it even if I did know what she likes.

The elevator glided to a stop with a barely perceptible hitch. For what seemed like an eternity, Stark thought the doors might not open. Then she found herself in the hallway outside room 2010 watching Renee slide the key card through the lock. She cleared her throat and resisted the urge to shuffle her feet. Instead, she dutifully followed Renee inside and stood waiting while Renee reached behind her, removed the Do Not Disturb sign, and hung it outside on the door handle.

Oh my God.

Uncertain of the next move, Stark remained statue-still while Renee locked the door, set the security chain in place, and moved around the room to turn on a few lights. Mouth dry, heart jackhammering in her ears, Stark searched frantically for something to say.

My legs are numb. I can't feel my hands. Jesus, what if I can't come. She'll think I don't like it. Don't like her.

Renee twisted the dimmer switch until the lights in the sitting area were barely a faint glow. Then she crossed back to Stark and slipped both hands inside the edges of the dark blue blazer, resting her palms against Stark's chest, her fingertips riding the edges of her collarbones. She gently smoothed her hands back and forth.

"This isn't a test. There's no right or wrong way to do it. There's just us...together...touching."

The sound of Renee's calm, kind voice, the brilliant light in her eyes, the warm welcoming touch of her hands—those were the things that quelled Stark's anxiety and left her smiling. She cupped her palm to the back of Renee's neck and leaned forward, skimming her lips over Renee's. Lost in the soft heat of Renee's mouth, she didn't think beyond the next caress or any further than the small nip of flesh and the moan of pleasure the gentle bite elicited. She couldn't be nervous when Renee was all she knew.

Wrapping her arms around Stark's solid waist, Renee sighed and tilted her head back, her eyes liquid. "You're so damn good at that."

"What?" Stark's voice was husky as she slowly worked her hand between Renee's sweater and the blouse beneath, circling her palm over Renee's lower back, loving the way the strong muscles tensed beneath her fingers through the thin covering of silk.

"Kissing. You're an amazing kisser."

"Yeah?" Stark grinned. "Then I have a suggestion."

Renee struggled to follow the conversation as the lower half of her body turned molten under Stark's hands. It wasn't even an intentionally seductive caress, just a steady massage of fingertips along her spine, and yet, her thighs trembled. *What will happen to me when those fingers finally touch my skin?* She moaned softly, then sharply caught her breath at the rapid flutter of excitement in the depths of her belly. She forced herself to focus. "What?"

"Since I'm doing okay in the kissing department, let's just lie down and start there."

"Good idea." Renee took Stark's hand. "I don't know why I didn't think of it myself." *Except none of my brain cells seem to be firing at the moment, and all the blood in my body is headed in the opposite direction.*

Renee left the lamps off in the bedroom, but enough illumination filtered through from the room beyond to light their way. Once at the bedside, she lifted off her cashmere sweater and tossed it onto the back of a nearby chair. Since she was in Paris on vacation, she wasn't carrying her weapon. But Stark was, and after removing her blazer, she slid the holster from her waistband with the kind of practiced move that was automatic and set it on the night table. Renee kicked off her shoes as Stark sat on the side of the bed and removed hers.

Stark looked up to find Renee watching her with a half-smile on her face. "What?"

"Still nervous?"

"Some."

"We don't have to rush."

"You don't have to go slow just for me, you know. I might fumble, but I'll keep up."

Renee moved closer to stand between Stark's parted thighs. She worked her fingers into the seated woman's hair, slowly drawing the thick dark strands between her fingers. "I have every confidence that you won't drop the ball, Paula." She tilted Stark's head back and leaned down, starting her own exploration of Stark's full, sensuous lips. She sucked lightly before sliding her tongue along the inner surfaces, closing her eyes as a wave of heat and longing washed through her. Her mouth still brushing Stark's, she murmured, "I'm going slowly for *me*."

Stark put both hands on Renee's waist and dropped back on the bed, bringing the other woman with her. Together, they rolled to the center until they were facing each other, gently embracing. Stark brushed her fingers through Renee's wavy hair. "In the academy I had a reputation for being the most persistent cadet—not the smartest or the fastest, but the one that never gave up. And I always finished everything I started."

"I'm not worried a bit about you finishing *anything,*" Renee whispered. "But I want to enjoy every minute of getting there."

"I think we can do that." Stark wrapped one arm more tightly around Renee's waist, drawing her close as she found her mouth again. At first, she kept her eyes open, hoping not to miss one second of the experience. After a few moments, however, the pleasure, carried on the rapid rush of blood through the muscles and sinew of her body, forced her to close her eyes. The sensations were far too sweet, the ache too deep, to do anything more than fly with them. Distantly, above the roar of her own heart thundering, she heard Renee moan softly. It was a high, sweet sound of longing and surrender. Desire surged from her depths, and without conscious thought, she rolled onto her back, drawing Renee on top of her, desperately needing to bring her closer.

"Oh God," Renee murmured as she fit her thighs and belly and breasts to Stark's, suddenly feeling her everywhere. They were both still fully clothed, but her skin tingled as if there were no barriers between them. "You feel so good."

Stark pulled the blouse from Renee's slacks and smoothed both hands up either side of her spine, fanning her fingers over the finely muscled back. She gasped when Renee pressed her hips into her, striking a spot that made her stomach clench and her breath catch on a groan. "You...too." She brought one hand between them and touched the top button of Renee's blouse. "Can I?"

"Oh...yes." Stunned by the sweetness of the question, Renee was forced to close her eyes against the swift surge of excitement that beat again between her thighs. *Too soon. Too soon to feel so much.* But she couldn't stop the feelings, either in her body or her heart. Shifting to straddle Stark's hips, she made room for the agile fingers that opened each button on her blouse with careful deliberation. She loved that about Stark—how careful she was with everything. As the silk parted over her breasts, exposing the scant lacy bra she wore beneath, she shrugged her shoulders and let the garment fall behind her. With one hand, she reached down and tugged Stark's shirt from beneath the waistband of her pants, pushing it up until her abdomen was bare. Then she lay back down upon her, moaning softly as their skin touched in that one small spot.

Instinctively, Stark cupped Renee's hips and pulled her tightly between her legs. She couldn't seem to get close enough to her. Her voice was a hoarse whisper as she gasped, "I feel like something inside of me is breaking apart, I want you so much."

Renee pressed her face to the curve of Stark's neck, fighting to still the motion of her hips. She wasn't ready to let go yet, but the movement was too stimulating for her to hold off for long. "The things you say...the way you touch me. You break my heart."

"Renee..."

"In a good way." Then Renee kissed her again, pushing up just enough to slip her fingers between them and pull open the buttons on Stark's shirt. As she slid a trembling hand inside, over the silk tank top beneath, Stark smoothed a hand up her back and opened the clasp on her bra. As her breasts were released, Renee moaned at the sudden freedom and the unexpected heaviness of the arousal swelling them. She arched her neck, her stomach quivering. "Touch me. Please."

Stark was very much afraid she might pass out. Even though she was lying down, she was breathing so quickly it felt as if no air was actually traversing her lungs. Her heart was a wild thing trying to tear its way from her chest. What had started as a distant pulse in the pit of her stomach had grown into a fist hammering between her thighs. Still, her hand seemed to move in slow motion as she raised her fingertips to brush lightly over the pebbled peak of Renee's breast. The small cry it drew from the woman in her arms tore through her like a knife. She could bleed to death on the beauty of that sound.

"I want..." There were no words. She wasn't even certain there was any way, any way at all, to possibly convey with her earthbound body the magnitude of her emotions. But she had no language beyond the touch of her hand and the caress of her mouth. She raised her hips and turned, carrying Renee to her back as she shifted upon her. At the same time, she lowered her head and tenderly took Renee's nipple into her mouth, enclosing it gently, carefully.

Even with Stark's weight upon her, Renee arched off the bed, lifting them both as the sweet agony centered in her breast. "Oh my God."

Startled by her own actions, Stark moved her mouth away. "Did I hur—"

Renee drove her fingers into Stark's hair and forced her mouth back onto her breast. Gasping, she pleaded, "Don't stop. Please. Please."

Stark closed her eyes, fearing that she couldn't have stopped even if asked. Renee's fingers dug into her shoulders and she was moving—*they* were moving—in urgent tandem now. Thigh between thigh, belly to belly, they drove each other higher. She sucked the stone-hard nipple, reveling in the small sounds that Renee made, finding the other breast with her hand and squeezing to the same rhythm as her lips played on the swollen breast in her mouth. She might have gone on forever, lost in the sweet power of the moment, except another ache clamored for attention. A terrible pressure, insistent and unrelenting, throbbed in her depths. She turned her face and pressed her cheek to Renee's breast. "Can we..." She lost her breath as Renee curled one leg over the back of her thigh and pushed up into her hard, striking the spot between her legs that threatened to explode. "Oh...jeez...clothes...can we get undressed?"

"Yes. God yes." Before the words had left her, Renee was tugging at Stark's shirt, desperate to strip it from her.

Rolling away, Stark fumbled at the buttons and zipper of her fly, her hands clumsy with urgency. It seemed to take forever, but it was only seconds before they were naked and reaching for each other again.

Time slowed. The room, the world outside it, even the susurrous rustle of the sheets beneath their bodies dissolved into silent wonder.

"Paula..." Renee cupped her palm against Stark's cheek, meeting her eyes as the lengths of their bodies touched for the first time. She caught back a sob of delighted surprise at the first brush of soft smooth skin.

"Renee." Stark cradled Renee's head in the bend of her arm and glided her hand down her side, over her hips to her thigh, imprinting every curve and line of her sleek, firmly muscled form in her mind. She'd imagined it—dreamed it—countless times, but nothing she'd conjured in her mind came anywhere close to the reality. "Tell me what you like."

"You," Renee murmured, quivering beneath Stark's hands. "You are exactly what I like."

Stark pressed her lips to the hollow at the base of Renee's throat, awestruck at the beauty of the pulse pounding through the vessels just beneath the skin. So fragile, so strong, so very much Renee. Tenderly, she brought her mouth to the scar slanting over Renee's left shoulder, shivering with the memory of the gunshot and her own terror as that precious life ebbed away on a tide of blood. "Don't let me hurt you—you're still healing."

"Oh, no." Renee stroked Stark's cheek. "You won't. I know it."

Stark raised her head, her eyes dark with yearning. "Help me please you. I want to so much."

Renee tightened her hold as she turned onto her back, drawing Stark above her. She wrapped her arms around Stark's shoulders and her legs around Stark's hips. Pressing her mouth to Stark's ear, she whispered, "I like you on top of me, pressing down into me. It makes me want to come."

That request was easy to fulfill, because Stark didn't have any choice but to rock into her. The pleasure inside of her was screaming to get out, to burst free, to explode from her on a flood of sweet agony. They found the rhythm easily, body to body, heart to heart, and together, they rode the wild edge of desire. Stark groaned. Renee was hot and wet against her own ready flesh, and she shivered as a familiar tingling began to ripple along her spine. "I think..." She struggled for breath. "I think if we keep this up, I might...come first."

"Oh, yes. *Yes.* Paula, let me feel you."

I shouldn't...I should wai...OhGodOh...God... "I'm coming," Stark gasped desperately, her breath sobbing out. "I'm...sorry."

"Oh sweetie." Renee fitfully stroked Stark's cheek, her hair, her back as her own passion rose. "It's okay. It's wonderful."

Still shuddering, eyes dim with the last shock of release, Stark braced herself on her forearms and watched Renee's face as, together, they continued their frantic thrusts. Hips churning, they pushed harder, rocked faster, slid against each other in a hot slick wash of need. Renee's eyes were nearly closed, her lips parted almost in surprise, her head tilted back. She looked vulnerable and glorious. In the distant reaches of her consciousness, Stark was aware of her own excitement condensing once more into a hard knot in the pit of her stomach, gathering force for another explosion that threatened to rend her soul beyond redemption. But that pleasure was nothing compared to the sight and sounds of Renee's desire. She wanted, hungered, for more.

"I want to be inside you," Stark implored.

"Hurry." Renee's stomach fluttered and her legs tensed. "I'm so close."

But Stark did not hurry. She eased onto her side and smoothed her palm down the center of Renee's body, over the hard quivering muscles in her abdomen and between her clenched thighs. Instantly, she felt the heat against the palm of her hand, and she drew gentle fingers through the wet, slick folds.

Renee's hips bucked as Stark circled her clitoris, and she gave a startled moan. "There. Oh, yes, there."

Stark forgot to breathe. She forgot her own need. She forgot that she'd never done this before. All she knew was the hard, full heart of Renee's desire and the terrible wonderful desperate longing to touch all of her, to the depths of her soul. When she slipped inside, she was immediately enclosed by hot smooth muscles. She heard Renee's breath catch as she pressed deeper. As she eased out and stroked back in, Renee came in her hand with one sharp cry.

Buried in her, Stark stilled her motion, letting Renee's orgasm play around her fingers. Then, as the ripples faded, she gently massaged the spot that made Renee whimper until she brought her once again to orgasm. She might have continued for the rest of her life if Renee hadn't finally grasped her forearm with a weak laugh.

"Paula, sweetie, stop. I have to catch my breath."

"Can I stay inside?" Stark brushed her lips over Renee's.

"Mmm."

"You feel...amazing."

"Oh God...you have no idea." Renee pulled Stark's head down onto her shoulder and rested her cheek against the top of Stark's head. She ran her fingers up and down Stark's strong forearm, marveling as she reached her own body and felt Stark's fingers disappear inside her. "You're wonderful."

"I've got this huge terrible...*ache*...inside." Stark shuddered, struggling to put words to the emotions that choked her. "Like if I can't be connected to you—not just connected, but *inside* you somehow—I might just die."

"You're inside more than my body, Paula," Renee murmured with a drowsy sigh.

I hope so. I hope I'm in your heart, like you are in mine.

"I'm sorry," Renee whispered. "I feel so good...so damn good. Tired."

Stark lay quietly, listening to Renee's breathing become deep and regular, feeling her muscles loosen as she relaxed into sleep. After a time, she tenderly withdrew from her, missing the joining immediately. She drew up the covers and closed her eyes, thinking that she might just have experienced her life's finest moment.

CHAPTER THIRTEEN

For the second time in as many days, Blair had the rare pleasure of awakening with Cam beside her. But the greater gift was that, as on the previous morning, Cam still slept. They'd awakened together infrequently, but Cam had always arisen first. Used to sleeping alone, Blair discovered that she enjoyed awakening to the comforting heat of another body pressed close. As long as it was Cam. She'd rarely spent the night with any lover, not because of protocol or caution—as was the case with the woman she loved—but out of choice. Finding herself in the arms of a stranger was not an experience she had welcomed. Finding herself with Cam's arm thrown possessively across her middle was joy.

Blair slid carefully from Cam's embrace to the edge of the bed and slowly slipped from beneath the sheets. Standing quietly in the small, still room, she glanced down at her slumbering lover. Even in repose, Cam's expression was intense. Dark brows slashed across a bold forehead, and the strong profile spoke of strength and determination. Blair loved the way Cam's body reflected her soul. She could never look at her without wanting to touch her, hoping somehow to convey the depth of her love when words failed. She resisted the urge now, because the sight of Cam asleep was almost as pleasurable as a caress.

At that moment, Cam appeared as carefree as Blair had ever seen her, and she was loath to disturb her. Scooping up her clothes, she stole to the bedroom door, hurriedly donned her blouse and slacks, and stepped into her shoes. After a quick trip to the bathroom, she made her way through the quiet house toward the kitchen in the rear. To her surprise, she found that she was not the only one already up. Bonita stood by an open door through which Blair could see a small courtyard with carefully tended flower beds and two wooden benches.

Bonita turned as Blair entered the kitchen. "Good morning. I didn't expect to see you up so early."

"Nor I you," Blair rejoined with a smile. "Didn't you say you were going to sleep in?"

"I'm afraid my mind had other ideas. I woke with a million thoughts in my head and decided I was never going to get back to sleep."

Blair laughed quietly. "I know exactly what you mean."

"I was about to go out to pick up a few things for breakfast. Are you in the mood for a walk?"

"Cam's still asleep."

"We shouldn't be long. It's only a block or so."

She doesn't know. She doesn't realize that I never just go out for a walk. Blair hesitated. She felt foolish saying no, and almost embarrassed to admit that she probably shouldn't do something as simple as walk to the corner store without notifying Cam or one of the other agents. *God, it's just for a few minutes, and the security detail is right out front. They'll pick me up as soon as I walk out the door. Cam can't be upset about that.* She realized that Bonita was waiting for her to reply.

"I'd love to."

"Good," Bonita replied, opening the rear door and holding it for Blair. "Let's walk through the courtyard. The bakery is on the street behind us."

Suddenly, Blair realized that if they went out the back of the house, the agents in front would not see them leave. *No one knows that I'm here, and no one is going to recognize me. It's safe.* Feeling reassured, she hurried to join her hostess.

The instant Cam opened her eyes, she knew that something was wrong. In a single, swift motion, she threw the sheets aside and bounded to her feet, scanning the room. Blair's clothes were gone. Heart pounding, she pulled on her pants, shrugged into her shirt, and, sockless, kicked into her shoes. She grabbed her shoulder harness from the chair and shrugged into it as she ran from the room. "Blair?"

The house was silent.

Ten seconds later, she was on the street and sprinting toward the black Peugeot parked five cars down from Bonita's front door. The passenger door opened and Felicia stepped out, her face calm but her eyes intense. "Commander?"

"Egret's not in the house."

"No one has been in or out of the house since I arrived at 0600," Felicia reported immediately, her tone crisp and controlled. "According to the night shift, everything was quiet after you and Egret entered the premises at 1949 last evening."

"Christ." A muscle in Cam's jaw jumped. "There's no way I would've slept through an abduction." She took a breath. "I'll check the house again. She may have left a note."

"Should we initiate a search?"

Cam shook her head. "Not yet. I want you here with the vehicle in case we need to pursue or relocate quickly. Stand by while I assess the need for backup."

"Yes, Commander."

Once inside, Cam headed directly to the rear of the house. If anyone had entered during the night, it would not have been through the front door, which had been under constant surveillance. She checked the door that she discovered in the kitchen, examining the lock and the frame for evidence of tampering. She found none. Eyes narrowing, she surveyed the tiny courtyard enclosed by the homes on Bonita's street and those on the block behind it.

I should've posted someone out here. Christ Almighty, I wasn't even thinking about it.

Why she hadn't been thinking about it was a problem for another time. Her stomach tight, a fierce headache beating just behind her eyes, Cam made a rapid but thorough reconnaissance of the rest of the ground floor and then returned upstairs. She found nothing disturbed and no evidence of a struggle anywhere. When she checked the bedroom she and Blair had shared, looking for a note, the crumpled sheets were a stark reminder of just how quickly passion could turn to peril. And how fleeting joy. *Blair. Jesus, where are you?*

Grimly, she started back down once more. It was time to institute a formal search. At the bottom of the stairs, she heard a faint sound coming from the rear of the house. It took less than ten seconds for her to reach the kitchen, weapon drawn and trained on the back door.

"Cam?"

Blair stood in the doorway, holding a paper bag with a long slender loaf of bread protruding from it, a shocked expression on her face. Behind her, Bonita stared, her eyes wide, her face pale.

"God, Cam!" Blair cried. "What's wrong?"

Weapon pointed at the ceiling now, Cam moved swiftly to Blair's side. "Step inside, both of you." Once the women were behind her, she turned sideways in the doorway and scanned the courtyard. It was empty. She looked up automatically, but all the windows facing the small, carefully tended common space were empty, nothing more than blank eyes gazing back. She holstered her automatic and closed the door behind her, then turned and met Blair's questioning eyes. "Are you all right?" Her voice was harsh, her gray eyes hard as granite.

"Yes." Blair spoke quietly, seeing with brutal clarity how her absence had been misinterpreted. "I'm sorry. We were only gone a few minutes."

"You should have told me. You should have alerted the team out front." Cam's voice was clipped, her body rigid with the lingering effects of adrenaline and fear. Fear was a sensation she had never before associated with her work. But Blair was her lover, not just her responsibility. *If anything happened to you...*

"We just went for a walk." Blair's heart ached to see the cold expression on her lover's face, devoid of tenderness and filled with fury. Fury, and something else she couldn't quite decipher.

"Alone. *Alone,* Blair. Unprotected."

"Cameron," Bonita said gently, seeing what Blair could not, "Blair's fine."

Cam spun toward her, her dark eyes snapping. "That's not the point!"

In a voice that sounded eerily like Marcea's, Bonita replied softly, "Isn't it?"

The gentle tone, the even gentler hint of a reprimand, instantly dissolved Cam's anger. She sighed and nodded, the tension suddenly replaced by weariness. "Yes." She looked from Bonita to her lover.

"That's *all* that matters."

"I'm sorry," Blair said softly again. "I thought—"

"No." Cam crossed to Blair and slipped her hand beneath the hair at the back of Blair's neck, caressing her tenderly. "*I'm* sorry."

As Bonita slipped from the room, Blair rested her cheek against Cam's shoulder and wrapped both arms around her waist. The automatic weapon in the shoulder holster against Cam's left side pressed against her breast, a harsh reminder of the complex boundaries that defined their relationship. "I meant to be back before you woke up. God, Cam, I didn't think about what would happen if you woke up before I got back."

"I can't believe I didn't feel you leave the bed—again." Eyes closed, Cam rested her cheek against Blair's hair, one hand stroking up and down her back. "That's completely unlike me."

"I love that you were still asleep when I left. I so rarely have the opportunity to see you like that." Blair pressed her lips to Cam's throat, whispered a kiss against her skin. "I liked to imagine it was our lovemaking that made you sleep so deeply."

"It did." Cam kissed Blair's temple. "When we make love, it always relaxes me." At Blair's short laugh, she added quickly, "Well, after it's over at least."

"Oh, darling." Blair tilted her chin and kissed the underside of Cam's jaw. "I never meant for you to worry."

"I know." Cam dipped her head and brought her lips to her lover's. The heat of Blair's mouth and the beat of her heart against Cam's chest helped to right her world. Blair was safe. "You didn't do anything wrong, Blair. It's not wrong to want to live like the rest of the world."

"Just not wise." There was sadness as well as resignation in Blair's voice.

"No. But I have no complaints." Cam caressed Blair's cheek, drawing her fingers slowly down Blair's neck. "I know how difficult it is for you to accept being guarded twenty-four hours a day, and I know that you've been trying. I appreciate it."

Blair shook her head. "God, Cameron. Don't thank me for being responsible. Not when you and the others put your lives on the line for me."

"That's not what this is about. This is about keeping you safe—" she pressed her fingers to Blair's lips to still the protest that she knew was coming. "And not just because you matter in some *theoretical* way. But because you, Blair Powell, are a special woman." She moved her fingers and kissed her lover's mouth again. "And I, among others, love you."

"You're the only one who matters," Blair murmured and she lifted a hand to Cam's neck, threaded her fingers into Cam's hair, and took the kiss deeper.

Cam groaned as Blair's tongue slid into her mouth and took possession. She was helpless when Blair touched her. Helpless when Blair smiled at her. Helpless just looking at her. Helplessly, hopelessly in love. The enormity of her need struck deep in the core of her, igniting her passion as well as her terror at how easily she could lose everything, and she trembled.

Blair felt Cam shiver and held her closer. She moved her mouth away, pressing herself tightly to her lover. "It's all right. I'm here, and I always will be."

Eyes closed, Cam nodded and fought for control. As her mind cleared and she banished the memories of loss, she laughed shakily. "You undo me."

"You seem to tilt my world too, Commander." Blair stroked her fingers through Cam's hair, tenderly now. "I have never before apologized to my security chief for breaking rank."

"I have an unfair advantage." Cam grinned. "You probably weren't sleeping with any of them."

"Mmm. Probably not." Blair's eyes danced when she saw her lover's spark. "Never wanted to—although there *was* this one state trooper..."

"Blair," Cam growled.

"All right." Blair laughed and patted Cam's cheek. "I won't tease you until after coffee."

"I need to advise the team that you're here."

Instantly, Blair's expression became serious. "Of course. Can we stay for breakfast with Bonita?"

"Blair, please," Cam said gently. "You don't need anyone's permission for something like that. I just need to know your plans so that I can do what needs to be done."

"I know. What I meant to say was, how do you feel about having breakfast with Bonita?"

Cam smiled. "I'd love that." She trailed her fingers over Blair's cheek and then kissed her lightly one more time. "I'll be right back."

On her return from advising Davis of the all clear, Cam came upon Bonita in the sitting room. "I'm sorry for frightening you earlier. Would we be overstaying our welcome if we had that breakfast you and Blair had planned?"

"That would be wonderful." Bonita rose from the sofa and linked her arm with Cam's. "Is everything all right now?"

"Yes. And...thank you, for helping me see what really mattered this morning."

"You're much too hard on yourself, Cameron. It's a difficult path that you've chosen to walk, loving her and protecting her at the same time."

"Aren't they always one and the same?"

"Of course, but in your case, the two are more at odds than they normally are." Bonita smiled as they began to walk. "If I were Blair and you were my lover, I would feel very well taken care of."

"Thank you," Cam said softly.

"You must try to let her take care of you, also. A lover needs that."

Cam stopped in the hallway just outside the kitchen and regarded Bonita with a raised eyebrow. "Have you and my mother been conspiring?"

Bonita laughed with delight. "When two people have been friends for as long as your mother and I, and have watched someone like you grow up, it's impossible for *either* of us not to mother."

"Like me?" Cam repeated, genuinely confused.

"Responsible and dedicated." Bonita patted Cam's cheek. "And so charmingly valiant."

Cam blushed. "I...thank you, Bonita."

"Come. Let's have our coffee and enjoy one another."

As they stepped into the kitchen and Cam's eyes met Blair's, she smiled. "Yes. Let's do that."

In Florida, in a domed, aluminum-sided hangar nearly the size of a football field, a man sat behind the controls of a flight simulator and practiced landing a jumbo jet. He had been enrolled in the flight school for six weeks and had very nearly perfected the techniques needed to alter the in-flight directional patterns of the huge aircraft. When the time came for him to put his new skills to the test, he knew that he would not fail. He had spent the last six years of his life planning for the grand moment that was soon to come. When he was called upon, he would be ready to play his part in the greatest holy war ever waged. Smiling, he reset the simulator to reflect the control panels of a commercial airliner cruising at 30,000 feet and continued to train for his mission.

Renee leaned on an elbow, her chin propped in her palm, and gazed at her hand resting in the center of Stark's abdomen. Her own coffee-colored skin stood out boldly against Stark's naturally pale complexion. The contrast reminded her of how different they were. Stark was so steady, so solid, so willing to give of herself.

And me? What am I, really? Not as trusting as I used to be, if I ever really was. When did I stop believing in someone like you? When did I stop dreaming?

Stark shifted and her lids fluttered. The twitch of muscles beneath Renee's fingers ignited an answering tremor in her depths. She remembered the way Stark had felt inside of her, taking her so effortlessly—knowing instinctively what she needed and giving her such sweet pleasure.

You were so good. So very good. And I fell asleep on you, didn't I, sweetie?

Need rose within her, tight and urgent. But as fiercely as the arousal gripped her, her touch remained gentle. Watching Stark's face, she stroked her abdomen, slowing when Stark murmured restlessly, then resuming when she quieted, moving lower with each tender caress. Touching her, recalling Stark's hands, she grew instantly wet. She caught her lower lip between her teeth, determined to ignore the sudden pounding between her legs. Cautiously, she inched down on the bed, smoothing her fingers along the inside of Stark's thigh.

She could feel the heat in Stark's skin, and the answering flames within her own yearning flesh soared. All thought fled. Only sensation remained. The rich scent of their desire, the satin-smooth skin slick beneath her fingertips, the soft sigh of Stark's breath in counterpoint to Renee's ragged gasps. Resting her breasts against Stark's thigh, she lowered her head and placed a single, careful kiss between Stark's legs.

"Renee," Stark said hoarsely, resting her hand on the back of Renee's head. She'd opened her eyes and nearly cried out with the sweet pleasure of Renee's mouth against her clitoris. "God. Oh... jeez."

Never moving her head, Renee reached up with one arm and placed her palm between Stark's breasts, holding her gently but firmly in place. "Don't move. Just feel."

At the words, Stark's hips twitched and her legs tightened. Her fingers trembled in Renee's hair. "Could you...do that again?"

"Mmm. I was planning to." Renee closed her eyes tightly against another surge of arousal. She was in danger of giving in to the insistent pulse of her own desire when she wanted so very much to please Stark this time. Careful to keep her body from brushing Stark's, uncertain that she could avoid the temptation to assuage her need with a few well-placed thrusts, she shifted until she lay between Stark's legs. Wrapping both arms around her lover's thighs, she glanced up to find Stark's eyes, wide and slightly glazed, upon her face. "Good morning."

Stark swallowed and traced her fingers over Renee's cheek. Her voice was a weak whisper, but her smile was brilliant. "The best."

Renee couldn't wait any longer. She needed to give; she needed to take; she needed to lose herself in the sweet ecstasy of her lover's excitement. She used her lips and mouth lightly at first, alternating kisses with languid strokes of her tongue. Each fleeting touch wrenched a small sound of pleasure from Stark's throat that struck hard in her own center. By the time Stark's clitoris had hardened with an approaching climax, she was about to explode herself. Still, she fought back the waves of release trembling in the pit of her stomach and teased Stark's passion to bursting in her mouth.

"Renee," Stark cried out in shocked surprise. "You're making me come."

The sound of Stark's pleasure and the pulse of her orgasm against Renee's lips brought an ache so sharp to her own flesh that she reached automatically to soothe it. At the first brush of her fingertips against her clitoris, she came.

Groaning with the spasms twisting through her depths, Renee caressed Stark with soft kisses and softer strokes of her tongue until the last pulsations dwindled away. Breathing heavily, she managed to move up the bed before collapsing on her side with one arm around Stark's waist. "God. God, you're so gorgeous."

Stunned, Stark pressed her cheek to Renee's breast and clung to her. "I can't...I feel...oh, Renee."

Laughing quietly, her heart feeling lighter than she could ever recall, Renee brushed her lips over Stark's forehead. "Good, right? You feel good?"

Stark leaned her head back, laughing too, and finally managed to focus on the beautiful face gazing at her with such tenderness that she wanted to weep. "No. Not good. Fabulous."

Renee's lips lifted into a satisfied smile. "Me too."

"We don't have to get up just yet, do we?" Stark nuzzled Renee's breast and drew the already taut nipple into her mouth. She smiled at Renee's quick gasp.

"Oh, sweetie...not if you're going to keep doing that."

"I was planning to."

CHAPTER FOURTEEN

Cam stood in a ballroom with a vaulted cathedral ceiling, centuries-old works of art lining the walls and adorning marble pedestals and a symphony orchestra playing in the background. The atmosphere was lush and elegant, the room filled with diplomats and all manner of European aristocracy. She saw everything, and yet, in a very real way, nothing at all. The key to effective surveillance was to train oneself to be aware of the gestalt, but not to lose oneself in the details. She had seen everyone in the room at least once, noting the particulars of their mannerism and dress—not because she was interested in them, but because she needed to discount them. As each individual was evaluated and deemed nonthreatening, they became as indistinct to her as cardboard cutouts, featureless shapes moving across her field of vision but making no particular impression. That night, as always, one woman stood out in sharp relief against the background of gray.

Blair had put her hair up for the formal affair, somehow taming her wild curls into an elegant twist held in place with a delicate comb that glinted with a hint of diamonds. Her strapless black evening gown dipped low between her breasts and revealed a tantalizing whisper of thigh as she moved. A diamond choker rested in the hollow at the base of her throat. Despite Cam's peripheral awareness of the other people in the room, Blair was the focus of her attention. Anyone who moved near her, spoke to her, or even appeared to be watching her for an unusual length of time garnered Cam's intent inspection. At the moment, she was watching her lover dance in the arms of a handsome, dark-haired man she recognized as France's minister of defense. His palm rested in the middle of Blair's back, against her skin, which was exposed by the gown's low-cut back. Nothing showed on Cam's face as she watched his hand move in an indolent caress.

Across the room, Mac systematically swept the huge space, pausing briefly at each exit to take note of who stood there— someone lingering near a doorway could easily be a lookout or a triggerman. He saw only the gently milling mass of suave men and beautifully adorned women. He also saw his colleagues—the six who were in the room. There were four additional agents on perimeter duty outside. His gaze halted on his chief as he followed her line of sight to Egret. From fifty feet away, he could see her dark eyes smoldering. Someone who didn't know her wouldn't notice her tension or her fury, but he had grown used to deciphering her state of mind by reading her body language and the message in her eyes. He had learned that she never voluntarily gave any indication of her feelings. Not for the first time, he was glad not to be in her shoes. He didn't shrink from the responsibility, and, in fact, was proud that he was usually the commander's first choice for team leader when she was off duty or otherwise unavailable. He did not, however, envy her, knowing that she was often forced to behave as if she had no personal relationship whatsoever with Egret. While never doubting that she could carry out her responsibilities in terms of Egret's security, he couldn't even guess at how much that restraint cost her emotionally.

"You're monopolizing Ms. Powell, Claude," a rich contralto voice complained playfully. A dark-haired, dark-eyed woman wearing a deep burgundy dress took Blair's arm and with a sly smile drew her away from the obviously displeased man. "How are you, darling?"

"I'm eternally grateful for the rescue," Blair murmured as she smiled and nodded to several individuals who greeted her as she walked slowly to the edge of the dance floor with her companion. "I was running out of polite conversation."

The woman, twenty years Blair's senior but still sensuously beautiful, tilted her head and laughed. "I'm surprised you lasted as long as you did. In the past, you would have sent him running with his tail between his legs in a matter of minutes."

"I was practicing diplomacy."

"You never saw the need for that before, as I recall." She drew Blair closer, brushing her breast against Blair's arm as she did so. When she felt no response from Blair, she laughed again. "You've changed."

Blair looked over to where she had last seen Cam and smiled softly as her eyes met her lover's. "Yes. I have."

"Ah..." Her companion followed Blair's gaze. In a voice verging on a purr, she said, "There's something about a long, tight body in a tuxedo that always makes me wet."

"Then I see *you* haven't changed, at least."

"She's the one all the fuss is about, I take it."

They stopped by a large marble pillar out of the stream of activity. Blair had a headache from making polite conversation with too many people for too many hours. All she wanted to do was shed her clothes, put her feet up, and enjoy a few quiet minutes with Cam. She sighed, seeing no point in denying what everyone was aware of.

"Yes."

The press had been waiting once again when she'd arrived at the presidential palace. They'd shouted variations on the same questions that they had bombarded her with the day before, and she once again made no comment. Although none of the guests mentioned the news articles, she had been aware of a few pointed stares during the evening.

"Is she anywhere near as good as she looks?" the woman asked.

Unoffended, Blair nevertheless ignored the question. "I'm going to make my way over to the president and his wife and pay my respects. I have an early-morning flight back to the States tomorrow, and I'm tired."

The dark-haired woman slid her arm around Blair's waist and leaned against her, her thigh pressing into Blair's hip. "We could slip away to my apartment for an hour or two. Remember how much fun that used to be?"

Blair couldn't. All she could remember was the empty pleasure of stealing a few hours of freedom that never truly felt free, and the moments of physical satisfaction that were even less gratifying. "I don't think so. Thanks."

"You can't mean to tell me that you're serious about this woman? An affair is one thing, but—really, Blair. Even if you don't care about the politics, it's social suicide."

"You know that's never mattered to me," Blair said quietly.

"I know that you always pretended that it didn't," her companion countered. "That's one of the many things I found so exciting about you. But you're young yet, and something like this could haunt you forever."

"You're absolutely right." A smile flickered across Blair's face. "Which is why I have absolutely no intention of letting her go."

The beautiful woman leaned close and kissed Blair lightly on the lips. "I'll miss those special moments with you, darling."

"Take care," Blair whispered before she slipped away.

Blair had crossed only a small part of the room when Cam appeared at her side. She slowed and smiled at her lover. "Hello."

"Ms. Powell," Cam replied quietly. She was close enough to touch her, but she did not.

"I'm ready to go home."

With a casual gesture that might have been interpreted as merely a brush of her hand through her hair, Cam murmured into the minuscule communicator on the undersurface of her left wrist, "Stark, bring the vehicle to the west entrance."

"I want to *really* go home," Blair said with a sigh.

"Yes," Cam admitted, allowing a rare break in her professional façade. "So do I."

"Come with me while I make my goodbyes."

"Of course. I'll be nearby."

"No," Blair murmured softly, curling her fingers around Cam's forearm and drawing her a step closer. "*Accompany* me."

Surprised, Cam stiffened. "Blair, I don—"

"Please."

The word was uttered softly, one lover to another, and Cam could not refuse. "It would be my pleasure."

As they approached the French president and his wife at the center of a small gathering of dignitaries, Cam scanned the crowd and took note of Mac on the left side of the room and Rogers on the right keeping pace with them. Assured that the appropriate surveillance was in place while her attention was diverted, she relaxed enough to appreciate how at ease Blair appeared in the midst of such exalted company. At the moment, Blair was thanking the French president and his wife for their gracious hospitality and commenting on how much she had enjoyed the evening. A few more polite words were exchanged, and then Blair smiled up at Cam. "May I introduce my escort, Cameron Roberts."

In French, Cam replied that it was an honor to meet them and a pleasure to be in Paris again. When the president's wife suggested that they return when Blair was not obligated by official duties, "to truly appreciate the beauty of Paris," Cam smiled warmly and said that she definitely hoped they would have that opportunity soon.

After the usual pleasantries, Blair and Cam turned to leave.

"I think she was flirting with you," Blair said under her breath.

Cam barely managed to stifle a laugh. "She most certainly was not."

"You're so damn charming, you're dangerous."

"As long as you think so, Ms. Powell."

Before Blair could reply, Cam eased away several steps. The few minutes between leaving the building and securing Blair in the vehicle were critical, and she needed to focus. Stark appeared with Blair's wrap and handed it to her.

"Here you are, Ms. Powell. The car is waiting at the curb."

"Thank you." Blair sensed several other people move close to her and knew that Mac and Rogers had just completed the circle behind her. With Cam slightly ahead and to her left, going through the door first as she always did, Blair stepped outside. Instantly, a bright light flashed in her eyes. As she blinked furiously to clear her vision, she was aware of a dark shape looming to her right. She cried out, more in surprise then fear, as Stark grasped her around the waist and pushed her back several steps while shielding her from the intruder with her body. At the same time, Blair saw Cam hurtling toward the shape, which she now recognized as a heavyset man in a dark cap and shapeless jacket. He held something in his hand.

The interloper came out of the shadows so quickly that he was within three feet of Blair before Cam saw him. When she did, all she registered was the speed of his approach and the fact that he held something in the hand that was extended toward Blair. *Gun.* Her reaction was automatic. She pivoted into him, bent her knees to lower her center of gravity, and shoved her shoulder into his chest. She clamped his leading arm—the one holding the weapon— between her fists, pulled him off balance, and threw him over her body onto his back. He landed with a grunt as the air was driven from his lungs by the force of his unchecked fall. Immediately, Cam planted her knee in the center of his chest and levered his arm into an elbow lock. With the slightest bit of pressure, she could break his arm. Without even looking up, she ordered sharply, "Get her back to the hotel."

Less than twenty seconds later, Blair was in the back of the Peugeot with Stark beside her and Mac at the wheel. With a screech of tires, they merged into traffic.

"Are you all right?" Stark asked quietly. Although she was breathing rapidly, her voice was completely calm.

"Yes." Blair looked back through the rear window, but she could see nothing. "What was that about, do you think?"

"Probably paparazzi or an autograph hound." Stark eased her weapon, which she had held by her side out of Blair's line of vision, back into her hip holster. *Or something worse, considering the commander's reaction.*

Blair sighed. "How long do you think Cam will be?"

Stark shifted uncomfortably. "I couldn't say."

"No," Blair murmured, closing her eyes as she wondered when she would see Cam again. "There's no way to know, is there?"

Renee rolled over and picked up the receiver on the second ring. "Hello?"

"Did I wake you?"

Smiling, she stretched out beneath the covers, enjoying the brush of cotton across her naked skin. "Well, I *was* having a very nice dream about a particularly sexy Secret Service agent..."

"I'm sorry."

"I don't mind."

"What are you wearing?"

Laughing in delight, Renee replied, "Why don't you come see for yourself?"

"All right."

Renee's stomach tightened with a jolt of anticipation. "Are you off shift now?"

"Uh-huh."

"How soon can you be here?"

Stark hesitated. "Two minutes too long?"

Oh, you are full of surprises, aren't you? When she spoke again, Renee's voice was throaty and warm. "Make it one."

"Roger that."

Renee threw back the sheet and stood as she hung up the receiver, reaching with her free hand for the robe that she had left lying across the foot of the bed. She shrugged into it on the way to the door, holding it closed with one hand, not bothering to tie it. When a knock sounded, she glanced through the peephole and hurriedly opened the door.

"Hi," Stark said as she slipped inside. She'd taken the time to change into a T-shirt and jeans.

Letting the robe fall open, Renee stepped forward and wrapped both arms around Stark's shoulders, pressing close. "Hi," she murmured as she brought her mouth to Stark's.

"Uh..." Stark's heart jumped into hyperdrive when she saw the quicksilver flash of moonlight on skin and then came to a complete standstill when she felt Renee's body mold to hers. She put her back to the door for support as she drew both hands up the back of Renee's thighs beneath the silk to cup her buttocks. When she automatically lifted her hips, Renee thrust back, and they both groaned. She closed her eyes, surrendering to all that was Renee. The ambrosial scent of desire filled her mind as a warm tongue filled her mouth and the flames within her danced high.

"Renee," Stark murmured when she felt fingers working at her fly. "If you touch me, I'll fall down."

"Mmm, I want to make you melt."

"Done," Stark gasped as fingertips brushed down her belly. Her legs shook and threatened to fold. "It's our last night in Paris. I want to spend it making love with you."

With effort, Renee stopped her downward quest and hooked

her fingers around the waistband of Stark's jeans. "How long do I have you?"

As long as you want. Forever. Stark circled her hand at the base of Renee's spine, holding her close. "0500."

A little more than three hours. And then we'll be on separate planes, going home to...what?

"Then let's get started," Renee murmured as she tugged her lover toward the bed.

"Commander?"

Cam turned at the sound of Mac's voice, leaning her hip against the waist-high railing of the balcony. "All quiet?"

Nodding, he joined her. "I didn't see you come back."

"Just got here."

He waited, knowing that she would tell him what she felt he needed to know. He wanted to ask about the shadows in her eyes that even the cover of darkness could not hide. But he didn't, because it would be an intrusion and because their relationship stopped somewhere short of friendship. The bond between them was professional, it was respectful, and it was one he would give his life for, but they had never invited each other into their hearts.

"What's the number one priority in your life, Mac?"

His surprise did not prevent him from answering immediately. "Egret's welfare."

Cam nodded. "Good. Because I don't want you worrying about your career if you find you have to tell me or someone else that you think I'm fucking up."

"You have my word on it."

"Thank you."

Simultaneously, they both turned and placed their hands on top of the iron balustrade that enclosed the balcony and looked toward the Arc de Triomphe a few blocks away. The fabric of their nearly identical tuxedo jackets brushed where their shoulders touched.

"I haven't noted any problems, Commander." He did not look at her when he spoke, but idly watched the stream of headlights flicker along the Champs Elysées.

"I took her to an unsecured location last night with the bare minimum of a team, and I didn't even have the foresight to check the perimeter myself. If someone had wanted her, I'm not sure we could have protected her."

What she had admitted to him would have been grounds for her dismissal if she'd confessed it to anyone else. That she trusted him with her concerns pleased him almost more than anything else in his career ever had. "Other than yesterday right after the press release in the States, we've only been on mid-level alert status. There hasn't been any suggestion of increased hostile activity in this area or undue attention directed toward Egret. There's been no reason to suspect she's at risk."

"It was sloppy," Cam muttered angrily. "I was so busy thinking of her..."

"Exactly," Mac said softly.

Cam rubbed her face briskly. "Just the same—"

"Commander, since you and Egret have been...together," he pointed out, choosing his words carefully, "she's been much more accepting of our security measures. She's much safer now than she ever has been."

"That's no excuse for me doing my job less well."

"Agreed. And if I thought that were the case, I would say so. To you."

"I'm counting on it." With a sigh, Cam turned back toward the comm center. "I'm going to review the itinerary for the return flight and the personnel placement—"

"Why don't you go to bed? It will keep until the morning briefing." After a second, he added, "I think Ms. Powell was concerned about the altercation earlier."

Cam blew out a breath. "Rogers and I worked him over pretty well. His ID checked out with the limited sources we could access—seems he's a legit freelance reporter. He said he was just trying to get a quote from her about her *lifestyle*. Wanted to scoop the other papers."

"You believe him?"

"I'd be happier if we had been able to run him through Interpol and the NSI database, but there was no way to do that tonight. And no reason to hold him." She stepped into the com center, which had already been partially dismantled in preparation for their departure.

"But the French have agreed to keep an eye on him and inform us if anything unusual turns up."

They both knew that interagency intelligence communication, especially international communication, was so poor that even if the French *did* discover something of concern in the reporter's background, the information might never filter down to those in the field. But it was the best that could be done.

"I'll see you at 0630," Cam said on her way to the door.

"Roger that." When Cam disappeared, Mac looked around the nearly deserted comm center. In the adjacent room, Cynthia Parker manned the computers for the remainder of the night shift. The glow of the monitors signaled her presence, but despite that, he felt completely alone. He sat down at the long empty conference table with a stack of computer printouts and began to skim through the random communiqués that came in twenty-four hours a day.

He imagined that Felicia was already asleep and hoped that the comfort of routine would carry him through to the morning.

CHAPTER FIFTEEN

Cam closed the comm center door quietly, nodded perfunctorily to Reynolds, who stood in the hall outside Blair's room, and walked toward the stairwell. It had been a long night, she was beat, and she was lonely. She'd hoped earlier for a few minutes alone with Blair after the formal affair, but the intruder had put an end to that wish. Now it was fast approaching dawn and a full day of travel awaited—another potentially hazardous time for Blair when Cam and the whole team needed to be sharp.

"Commander?"

Turning, Cam answered, "Yes?"

Reynolds held out an envelope. "For you, ma'am."

Silently, Cam stepped forward and extended her hand. Angling with her back to Reynolds, she opened the envelope and withdrew the single sheet of cream-colored stationery bearing the watermark of the Hotel Marigny. In her lover's bold script she read, *Please come to me—no matter how late. B—*

Carefully, Cam replaced the notepaper in the envelope and slipped it into her jacket pocket. Then she walked directly past Reynolds, who gave no sign that he even saw her, used the master passkey to open the door, and stepped inside. The sitting room was dark, as was the bedroom beyond the open door opposite. Moving slowly in the moonlight, Cam removed her tuxedo jacket and dropped it onto the arm of the sofa as she passed. She loosened the tie from around her neck, folded it, and slid it into her pants pocket. By the time she reached the bedroom door, she had removed her cuff links and studs from her shirt and placed them into the opposite front pocket. Once inside the bedroom, she bent down, untied her shoes, and pushed them off along with her socks. She pulled her open shirt free from the cummerbund at her waist and let it fall over the holster on her hip. Standing beside the bed, she looked down on Blair, who slept nude beneath a pure white sheet.

She'd taken the comb from her hair, and waves of gold framed her face in the silver light. A pain struck deep in Cam's heart, the kind of ache she always felt when she looked at beauty. Faced with both beauty *and* love, she was rendered helpless with awe. She freed her weapon from her waistband and rested it on top of the antique nightstand, then removed her shirt, unzipped her pants, and stepped out of the remainder of her clothing. Gently, she drew aside the sheet and eased down onto the edge of the bed. Before she could stretch out, Blair curled around her from behind with both arms encircling her waist and pressed her cheek to the center of Cam's back.

"You came. I hoped you would," Blair murmured, her mouth against Cam's skin, her palm flat against Cam's abdomen.

"I tried not to wake you," Cam whispered, covering Blair's hand with her own. Their fingers linked automatically.

"Mmm, no. I'm glad you did. I was worried."

"Everything is fine."

As they talked, Blair stroked her fingers up and down Cam's abdomen. The touch, casual and possessive, was both comforting and arousing. Blair's hand still in hers, Cam gave a weary sigh and leaned back onto the pillows. Blair shifted with her until she was lying against Cam's side, her head on her lover's shoulder.

As she continued her soft caresses, Blair asked quietly, "Who was he?"

Cam stroked the thick blond hair, soothed as she always was by its fragrant softness drifting through her fingers. "Just a reporter, it looks like."

"That light was a camera flash, then, when I first walked out?"

"Yes—and he was equipped with a minirecorder, too. That's what he had in his hand—the microphone." *That I took for a gun.* Cam considered how close she'd come to dislocating his elbow, more out of fury than necessity. He'd been the last person in a too-long line of people who had overstepped their bounds that evening where her lover was concerned—the throng of media who had descended upon them the instant they had stepped from their vehicle; the men who found Blair desirable and who took the opportunity to hold her and caress her as if it were their right; the ex-lover—because she couldn't have been anything else considering the way she had looked at Blair and touched her with a knowledge born of intimacy—who had clearly been interested in another interlude. By the time this intruder had lunged from the darkness to accost her lover, Cam had been ready to fight. It had taken all her control merely to immobilize him without assuaging her anger by breaking his arm.

Blair pressed her lips to the tight muscles just below Cam's collarbone. "What's wrong?"

"Nothing—just wound up."

"I know. I can feel it." Blair raised up on an elbow and studied her lover. Cam's eyes were dark pools, and in the dim moonlight, she could not read what lay in their depths. Without being able to see Cam's eyes, she was at a disadvantage, because that was the one place Cam's secrets were exposed. She placed her palm in the center of Cam's chest, felt her heart beat steady and sure, and eased her leg over Cam's thigh. "Want to tell me why?"

Cam hesitated, reluctant to burden her lover with concerns over a situation she could not change. Then she recalled what Blair had said to her only weeks before.

I love you. It's not just about sex and it's not just about common ground. It's about needing to be with you. It's about needing to be in your life.

Resting a hand on the back of Blair's neck and drawing her back down, Cam replied quietly, "I was thinking about how much I don't like other people touching you, or even trying to."

"Other people." Blair was silent for a long moment. "Other people like Margot Fallon?"

"She would be one," Cam noted nonchalantly as she thought of the striking wife of the French ambassador.

"I should have realized that you would know exactly what she was doing." Blair sighed, aware as well that her previous liaisons with Margot must have been documented somewhere and that Cam would have read all about them. "You do know that I wasn't tempted, don't you?"

"Temptation is not a sin."

"No," Blair mused, "I suppose we can't be expected to control how our bodies respond."

"I'm going to kill her."

Cam's tone was absolutely serious, but Blair merely laughed and fit herself more closely to Cam. "As it happens, I was tempted in neither body nor spirit. But I'm sorry if it bothered you."

"It's not your fault, and there's no need for you to apologize." Cam turned her head and kissed Blair's forehead, shifting on her side until their bodies touched along their lengths. "I can see why it's so hard for you to constantly be the center of attention. So many people take liberties."

Blair caught her breath as her heart filled with a combination of wonder and surprise. "Every time you say something like that, I fall in love with you all over again."

Before she could change her mind, Cam pushed on. "I talked to Mac tonight about whether my being in love with you was compromising my ability to run the detail."

"Oh, Cam. I'm sorry. I'm sorry that anything about tonight made you feel that way." Blair laughed softly and kissed the side of Cam's throat. "A few months ago—hell, a few *weeks* ago, I would have been delighted to think that you weren't happy with your performance. Then, maybe I could've taken advantage of your momentary, and extraordinarily rare, insecurity to get you to resign."

"And now?" Cam asked curiously.

"As much as I still hate the thought of you placing yourself in jeopardy to protect me, I love having you around." Blair took a deep breath and finished before she could change her mind. "More than that, I love having you as my security chief. I trust you."

"That means everything to me," Cam murmured, tracing her fingertips along the undersurface of Blair's jaw before tilting her head up for a kiss. She lingered on the softness of Blair's lips, gliding her fingers over the elegant bones of Blair's face as she explored the warmth of her mouth with her tongue. When she drew back, she added huskily, "If I ever thought I couldn't take care of you, I'd quit."

"I can't imagine that will ever happen," Blair whispered, "but as long as you let me take care of you, too, I won't ever ask you to stop doing what you need to do."

Cam rested her forehead against Blair's, a feeling of ultimate peace and rightness stealing over her. "I need you so much."

For the second time that evening, Blair was speechless. She pressed even nearer, her breasts against Cam's, a leg insinuated between Cam's thighs. The surge of pleasure that streaked through her had as much to do with happiness as arousal. If it had been physically possible, she would have climbed inside of Cam's body and curled up—she wanted to be that close to her. As it was, she had only her inadequate words and her body with which to convey the depths of her love. She smoothed her palm down the center of Cam's back to her hips, then pulled Cam more firmly into her. Her voice held a desperate plea. "I love you so much and I don't know how to tell you, to show you. I want to make love to you, but I know it won't be enough. God...nothing will ever be enough."

"Hold me tightly," Cam whispered hoarsely against Blair's ear, needing nothing more than the beat of Blair's heart against her skin. "Just hold me like this until morning, and I promise, it will be enough."

The faint tremor in Cam's voice brought a surge of protectiveness, and Blair tightened her grip. "Oh yes, darling. Oh yes."

"It's almost dawn," Renee whispered, leaning on her elbows with her hands gently framing Stark's face. "You should get some sleep."

"I can sleep on the plane." Stark drew both hands down Renee's back to her hips and lifted her own pelvis, the contact striking fire to her blood. "I can't seem to get enough of you. I don't want to sleep when I can be touching you."

"This doesn't have to end tonight." Renee kissed her softly. *Does it? Tell me that it doesn't. Tell me that this isn't just about being in Paris.*

"I know," Stark sighed. "But once we're home, you'll go back to work, and I'll be traveling with Egret. I won't be able to see you as much."

Renee laughed softly as relief lifted her heart. She threaded her fingers into Stark's hair and edged her leg higher between Stark's strong thighs, reveling in the surprised groan from the woman beneath her. Although she'd thought herself satisfied—*beyond* satisfied—by the soaring orgasm she'd experienced only moments before, she felt herself pulse and grow hard again. "We'll find time. We'll make time." She leaned down and took Stark's mouth with a hunger that surprised them both. She rocked on Stark's thigh, teasing them both as she slicked Stark's skin with the hot essence of her desire. Gasping, she forced the words out. "This is *our* life."

"Sit up," Stark urged desperately, her breath barely moving as she watched Renee's face dissolve with pleasure. "I want to see you come. I want to remember how beautiful you look."

Renee gave a small cry and forced herself upward to sit astride Stark's leg, grasping the hands that Stark offered in support. Their fingers clenched and her hair fell forward on either side of her face as her head dropped. Her hips pistoned as her stomach tightened and her vision dimmed. "Oh God," she cried, her head snapping back. "Oh God, Paula."

"That's it," Stark groaned hoarsely. Her own body throbbed with an answering swell of passion as she watched Renee near orgasm, but that pleasure was only a pale echo of the sheer glory of watching Renee's surrender. "So beautiful."

Trembling at the peak of her release, Renee implored, "Hold me."

Stark reared up and enfolded Renee in her arms as Renee shuddered and sobbed out her name. Together they fell back to the bed, wrapped tightly in each other's embrace.

Stroking Renee's hair, Stark murmured, "You okay?"

"Oh," Renee laughed unsteadily, "I have no idea." She rubbed her cheek against Stark's breast. "I've never been like this with anyone before."

"Like what?" Stark kissed her forehead, her eyes, her cheeks. "Huh? Sweetheart?"

"So crazy, so free." Renee cupped Stark's breast gently. "So *safe*. You're a remarkable lover."

"Uh," Stark mumbled, trying to ignore the swift tightening of her nipple beneath Renee's hand. "I'm not doing anything. I'm just...you, it's you...I'm just touching you."

Then please don't stop. Renee sighed languorously. "It's working very nicely."

"Good." Stark stilled the motion of Renee's hand. The slow brush of fingers was driving her crazy. "Will you call me as soon as you land tomorrow?"

"Mmm-hmm. Where are you going to be?"

"We're *supposed* to be headed back to New York City, but you never know."

"I'll tell you what—I'll call your cell when I land, then *you* call me when you're free."

"Okay." Stark let out a sigh. "I miss you already."

"I'm not gone yet." Renee replaced the fingers on Stark's nipple with her lips while at the same time smoothing her hand down Stark's stomach and between her legs. She moaned softly as Stark arched beneath her hands. Carefully, she fondled the length of the firm clitoris, timing her strokes to the rhythm of Stark's murmured pleasure. When the first ripple of Stark's climax coursed beneath her fingertips, she carefully entered her.

"Feels so good." Stark jerked and buried her face in Renee's hair, trying hard to hold out against the sudden surge of sensation. She hadn't known she could feel this way, so full and yet so hungry for more. "Do it...harder."

"Next time, sweetie," Renee whispered, drawing her fingers tenderly in and out. "Just come for me now."

"I am," Stark sobbed. "I...oh...I am."

Through a haze of excitement, Renee contained her desire to push harder and deeper, knowing that this act of love was new to her lover. She stilled her hand when the orgasm played around her fingers, moving only enough to encourage the last final spasms of pleasure. When she felt Stark's taut muscles soften and her body relax, she slowly withdrew. At the sound of a small cry, Renee swiftly gathered her lover close.

"Sweetie, honey? Are you okay?"

Weak with the aftermath of pleasure, Stark rested her forehead between Renee's breasts, her voice barely a whisper. "Okay? I could die happy now."

Renee's heart lurched, though she knew the words carried no portent, and she managed a small laugh while stroking Stark's damp face. "Well, since that was only the beginning, I suggest you stick around for a while longer."

"Oh, I intend to."

At 0610, Felicia looked up from her newspaper as the hotel room door banged open. Stark came flying through with a look of dazed panic on her face.

"Oh man," Stark exclaimed, her eyes faintly wild. "I'm going to be late, and the commander is going to bust me."

Felicia, in a dusky gray, blended-silk suit, sipped coffee at the small table before the open French doors that led to the small balcony. She lowered her cup and regarded Stark with a hint of a smile. "Go take a shower. I packed your gear already."

Stark skidded to a halt, breathing heavily. "You did? Oh God, you *did?* I owe you. I owe you so big."

"You're right. You do." Felicia went back to her newspaper, suppressing a laugh.

Fifteen minutes later, she and Stark headed for the comm center where, within a matter of thirty seconds, the rest of the team arrived as well. The agents took seats around the conference table and waited silently, most with coffee in one hand and a PDA in the other, for Cam to walk to the head of the table and open the morning briefing.

"There's been a slight change in plans," Cam announced at precisely 0630. "We're flying into Washington Dulles instead of LaGuardia. Those of you on temporary assignment for this trip can make arrangements there to return to your home base. The permanent team will remain in DC until further notice. Mac will update shift assignments en route."

No one commented. Last-minute changes in the itinerary weren't at all unusual, especially on a return leg. Disruption of personal plans was a routine part of the job. After Cam reviewed the timetable for transport to De Gaulle Airport, along with the vehicle assignments, she dismissed the team to prepare for departure. After everyone had left, Mac approached her.

"Let me guess. Lucinda Washburn?"

Cam nodded with the barest trace of a grimace. "I don't think she ever sleeps. She called Blair at 0500 and demanded a personal appearance at the White House this evening."

"I take it this was prompted by the press release?"

"Presumably." Cam bit off the words as she tried to control her temper. "It isn't as if Lucinda didn't know this was coming. Blair advised her of the interview when it was scheduled."

"Anything I can do?"

Cam shook her head. "Thanks. Blair will handle it, I'm sure." *I just wish she didn't have to. All she wants to do is get back home so she can paint. She's paid her dues with this trip, and the least Lucinda can do is leave her in peace for a few weeks.*

With a conscious effort to focus on the details of the last leg of their journey, Cam sighed. "Let's go home, Mac."

"Roger that, Commander."

18Aug01
Just off Interstate 95, Florida

A beefy redhead in olive green cammies entered the restaurant and looked around the nearly empty seating area. His flat blue eyes settled on the thin, bearded, dark-haired man attired in casual tan chinos and an open-collared white shirt. The faxed photo he had been provided of his contact wasn't very good, but the man in the booth staring back at him fit the description. He walked across the room and settled heavily into the booth opposite the smaller man.

"Is your team ready?" he asked without preamble.

Arrogant Americans. The bearded man's eyes sparked with indignation, but he answered quietly in lightly accented English, "We are."

"What about the others?"

"They await only the final instructions to move into place."

The redhead passed a single sheet of paper across the table. "These are the flight details."

The targets weren't listed, but he knew them. New York City, Washington, DC, Chicago, Los Angeles. And a very special one of which his bearded "friend" was unaware.

After a moment of studying the printout, the first man lifted surprised eyes. "We understood it was to be sooner."

"The personnel for one of the critical flights were changed. If Hydra command wants all six targets, this is the date." The second man's tone was condescending. They were on *his* turf, even if it was their show. They'd come to *his* organization with an offer to combine resources for a preemptive strike that would send a message once and for all that in America, the *true* Americans were coming to power. Ultimately, their groups might have different agendas, but a blow to their common enemy would strengthen them all. Allies today, enemies tomorrow. That was the way of war.

"When *my* leader gives the word, we will not hesitate." The bearded man carefully folded the sheet of paper listing the departure times and flight numbers of the airplanes that would carry him and his brothers to glory.

CHAPTER SIXTEEN

The Suburban slowed as it passed the security gate and proceeded to the first family's private entrance. Blair leaned across the seat and touched Cam's arm. "Will you be at your apartment?"

"Tonight?" Cam inquired. She'd dismissed the auxiliary agents who had accompanied them to Paris at Dulles, and her core team had the night off. The White House security patrol would be responsible for Blair's security while she was at the White House, as they were for the president when he was in residence. It wasn't an arrangement Cam was particularly fond of—she considered the White House security patrol to be essentially gatekeepers, not security agents. But politically, she had nothing to say about it. "I'll be there tonight. Will you be staying here?"

Blair nodded. "I don't know how long this meeting with Lucinda will take, but I'm hoping to catch my father later. I haven't seen him since before we left for Paris."

The vehicle had stopped, but since she and Cam had made no move to get out, Phil Rogers remained behind the wheel on the other side of the privacy panel. Nevertheless, Blair lowered her voice. "I'll miss you. I've gotten used to having you in my bed at night."

"I know." They had a certain amount of freedom when traveling, and even home in New York, because Blair's security team existed for one purpose—to protect her. The agents were trained to look the other way where the private lives of their protectees were concerned. Even when that included sleeping with one of them. Still, she and Blair valued their privacy and tried to shield their personal relationship from too much scrutiny, which meant there were times when they could not reasonably find a way to be together. This was one of those times.

Cam sighed. "It's getting so I can't sleep well without you."

Blair smiled. Although Cam's discomfort was the last thing she wished for, she was enormously pleased to know that she was not alone in hating their forced separations. "I'll call you as soon as I can after the meeting with Lucinda."

Cam raised an eyebrow slightly as she shook her head. "I'm coming with you for that."

"What?" Blair sat up straighter.

"If Lucinda Washburn wants to talk to you about your relationship with me, then I want to be there."

"I don't think that's a very good idea," Blair said immediately. "The last thing we want to do is keep underscoring the fact that you're both my security chief and my lover. I don't want to put you in the spotlight."

"You can't put me in the closet, Blair," Cam said succinctly. "Lucinda knows who you're sleeping with. My superiors know I'm sleeping with you. The president of the United States knows that we're lovers. There's no closet big enough to fit all that."

"I'm not trying to put you in the closet, Cameron." Blair was jet-lagged and bone-weary from the constant stress of deciding how much to reveal about her personal life, and to whom. Her words had come out more sharply than she had intended.

"Then what are you trying to do?"

"*Protect* you." Blair reached for the door handle. "That *is* something you understand, isn't it? *I'm* certainly supposed to understand it when you've decided to stand between me and danger. I'm even supposed to be happy about it!"

Before Blair could step from the vehicle, taking with her their last chance for privacy, Cam reached out and caught her arm. "Blair, wait."

Because she already missed her, and because she knew her heart would ache for the rest of the night if they parted this way, Blair stopped. With a sigh, she settled back into the seat. "God, sometimes you make me so crazy."

"Then we're even." Cam rubbed the bridge of her nose and then ran her hand through her hair. In a calmer voice, she said, "If Lucinda Washburn or anyone else is going to dress you down for your relationship with me, I want to be there. We need to deal with that together. If we're a couple."

If we're a couple. A couple. Blair regarded Cam intently, searching her eyes for the answer to the question she was afraid to ask. This time it wasn't enough to *see* the determination and the caring in Cam's eyes. This was something so essential to her soul that she needed to hear the words. "Is that really what we are? What you want?"

Nothing ever defused Cam's temper faster than the slightest hint of insecurity in Blair's voice. The moment they'd met, she'd fallen in love with Blair's strength and her indomitable will. To know that anything, but most especially something about their relationship, could shake that certainty was like a fist in the gut. She extended her hand and took Blair's. "I love you. You're my life."

For an instant, Blair closed her eyes. When she opened them, even the dim light inside the vehicle could not hide the shimmer of tears. "I can't say no when you say something like that. No one has ever been able to reach inside me the way you do."

Cam lifted Blair's hand to her lips and kissed it gently before rubbing the backs of Blair's fingers against her cheek. "That's because I'm the only one who belongs there."

"It's true, and it still scares me to death." Blair spoke softly, almost to herself. Then she straightened and fixed Cam with a steady gaze. "You'll have to be careful with Lucinda. She's used to chewing out the Joint Chiefs and assorted cabinet members before breakfast."

"I shouldn't think she'd be any worse than the president's daughter before coffee."

Blair laughed out loud. "You do like to live dangerously, don't you, Commander?"

"Let's say I enjoy living life with you." Cam merely grinned as she pushed open the door and stepped out before extending her hand to Blair. "Shall we?"

With you, anything. Blair slid from the Suburban and linked her fingers with Cam's as she gazed up at the White House. Another fragment of her life slipped into place as she walked up the stairs to the entrance with her lover.

"Just one minute while she finishes this call," Lucinda's harried assistant said to Blair as he fielded three other calls at once. "She wants to be interrupted for you."

Three minutes later, he waved Blair and Cam into the chief of staff's office. Lucinda was behind her desk, her reading glasses hanging on a colorful braided cord around her neck. She looked up at the sound of their entrance and then regarded Cam with an intense stare before turning her attention to Blair. "You might prefer that this meeting be private."

"No, I don't prefer that." Blair reached out and took Cam's hand once again. "You know my lover, Cameron Roberts. Cam, Lucinda Washburn."

Cam quickly squeezed Blair's fingers before stepping forward to extend her hand across the desk. "Pleased to meet you, ma'am."

Lucinda, a formidable woman in her mid-fifties wearing an impeccably tailored suit and just the right amount of expensive but understated jewelry, stood and returned Cam's handshake. Then she walked around the side of the desk, gesturing to the small seating area. She took the chair opposite the sofa, allowing Blair and Cam to sit together. Then she once again focused on Cam.

"Are you interested in marrying the president's daughter, Agent Roberts?"

"Lucinda, what the hell?" Blair sat forward indignantly, her eyes blazing.

The chief of staff gave a nonchalant shrug. "Just one of many questions I have."

"Our private life is none of your business." Blair had known Lucinda Washburn since she was a child, and she'd often been intimidated by Lucinda's power and status, not only within her father's political machine but also within the small social circle of family friends. She rarely had occasion to argue or take issue with Lucinda, even though she sometimes resented the woman's central position in her father's life. A position that *she* never seemed to occupy.

"First of all," Lucinda said mildly, "you don't *have* a private life. Not for at least the next three—God willing, the next *seven*—

years. Secondly, even if you did, it *is* my business. Everything that impacts on your father's position is my business."

"I fail to see—"

Cam's deep voice interjected quietly, "A year ago I never could have imagined loving anyone the way I do Blair. I haven't thought about marriage, but I believe in it as an institution. And I love the president's daughter, so the answer to your question is yes."

While Lucinda studied Cam speculatively, Blair regarded her with stunned astonishment. Finally she spoke, her voice thick with emotion. "Cameron, are you proposing?"

"Not at the moment." Cam's expressive mouth quirked into a grin as she met Blair's eyes. "When the time comes, I'd like to do that in slightly more intimate surroundings."

"When the time comes," Blair repeated, still trying to absorb the concept of that kind of commitment. After the first wave of surprise, she felt a flush of pleasure, and she leaned her shoulder gently against Cam's.

"Interesting answer, Agent," Lucinda allowed. "It's just one of many questions that our press secretary has had to field so far." She looked down at the sheaf of papers she had carried with her from the desk. In a matter-of-fact tone, she read, "Will President Powell support legalizing gay marriage? Does Blair Powell plan on having children? How does the president's daughter plan to become pregnant? How many of her security staff has she slept with?" At that, Lucinda shook her head in disgust. "Some of these fools have no sense of propriety at all." She looked up from the papers, her expression guarded. "There are a dozen more like this, and worse. You need to review them and formulate answers."

"Why?" Blair snapped. "I'm not obligated to respond to this kind of interrogation."

"No, you're not," Lucinda agreed in a surprisingly calm voice. "But these questions are going to keep being asked, and it's better that we all know what the answers are going to be. Then I can handle—"

"You mean *spin,* don't you?" Blair's tone dripped sarcasm.

Lucinda shrugged. "In politics, image is still one of our most important assets. You may call it anything you desire. I can't afford to be taken by surprise, so I need to know if you're going to answer one of these questions someday in a manner that puts us all on the defensive."

"Our *private* life is our own business."

Cam gently placed her right hand over Blair's left. "Surely you can't expect Blair to answer such intrusive and inappropriate questions." Her tone suggested fact rather than query. "Blair has already made it clear that we are romantically involved. If that requires further explanation, then feel free to say that we are in love, monogamous, and planning a long-term relationship."

"You're remarkably astute for a federal agent, Commander."

Cam held Lucinda's gaze steadily. "As I'm sure you know, I grew up in Italy where my father was this country's ambassador. No one practices politics quite like the Italians."

Lucinda laughed with reluctant pleasure. "Are you sure you want to waste away in obscurity toiling for the Treasury Department? I can put your talents to much better use."

"I'm doing exactly what I want to be doing. But thank you."

"Give me the questions," Blair said sharply, reaching for the papers that Lucinda still held. "I'll look them over and if there's something I feel is pertinent and appropriate, I'll give you our response."

"What am I missing?" Lucinda eyed Blair curiously. "You might be in love, but that's hardly cause for a sea change."

Blair stood, drawing Cam up beside her. "I *am* in love, and it changes everything."

In a rare show of emotion, Lucinda gave Blair a quick hug. "I'm happy for you," she murmured against Blair's cheek. Then she stepped away and strode back around her desk. She placed both hands flat on the top and leaned forward. Her command voice had returned. "No surprises, Blair. I mean it."

"The only thing I want to do is go back to New York and be left alone. Since I know that's not possible, we'll *all* just have to do the best we can." Blair sighed. "Is my father busy?"

"He's always busy, but he knows you're here, and he wants to see you." Lucinda glanced down at another printout on her desktop. "He's in the residence now."

"Thanks," Blair said softly.

"Nice meeting you, Ms. Washburn," Cam said as she walked to the door with Blair.

"I'm sure we'll meet again, Agent Roberts." Lucinda regarded the president's daughter and her lover contemplatively as the door closed behind the pair. *You've made an excellent choice, Blair. She can handle herself, and she loves you. How very fortunate.*

"Blair," Andrew Powell exclaimed with a smile as he rose from the reading chair in his study. "Welcome back."

"Hello, Dad," Blair said as she kissed her father's cheek.

The president turned to Cam and extended his hand. "Good to see you, Cam."

"Sir."

Andrew Powell pointed to the nearby sofa. "Sit down. Are either of you hungry? Do you want anything to drink?"

"I think we're more tired than anything," Blair responded, sinking gratefully down into the plush cushions. "The trip was hectic."

"But...uneventful?" The president spoke quietly, watching his daughter's face carefully. Even her admission of being tired was unusual.

"Basically, yes," Blair replied. "The early press release about my interview here in the States got us a little more media attention than we had expected, but it was manageable."

Powell shifted his gaze to Cam. "Did you have enough people to handle the situation?"

"Yes, sir. Our team is well prepared for that kind of eventuality, and we had the cooperation of the local security forces."

"If there's anything you need...more personnel, more—"

"Dad," Blair cut in firmly. "Everything is fine."

"I'm allowed to worry. It's a father's prerogative."

Surprised by his serious expression and the sincerity in his voice, Blair colored with pleasure and embarrassment. "First of all, there's nothing to worry about. Secondly, Cam knows exactly what she's doing."

"Then I'll consider the issue closed," the president conceded graciously. He reached for his nearby cup of coffee and sipped. "I suppose you've seem Lucinda already?"

"First thing," Blair informed him with the barest hint of a grimace.

"I asked her not to pressure you into anything regarding a personal statement about your private business, but..." He lifted his hands in a helpless gesture and shook his head. "She never listens to me."

Cam laughed.

"Ah, I can see that the chief of staff is still ignoring the commander in chief's directives." Powell studied Blair with concern. "Has it been bad?"

Once again, his directness and the affection in his voice caught Blair off guard, and she automatically reached for Cam's hand. She drew their joined hands to her thigh as she spoke. "It's infuriating and at times embarrassing. But all in all, not really as bad as I anticipated."

The president glanced at Cam. "Have you had any problems from your director?"

"Sir, that wouldn't be something I would expect you to trouble yourself over."

"So I'm not to be concerned about my daughter's partner's welfare?"

Cam met the president's eyes steadily, her hand loosely clasped in Blair's. "I appreciate your concern, sir. I also feel that if I were to take advantage of your influence to protect my career it would call my affections for Blair into question. That is unacceptable to me, sir."

The president smiled but his eyes were intent. "I'm not asking as the president, but as a father."

"Sometimes, sir," Cam replied softly, "our responsibilities make it impossible to act on what's in our hearts."

"Are you always so certain of your responsibilities, Agent Roberts?"

"No, sir. Sometimes my heart wins."

Blair released Cam's hand and slid her arm around Cam's waist. "Dad, is this some kind of a traditional rite known only to men where the father questions the daughter's suitor?"

Powell laughed. "No, I'm just enjoying the opportunity to get to know your partner."

"I don't want Cam to think that every time she comes to the White House, she's going to be interrogated. First Lucinda, now you."

"Have I made you uncomfortable, Cam?" the president asked with genuine concern.

"No, sir." Cam smiled briefly at Blair. "There's nothing about my feelings for Blair that I have any problem discussing."

"Even with the news media?"

Cam's expression hardened. "If I had my way, sir, a reporter wouldn't get within twenty yards of your daughter. If they question me, *I'm* under no obligation to be polite."

Powell nodded contemplatively, impressed by the woman his daughter had chosen. "How do you two feel about spending Labor Day weekend at Camp David with me?"

Blair glanced at Cam questioningly. "That would be great. Don't you think?"

"Of course," Cam replied. Wherever Blair went, she would be.

"I expect you to be off duty for that weekend, Cam," the president added.

"Sir?"

"You can hardly relax and enjoy the time away if you're working. Turn the detail over to your second in command. We'll have plenty of security at the retreat."

Cam opened her mouth to argue that she didn't command *his* agents and that Blair's security was *her* responsibility, then simply nodded. One did not argue with the president of the United States.

"Good," Powell said. "Are you staying in the residence tonight, Blair?"

Blair looked from her father to Cam. "If it's all the same to you, Dad, I'd rather spend the night with Cam, and I don't think we can really do that here. There's no use giving the media more ammunition so soon after the release of the interview."

"You're probably right. I'm sorry about that."

"Thanks," Blair said as she rose and crossed to her father. She leaned down and kissed his cheek. "That's all that really matters— that you understand."

The president rose and walked them to the door. "I may not see you again until Labor Day weekend. My schedule is very full."

"Then we'll see you at Camp David."

Once in the hall, Cam said in a low voice, "Do you think I passed inspection?"

"I can't believe he did that." Blair stopped walking, turned, and kissed Cam lightly on the lips. "But you did fine. So well, in fact, that I can't wait to get you alone."

Cam grinned, ignoring the impassive expression of the security guard who stood ten feet away by the side of the elevator. "Good. I was hoping that *you'd* be impressed."

"Oh, Commander. I was. I most certainly was." Laughing, Blair took Cam's hand and drew her into the elevator. "And as soon as we get to your apartment, I intend to show you just how much."

CHAPTER SEVENTEEN

Cam sat in the dark on the wide leather sofa in a loosely belted gray silk robe, a short heavy tumbler of Glenlivet in her left hand. Blair lay sleeping with her head pillowed in Cam's lap, her cheek pressed to Cam's abdomen while the fingers of Cam's right hand curled gently in her hair. Outside the night was dark, the black sky hazy with a faint glow in the distance that Cam knew was a reflection from the security lights surrounding the White House. She'd sat in this position dozens of times before—at the end of a long day when she was too tired to sleep and too lonely to seek company—but she couldn't recall a single instance when she had ever been so satisfied or so content.

"Mmph," Blair muttered as she shifted onto her back and opened her eyes with a long sigh. Blinking, she stared up at Cam. "I fell asleep. I'm sorry."

"Don't be," Cam murmured, stroking her lover's cheek. Her eyes swept over Blair's sleekly muscled body, clothed now in a loose-fitting T-shirt and boxers that Blair had pulled from Cam's bureau after taking a shower earlier. "It's nice to relax with nothing to do except be together."

Neither mentioned that in the morning Cam would assemble the team and they would fly back to New York. Nor that despite being home, they would still be separated for the better part of every day. Blair nuzzled her face against Cam's stomach, breathing in her distinctive scent. "What were you thinking of while I zoned out?"

Lazily, Cam drew strands of gold through her fingers. "About how good I feel—how right it is to be with you."

"Yeah?" Blair's voice was husky as she reached up to trail her fingers along Cam's forearm. "Even here, like this? With me drooling on you?"

"*Especially* here like this." Cam set her glass down on the end table. She leaned over and kissed Blair softly. "We can probably dispense with the drool, but I particularly like the boxers."

Blair laughed.

"And," Cam added, "I like holding you while you sleep."

"You know, I made a few promises back at the residence which I've failed to carry through on," Blair noted lightly. "Should I worry that we've been alone together for almost four hours, and we haven't made love?"

"In all the months we've known one another, I've never once looked at you without wanting you," Cam replied pensively. "I want you now. But the nicest thing about the last hour or so, sitting here with you sleeping in my lap, has been knowing that beneath the passion, there was peace—and that we'll always have both."

"Oh, Cam," Blair breathed. She turned her face hard into Cam's body, bringing her arm around Cam's waist to hold her tightly. "Doesn't this scare you even a little?"

"No, baby," Cam murmured, still softly stroking Blair's hair. "The only thing that scares me is the thought of losing you."

"Not possible." Blair pushed herself up until she was cradled in Cam's arms, her face close to Cam's. "I am completely crazy in love with you. What you said to Lucinda today? About marriage?" She took a shaky breath. "You might find this hard to believe, but I believe in it, too."

Cam kissed her again, one hand caressing the back of her neck beneath her hair, the other smoothing the length of her thigh to trail beneath the edge of the cotton boxers. Exploring Blair's mouth until she'd satisfied her hunger for the taste of her, Cam drew away. "I *do* believe you, because I can feel it every time you touch me."

"So maybe someday we can talk about it again," Blair whispered as she gently parted the silk over Cam's chest.

"Mmm, someday. Definitely." Cam leaned her head back, her lids heavy with pleasure as Blair stroked her breasts. "You're making it hard for me to think about much of anything right now."

"Am I?" Blair rolled a hard nipple between her fingers, biting her lip and stifling a moan as Cam arched against her. "*I'm* thinking about all the things I've wanted to do to you since this afternoon."

"This afternoon, huh?" Trying to recover her breath, which had fled with the first teasing touch of Blair's fingers, Cam eased her hand beneath the wide leg opening of the boxers, drawn to the heat between Blair's thighs. "You're not supposed to think about sex in the presence of the president."

"Especially not," Blair nipped at Cam's lower lip as she tugged harder on the erect nipple, drawing a deep groan from Cam, "when he's your father."

"I don't want to think about *that* right now," Cam said urgently, her head spinning as her hand glided over hot ready flesh. "God, you're beautiful."

"That feels so good," Blair said, resting her forehead on Cam's and unconsciously squeezing Cam's breast harder.

"Yes," Cam grunted as another jolt of excitement streaked downward through her stomach. She circled Blair's clitoris firmly, feeling her grow harder.

"Don't make me come," Blair whispered as she eased her hips away from the talented fingers that fondled her knowingly, her control too brittle to tolerate the exquisite pleasure. She ran her tongue over the underside of Cam's lip. "I want to want it until I beg."

"I want you now," Cam groaned, shifting her hips restlessly beneath Blair.

"Then I'll have to distract you." Blair edged down off the sofa to kneel between Cam's thighs. She opened the covering of silk to reveal Cam's body in the moonlight, catching her breath as if witnessing the glory of her for the first time. She drew her fingers lightly down the center of Cam's abdomen, watching her lover tense and tremble, then leaned forward to place a gentle kiss between her thighs. "I love you."

"Blair," Cam whispered softly, helpless with love and need. In this same place, a lifetime ago, she'd closed her eyes and willed a stranger to assuage her pain. Now there was only joy. With effort, Cam raised her head and focused on Blair's face, lifting an unsteady hand to cup her lover's face. "Let's...go to bed."

"You're already so close. Let me finish."

Blair's breath, hot on her fevered flesh, made Cam shudder. "I want...to come lying beside you...in your arms. Please."

"Yes, darling," Blair murmured, rising with Cam's hand in hers. Cam so rarely asked her for anything, and she would deny her nothing. She wrapped her arm around Cam's waist and held her close. "Come let me love you."

"'Lo?"

"Hey, sleepyhead."

"Hey," Stark replied. "Did you just get in? I was worried."

"Yes, just a few minutes ago." Renee checked her watch. 0150. She sighed with exhaustion. "We sat on the ground at De Gaulle for a couple of hours while they checked over the electrical system. Finally we ended up changing planes. By the time we got to JFK, the incomings were so backed up we almost had to divert to Dulles."

"That might not have been so bad. *We're* in DC."

"For how long?" Renee couldn't hide her disappointment. She'd been hoping to see Paula in the morning for just a few minutes before she reported for her new assignment.

"Not sure yet. The whole team is still here, and I guess we'll be briefed in the morning. What about you?"

"There was a letter waiting for me at my sister's." Renee propped her feet on the cluttered coffee table and lifted the single sheet of paper. "I've been temporarily assigned to the New York Bureau office. I'm to report tomorrow for limited duty."

"That's good, then, right? At least we'll be in the same city."

"*That* part's good," Renee agreed immediately. "The part I don't like is the term *limited*. I didn't join the Bureau to be a paper pusher."

"It's only been a few weeks since you were shot," Stark pointed out.

"Yeah, yeah. I know." Peevishly, Renee nudged a can of Coke around on the top of the coffee table with her toe. "One of the biggest branches of the counterintelligence division is located here in New York. If I'm lucky, that's where I'll be assigned."

"So, uh, are you going to stay with your sister?"

Renee was silent, staring around the tiny, crowded apartment. She'd been sleeping on the couch before she left for Paris. Her sister was a good sport, but the space wasn't designed for two. "Probably for a couple of days, then I'm going to need to find something else. Chloe hasn't complained, but I think her boyfriend will be glad to see me go."

"I...well...I'm hardly ever home. You know, with the split shifts and Egret traveling." Stark fidgeted beneath the sheets, her heart pounding as hard as it had the first time she'd realized that Renee was about to kiss her. In a rush, she blurted, "You could stay at my place."

This time the silence was heavy with the sound of unspoken words.

Inwardly, Stark cursed herself for being a clumsy, inappropriate dolt. "I'm sorry. That was dumb."

"No," Renee said softly. "That was nice. And it's tempting... and *not* just because it would solve my problems. I can't think of many things—*anything*, really—that I would like more than being in the same space with you as much as possible. And because I feel that way, I need to be careful."

Stark plucked at the covers restlessly. They might have been flirting with a relationship for weeks, but they'd only been sleeping together a matter of days. "I understand. I didn't mean to put you on the spot." She intended to drop the matter, and then the next words popped out. "You wouldn't have to stay, if it didn't work out."

"What if it does? Are you ready for that?"

"We'd kissed once," Stark noted solemnly, "before the Loverboy operation went down in New York. I remember that kiss. It was beautiful. It was over in a second, and you just brushed your lips over mine, but I knew it was more than just a friendly kiss." She drew a breath, remembering that Renee had just finished a workout and had still worn her boxing gloves. Her T-shirt had been damp with sweat and her caramel skin misted with its shine. She'd looked strong and feminine and so sexy. "Less than twenty-four hours later, I was kneeling on the ground with my hands pressed to your chest, afraid that you were dying."

"Paula, sweetie," Renee breathed, heart aching to hear the tremor in Stark's voice. "Honey—"

"No, I'm okay." Stark pushed on, needing to give voice to

the well of emotions springing within. "What's between us, it started *before* that kiss, before we'd even touched. Because when I thought that you might die, I hurt somewhere inside that I hadn't even known was there. I hurt in some place that felt like it would bleed forever."

"Oh my God. Paula." *I love you.*

"So, yeah, I'm ready." Stark spoke quietly, gently. She'd never said anything like what she had just said before, never even thought the words. But she knew without question that they were right and true. That knowledge gave her strength, and from that strength, came patience. "But maybe it would be smart if we said from the beginning that it would just be a temporary arrangement. Three weeks."

"Three weeks." Renee's voice trembled now. "That seems... reasonable."

"By then, you'll have a better idea what your permanent assignment will be, and we'll have had a chance to check things out."

Renee laughed, sounding almost giddy with happiness and wonder. "I'm all for checking things out with you, sweetie."

"Yeah? So you think that might work...temporarily?"

"I think it just might. Call me when you get back to the city and you're free, and I'll come over. Okay?"

Stark sighed and slid down under the covers. She was tired, but she felt great. The only thing that was missing to make the night perfect was Renee lying beside her. "Roger that."

"You sleepy, sweetie?"

"Yeah. Some. How about you?"

"I'm still wired from the trip," Renee replied, swinging her feet over to the sofa and stretching out.

"I don't have anywhere to go for a few hours," Stark murmured.

"Oh yeah?" Renee reached up and clicked off the light on the end table. With a tiny laugh, she said, "So, sweetie, what are you wearing?"

0200 20Aug01

A cell phone rang in a paramilitary compound deep in the mountains of Tennessee. The duty officer—a twenty-year-old white man with his hair clipped to within a breath of his skull, dressed in battle fatigues, and weighted down with his sidearm, extra ammo in magazine clips hanging from his belt, a bush knife in a leather sheath, and night glasses on a thick leather strap around his neck—answered the call. "Sergeant Wilson."

"This is red team leader. Have the general call me at this number."

Wilson, the weekend duty officer who worked during the week as a gas station attendant at one of the rest areas on the interstate, knew better than to question the order and dutifully repeated the ten digits. He'd never met the person who belonged to the voice on the phone, but he was familiar with the deep rumbling tone. "Yes, sir. Right away, sir."

When the caller terminated the connection, Wilson used the landline to ring through to the general's quarters, one of the cabins that once composed the mountain resort that now formed the heart of the compound. The central lodge had been converted into the organization's headquarters, while the officers were housed in the cabins scattered in the surrounding woods. The volunteer personnel bivouacked in tents in areas they had clear-cut themselves. The entire five-acre compound was surrounded by a ten-foot barbed wire fence and protected by motion sensors and floodlights. Some of the officers, like the general, spent the better part of every month on base. The rest of the troops were only weekend warriors like himself, but those core members were dedicated and determined to take part in the struggle to reclaim the nation for the people.

"General Matheson, sir. I have a priority call for you."

"Give me the number, soldier."

Five minutes later, the dark-haired American flipped open his cell phone as it vibrated. "Good morning, General."

"Is it? Maybe in whatever cushy hotel you're in," the gravelly voice barked. "It's hotter than hell up here in these mountains, even with the windows open. You end up trading a dozen mosquito bites for a piss-poor bit of breeze."

"My sympathies, General."

"Yes, well, let's not waste these high-security minutes." They'd learned a valuable trick from their Middle Eastern colleagues—by anonymously purchasing disposable memory chips, usually from Switzerland, for their cell phones, they could communicate by satellite links with no danger of their calls being traced. Those with sophisticated equipment could even use the chips to uplink their computers for more extensive data transfer or to insert maps, photo images, and other intelligence data into dummy Web sites. "What the hell happened over there? That mission was planned down to the second—it should have gone off flawlessly."

"I was hoping you could tell *me*," the other man snapped, his patience frayed by the months of planning that had nearly culminated in disaster. "We were minutes away from completion of the operation when we had to abort. The premature release of the target's newspaper interview increased media attention to the point that our extraction route was unacceptably compromised."

The general grunted in disgust. "We had nothing to do with that. We don't *want* undue focus on the target at this point in time. Not when the larger operation is about to commence."

"This is not the time for miscommunication," insisted the agent who had spent the last six years of his life infiltrating one of the most secure organizations in the world. "Timing is critical now."

"You think I don't know that? What the hell do you think we've been doing here for the last year?"

Silence hung thickly while each man struggled with his temper.

"Are we abandoning this target?" the agent demanded.

"No. But the mission has changed...from abduction to termination," the general replied stonily. "It will be a coordinated strike to coincide with that of our *friends*."

The dark-haired man's stomach tightened. He kept his response short to avoid the possibility of revealing his surge of anxiety. "When will I get the details?"

"When you need them."

The American agent standing on a corner in Washington, DC within sight of the White House, making plans to commit treason, nodded as if the man on the other end of the line could see him. "I understand. I'll be waiting."

CHAPTER EIGHTEEN

22 August 2001

Cam leaned against the stone pillar that supported the wrought-iron gate on the east side of Gramercy Park, surveying the entrance to Blair's apartment building. At 11:30 a.m., a stylish blond in a navy blue linen dress, the hemline high enough to accentuate elegantly sculpted calves, exited and walked to the curb. Brushing her shoulder-length hair back with one casual sweep of her hand, the woman glanced down the street, apparently in search of a cab.

"Diane," Cam called as she pushed away from the wall and crossed the street.

Diane Bleeker looked around in surprise and smiled curiously as Cam approached. "Why, hello, Cam." Her voice was whiskey warm and her gaze leisurely as it traversed Cam's face and then did a slow appraisal of her body. She curled her fingers into the crook of Cam's arm with casual affection. "I haven't seen you in far too long. How are you?"

"I'm fine." The unusual absence of flirtation in the blond's tone instantly raised Cam's suspicions. Diane, Blair's business agent and best friend, was seductive by nature, and although Cam never took her seriously, she had come to expect a certain amount of suggestiveness in her manner. Its absence confirmed her concerns that something was not right—and seriously so. "Would you walk with me for a few minutes? I'll see that one of my agents takes you home after that."

"Only if you promise that it will be the beautiful Felicia," Diane responded with her winning smile.

Cam shook her head as they began to walk north, grinning despite the uneasiness churning in her depths. "Actually, Felicia isn't on duty. How about John Fielding?"

"Oh, really. He's hardly an appropriate substitute." Diane gave an elaborate sigh, but her eyes were devoid of merriment. "You don't have to take one of your agents away from their duties, Cam. I'll get a cab when we're done. Now, not that I mind you lying in wait to spirit me off, but I suspect it's more than a stroll you have in mind."

"Yes," Cam said quietly. "It's Blair. I'd hoped you could tell me what's wrong." The change in Diane's expression was barely perceptible, but Cam sensed her withdrawal and fought back a surge of temper born of two days of confusion and worry. "We've been back in the city since Monday, and she hasn't left her apartment once. I haven't seen her, even for briefings. She's canceled them all."

"Surely you've talked."

"On the *phone*." Cam shook her head in frustration. "Several times a day, in fact. But every time I've asked to see her, she's given me an excuse."

"You do know that she's working on the paintings for her show on the eighth, don't you?"

"Yes, I know that, and I know how consuming that can be. My mother is an artist—so are most of her friends. I've spent my life around them. But I've seen Blair work against a deadline before, and she's never shut herself away so completely." *Not away from me.*

"And she hasn't said...anything?"

"No. When we left DC, everything seemed fine." *We made love almost all night. We were happy.* She'd asked herself a dozen times what could have caused the abrupt change, and each time she'd come up empty. They hadn't had much time for conversation in the rush to get the team briefed before the short flight home. Blair had been quiet during the journey, but they certainly hadn't fought. Cam ran a hand through her hair, cursing herself under her breath. "I feel like an idiot even talking to you about this. But today she called to see *you,* so I thought—Christ, I don't know what I thought."

"Love makes fools of us all," Diane murmured in a surprisingly gentle voice. "You must remember that Blair and I have been friends since we were barely more than children. Despite the fact that we often argue and have been known to compete over...all manner of things, we love each other. She feels safe with me."

It was the kindness in Diane's voice's that brought a chill to Cam's heart. She stopped walking and drew Diane under the awning of a hotel, out of the way of pedestrian traffic on the sidewalk. She stared into Diane's eyes and thought she glimpsed sympathy there. "There *is* something wrong, isn't there? What is it?"

"Cam." Tenderly, Diane stroked the tight line of Cam's jaw. "Give her just a little more time. She's not used to being loved the way you love her."

"The waiting is killing me," Cam confessed in a tormented voice.

"I know. And so does she." Diane leaned close and kissed Cam's cheek. "I'm going to get that cab now. You have my number. Call any time."

Cam waited on the sidewalk until Diane disappeared into a cab, then turned to walk back toward Blair's apartment. If she'd thought Blair was being thoughtless or intentionally disregarding her feelings or just simply ignoring her, she would have insisted that Blair see her, explain what the hell was going on. But she'd heard the hesitation in Blair's voice when they had talked, as if Blair was struggling to be close but couldn't find a way. And some sixth sense told her that she had to let Blair be the one to break the silence. She just didn't know how long she could endure it, because she had never been so lonely in her life.

"Commander?"

"What?" Cam barked, not looking up from the reports she'd been reading all afternoon. Mindless, tiresome, boring work. Anything to pass the time.

"Ms. Powell just called. She asked if you were available to see h—"

Cam stood so quickly her chair rocketed backward and hit the wall. "Thank you, Agent Wright."

"Yes, ma'am." Barry Wright stepped hastily aside as Cam charged past.

Two minutes later, Cam knocked on the door to Blair's penthouse loft. Almost immediately, the door opened and she stepped inside. The huge space, partitioned only in one corner for Blair's sleeping area and bathroom, was suffused with the golden glow of evening sunlight. In the sleeveless T-shirt and loose cotton drawstring pants that she favored when painting, Blair stood backlit, her face in shadows. It didn't seem possible, but Cam thought her lover looked thinner than the last time she'd seen her, only two days before. Uncertain if she had been summoned as Blair's lover or as her security chief, Cam did not move to touch her. "Hi."

"Hi," Blair said quietly, an edge of exhaustion in her voice. After a few seconds' hesitation, she stepped closer and reached for Cam's hand. "Thanks for coming."

"How's it going?" Cam asked cautiously. Now that Blair was nearer, Cam noticed that there were deep shadows beneath her eyes and that their usual vibrant blue was dull with fatigue. The fingers that loosely clasped her own trembled slightly. With her free hand, Cam gently lifted Blair's chin until their eyes met. "You look beat."

"I've been working pretty much nonstop since we got back." Blair gestured over her shoulder toward her studio at the far end of the loft. "I finished two more canvases."

"Are you happy with them?" Cam felt as if she were walking across a minefield in the dark. There was a barrier between them as tangible as a stone wall, and she didn't know how to breach it. The separation, so real she could almost touch it, produced a nearly unbearable ache in her chest.

"Yes, I am. I think." Blair sighed and unconsciously rubbed at the headache that pounded between her brows. "I am pretty tired, I guess. I'll show you what I've done later, if you like."

"I'd like that very much." Cam drew Blair across the room to the sitting area. It was a testament to the depth of Blair's fatigue that she didn't protest when Cam guided her down to the sofa and then sat beside her. "I was starting to worry. You've been pretty quiet since we got back."

Uncharacteristically, Blair looked away. When she spoke again, she focused on their joined hands, which rested on the soft leather between them. "I called you because I need to go back to

DC tomorrow."

Cam grimaced. "What is it this time? Lucinda or some other West Wing command performance?"

"Neither," Blair said in a subdued voice. "I have an appointment at Walter Reed Hospital tomorrow afternoon."

It took a moment for the words to register, and then Cam's blood turned to ice. "Why?"

Blair raised her eyes to Cam's. "I found a lump in my breast."

A million voices screamed inside Cam's head. *Jesus, how long have you known? How could you wait to tell me? This isn't happening—not to her, not to us. Oh God, baby, are you scared? Christ, how am I going to fix this.* And loudest of all, the desperate entreaty: *Please, please don't let anything happen to her.*

Throat so dry the words sliced her flesh as she spoke, Cam asked, "When? When did you...find it?"

"Monday morning..." Blair swallowed, struggling to fight back the terror. In some part of her mind, she had always known this was possible. Perhaps even probable. After all, she could recite the statistics from memory. But numbers and probabilities were so very different than the reality. Still, she reminded herself that this *thing* inside her could be nothing. And even if it *was* what she feared, she knew, too, of all the progress that had been made in treatment since her mother had been diagnosed. Since her mother had died. But despite what she *knew,* the experiences forged in childhood and burnished by loss rode roughshod over any rational thought, and all she could see was her mother's face and her father's sorrow. "I noticed it while I was showering."

"Why didn't I feel it?" Cam's words were more self-recrimination than question. *Jesus, why didn't I know?*

"It might be nothing," Blair said, forcing optimism into her voice. "It's probably nothing. It's just...it has to be checked."

"Of course." Cam edged closer on the sofa and placed her hand gently on the small of Blair's back. Their thighs lightly touched, and their hands, still clasped, remained joined. "Which side?"

Wearily, Blair rested her head on Cam's shoulder. "The left."

The left. I touch you there all the time. Why couldn't...why didn't I feel it? If I had, would it have made a difference? Does it make a difference now? Oh, Christ. What does this mean? Cam feathered a kiss into Blair's hair and moved her hand up to cup Blair's neck, smoothing her fingers up and down the rigid muscles along her spine. "Can I...can I feel it? Will it hurt you if I do?"

"No," Blair rasped. "It won't hurt." She leaned her head back into Cam's palm, grateful for the strength in the long tender fingers. She searched Cam's eyes and saw something she'd never seen before, something she knew Cam would never let her see if she'd known it was apparent. Fear. She lifted a hand and stroked Cam's cheek. "It's all right."

Swiftly, Cam turned her face and pressed her lips to Blair's palm. "I know, baby. I know."

"I'm sorry I worried you."

Cam shook her head. "It's all right." She drew Blair close. "I wish you would have told me sooner...right away."

"I wanted to. I *tried* to." Blair's voice held a hint of confusion. "I just couldn't make myself say it." She shook her head. Her grip on Cam's fingers tightened. "That sounds crazy, doesn't it? I'm not naïve. I knew it wasn't going to go away. I just wanted to come home and paint."

"Can we go into the bedroom?" Cam was desperate to hold her. Really hold her. She ached to shelter her, to somehow put herself between Blair and anything that could hurt her. She knew how to do that in the world outside these rooms. She trusted in her ability to keep Blair safe. But this...how did she protect her from this? She'd never felt so helpless or so frightened in her life—not even when she'd watched her father's car burn after the explosion, because she'd known, as much as she'd wanted to deny it, that he was already gone. "I want to hold you."

"Yes. God, Cam, I've missed you so much."

Cam fingered the Handie-Talkie on her belt. "Stark?"

"Yes, Commander?"

"You're in charge of the detail. I don't want any calls put through to me or Ms. Powell for any reason other than a Priority One."

"*Yes,* Commander," Stark snapped.

Thumbing the off button on the radio, Cam stood and guided Blair up. Arms around each other, they walked to the bedroom.

By the side of the bed, Cam swiftly shed her jacket and shoulder harness. As she reached to unbuckle her belt, she said, "Let's get into bed."

Wordlessly, Blair loosened the drawstring at her waist and pushed down the cotton pants. She hesitated only a second before grasping the hem of her T-shirt and drawing it off over her head. Naked, she slipped under the covers and held them back for her lover to join her.

Cam settled on her side beneath the sheets and faced Blair. "Show me where it is."

Blair took Cam's hand and drew it to her breast, pressing her fingers gently over a spot on the upper outer aspect of her left breast. "Here."

Carefully, Cam circled her fingertips over Blair's smooth skin. After a moment, she felt an area the size of a nickel that was firmer than the surrounding tissue. Hoarsely, she asked, "Is that it?"

"Yes."

It seems so small. That can't be anything, can it? Cam leaned down and kissed Blair's breast directly over the tiny mass. "I love you, Blair." Then she lay back and drew Blair into her arms, guiding Blair's head to her shoulder. With her arms wrapped tightly around her lover, she pressed her cheek to the top of Blair's head. "What should I do to help you?"

"Will you stay with me tonight?"

"*Every* night." Cam's voice was fierce. *Let protocol be damned. Let the media and the Treasury Department and the White House be damned. Nothing is going to keep me from Blair's side. Not now, not ever again.*

Blair felt Cam tremble and heard the rage simmering beneath the surface. She drew her leg over Cam's thigh and fit herself more closely to the curve of Cam's body. She feared the anger was with her. "I'm sorry I didn't tell you right away."

"No," Cam rasped, closing her eyes tightly against the tears of anguish and fury. "I understand. You have nothing to apologize for."

Blindly, Blair reached up and pushed her fingers into Cam's hair, drawing her head down for a kiss. With the first touch of their lips, she felt the terrible weight lift from her spirit and sensed the strength returning to her soul. With a small sob of joy and welcome, she gave herself to the tender caress of Cam's mouth on hers. Their touch spoke of joining and belonging and trust, and Blair drank of their union until the pain loosed its hold on her heart. With a sigh, she settled her cheek once more against Cam's shoulder. "I didn't realize how much I needed you. Not until just this moment."

"You won't forget that, will you?" Cam stroked Blair's hair. "I can't bear to be away from you. Not just now. Ever."

Blair was silent, wondering how it was that she believed those words. Wondering why she trusted that Cam would not leave her, no matter what came. *Is this what love truly is? Believing without question? Knowing beyond doubt?*

"I never thought about *not* telling you. I never thought that you wouldn't be here for me." Blair's voice held a hint of wonder. "That's because I know you love me."

"I do," Cam murmured, turning her face into Blair's hair to hide the tears she could not hold. "I do, Blair. With everything I am."

CHAPTER NINETEEN

23 August 2001

Cam lay awake, the first hints of sunlight streaking through the skylights onto her face. Blair lay curled against her, her head on Cam's chest, one arm and a leg thrown possessively across Cam's body. Miraculously, Blair had fallen asleep shortly after seven the previous night and had slept soundly for almost ten hours. Cam, however, had barely dozed. As the light had slowly seeped out of the loft and darkness taken its place, she had stared at the ceiling, stroking Blair's hair, listening to her soft, even breathing, and concentrating on the heat of her lover's body against her skin.

It seemed impossible that only a few days before, she and Blair had stood together in the White House declaring their love for each other and contemplating a future, speaking of marriage. She wondered why those moments seemed so much less real than the awareness that she could lose everything in the fragile time between two heartbeats. Why loss seemed so much more possible than happiness. Cam sighed and gently kissed Blair's forehead.

No point in asking questions that can't be answered.

Eyes closed, Blair drew her hand up Cam's body until it rested between her breasts and softly stroked the center of her chest. "Don't worry so much. Not yet."

"It's hard not to, but," Cam tightened her hold, "I'm reminding myself of all the positives—that you're young and it's probably nothing too serious; if it *is* serious, it's treatable; and most importantly," she kissed Blair's temple, "I know you, and you're a winner."

"I love you," Blair murmured softly, tracing her fingertips along Cam's collarbone. "I asked Diane to come over yesterday so we could catalog the paintings for the show. I didn't know I was going to tell her about this until she was here."

Cam continued to stroke Blair's shoulder and back—long, smooth, tender strokes. "It bothered me, at first, thinking that you didn't tell me right away and that you'd told Diane first."

"Cam—"

"It's okay," Cam said quickly, meaning it. "The most important thing is that *you* know that you're not alone, and that..." She stumbled as she worked to steady her voice, "we love you."

"If you only knew how much I need you."

"I'm here."

At 5:00 a.m., Cam ran north along her familiar jogging route into Central Park. She ran automatically, mindlessly, the rhythmic sound of her feet meeting earth a distant partner to the pain that thundered through her with each pulse of her blood. Her pace was faster than normal, but she was unaware of her breath rasping harshly in and out of her chest or the cramps knotting her overworked muscles. By the time she reached the reservoir and started around, her head was light from oxygen hunger and her limbs shook with the buildup of lactic acid.

She'll be fine. She has to be fine. Nothing will happen to her. I won't let it. God, how can I stop it? What can I do? What can I... how can I...this can't be happen—

Gasping, Cam vaulted off the path into the thick underbrush that bordered the jogging trail, braced herself with one arm against a tree trunk, and vomited until her stomach muscles gave out. Then she turned and slid to the ground, her back scraping against the rough bark. She leaned her head back and watched the early morning sun dapple the canopy of leaves overhead. With hands that shook, she fumbled her water bottle from the pack around her waist and rinsed the taste of fear from her mouth. When her vision cleared, she pushed herself upright and headed back at a steady pace to her duty and to the woman who was her destiny.

Stark pressed close to Renee's back, one arm around her waist and her face pressed to the soft spot between Renee's spine and shoulder blade. She kissed the warm skin and murmured, "Five more minutes?"

"We should get up," Renee sighed, pushing her hips back into the curve of Stark's body. "Mmm. God, you feel good."

"Uh-huh," Stark mumbled, caressing Renee's stomach. "I do."

Renee murmured contentedly. It was the second morning they had awakened together, and it felt as unfamiliar and as exciting as it had the day before. "I like the way you do this."

"What?"

"Snuggle."

"Snuggle?" Stark's voice held a note of uncertainty. "That doesn't sound very sexy."

Renee laughed quietly and drew Stark's hand to her breast. Her breath caught as Stark's fingers closed around her nipple, tugging lightly. "Oh, but it *is*. There's something very sexy about the way you hold me."

"*Everything* about you is sexy." Stark rubbed her cheek against Renee's shoulder and then lifted up to kiss a spot just below her ear. "And you smell really good, too."

Renee turned onto her back and drew Stark down upon her. She fit a leg between Stark's and lifted her hips. The teasing touch on her breast had made her wet, and she knew that Stark would feel it. She smiled, a slow pleased smile, as she saw Stark's eyes widen at the first touch. "Feel me?"

"Oh, yeah," Stark said breathlessly. Her heart pounded like a wild thing trying to escape from her chest and all she could think, feel, sense was Renee—everywhere. Filling her mind and her heart and her body with wonder and desire. "I want to make you come."

"We have to get ready for work." Renee squeezed her thighs around Stark's leg, teasing them both. Then a trembling began deep in the pit of her stomach and she knew she would need to stop soon or come.

"Give me five minutes," Stark insisted. She kissed the corner of Renee's mouth, then flicked her tongue over the surface of Renee's lips. "Come on. Five. Minutes."

Renee ran her fingers through Stark's hair, laughing shakily. "Take ten."

Smoothly, Stark pushed down on the bed until she rested between Renee's legs. Gently curling her arms beneath Renee's thighs, she lowered her head and eased her lover into her mouth.

Then she took her time, because some things were too precious to hurry.

At 0700, Cam walked into the command center one floor below Blair's penthouse apartment. After her run, she'd showered in her own apartment diagonally across the square from Blair's building and dressed in her customary tailored dark suit and slightly paler shirt.

Like Blair's loft, the area housing the command center was a single open space. Workstations enclosed by aluminum-framed gray partitions occupied the central area, a monitoring station crammed with computers, monitors, and communication links to all of New York City's emergency service offices filled the near end of the room, and a glass-enclosed conference area was located at the opposite end. Per routine, Cam strode to the head of the table in the conference room and remained standing while she addressed the agents gathered for the morning briefing.

"There will be new shift assignments beginning today." She waited while the agents shuffled through their papers to find the week's itinerary. "The following agents will be assigned to the first team until further notice—Stark, Davis, and Parker. Stark is lead. Second team will be Fielding, Foster, and Reynolds. The rest of you will be assigned to shifts as the schedule demands. Mac will coordinate as usual."

Cam had had only a few minutes to glance through the daily reports, including the routine intelligence reports. She looked to Mac. "Anything pertinent in the dailies?"

"No, ma'am," Mac replied. He was too experienced to ask her anything about the assignment changes during the main briefing. She would tell him privately what he needed to know. He also knew better than to ask her what had put the shadows in her eyes or the subtle tremor in her hands.

"Good," Cam said abruptly. "Mac, we need to be in DC by 1100 today. I'll be in the Aerie. Make arrangements for the team at the usual hotel and call me when you have the flight details. Leave the return date open."

"Yes ma'am."

"Thank you. That's all." Cam turned around and walked swiftly through the command center to the outer hallway and keyed the private elevator that led to Blair's apartment.

When she knocked, Blair answered immediately. She wore the royal blue robe that Cam had first seen her in, and, like that first day, her hair was down and wilding around her face. Despite the stress of the last three days, Blair's eyes were clear and her full lips their usual sensuous deep rose. She was the most inspiring woman Cam had ever seen. Love, wonder, need, fear—every emotion that Blair invoked boiled within her.

As the door swung closed behind her, Cam framed Blair's face in her hands, her fingers drifting into the thick golden curls. She lowered her head and smoothed her tongue over the surface of Blair's lower lip before gently sliding inside. As the kiss deepened from greeting to urgency, Cam felt Blair's arms wind around her waist beneath her jacket and Blair's body press tightly to her own. She groaned faintly and swayed against the onslaught of sudden desire.

Blair gripped Cam's back fiercely, her hips rocking from side to side between Cam's spread legs. She pulled her mouth away, gasping. "You make me feel so much. So *alive*."

Without realizing it, Cam tightened her grip in Blair's hair, tilting her head back as she dragged her teeth down the side of Blair's neck. She hungered for her, not just physically, but in the far reaches of her being, with a need as critical as breathing. She dipped her tongue into the hollow at the base of Blair's throat and murmured, "You're everything."

"Don't stop," Blair whispered, her plea almost a prayer. She pulled Cam's shirt from her waistband and smoothed her hand over Cam's spine, then around her side and onto her abdomen. The muscles beneath her fingers rippled and tightened and her own body quickened. Head thrown back, eyes closed, she moaned as Cam's mouth moved down the center of her chest. She felt the air, cool on her hot breasts, as her robe fell away. "Yes."

"I love you," Cam choked as she lifted Blair's breast in the palm of her hand and pressed her mouth to the tight nipple. Without thinking, nearly *beyond* thinking already, she bit gently. Through the fog of arousal, she heard Blair whimper.

Everything stopped.

Ice filled her veins as Cam's head snapped up. "Oh my God. *Blair*. Did I hur—"

"No."

Before Cam could speak again, Blair put both palms against her chest and pushed her back against the door, following close with her body. She found Cam's hand and put it back to her breast, squeezing Cam's fingers closed around it. "Touch me. Here." Her stomach clenched at the piercing pleasure. Blindly, she found Cam's other hand and drew it between her thighs, her vision dimming at the rush of heat and pressure against her swollen flesh. Voice breaking, she gasped, "And here." *God. Don't go away. I need you now.*

Always, even when they had feared to put words to their emotions, their bodies had spoken...of passion, of need, of love. Cam felt her lover's cry—through her skin, beneath her fingertips, against her lips—and she answered without hesitation or restraint. She took Blair's breast into the warm haven of her mouth as she entered her body, claiming her, deep and full, carrying her on the tide of their passion beyond fear and uncertainty and loss.

As the climax crashed through her, Blair felt as if she might fall, but she knew absolutely that Cam would not let her. Crying out, back arched and trembling uncontrollably, she came around Cam's fingers, clutching her shoulders to stay upright. When her muscles turned to jelly, she sagged in Cam's arms, her head on Cam's shoulder.

"Oh God. I...don't know where...that came from."

"Us. It came from us." With an arm around Blair's waist, holding her tightly to her chest, Cam brushed her cheek over Blair's hair. She ached with loving her and had trouble catching her breath. She felt the start of tears and, horrified, blinked them away. Kissing the top of Blair's head, she whispered, "Everything is going to be all right."

"Yes," Blair murmured wearily, her eyes closing as she listened to Cam's heart rate slow into the steady, strong cadence that personified everything about her lover. Everything she had come to rely upon. *No matter what comes, it will be all right—as long as I have you.*

Renee picked up the phone on the first ring. "FBI, Special Agent Savard. How may I help you?"

"You busy?"

"Hey." Unable to hide her smile of pleasure, Renee swiveled her chair away from the man who sat at the desk opposite her in the office that she shared with six other FBI agents. The New York City division of the FBI, on floors 22 through 24 of the North Tower of the World Trade Center, was one of the agency's largest divisions outside of DC. A posting there was a much-sought-after assignment, as was the counterintelligence unit where Renee had worked for the last two days. Currently, she was doing little more than reading case files and report summaries to acquaint herself with the scope of the investigations undertaken by her new division. For many reasons, professionally *and* personally, she wanted this posting to become permanent. "Trying to *look* busy, anyhow. How about you?"

"We're headed back to DC."

"Oh?" Renee kept the surge of disappointment from her voice. "For how long?"

Stark sighed. "Don't know. I don't have any details."

"Will you call me, when you know?"

"Yes. Sorry about this."

"No need to be. I understand." Renee glanced quickly over her shoulder, but no one was paying any attention to her. Lowering her voice even further, she murmured, "I'll miss you."

"Me too. I really liked coming home last night and having you be there."

"None of *that* during working hours," Renee chided with another smile.

"What?" Stark asked in an innocent tone.

"You know what."

"Okay, maybe I do...a little."

"I should go," Renee said softly. "By the way...*I* really like waking up with you."

Stark made a sound halfway between a groan and a laugh. "Now look who's not playing fair."

"Call me soon. Be safe."

"Roger that." Stark hung up the phone gently, wondering when she would see her new lover again. *Be safe.*

You have one voice mail message. Please enter your password now.

The iron gray–haired man, flat stomached and tight jawed, followed the electronic commands and thumbed in the numbers on his cell phone as he navigated the Beltway. He had business meetings scheduled the entire day and another kind of meeting that evening. *That* meeting was with a group of men he swore he would never associate with five years ago. The old adage was true—war made for strange bedfellows.

He kept his eyes on the five lanes of traffic as he listened to the message.

Target relocating unexpectedly to Zone One, precise destination undetermined. Duration unknown. Will advise.

A souped-up Mustang cut in front of him, forcing him to brake sharply. His violent curse, however, was not directed at the driver ahead of him but at the possible disruption of his carefully orchestrated plans. There had been far too many false starts brought about by inexcusable mistakes and occasionally by pure and simple bad luck—foreign operatives denied visas because of lost paperwork or key domestic militiamen arrested for domestic violence or assault and battery. Now that the operation was officially underway and the great machinery of war had been set in motion, he could no longer influence the timing of events. If his forces could not strike their primary target in concert with the attacks of their allies, they might not get another chance.

The decadent régime that held the reins of power in Washington was weak now due to years of ignorance and hubris. But he was not fool enough to think it would remain so after the first attack was launched. The advantage was his now, and he could not lose it.

He punched the number to leave a return message.

"Target location change immaterial. Plan and timetable unchanged."

CHAPTER TWENTY

Cam stood in profile at the window, shafts of sunlight streaming around her body and highlighting the sculpted planes of her face. From her position in the doorway of Cam's bedroom, Blair thought her lover looked like a warrior goddess carved from gold. There was an utter stillness in her body and a distant expression on her face that Blair had come to recognize as Cam preparing herself for battle. This time, Blair knew, Cam was readying herself for whatever foe Blair might need to fight.

I love you for that look. I love you for being willing to face what comes next. I wish you didn't have to, but I don't have the strength to send you away.

"Darling?" Blair murmured softly as she crossed the room.

Immediately, Cam turned from the vista she had not actually been surveying and greeted her lover with a smile. "Hey. All settled?" She held out her arm and drew Blair close, stroking Blair's back.

"I only unpacked a few things," Blair replied, curving into Cam's side. She slid a hand beneath Cam's jacket and rested it on the crest of her hip. "Just in case we're not staying."

"Are you ready?" It was 1150 and Blair's appointment with the breast specialist at Walter Reed Army Medical Center was scheduled for 1300. Cam had reviewed the itinerary with Mac on the short plane ride earlier that morning. The first team was waiting in front of her apartment building now.

"In just a minute." Blair shifted away and caught Cam's hand, drawing her to the sofa where they had made love only days before. Those few hours of peace and passion seemed very far away. Blair brushed the anger aside and focused on the present. "There's something I want to talk to you about before we leave."

Cam regarded Blair intently, searching the familiar cobalt blue eyes for signs of fear or withdrawal. Gratefully, she found neither. Since the previous afternoon when Blair had told her what was wrong, she had been half expecting Blair to try to push her away. That's what the woman she had met less than a year before would have done. Her relief at discovering that Blair trusted her to stay—trusted in the strength of their love—was profound. She took her lover's hand and cradled it between her own. "What is it?"

"I have some idea of what's going to happen this afternoon." Blair traced her thumb over the top of Cam's hand. Her voice was steady and calm. She *was* ready. The initial shock had finally dissipated and her strength of will had returned. She, too, was prepared for battle. "If the surgeon has the slightest doubt about what this might be, I want it out of my body."

"Yes. So do I." As far as Cam was concerned, the upcoming examination couldn't be done soon enough. It was as if she could see a bullet streaking toward Blair's body, and she couldn't do anything about it. She couldn't get in front of it, and she couldn't push Blair out of the way. Her helplessness was eating holes in her gut. If there was the slightest chance of an enemy within Blair's body, she wanted it killed. Dead. Destroyed. Immediately.

"There's something else I want you to know," Blair said quietly.

Cam brushed her fingertips over Blair's cheek. "Tell me."

"If this is cancer, there might be several treatment options." Blair watched Cam's eyes as she spoke. "But even if there are alternatives to surgery, I want a mastectomy."

"All right." Cam's expression never changed and her voice never wavered. "Whatever you want, as long as it's the best chance of cure."

"Apparently sometimes radiation therapy is as good as surgery, but there is always a small chance that another tumor could develop later on down the road. I don't want to face that, not after what happened to my mother."

Cam's throat tightened as she saw the pain swim in Blair's eyes. Voice husky, she said, "I understand."

"Cam...I saw what my father went through. I don't want you—"

"Don't," Cam said gently, brushing her thumb over Blair's lips. "We're not there yet—nowhere *near* thinking about that. And no matter what happens, I need you. And I need to be with you."

Closing her eyes, Blair pressed her cheek to Cam's hand. "God, I wish this wasn't happening."

"So do I, baby." Cam leaned forward and kissed Blair gently. "But let's find out what we're facing first. This may very well turn out to be nothing at all."

Blair nodded. "I know. But the numbers are not on my side— if not now, five years from now, or ten, or twenty." She sighed and met Cam's eyes. "I've always known it. I just don't think about it."

"None of us can predict the future. The best we can do is make the most of the life we have." Cam kissed her again. "I love you so much, Blair."

With a small cry, Blair took Cam's face between her palms and found her mouth, taking the kiss deeper with almost desperate force. When she drew away, tears danced on her lashes. "I count on it. I count on *you*. I never imagined having anyone like you in my life."

Cam kissed her forehead, her eyelids, her mouth, tenderly but with trembling intensity. "I feel like I was born to love you. Just let me, and I'll be happy."

With a shaky laugh, Blair threaded her arms around Cam's waist and pressed into her. "As if I could help it."

A trim redhead in a United States Army uniform bearing the insignia of a lieutenant colonel stepped into the spare, functional office and crossed the gray carpet to where Blair sat in one of the two chairs facing a plain, dark wood desk. Cam sat beside her. Extending a hand to Blair, the woman said, "Ms. Powell, I'm Dr. Leah Saunders."

"How you do, Dr. Saunders," Blair replied, shaking the doctor's hand. She indicated Cam. "My partner, Agent Cameron Roberts."

"Doctor," Cam said as she shook Dr. Saunders's hand as well.

After the introductions, the surgeon walked around behind her desk and sat down. She slid a plain manila folder to the center of the dark green leather blotter and picked up a nearby pen. As she opened the folder, she met Blair's eyes. "I need to get some medical history before we proceed to the examination. I have your basic data here, so we can concentrate on the present problem."

"Of course." Blair's throat felt dry but her voice was steady.

"You're concerned about a lump in your left breast?"

"Yes."

"When did you first notice this?"

"Three days ago."

"Any tenderness or history of trauma to the area?"

"No. I just happened to feel it while I was showering."

The doctor scribbled a note. "Have you ever had any problems with your breasts previously—lumps, drainage from the nipple, rashes on the skin?"

"No, never."

"Have you ever had a mammogram?"

"No."

Again, Dr. Saunders paused to enter the information. Then she looked up, her eyes intently focused but her expression kind. "Ordinarily, I wouldn't order a mammogram on someone your age. However, given the family history, if it turns out you *do* have a palpable lesion, I'd like to image both breasts just for completion's sake."

"Yes," Blair replied quietly. "That would be fine."

"Are you having any other health issues I should be aware of?" At Blair's negative head shake, Dr. Saunders added, "Any medications or drugs of any kind?"

"No."

"Okay." Dr. Saunders stood and gestured to a door on the opposite side of the room. "The examination room is this way. I'll have a nurse bring you a gown, and then I'll be in in a few minutes. Your partner is welcome to accompany you."

"Thank you." Blair reached for Cam's hand, and together they followed the surgeon.

In less than five minutes, Blair was naked from the waist up, covered only by a thin paper gown, and seated on a vinyl-covered examination table. Dr. Saunders arrived, washed her hands rapidly in the sink in one corner, and turned to Blair.

"All set?"

"Yes." Blair looked past the surgeon to Cam and smiled weakly.

Cam stood just inside the door of the ten-by-ten-foot white tiled room as the surgeon instructed Blair to lie down, sit up, and raise her arms while she observed and palpated Blair's breasts. As she watched the examination, sweat broke out between Cam's shoulder blades, although the room was not overly warm. She'd never seen Blair's eyes quite so blank before, as if her body was present but her mind was somewhere else. The surgeon was proficient and professional and apparently gentle, but Cam couldn't help but see Blair as victimized by the entire process. She clenched her fists at her sides and fought back the surge of fury. She had no one with whom to be angry and nowhere to vent her frustration.

"You can close your gown now," Dr. Saunders said as she stepped back. She waited for Blair to retie the paper strips that held the gown closed before she continued. "You have a one-centimeter density in the upper outer quadrant of your left breast."

Blair's face registered no change. Cam's stomach turned over, but she forced herself to listen.

"It's in an area of the breast where many women your age normally have unusually dense tissue. However, this is a discrete mass and warrants further evaluation."

"What kind of evaluation?" Blair asked in a low, controlled tone.

"The mammogram, first of all. I want to be sure there aren't any other abnormalities that I can't feel."

The doctor's tone was matter-of-fact and straightforward. Nothing she'd said so far surprised Blair. She'd known from the first instant that what she felt in her breast was not her imagination. She had read about the disease, lectured about the disease, and lived through it, even though at the time of her mother's illness, she had not understood all the nuances of treatment. "And then?"

"Assuming that nothing else shows up on the films, that area needs to be biopsied."

As Dr. Saunders spoke, Cam stepped around her and moved

to Blair's side. She rested her hand at the small of Blair's back on top of the baby-blue paper gown. Beneath her fingers, she felt her lover tremble. Cam asked quietly, "What if the mammogram is normal? Does she still need the biopsy?"

"Good question," Dr. Saunders replied. "The answer is yes, because a mammogram is not 100 percent accurate. Even if it's normal, in the presence of a discrete palpable mass, a biopsy is still indicated." She looked from Cam to Blair. "I could do a needle aspiration biopsy here in the office. It's simple and relatively painless. The problem is it will only sample a small portion of the mass. If it comes back normal, we can't be sure that there isn't an adjacent area of abnormality which the needle biopsy missed."

Blair didn't hesitate. "I want it out. All of it."

"Very well," the surgeon said. "I'll arrange for the mammogram this afternoon to be certain that there are no problems in the rest of the breast or the right side. We'll plan on an open biopsy of the left breast at 7:00 a.m. tomorrow morning. I'll need to make a small incision directly over the lesion. You'll be sedated, but not completely anesthetized. The incision will be about an inch long. It will leave a scar, but it shouldn't be too noticeable given time."

"Yes. That's fine."

For the first time, Dr. Saunders looked the slightest bit uneasy. "Ms. Powell, would you like me to brief your father?"

Blair met the surgeon's eyes. "I'd rather he not know right now."

After a second's hesitation, the surgeon nodded. "If you leave your phone number with my secretary, I'll call you as soon as I've reviewed the mammogram. Someone will be by in just a few minutes to give you instructions regarding the surgery tomorrow and to take you to radiology. Do either of you have any questions?"

"No. Thank you," Blair said quietly.

Cam shook her head.

"I'll speak to you later then."

As soon as Dr. Saunders left, Blair let out a long breath and leaned into Cam's side. "Well."

Cam wrapped her arm around Blair's shoulder and kissed the top of her head. "Are you okay?"

"I guess so. It's what I expected." Blair closed her eyes and pressed her cheek to Cam's chest. "I'm so glad you're here."

"Me, too," Cam whispered.

Renee glanced around the still-unfamiliar apartment. Like Stark, it was neat and tidy. And like her, here and there were surprising touches of sweetness. A hand-embroidered pillow on the sofa bearing the words "Home is where the heart is." It looked like something done by a grade-schooler, and Renee was willing to bet it was a gift from some friend or family member. The fact that Stark actually kept it out was testament to how tender at heart *she* was. A small, carefully tended aquarium filled with colorful fish sat on an ornate pedestal table in one corner of the room. A list of specific instructions as to the care and feeding of the inhabitants sat nearby with an assortment of food and medicinal agents. Obviously, some friend or neighbor looked after them when Stark was away on assignment. For some reason, the touching attention that Stark paid to these small creatures stirred Renee's heart.

You are such a sweetheart. God, how did I ever find you?

As if in answer, Renee's cell phone rang and the readout indicated it was Stark. With a quick smile, Renee answered. "Hey! I was just thinking of you."

"How you doing? Are you home?"

Home. Renee glanced around the apartment. She'd unpacked the suitcases she'd brought from her sister's. There was very little else of hers in the apartment, other than a few books that she'd acquired during her convalescence. *Is that what this is? Home? Am I ready for that?*

"I just got in," Renee said quickly. "How about you?"

"I'm at the hotel. Probably in for the night."

"How long will you be there?"

"I'm not sure," Stark said pensively. "For some reason, we're in an information blackout. I don't even know what we're doing in the morning. The commander is assembling the first team at 0530 for a briefing."

"Just the first team?" Renee asked curiously. "That's not SOP, is it?"

"No. Usually the whole team gets briefed on the complete

itinerary and schedule for several days in advance." Stark was silent for a moment, then said quietly, "We spent all afternoon at Walter Reed. Just the first team."

Renee inhaled sharply in surprise. "Blair?"

"Yeah."

"Oh God."

"Yeah," Stark agreed glumly. "I have no idea what's going on, but it can't be good if we had to rush down here for...something."

"What about the commander?" Renee asked, thinking how much she liked both women and how much they had already been through.

"Same as always, totally in control. Except...I don't know, she looks...*too* controlled, you know? Like something might crack."

"Yes." Renee slumped onto the couch and leaned her head back, staring at the ceiling. "Are you okay?"

"Just worried."

At that, Renee smiled faintly. "I wish I were there with you."

"Yeah, I miss you."

"Me too, sweetie," Renee breathed softly. *More than I imagined possible.*

On the TV screen, Sigourney Weaver's Ripley stalked through the bowels of the *Nostromo* searching for the alien life form that had killed most of her crew. Cam was stretched out on her bed in a faded gray T-shirt and gym shorts. In a matching outfit, Blair lay curled against her, her head on Cam's shoulder. She was so quiet she might have been asleep, but Cam knew that she wasn't. Her heart was beating too rapidly for that.

"I think you should tell your father," Cam said softly.

"He's got enough on his mind. We don't even know anything yet."

"That's not what matters." Steadily, Cam stroked Blair's bare arm. "He'd want to be here for you."

"I know, but I don't want him to worry if there isn't any reason to."

"Baby," Cam murmured, dipping her head so that she could kiss Blair's lips. "I got the sense that being your father is very important to him. I think he'd want the chance to worry."

Blair squeezed her eyes closed. "I can't even imagine what it will bring up for him."

Cam's heart twisted, but she continued softly, "The same pain it brings up for you. That's why the two of you need to be together for this."

"God, I keep hoping this will just go away."

"I know. And maybe it will." Cam held her fiercely. "*Probably* it will. But until then, we need to be together. All of us. Like a family."

For the first time since she'd brushed her fingers over her breast and felt something that had never been there before, Blair cried. Cam kept her in her arms, rocking her very gently, until the tears abated. Then she pulled up the hem of her T-shirt and carefully dried her lover's cheeks.

"I'm not blowing my nose on your T-shirt," Blair mumbled.

"Oh, good. Sweat and tears are one thing, but sn—"

Blair's cell phone rang, causing them both to jump. Before it rang a second time, Blair snatched it up.

"Hello?...Yes, this is she...all right...yes. Yes, I understand... I'll be there. Thank you."

Cam held her breath while Blair closed the phone and set it aside.

"Except for some increased density in the area of the mass, the mammogram is normal," Blair said in a rush.

"Oh, thank Christ." Cam pulled Blair back into her arms and kissed her. "God, that's good news."

"Yes." Blair gave a shaky laugh. "Now, all we have to do is get through the biopsy tomorrow."

"We will, baby," Cam murmured. "We will, I promise."

CHAPTER TWENTY-ONE

24 August 2001

It was still dark when Cam felt Blair leave the bed. When she heard the shower running in the bathroom, she threw back the covers and made her way into the adjoining room. Once inside, she tapped gently on the glass door of the shower before sliding it open a few inches. Blair stood beneath the steaming water, her hair streaming back from her face, her eyes closed. There were smudges beneath her eyes, testament to the fact that she had slept little, if at all, the night before.

"May I join you?" Cam asked softly.

Without opening her eyes, Blair pushed open the door and extended her hand. "Please."

Cam stepped in behind her lover and reached for the soap. Circling Blair's waist with one arm, she drew Blair back against her chest. Resting her chin on Blair's shoulder, she lathered the front of Blair's body with her other hand.

Neck arched, Blair rested her head back against Cam and sighed. "You have the best hands."

Chuckling softly, Cam smoothed her soapy palms over Blair's breasts, then down her abdomen. "And you are a beautiful woman." When she felt Blair stiffen, Cam continued evenly, "*And* there isn't one part of you I don't love." She pressed her fingers above the spot where Blair's heart beat. "But this is what I love most about you, Blair. What's inside...here."

Blair turned in the circle of Cam's arms and wound her arms around Cam's neck. Pressing her face to the soft warmth between Cam's neck and shoulder, she leaned into her lover, welcoming her solid strength. "With any luck, there'll just be a little scar. If there's more..."

"No scars, no matter how many or how big, are going to make me love you any less." Cam cupped her palm beneath Blair's chin and lifted her face until she could bring her mouth to Blair's. She took her time kissing her, exploring her lips, and then the inner surface, and then the inside of her mouth. She stroked and caressed and worshipped until she felt Blair tremble in her embrace. Then she drew away and whispered, "And *nothing* will ever make me want you any less."

"How is it that you always know what to say?"

Cam shook her head, her eyes dark as they held Blair's. "I don't. I just try to tell you how much you mean to me. I always feel like I come up short."

"Oh, Commander," Blair laughed tremulously as she brushed her fingers through Cam's wet hair, "believe me. You *never* come up short."

"Are you all right?" Cam asked as they stepped from the shower and she handed Blair a thick turquoise bath sheet.

"Yes, I think so." Blair wrapped herself in the oversized towel and knotted it just above her breasts. "I know I would have gotten through this no matter what." She reached out and caressed Cam's face. "But your being here for me...I don't think I've ever felt so loved."

Cam tossed aside the towel she had been using to dry her hair and stepped close to Blair. Tenderly, she took Blair's face in her hands and kissed her very gently. "I think I'd go crazy if I couldn't be with you right now."

Blair's gaze softened as she searched Cam's face. "Are *you* all right? God knows you're not indestructible, even though sometimes you *do* make it hard to remember that."

"Thank you." A smile twitched at the corner of Cam's mouth. "And I'm fine."

"Then everything will be all right." Blair kissed Cam swiftly one last time and turned to leave the bathroom. "I'll be ready in just a few minutes."

A few seconds later through the open door, Cam heard the quiet sound of Blair talking on the phone. Then very clearly, she heard her lover's words.

"Hi, Dad? Listen, there's something I need to tell you."

The four Secret Service agents gathered in the sitting area of the hotel suite stood automatically when Cam entered with the first daughter by her side.

"As you were, please," Cam said to Mac, Felicia, Stark, and Parker. "Ms. Powell asked to be included in the briefing this morning."

All four nodded respectfully. Stark's expression, however, was worried, and Mac's blue eyes were particularly intense. Felicia appeared serene as always. Cynthia Parker, the newest member of the team, took her cue from the others and waited patiently, her attention on Cam.

"Ms. Powell is scheduled for an outpatient surgical procedure at 0700," Cam said evenly. "I want an absolute information blackout on this. *No one* gives a statement. *No one* gets close to her with questions."

Blair settled one hip on the arm of an overstuffed chair as Cam spoke. She was used to Cam's command mode and felt oddly comforted by it, even while struggling with the sensation of being disconnected from everything around her. She was acutely aware that the entire shape of her future could change in the next few hours. Plans she had made, dreams she had nurtured since childhood, and the joy of a newfound love could all be altered by a tiny clump of cells growing uninvited in her body. Those facts were nearly impossible to absorb, and yet she knew she must. Only by embracing the reality could she hope to emerge victorious. She *would* have her life back, no matter what the outcome of the biopsy. Blinking, she realized that Cam had stopped speaking.

"Sorry." With an apologetic smile, Blair rose. "I just wanted to be here when the commander explained the situation. I know you'll do your best to keep this from the press." She shrugged. "But I also know how persistent they are. If it gets out..."

"It won't," Stark said vehemently, looking from Blair to her colleagues. "Right?"

The series of *Roger that*'s made Blair smile. She reached out to clasp Cam's hand.

"Well, then. Let's get this over with."

Nude except for a thin cotton gown tied in the back, Blair lay on a stretcher with the back elevated to forty-five degrees, a sheet pulled to her waist. Cam waited by her side, their fingers entwined. Stark stood guard just inside the door of the holding area—the anteroom where patients were readied to be taken back to the operating room. Felicia and Cynthia were posted in the hallway just outside, and Mac waited with the vehicle in an underground parking garage. There were no other patients in the holding area. It was 6:45 a.m.

Cam heard a voice in the hallway shout *Attention* just as Stark snapped into position, hands at her side and eyes front. Andrew Powell stepped into the room with three men close behind. He stopped abruptly and then turned to say something to the man closest to him. His lead security agent looked unhappy but he and the other two men backed out into the hallway. Then the president rapidly crossed the room to stand on the side of the stretcher opposite Cam. He leaned down and kissed Blair's forehead.

"Hi, honey."

"Hi, Dad."

The president glanced over at Cam. "Cam."

"Sir."

"How are you doing?" he asked gently as he brushed a nonexistent strand of hair from Blair's cheek. His blue eyes, exactly the same shade as Blair's, swirled with emotion.

She smiled up at him, her gaze calm. "I'm okay. Really."

"Of course." He regarded her solemnly. "I'm glad you called."

Blair glanced at Cam, then at her father. "I should've called sooner. I'm sorry."

The president shook his head slightly. "I'm sure you had a lot on your mind." He cleared his throat. "Do you mind if I talk to the doctor?"

"No, but there isn't anything to tell just yet. After the biopsy, then we'll know." Blair took a deep breath. "Dad, it's probably going to turn out to be nothing. This is just a precaution."

"I know that," he said with certainty.

At that moment, Leah Saunders, dressed in navy blue scrubs, walked in through a door at the rear of the room. When she saw the president by Blair's side, she saluted smartly. "Sir. I'm Colonel Saunders, your daughter's physician."

"Doctor," Powell said.

"We're about set," Dr. Saunders said, her focus now on Blair. "Ready?"

"Yes."

"I'll just give you a minute then, and the aides will take you back. I'll meet you there."

Andrew Powell kissed Blair's forehead once again. "I'll see you in a little while, honey."

"Dad," Blair protested, "you don't have to stay."

"I can take phone calls here as well as anywhere else." He smiled and stepped back a few paces to give his daughter and her lover privacy.

Cam kissed Blair gently on the lips. "I love you, baby."

"I love you, too."

"See you soon," Cam whispered, feeling helpless and useless and furious at her impotence.

As the assistants pushed the stretcher toward the doors to the operating room, Cam walked alongside, still holding Blair's hand, until they reached the restricted area. Then she stood in the doorway until Blair was out of sight. Turning back, she saw that the president still waited, and she rejoined him.

"Can I buy you a cup of coffee?" he asked.

"Yes, sir. I just don't want to go very far." What she *wanted* to do was shove back through the double doors with the big red Restricted sign, find Blair, and get her the hell out of there.

Something of what she was feeling must have shown in her face, because the president's expression softened and sympathy flickered in his eyes. "They'll take good care of her here. Plus, it will take more than this to knock Blair down."

Cam smiled faintly. "I know. She's amazing."

The president nodded. "Yes, she is."

With her coffee growing cold in a cup on the end table, Cam paced in front of the window in a private waiting room while the president sat on a sofa in the far corner talking on the phone. His security agents flanked the door. Cam had stationed Felicia and Stark in the recovery room where Blair would be taken after her surgery. She glanced at her watch for the tenth time. 0725.

She tried to visualize what was happening to Blair while *she* stood powerless to help. Hospitals were such cold, impersonal places. She remembered what it had been like when she'd been shot the last time. The lights in the ICU were so bright and the muffled voices so confusing and the disorientation so frightening. And the pain. Jesus, the pain. "I just don't want her to hurt."

"The biopsy shouldn't be too bad," Andrew Powell said quietly.

Jerking in surprise at the sound of his voice, Cam met his eyes. "Sorry. I didn't mean to disturb you."

"You didn't." He set his papers aside and joined her at the window. "She'll be sore for a few days, but I doubt it will bother her much."

Cam stared at the expanse of green lawns visible through the window, thinking that she was only experiencing a fraction of the anxiety and anguish this man had endured when the woman he loved had gone through something far worse. "I hate not knowing what to do to help her."

"Yes," the president said quietly. "I know."

They stood silently a moment longer until the president's phone rang again, and he turned away with a brief pat on Cam's shoulder.

At 7:50 a.m., Dr. Saunders appeared. The president hastily concluded his phone call and stood. The surgeon looked first at Cam and then at the president.

"Ms. Powell is fine. She's in the recovery room and resting comfortably."

Cam and Andrew Powell both spoke at once.

"What about—"

"Did you—"

The president motioned to Cam. "Go ahead."

"Can you tell anything yet?" Cam's heart was racing and her throat was dry. Even in the midst of a crisis, her heart rate never rose above sixty. Now it felt like it was going to beat out of her chest.

"Nothing definitive," the surgeon said apologetically. "We really can't tell anything without a thorough pathologic examination, but I will say that the lesion was small, and I'm quite sure I removed it all. There was a small lymph node in the area that I removed as well. That appeared perfectly normal."

"How long until the pathology report is available?" the president asked.

"I put a rush on it, sir. Sometime tomorrow."

"Can we see her?" Cam asked.

"Yes. She's been sedated, but I'm sure she'll be happy to see you both."

Cam extended her hand. "Thank you."

Dr. Saunders smiled. "Of course." She turned to the president and saluted. "Sir."

"Thank you, Colonel," the president replied as he returned her salute.

"Hey," Blair said thickly, blinking to focus her eyes. "You guys still here?"

"Yes," Cam murmured as she leaned down to kiss her lover's forehead. "How are you feeling?"

"Fine. Hurts a little but...I've taken worse hits than this...in the ring." With effort, she turned her head and regarded her father. "You okay?"

"Just fine, honey. I have a meeting scheduled so I need to leave in a minute. The doctor says you did great."

"I can't...remember anything." Blair frowned. "Damn drugs."

Cam grinned. "Why don't you close your eyes and get some sleep."

"Does she...know anything yet?" Blair struggled to clear her head and failed. "Hate...the waiting."

"I know, baby," Cam murmured soothingly, reaching over the

rail to stroke Blair's hair. "We'll know soon. And then we'll take care of it."

"You sure?"

"I promise," Cam said fiercely. She continued to stroke Blair's cheek as her lover's eyelids fluttered closed. Once she was certain Blair was asleep, Cam straightened and found the president's gaze fixed intently upon her. "We'll be at my apartment tonight, sir. I'll call you with an update, if that's all right with you."

"That sounds fine. I can see that she'll be in good hands."

"Thank you, sir."

He shook his head, saying quietly, "No, Cam. Thank you."

Alone, Cam pulled a chair over and settled down to wait. Stark and Davis stood at the door, quietly keeping guard.

"I feel *fine,* and I'm sick of lying in bed."

Cam had never heard Blair sound petulant before, and she found it rather endearing. However, she hid her smile, preferring not to incite her reluctant patient any further. "How about if we just have our pizza in bed while we watch a movie? You don't have to sleep."

Blair regarded her lover suspiciously. Her breast ached, her head felt fuzzy, and Cam had been so sweet all afternoon, it was making her cranky. She didn't like being taken care of—well, maybe she did, a little. And that was annoying her, too. "What kind?"

"Cheese."

"No pepperoni?"

"Ah—I thought that might be a bit much after the anesthesia and all." Cam eased onto the bed and settled her hand on Blair's thigh. In a husky voice, she murmured, "I got *The Mummy Returns.*"

"Letterbox?"

"Uh-huh."

Carefully, Blair shifted over to make room on the pillows piled at the head of the bed. "Okay. Cheese sounds good."

"Want a pain pill?"

"No."

"Maybe after you eat?"

Blair started to protest, but caught a glimpse of the worry in Cam's eyes. She covered Cam's hand with her own and squeezed gently. "I will if I need it. Promise."

"Deal. I'll get some paper plates and more soda."

Halfway through the mummy's rampage through London, Blair fell asleep. Cam rose gingerly, gathered up the leftovers, and carried the lot to the kitchen. Her head throbbed, and yet she didn't feel tired. Now that Blair was home, and safe, the last few days felt more and more like a bad dream. It was hard to believe that there could be *anything* wrong with Blair, let alone something life-threatening. Still, Cam knew it wasn't quite over yet. And the waiting was pure torture.

Leaning against the counter, she rubbed her hands over her face in a vain attempt to chase away the headache and settle her nerves. Then, abruptly, she reached for the phone and punched in a number.

"Mother? There's something I want to talk to you about."

CHAPTER TWENTY-TWO

25 August 2001

Blair sat curled up in the corner of the couch, a pillow behind her back and a blanket over her knees. She sketched on a pad that lay in her lap, her eyes drifting between the paper and the woman who sat across from her at a small table by the windows. Cam wore a faded, nearly threadbare work shirt and red boxers. Only two buttons just below her breasts held the shirt closed. Her dark hair was unruly and her profile pale and remote, as if chiseled from stone.

"You have a face to make an artist weep," Blair muttered as she drew rapidly.

"Huh?" Cam glanced up and turned in Blair's direction. "Need something?"

A slow, suggestive smile lit Blair's face. "Maybe."

"Feeling better?" Cam grinned back, one brow arching. She was glad that Blair seemed able to lose herself in her work, because all *she* had wanted to do since wakening was call the doctor to ask if the pathology report was finished. She hadn't, knowing that as soon as Dr. Saunders had any information, she would contact Blair. One did not keep the first daughter in the dark about something like that any longer than necessary.

"Just fine." Blair indicated the empty space on the other end of the sofa. "Except I'm kind of lonely."

Cam set the newspaper aside and crossed the room to join her lover. Once seated, she drew one leg up on the cushion and extended her arm along the back, facing Blair. Her bare foot just brushed the bottom of the blanket draped over Blair's bent knees. "Are you going to be all right for the show in terms of finishing everything up?"

"Mmm," Blair replied absently, flipping to a fresh page on her sketch pad. "I might not finish one or two...depending on...how long we stay here. But even without them, I should be okay." She looked up, meeting Cam's eyes. "Would you mind unbuttoning your shirt?"

"All right," Cam replied slowly, her tone pitched low. Moving nothing except her hand, she loosed the two buttons and allowed her shirt to fall open between her breasts. "Good enough?"

"For the moment."

They were silent as Blair's hand moved in sure, swift strokes over the surface of the paper, her blue eyes, dark with purpose, flicking back and forth between her lover and her art.

"Shrug it off your left shoulder just a bit, so your breast is exposed," Blair requested without looking up.

Again, being careful not to move the rest of her body, Cam pushed her shirt aside so that part of her chest was bared. The room was warm, yet her nipple contracted not from the touch of the air against it, but from the sweep of Blair's eyes over her skin. As a child, she'd sat in on classes her mother taught using nude models. When older, she'd posed nude as well. Neither experience had felt sexual, and she had learned to love the human form in a purely aesthetic way as a result.

She'd known that posing for Blair would be different, but she hadn't anticipated just how much. Despite the fact that she knew Blair saw her body now only in the context of light and shadow, texture and line, angle and curve, being the object of Blair's intense focus stirred her nonetheless. Her pulse jumped, her skin tingled, and, despite herself, arousal fluttered in the pit of her stomach. She worked to keep her breathing even.

"Doing okay?" Blair murmured, her eyes on her sketch pad as she turned to another page.

"Yes."

"Can you slip off your boxers and then return to the same position."

"Sure." Cam's voice was husky.

Blair seemed not to notice as she switched from pencil to charcoal. Head bent, she sketched effortlessly, concentrating on the curve of Cam's breast against the long line of her arm in one view, drawing the angles and contours of her profile in the next. Suddenly she raised her head. "Now the shirt."

Wordlessly, Cam obeyed.

As Blair prepared to start a new sketch, she paused to let her eyes travel from Cam's face down the column of her neck and over her chest to the long plane of her abdomen. One lean leg angled over the edge of the sofa to the floor, while the other was bent at the knee and extended along the seat toward Blair. There was only a shadow of the dark triangle between her thighs.

"I've sketched women in the nude before," Blair remarked quietly, her gaze returning to Cam's face.

"I know," Cam said, her thighs tightening. "I've posed before, too."

"I've never become sexually aroused while I was doing it." Blair's hand rested on the surface of the paper, immobile.

Cam swallowed around the sudden need in her throat. "Neither have I."

"I am now." Blair's breath caught as she saw the flush of excitement rise on her lover's chest.

"Me, too."

"You are so beautiful," Blair whispered.

"No," Cam said quickly when Blair moved to put down her charcoal and pad. "We can't."

Blair's eyes flashed with frustration, but she nodded. Just the action of leaning over had sent a twinge of pain shooting through her breast, reminding her of the recent surgery. She sighed, carefully placing the articles on the coffee table beside her. "I've lost my concentration."

"Should I get dressed?"

"I don't know," Blair said suggestively, poking a leg out from beneath the blanket and rubbing her foot up the inside of Cam's thigh. "How adventurous do you feel?"

Laughing, Cam grabbed Blair's ankle before the questing foot could reach higher. "Right this minute, I'm on simmer. Touch me *there,* and I'm going to get uncomfortably warm."

"I wouldn't mind watching you put the fire out."

Shaking her head, Cam reached for her shirt, which she had

dropped on the floor. "I don't trust you to just watch."

"I've been known to show restraint at times," Blair protested, "even though I seem to have little where you're concerned."

Standing to step into her boxers, Cam gave Blair a sidelong glance. "Let's test your restraint some other time, when it won't matter if you weaken."

"I'll hold you to that."

"No argument from me." Cam leaned down to kiss her. When Blair curled fingers in her hair, held her head firmly, and sucked on her tongue, the heat in Cam's belly burst into flames. She pulled back, gasping. "Not fair."

Blair regarded her with a combination of hunger and ferocity. "I love the way you want me. I couldn't stand to lose that."

Swiftly, Cam knelt by Blair's side and gentled a hand against her cheek. "You won't. I promise. But I don't want to hurt you, either."

With a sigh, Blair rested her forehead against Cam's. "I know. I know you're right."

"The next time I pose for you," Cam whispered, "let's make sure we have time to finish *everything*."

"I love you," Blair said with a smile.

Cam smiled and stood. "Are you hun—"

The phone rang and they stared at each other for a millisecond before Cam grabbed it. "Roberts." She listened, then extended the phone to Blair. "Marcea."

"Hello," Blair said with affection, watching Cam as she crossed the room and disappeared from her view. "Yes, she told me she called you...No, of course I don't mind...No, not yet. Some time today, we hope." *Thank you,* Blair mouthed as Cam set a fresh cup of coffee beside her. "Oh, I'd love to see you, but it's not necessary for you to come East just for this." She lowered her voice, although Cam had already returned to the kitchen. "If I should need more surgery, it might be good. I wouldn't worry so much about Cam then." Listening to the warm, gentle voice, her eyes brimmed with sudden tears, and she struggled to keep her voice even. "I'm all right. Really...We'll call you when we know something more." She blinked and whispered, "Thank you."

"Everything all right?" Cam asked in concern when she

returned carrying a tray with toasted English muffins and more coffee.

Blair nodded, brushing at her cheeks. "Your mother is wonderful." She smiled tremulously at Cam. "She said she loves me."

"If she did, then she means it," Cam replied quietly. "Is that okay?"

"Oh, yes," Blair murmured. "I—"

The phone rang again. This time when Cam held it out to Blair, her expression was solemn. "Dr. Saunders for you."

Quickly, Blair took the phone. "Yes, this is Blair Powell. All right. Yes. Thank you."

"Well?" Cam asked before Blair had even pushed the off button, her stomach tight to the point of pain.

Blair pushed aside the blanket that still covered her knees and stood, extending her hand to her lover. "She expects the pathology report within the hour and asked me if we can come in."

Heart thundering, Cam squeezed Blair's fingers gently. "Let's get ready, then."

Less than an hour later, Blair and Cam once again sat side by side in the chairs facing Dr. Leah Saunders's desk. The otherwise empty room seemed to echo with their unspoken thoughts. Cam edged her chair over so that she could rest her right forearm on the arm of Blair's chair and clasp her lover's left hand.

"Are you okay?"

Blair gave Cam's hand a squeeze. "Just a little nervous."

"No matter what—"

The door opened and the doctor strode in, a folder under her right arm. She nodded to Cam and Blair and said immediately, even before reaching her desk, "The biopsy is benign."

Cam felt light-headed, as if she'd suddenly taken a punch to the gut. She barely had enough strength to murmur, "Thank God."

Blair's breath whooshed out on a relieved sigh, but she remained rigid, her gaze fixed on the surgeon's face. "What else?"

"Nothing specific," Dr. Saunders said as she sat. "The histology mostly shows the expected cellular pattern for a woman your age." She paused, studying first Blair, then Cam. "There *are*, however, a few areas of atypical ductal hyperplasia, which some authorities consider precancerous or, at the very least, a potential marker for the later development of breast cancer."

"What does that mean for me in practical terms?" Blair's voice was steady but her grip on Cam's hand was fierce.

"Unfortunately, we don't really know." The surgeon shrugged in frustration. "If the entire specimen were involved, I'd be much more concerned. In your case, it was a very small percentage of the tissue examined. However, with your family history, we have to be cautious."

"Meaning *what?*" Cam asked sharply, unconsciously assuming her command tone. Her lover's well-being was at stake, she was tired and edgy, and she could no longer tolerate feeling so helpless.

Blair shifted her attention to Cam, smiling softly. "It's all right, darling. We'll sort it out."

"Sorry," Cam whispered, her eyes holding Blair's.

"You don't need to be," Blair murmured before turning back to the surgeon. "What do you recommend?"

Dr. Saunders, used to the anxieties of patients and family members, continued in a quiet voice. "Because your mother developed breast cancer at an early age—premenopausal breast cancer—we have to be concerned about genetic inheritance. I would recommend that you have genetic testing to determine if you have the BRCA1 or BRCA2 gene for breast cancer."

"And if I do?" Blair asked.

"Then you have a 20 percent chance of developing breast cancer by the age of forty, and a 50 percent chance by the age of fifty." Still regarding Blair intently, Dr. Saunders added, "And you would be a candidate for elective mastectomies prior to the onset of the disease if you desired."

The nightmare, it seemed, had not ended, but Blair had not expected it to. She was incredibly thankful that she was not facing a diagnosis of breast cancer at this point in her life. But hearing the numbers applied to *her* so matter-of-factly only reminded her that she would never be free of the threat. She realized for the first time that she was crushing Cam's fingers and willed herself to relax.

"How likely am I to have the gene?"

"I can't speculate, because we have no way to determine if your mother had the gene or not. If she did, you have a 50 percent chance of having it as well."

"How do I find out?" Blair asked with determination.

"DNA testing can be done on a blood specimen."

"Can we do that today? I'd really like to go back to New York as soon as possible."

Colonel Saunders nodded. "I can have one of the technicians take the sample. It will take several days for the results, but I can call you with that. Once I check your incision, if everything looks to be healing satisfactorily, I don't see why you can't go home."

Blair looked at Cam. "All right?"

"Yes," Cam replied instantly. Knowing the foe was infinitely preferable to being taken unawares by an enemy cloaked in shadow. "Absolutely."

Stark called Renee while she waited by the passenger side of the lead car in front of the commander's apartment building. Mac was driving on the way to the airport, and she would ride shotgun.

"Hi! You busy later?"

Renee drew a sharp breath. "Are we talking about an in-person or a phone date?"

"I don't know," Stark mused. "I'm getting kind of addicted to the sound of your voice."

"I promise," Renee murmured, lowering her voice seductively, "I'm better in the flesh."

Stark's stomach did a flip and things lower down started throbbing. "Jesus. I'm on duty here."

"You started it." Renee laughed.

"Yeah, but it feels really good."

"Stop, now. We *both* have to work. And in case you've forgotten, the sound of *your* voice does very nice things to me, too."

Grinning, Stark said, "We'll be back in the city this afternoon, and I'll be off at seven. Do you want to have dinner somewhere?"

"Uh-huh. In bed."

Stark blinked and felt herself get wet. "Oh, man. That did it."

"Did you say something, sweetie?"

"Yes." Stark heard her voice waver and repeated more firmly. "I said yes. Definitely, yes."

"Mmm," Renee chuckled. "Can't wait."

1510 25Aug01
Falls Church, Virginia

A rental car carrying four men pulled into a parking lot next to a twenty-four-hour convenience store. A middle-aged Salvadoran man emerged from a battered Mercury and walked to the driver's side window.

"You are the gentleman sent by our mutual friend?" he asked in concise, polite tones.

"The general told us you would provide papers," the bearded driver said curtly.

"That is correct, for $50 apiece, U.S. currency. And I do not provide papers, only the assistance for *you* to obtain them."

Perturbed, the driver glanced at the other men in the car, then back to the Salvadoran. "We were told you would provide legal identity papers for all of us."

"In Virginia, all that is required to establish legal status is a sponsor to affirm that you have a permanent address in the state. I will do that for you, and the commonwealth of Virginia will provide your identity papers." He glanced at his watch. "If we go now, we will be done by sundown."

Once the men had obtained their American driver's licenses, the driver stopped at a Kinko's and paid cash for ten minutes of computer time. There, he sent the same e-mail to two different Yahoo addresses. The recipients were both in Las Vegas and had been there for weeks while the final plans and timing for the operation were determined.

Credentials obtained. We leave tomorrow. Rendezvous in three days.

The summit meeting for the six pilots was confirmed.

CHAPTER TWENTY-THREE

Paula Stark sat nude at the head of the bed with Renee Savard snugged sideways between her legs, Renee's head on her shoulder. The remains of their deli sandwiches rested on plates on the bedside table along with an empty bottle of wine. With an arm wrapped around Renee's waist, Stark rested her cheek against Renee's temple and lazily circled a palm over her abdomen. "Hungry? There's some food left."

"Uh-uh," Renee replied in a slow, somnolent drawl. "Right now, I can't think of anything except how damn good I feel."

"I really missed you."

Renee laughed quietly. "I noticed."

After the security team had reached Manhattan and Egret was settled in for the night, Stark had returned to her apartment to find Renee waiting. They'd kissed hello, carried the thick sandwiches that Renee had picked up on the way home from the FBI offices directly into the bedroom, and made small talk for ten minutes while they shared the wine and nibbled at the food. That was as long as Stark had lasted. She'd put her sandwich down, slipped her hand beneath the hem of the knee-length skirt that Renee had worn to work, and run her tongue slowly across Renee's lower lip. Halfway through the kiss, her hand had been most of the way up Renee's thigh. The rest had been a flurry of urgent motion and insistent caresses.

"I can't help it," Stark confessed, rubbing her chin softly back and forth along the tip of Renee's shoulder. "I can't think of anything better than touching you. Well, you touching *me,* maybe, but you know what I mean."

Eyes closed, Renee drifted in the hazy aftermath of passion, her hand covering Stark's as Stark stroked her. "When I'm with you like this, it's as if nothing else exists. Nothing outside this room, this bed, your arms around me. It's so peaceful." What she didn't say, what she was afraid to even *think,* was how perfectly right it felt. These moments with Stark refreshed her spirit and replenished her soul, reminding her that it was possible to trust, and to love and be loved.

"Sometimes," Stark whispered with her lips against Renee's ear, "I think about you—about the way you touch me. No one else has ever made me feel what you do. And I think that I'll never want anyone else but you to touch me."

Renee's body tensed as her heart shuddered in her chest. "Paula." She felt warm breath against her neck, the sturdy body supporting hers, the strong arms holding her safe. Picturing the gentle woman who had taken her with such fierce passion only moments before, she trembled, fighting what she most desired. Quietly, she said, "I haven't been very lucky in love." She shifted until she could meet Stark's gaze. "Until now."

"Did someone hurt you?" Stark's dark eyes were soft with sympathy. "Someone you loved?"

"Hurt me? Oh," Renee said with a small laugh, "I suppose it was more a case of someone not sharing my vision of love."

"Which is?"

Renee sighed. "I grew up believing the things I'd read in books—that love would be a wondrous thing of endless intensity and deep connection. A grand passion to end all passions. When I fell in love for the first time, I thought I'd found that. Her idea of a relationship turned out to be...different." She forced a smile and tried for a lighter tone. "I chalked that failure up to us both being too young, but I've tried it a couple more times without much success."

"So you don't believe in that kind of love anymore?" Stark's question was gentle as she continued to trace her fingertips over the smooth skin of Renee's abdomen.

"I didn't think so." Renee reached back a hand and cupped the nape of Stark's neck, drawing her close for a kiss before murmuring against her mouth, "You're making me change my mind."

"Good." Hearing the sadness and longing in Renee's voice, Stark wanted to heal the hurt that had been none of her doing, just because she couldn't bear the thought of Renee in pain for any reason. She kissed the corner of Renee's mouth and embraced her more tightly, cradling one small, firm breast in her palm as if holding a fragile objet d'art. When Renee moaned softly and wrapped both arms around Stark's neck, Stark unconsciously smoothed her palm down the tight plane of Renee's abdomen until her fingers brushed the down between Renee's thighs.

"Paula," Renee breathed, her hips lifting to the promise of her lover's touch.

Stark trailed the tip of her tongue over the inner surface of Renee's upper lip before pressing deeper into the warm welcome of her mouth. As her tongue caressed her lover's, she eased a finger along either side of Renee's clitoris, squeezing gently.

Renee's body jerked, and she gasped, fingers closing convulsively on Stark's shoulders. Her hips rocked between Stark's legs in time to the pulse that beat between her own thighs. "I'm still so sensitive...I don't know if I can take it..."

"I'll go easy," Stark promised, a note of desperation in her voice. "I want to touch you so much. Please." She slid her hand lower into the slick heat, and Renee whimpered quietly against her neck. Stark's heart pounded and her stomach clenched around the sweet ache of arousal deep inside. "Okay? Honey, okay?"

Shuddering, Renee pressed her lips to Stark's ear. "Do it harder. Do it harder, just like that..."

Scarcely breathing, Stark followed the rise and fall of her lover's questing hips as she stroked over swollen flesh and circled the stiffly prominent bundle of nerves. When she flicked the rigid shaft, Renee made a keening sound and Stark pulled away, afraid she had hurt her.

"No!" Renee cried. "Don't stop. You're...making me... come."

"Oh God," Stark choked, burying her face in Renee's neck as she fondled her to orgasm. *I love you.*

Renee came with a high thin wail, color bursting behind her eyes and heat blasting along her spine. Back arched, eyes tightly closed, she rode the edge of forever in her lover's arms.

"Ohh," Renee sighed, slumping limply against Stark's chest, her head dropping onto Stark's shoulder. "You have amazing hands."

Arms around her lover, Stark kissed Renee's forehead, the corner of her eye, the tip of her nose. "You're so beautiful when you come. I just want to keep doing it."

Shakily, Renee laughed. "Okay. Sure. Why not. Only... give me a minute to catch my breath." She snuggled closer, then gradually became aware of the staccato rhythm of Stark's heart beating beneath her cheek. "You okay, sweetie?"

"Mmm-hmm."

Renee raised her head and searched Stark's face. She rocked her hips slowly between Stark's thighs. "Sure?"

Pupils dilating with the unexpected pressure, Stark caught her breath at the shaft of pleasure that shot through her. "Uh...that's really nice."

"You know," Renee said quietly, resting her cheek in the curve between Stark's neck and shoulder, "I love to hear you come."

"Yeah?" Stark grew very still.

"Uh-huh. A *lot*." Renee found Stark's fingers and clasped them in her own, drawing their joined hands between Stark's thighs. She guided their intertwined fingertips over the prominence of Stark's clitoris, her pulse racing as Stark moaned quietly. "Yes," she breathed, "like that."

Eyes closed, Stark nestled her face in Renee's hair, one arm holding her close as the excitement of their twin touches brought her rapidly to a peak. "Feels good...so good. Stay there..."

"You're beautiful," Renee whispered through a throat tight with expectation. Their hands moved in rapid synchrony, and she heard Stark groan again. "Tell me. Tell me what you feel."

"Aches...nice...I want to come." Stark's thighs jumped with the first whisper of release. "It's starting..." Her stomach twitched and jerked and thunder roared through her head.

Renee stopped breathing, her senses completely focused on the hard heat beneath her fingers and the tight stillness of Stark's body. Afraid to break the moment, she remained silent while her mind screamed for Stark to surrender. Her own heart pounded as if she were about to explode. When Stark gave a startled shout and threw her head back with the first shock of orgasm, a cry tore from Renee's throat. "Oh, Paula, *yes.*"

"Oh God, oh God," Stark murmured over and over as she clung, shuddering, to Renee.

"Ahh," Renee said on a long breath when Stark collapsed against the pillows. "It's even better when I can hear you *and* feel you." She scooted around to stretch out beside Stark and then drew her lover into her arms. "I missed *you,* too."

Pillowing her face against Renee's breast, Stark mumbled, "How long does this last?"

"Does what last, sweetie?" Softly, Renee stroked Stark's face.

"This...incredible happiness."

Renee bit her lip and held Stark's face more closely to her breasts. When she could trust her voice not to quaver, she whispered, "Just as long as we remember how precious these moments are."

Cam leaned a shoulder against the partition that separated Blair's bedroom from the rest of the loft, watching her lover unpack. "Are you sure you're going to be all right?"

"Yes," Blair said without looking around.

"What about changing the dressings? Can I help you do that?"

"I'm going to wait until bedtime when I take a shower. The doctor said I could get it wet tonight." Blair reached for the last of the clothes. "It shouldn't be that difficult."

"Will you call me, if you need something?"

"I'll be fine, darling." Suddenly, Blair stopped in midmotion and sat down on the side of her bed, a stack of T-shirts in her hand. "No, I won't. Hell. I miss you already."

"I can stay." Cam pushed away from the wall, her voice low and intense. *I want to stay. Especially now—it's so hard to be away from you.*

"The only good thing about the last few days was that we could be together all the time." Blair shook her head, her voice a monotone. "But it's harder here—I don't know why, but it feels like we'd be compromising you professionally."

"That's not what matters." Quickly, Cam closed the distance between them, sat on the bed beside her lover, and encircled her waist with an arm. "I love being with you. I love going to bed with you, waking up with you, just knowing that you're somewhere nearby. I love being able to look up and see you sitting across the room, absorbed in a sketch."

"I love all those things, too." Blair rested her cheek against Cam's shoulder, her fingers curled on the inside of Cam's thigh. "My breast is fine, and there's nothing I can do to hurt it since I don't really even have time to go to the gym. I need to finish two or three canvases by the middle of next week so Diane can get them to the gallery and hung for the show. I've got a ton of things to do around here before we get ready to leave for Camp David."

"And there are probably six piles of paperwork waiting on my desk for me to wade through," Cam agreed. She kissed the corner of Blair's mouth. "But that doesn't mean I'm not going to miss you when it's time to go to bed."

"I know," Blair said with a rare note of discouragement in her voice. "Still, with the entire team downstairs and the occasional reporter wandering in and out, I don't think we should start cohabitating up here."

"You're right. I know you're right." Cam sighed, knowing, too, that it would only be harder on them both the longer she stayed. "I'll be downstairs for a few hours, then I'll stop up here before I head over to the apartment."

"That will work out just right," Blair replied, forcing a lighter note into her voice. "When I called Diane from DC to give her the news about the biopsy, she said she wanted to drop over tonight."

"Good." Cam kissed Blair gently, then stood. She settled her hands in her trouser pockets and observed her lover critically. There were shadows under Blair's eyes, and she was pale. "Promise you'll get some rest tonight, okay?"

Blair tilted her head and looked up at Cam with a small smile. "You look a little done-in yourself, Commander."

The corner of Cam's mouth quirked. "Never been better."

"Uh-huh." Blair laughed, stood quickly, and brushed her mouth over Cam's. "You'd better leave now, because I'm starting to get ideas about how I'd *really* like to spend the evening. It's been far too long since we've been able to make love."

Cam laughed. "I think it's only been a couple of days."

"Like I said," Blair replied, her voice husky as she drew

her hand up the inside of Cam's thigh and cupped her. When she squeezed, Cam gasped. Blair smiled. "*Far* too long."

Carefully, Cam placed both hands on Blair's waist and bent her head to capture Blair's mouth. Taking care not to press her chest to Blair's breasts, she kissed her deeply, letting her probing tongue satisfy some of her hunger. When she drew away, her heavy-lidded eyes were smoky with desire. "Don't do anything tonight except relax. Promise?"

Blair nodded, stroking Cam's cheek. "I love you. You've been wonderful through this. Thank y—"

"Blair," Cam murmured, catching Blair's fingers in hers and turning her head to press her lips to her lover's palm. She closed her eyes and rubbed her cheek against Blair's fingers. "Don't thank me for loving you, baby. Nothing has ever made me happier."

"I know you say that," Blair said, tilting her head back and studying Cam's face. "I'm not sure I understand *why* it makes you happy, but I know that you make me feel like I'm the center of your world."

"You are," Cam said quietly. She brushed her thumb over Blair's lower lip, then along the edge of her jaw until her fingers rested lightly on Blair's neck. "Do you mind?"

"God, no." Blair gave a shaky laugh. "It scares me sometimes." She saw Cam's brows furrow and added hastily, "Oh, not because I don't want it. Definitely not that. But...because I'd be lost if you stopped."

Cam smiled tenderly. "I won't."

"Funny," Blair murmured just before she kissed her, "but I believe you."

At 2330, eight men assembled in the ready room at the compound in Tennessee. The general was present, as were his four top men. The three newcomers were men who headed their own paramilitary factions—one in South Carolina, one in Nebraska, and the last in Michigan. Each had played a small part in the larger plan that had been underway for over three years. They'd worked together before, including planning the bombing at the federal building in Oklahoma City. Despite the fact that several members had been captured, that had been the first action of the Patriot network on native soil, and they'd had great success recruiting personnel and raising money as a result. Now, an even more daring plan was underway.

"We are prepared to execute our arm of the operation," the general stated with certainty. He glanced at his men. "And these are the *patriots* who will carry out the ground action."

There were sounds of congratulations as the men shook hands and made introductions. The general continued, "According to the undercover agent's latest report, the target has returned to home base. At this point, our focus must be on her."

"What if there's another snag like there was in France?" the rail-thin, jittery Nebraskan asked. "Those foreigners have mapped out an awfully ambitious plan, and there's lots of ways for it to get fucked up."

"That's true," the general said. "But even if only *part* of the main operation comes off the way they've laid it out, it will be enough. And regardless of what happens, come September, we *will* implement our part of the plan." He took his time and met each man's gaze. "Are we all agreed?"

Everyone nodded.

"Very well, then. And may God bless America."

CHAPTER TWENTY-FOUR

0015 26 August 2001

Cam tapped quietly on Blair's door. She had a key; so did Mac and each team leader. She had never used hers, and wouldn't, unless it was an emergency. When the door opened, she was surprised to find that the woman standing on the opposite side, bare-legged in nothing but an oversized T-shirt, was not her lover.

"Hello, Commander," the stunning blond said quietly, a playful smile on her full mouth.

"Diane," Cam replied with a hint of a question.

Finger to lips, Diane moved aside and gestured with her head toward the couch. Cam took two steps into the loft, stopping when she saw Blair curled up on the sofa, eyes closed, a brightly colored cotton throw covering her. Cam gave Diane an inquiring look and eased back into the hallway.

"She fell asleep in the middle of a sentence," Diane explained quietly as she pulled the door partially closed behind her.

"Is she all right?" Cam's voice vibrated with tension. She'd only been gone a few hours, but it felt like a month. "Was she complaining of any pain? She doesn't have a fever or anything, does she? Is—"

"Hey, slow down," Diane said in a surprisingly gentle tone. "I think she's just worn out." She tilted her head, her long blond hair swirling around her elegant neck, her azure eyes traveling from Cam's face down her body and back again. "*You* look ready for bed, too. I was going to spend the night in case she needs anything, but—"

"No," Cam interrupted. "You go ahead and stay. It will be good if you're here in the morning."

"I'm not so sure about that. She's likely to shoot first and ask questions later when she discovers that you were here just now and I didn't wake her."

Cam grinned. "Just keep your head down until I can talk to her. I'll tell her you were just following orders and didn't have any choice."

"Sounds good to me—I'd rather you take the heat." Diane reached out and squeezed Cam's hand, then released it. "Are you okay?"

"Sure."

Diane made an exasperated sound. "You know, that macho stuff might work with some people, but I've watched the two of you fall in love. I know what she means to you." *And I'd give anything to have a woman look at me the way you look at her.*

For the first time, Cam admitted to herself how tired she was, and how worried. "I'll be better when she gets the results of the genetic testing. Otherwise, I'm good."

"I meant it when I said you could call me, Cam. Just because Blair and I are friends doesn't mean that you and I can't be as well. We both love her."

"I know you do, and I'm glad."

Something in the way Cam said it, as if she really *did* know, brought Diane up short. Looking for a hidden message, she studied the calm charcoal eyes. She couldn't read a thing in them. "You don't mind?"

Cam shrugged and leaned a shoulder against the door frame. "She's an amazing woman. I can't imagine loving her and *not* wanting her."

"That's the difference between us, Cam. When I had the chance, I was afraid to do both at once. You never were." With a sigh, Diane leaned up and kissed Cam's cheek. "Go home. Go to bed. You look like hell."

"Ask her to call me when she wakes up. And...tell her I love her."

"That, Commander, will not be a news flash," Diane said with a small laugh, the sorrow leaving her eyes. "But I will be sure to pass along the message."

"Why didn't you wake me?"

Wisely, Diane didn't answer, but merely passed a steaming cup of coffee to her friend as she sat beside her on the sofa. She waited until Blair, looking grumpy under the incongruously bright and cheery cotton throw, had taken a few sips. She'd had an hour or so before falling asleep the night before to prepare her story. "Cam looked like she was really beat. The only way I could get her to go home to bed was to tell her that I thought *you* should sleep."

Blair frowned. "I think there's some trickery at work here, but I haven't had enough coffee yet to figure it out."

"She said she loves you and for you to call her when you're civil."

"She didn't say civil." Blair narrowed her eyes. "Did she?"

Diane smiled demurely.

Blair laughed. "God, I'm glad you're here."

"So am I." Diane reached across the space between them and briefly stroked the back of her fingers over Blair's cheek. "Are you going to be all right alone here today? I can stay, or you can come to my place."

"No, thanks. Really. I have to work, and Cam will be in and out. I'll be okay."

"Will you phone me as soon as you hear from the doctor?"

"I will. She said she'd rush the lab, but I don't know when we'll get the word."

"Whenever—day or night." Gently, Diane took Blair's hand. "And if you want to talk about anything, any time, just call, okay?"

"I promise." Blair leaned over and kissed Diane's cheek. "Thanks. I love you."

"I love you, too."

27Aug01
Panther Motel, Deerfield Beach, Florida

Report – Strike Team One. Confirm five

```
core members and pilot, Strike Team Two,
rendezvoused  on  schedule.  Operation
date established: September 11, 2001.
Departure  point:  Boston.  American
Airlines  Flight  11  to  Los  Angeles.
Target: NYC. Tickets purchased via Sun
Trust  debit  card  for  delivery  to  POB
in Hollywood, Florida.
```

0615 27 August 2001

"I really like the way you look when you get ready for work," Stark commented as she sat cross-legged on top of the covers, a yellow terrycloth robe loosely belted around her waist.

"Yeah?" Renee turned from the dresser where she had been sorting through her travel jewelry box in search of the small gold hoops she intended to wear that day. She'd already donned a plain white shirt and dark trousers and clipped her weapon holster to her right hip. A matching blazer lay over a chair next to the open closet. "How come?"

Stark leaned back on both arms, unmindful of her robe opening to expose her chest. "You just look so...capable. I like it. It's sexy."

"Sexy?" Renee shook her head with a fond smile. "I'll tell you what's sexy. *Sexy* is you lounging around in that robe with nothing on under it and most of you on display. Come on, have a little mercy—I have to leave for work in five minutes."

Stark followed her lover's gaze down her body and grinned. "You can't see anything."

"Sweetie," Renee said in a threatening tone as she stalked closer to the bed. "I don't need to see—I *know* what's underneath. Being reminded is what's dangerous." She leaned over and kissed Stark on the mouth, finishing with a small nip to her lower lip before straightening up.

Eyes slightly unfocused, Stark let out a shaky breath. "I don't think that was a very nice thing to do. Now I'm totally excited."

Renee slipped into her jacket and pocketed her badge. "Good.

Think of me today."

"As if I wouldn't anyway," Stark mumbled. She closed her eyes and lay back on the bed, listening to the soft sound of Renee's laughter lingering in the air.

0730 27Aug01
Delray Beach, Florida

> Report - Strike Team Two. Confirm
> departure point: Boston. United
> Airlines Flight 175 to Los Angeles.
> Target: NYC. Two one-way, first-class
> tickets booked at a cost of $4500.00
> each; contact address Delray Beach,
> Florida.

0910 27 August 2001

Blair set down her brush at the sound of a knock on her door and glanced at the clock. She'd been working since five a.m. in a faded red T-shirt and jeans, her hair tied back with a blue bandanna. She pulled the bandanna from her hair and wiped her hands on the way to the door. Out of habit, she checked the peephole and saw her lover on the other side. Quickly, she released the locks and pulled open the door. "Hi. You're early."

"Did you hear anything yet?" Cam stepped inside and waited for Blair to close the door before kissing her. "I finished the briefing early...well, actually I *started* the briefing early. I didn't want to miss Saunders's call."

"Nothing yet. We might not even get the test results today." She took Cam's hand and led her to the breakfast bar. "Sit down. I'll get you some coffee. Have you eaten?"

Cam shook her head. "Just coffee is fine."

Blair narrowed her eyes. Cam had never looked anything less than 100 percent fit, even when she'd barely been recovered from a near-fatal gunshot wound. Now, her color was ashen, fatigue lines etched her cheeks, and her normally vibrant voice was tinged with weariness. "Cam, have you eaten anything?"

"I'm not really—"

"We haven't even been back two days, and I'm going out of my mind," Blair said, her tone low and edgy. "If I *could* have you around all the time, I probably wouldn't want it. But *not* being able to have you around all the time is destroying my concentration. And sleeping without you..." She held up her hands in frustration. "*Now* I have to worry that you're not taking care of yourself."

"I'm sorry," Cam said quietly.

Blair stopped abruptly, the coffee carafe in her hand poised over the glazed blue mug that sat alone in the middle of the white tiled counter. "Which part of all of this is keeping you awake at night?" *What is tearing you apart?*

A muscle in Cam's jaw jumped.

"We haven't talked about what we'll do if the tests come back positive," Blair said evenly as she poured the coffee and then passed the mug to her lover. "We haven't talked about the fact that sooner or later, I'm likely to develop breast cancer." She met Cam's eyes, her own sad. "I haven't asked you what this is doing to you. *I'm* sorry."

"Blair—" Cam said, starting to rise.

"No." Blair held up a hand. "Stay on the other side of the counter. Something happens to my reason when you touch me."

Although her eyes were dark, Cam's lips twitched in a fleeting grin. Then she took a long breath as concern eclipsed the humor in her expression. "If the tests come back negative, then it won't be much different for you than for any other woman, right? Breast cancer is something we all have to think about. You'll just have to be vigilant—self-examination, routine mammograms, checkups with the doctor—SOP."

Silently, Blair nodded, watching Cam's face intently. Cam was so very good at being strong. It wasn't an act. But sometimes, that strength shadowed her pain so well that even Blair could miss it.

"And if the tests come back positive," Cam continued steadily, "we'll do whatever you decide."

"You know what the recommendations are if I have the gene, don't you?"

"Yes." For the last day and a half, when she hadn't been working, Cam had been reading everything she could find on the Internet about breast cancer. She understood that with Blair's family history, if her lover turned out to have the gene for breast cancer, the likelihood was extremely high that she would develop the disease—possibly an aggressive form—before her fortieth birthday. She understood, too, that many authorities recommended bilateral mastectomies to prevent that. "I know about the surgery."

"How would you feel if I decided to do that?"

"Is that what you want to do?"

Blair shook her head. "You're *so* damn good at taking care of me that sometimes I don't even realize it. I want to know how *you* feel." For the first time, she reached across the counter and took Cam's hand, linking their fingers. "Let me be the comfort for you that you are for me."

In a gesture so rare that Blair's heart turned over, Cam broke eye contact and lowered her head. With a trembling hand, she covered her eyes.

"Oh God," Blair uttered, moving quickly around the counter. She wrapped her arms around Cam's shoulders and with one hand, guided Cam's face against her breasts. She kissed the top of her lover's head. "Sweetheart, it's okay."

Eyes tightly closed, Cam held on, her fingers spread over the strong muscles of Blair's back. "I don't know what to do. I can't stand to think of anything hurting you."

The words came so quietly that Blair had to strain to hear them. Cam's heart thundered against her, and she felt the tension ripple through Cam's body. "Nothing is hurting me now." She spread her fingers into the thick hair at the back of Cam's neck and gently tugged her head back. The anguish in Cam's eyes brought a flood of tears to her own. "If I need to have the surgery, I can handle the pain. I'm pretty sure I can even handle the...results." She brushed at Cam's hair with her fingertips. "I don't think I can stand it if it changes anything between us."

Swiftly, Cam surged upright, bringing their bodies into full contact, her arms still tight around Blair's waist. "There is *nothing* that will ever change how much I love you." She kissed Blair tenderly, but her body trembled with fierce urgency. When she drew her mouth away, she whispered hoarsely, "Not one scar, not two, not a hundred will ever make you less beautiful to me."

Blair pressed her face to Cam's neck, sliding her hands beneath Cam's jacket, fitting herself to every inch of her lover's body. Voice muffled, she murmured, "I need you so much."

"I need you, too." Cam kissed the wisps of hair at Blair's temple. "I should've stayed with you this weekend."

"I know. We'll figure out how to make this work." Having Cam next to her, sensing their love healing their shared pain, Blair felt her heart lift. With a small laugh, she added, "But at least I got work done."

"Well, I'm glad to hear *that*." Cam eased a hand under Blair's T-shirt and dipped her fingers beneath the back of Blair's jeans, circling her fingertips in the small hollow at the base of Blair's spine.

"Mmm." Blair kissed Cam's neck, then the undersurface of her jaw, then a spot just below her ear. She smiled when Cam's heartbeat raced hard against her breast. Thighs pressed tightly to Cam's, she leaned back in her arms. "I missed you, though."

"Did you?" Cam shifted until her thigh rested between Blair's. "Did you suffer?"

"Sexual frustration can be sublimated, you know." Blair gripped Cam's shirt and pulled it from her trousers, then walked her fingers up Cam's bare abdomen. The muscles twitched beneath her fingertips and her own stomach clenched. "I got a *lot* of work done."

Cam's vision wavered. With the sudden swell of desire came the crushing need to keep Blair close, safe, *hers*. It took every ounce of Cam's willpower to fight back the aching urge to strip down, tear apart—*destroy*—every single barrier that threatened to separate them. Their clothing was the most accessible, but it was the intangible, the things she couldn't get her hands around or her body in front of, that were driving her crazy. Rumor, innuendo, public opinion—if those things weren't amorphous enough—now the specter of a lethal killer *inside* her lover's body stalked her waking and sleeping moments.

"Jesus, Cameron, you're shaking all over." Passion gave way to concern, and Blair pulled away a fraction.

"No," Cam protested. "Please, don't go."

"Oh, darling," Blair soothed, stroking Cam's cheek. "I'm not going anywhere." She reached behind her and found Cam's hand, holding tightly as she stepped back another pace. "Come into the bedroom. I need to hold you. I need you to hold me."

Mutely, Cam followed, needing only the touch of this one woman's hand to center her universe.

Standing in a shaft of sunlight by the side of the bed, they undressed slowly, no urgency now, only peace. Blair pulled back the sheet, slipped beneath, and held it open for her lover to join her. Facing each other, bodies lightly touching, they kissed again. A soft sigh, a quiet moan, the thunder of two hearts beating as one drifted on the air. Hot skin, tight muscles, and the wonder of passion made flesh united heart and soul. Devotion, desire, the sweet ache of need shimmered as blue eyes met gray.

"Touch me," Blair whispered against Cam's lips, smoothing her fingers down Cam's abdomen and between her legs. She waited until Cam mirrored her before gliding her fingers through the waiting warmth, pausing for a heartbeat as Cam's hips lifted into her palm. The answering brush of Cam's hand over her clitoris nearly made her come, and she clung to sanity with a thread. "Fill me now...as much as you can."

Dizzy with the scent and sensation of Blair's arousal, Cam slipped inside as Blair echoed the movement. Instantly, her orgasm surged, and she stiffened, struggling to stem the tide of pleasure already loosed. When Blair withdrew and then pushed deeper, she couldn't hold on. Shuddering beneath the onslaught rising from her depths, Cam felt Blair pulse around her fingers. Her lover's cry of release triggered another peak and she buried her face in the curve of Blair's neck, sobbing softly.

Still coming, Blair gripped Cam tightly, stroking her face fitfully as she gasped, "I love you. I will always love you."

When her vision cleared and her breath returned, Cam settled onto her back and pulled Blair into her arms. "Can you tell that you're all I need?"

"Yes." Blair rested her cheek on Cam's breast. The ridge of scar tissue, harder than the soft skin surrounding it, reminded her of how it felt to nearly lose the woman she loved. She ached to think that Cam would ever experience that terrible pain because of her. There was no answer for that, no protection against it, no promise or guarantee that she could make that might not be a lie. There was only this moment and the hope of those to come. "While I live, you will always have my heart."

"And you mine," Cam whispered, "as long as I live."

The phone rang, shattering the stillness, but not the calm that suffused their souls.

Blair reached behind her for the receiver, and returning her eyes to Cam's, said steadily, "This is Blair Powell."

CHAPTER TWENTY-FIVE

1000 27 August 2001

Blair spoke only a few words, listening with no change in her expression, as Cam, breath held, searched her lover's eyes for the truth.

"Yes, thank you, I'll do that. No, I'll see someone here," Blair said quietly.

See someone here. The ache in Cam's chest exploded with greater force than when the bullet had torn through her. That day as she had lain bleeding on the sidewalk, staring at the bluest sky she'd ever seen, she'd had one brief instant of awareness that she was dying. But just before she'd gone down, she'd seen Blair dragged back inside the building out of harm's way. With that image in her mind, she'd had no fear and no pain. Her duty was done, and Blair was safe.

Now, all she felt was pain.

Struggling for calm, desperately searching for the reservoir of strength that had carried her through her father's death, her own near-death, and the loss of an agent under her command, Cam lay very still, afraid that if she moved at all Blair would feel her shaking.

"I'll let you know where I need my records sent. Thank you again. You've been wonderful." Blair pushed the off button and held the receiver against her chest. She met Cam's eyes, her pupils so wide her blue irises were nearly as dark as Cam's troubled gray ones. "I'm..." Blair's voice cracked and she swallowed. "I'm negative. I don't have the gene."

"Oh, good Christ." Cam closed her eyes for a fraction of a second, then reached for her lover. There was only an inch between them, but it was far more than she could bear. Still, she was mindful of Blair's recent surgery and as much as she wanted to hold her tightly, she contented herself with easing her palm over Blair's neck and down her back. "God, baby, I'm so happy."

Blair laughed unsteadily. "I can't believe it. I was so *sure* I'd be positive." She caught Cam's hand and held it tightly. "I was trying to convince myself that it would be okay if I had to have more surgery."

"It *would* be okay." Cam kissed her forehead, her eyelids, her mouth. With her fingers gently caressing Blair's face, she murmured, "No matter what, it would be all right. But I'm just so damn glad you don't need it."

"She'll send my test reports to my gynecologist, and I'll just go back for my regular twice-yearly checkups." Blair kissed Cam, long and deep. When she pulled away, her eyes were hazy with love and desire. "It's over, darling. It's really over."

"Yes." Cam leaned up and guided Blair onto her back. Very carefully, Cam leaned down and kissed the inside of Blair's left breast, just opposite the biopsy site. Then she raised her head and kissed Blair's mouth. "I love you."

With a hand cupped behind Cam's neck, Blair drew her lover back down to her other breast. As she felt Cam's lips enclose her nipple, she murmured, "Love me again."

1015 28Aug01
Miami Beach, Florida

> Report - Strike Team Two. Pilot confirms purchase of one-way ticket at United Airlines ticket counter without incident. Cost $1600.00. UA Flight 175 to Los Angeles.

2230 30 August 2001

"Here," Cam said abruptly, "don't lift that. I'll get it."

"Cameron," Blair said irritably, "it's a *painting*. It's not heavy."

"Why don't *I* get it," Diane said smoothly, reaching between the two women to pick up the four-by-five-foot bubble-wrapped canvas. She smiled benignly at Cam and shooed away Blair, who was flushed and sweaty, with an impatient motion. "Why don't you two sit down somewhere and have a drink while I supervise loading the rest of these."

"I'm perfectly capable of doing it." Blair was tired and cranky and unreasonably anxious about the upcoming show. She'd been working nonstop for three days on too little sleep and too much caffeine, and her nerves were frayed. It didn't help that Cam was uncharacteristically edgy as well. It *especially* didn't help that they'd had little time alone together, and when they had, they were both prickly.

"Of course you are. Wonderfully capable—but they're mine now, and I'll see to them." Ignoring Blair's snarl, Diane pointed to a stack of similarly wrapped paintings against the wall when her gallery assistant and another employee arrived, escorted by Paula Stark. "Jamie, these are the ones that are going. Make sure to take them directly into the storeroom. Do *not* leave them in the van unattended."

"You got it," the young woman replied good-naturedly. She nodded to Blair. "Good evening, Ms. Powell."

Blair raked a hand through her hair and smiled. "Hi, Jamie. How are you?"

"Terrific. Really looking forward to your show." Jamie directed the young man with her toward the canvases. "Take the smaller ones last, Dick. Thanks."

Within a matter of minutes, the paintings, the culmination of a year's work, were gone. As Diane waved goodbye, Blair surveyed the nearly empty studio with a conflicting mixture of trepidation and anticipation. Some critical part of her soul was about to be exposed, and she could no longer protect, defend, or explain that part of herself. Her art would have to speak for itself. *Why am I doing this? I'd be just as happy painting even if my canvases never left this room.* For one insane moment, she wanted to follow Diane out to the elevator and tell her to bring the paintings back.

"You okay?"

"No," Blair snapped, jerking around to face Cam. "I can't believe I'm doing this. I don't even *want* to do this." She saw the surprise in Cam's face at the heat in her voice, and the fire instantly left her eyes. She leaned her hips against the back of the sofa and shook her head. "God, I'm being a bitch. Sorry."

"It's all right," Cam said as she walked over to her lover. "This last week has been hell."

Blair ran her fingers along the edge of Cam's silk lapels, then smoothed her palms over Cam's chest beneath the jacket. Her hand brushed the leather strap that crossed Cam's left breast to the weapon harness snugged beneath her arm. "It hasn't been a picnic for you either." She fingered the leather as she rested her forehead against Cam's shoulder and closed her eyes. "I thought after the news that I'm BRCA-negative I'd feel better, but I'm still all churned up inside."

Cam softly caressed Blair's neck before kneading the tight muscles in her shoulders. "It has to have brought up a lot of painful memories for you. That, and the surgery, and the pressure to get things ready for the show—no wonder you're a bit..." She stopped, searching for an appropriate word.

"Bitchy?" Blair suggested with a faint laugh.

"Well, that might be one term for it." Cam grinned.

"Okay, fair enough. But what about you?" Blair tapped Cam's chin with a fingertip. "What's bugging you?"

"Me?"

"Yes, Cameron. You. You're never restless, but every time you're up here you've been wearing a path in front of my windows."

"Uh," Cam flushed.

"What?"

"I'm nervous about this weekend."

Blair blinked. "Why?"

"Blair." Cam shook her head in fond exasperation. "I'm about to spend the weekend with my lover in the company of her father. For the first time. And oh, by the way—her father happens to be the president of the United States. Don't you think that entitles me to be a little bit nervous?"

Delighted, Blair laughed. "I can't believe it. That is so cute."

"Cut it out," Cam growled just before she dipped her head and unceremoniously bit Blair's neck.

Blair arched her head back. "Mmm, now *that's* more like it."

"Well, since we're leaving in a few hours, that's about all we're going to have time for."

"Yes," Blair murmured, "but now that I don't have to worry about my health or my work, I can concentrate on what I've been missing." Deftly, she opened the top two buttons on Cam's shirt and slid her hand inside. Fingers drifting over the top of Cam's breast, she noted in a husky voice, "And that, Commander, would be you."

Cam slapped her palm down over Blair's hand, pinning it to her chest. "I have absolutely no intention of having sex with you if your father is anywhere in the vicinity."

"Well," Blair danced her fingers lower to stroke Cam's nipple, purring faintly when she felt it hardening beneath her touch, "it's a big compound."

Gasping, Cam protested, "Not big enough."

"So you say."

0700 2 September 2001

Naked, Cam rested her butt against the sink in the spacious bathroom and watched Blair towel dry. She noted with satisfaction that her lover's breast was barely swollen now. "How's it feel?"

"Itchy. I wish the rest of the goddamn stitches would fall out."

"You're a terrible patient."

Blair cocked an eyebrow. "Look who's talking. As I recall, you had second-degree burns on your entire arm and shoulder and—"

Cam held up both hands in surrender. "Okay. Okay. You win." Laughing, she took a step closer and cupped her palm beneath Blair's breast, lifting it gently to peer at the suture line. "It looks really good. Just a faint line. Do you think I should—"

"Darling," Blair interrupted quietly. "That's my breast you're holding up for inspection."

"Is it?" Cam inquired, raising her head. The corner of her mouth lifted. "I hadn't noticed that."

Blair tightened inside as her nipple tightened beneath Cam's thumb. "My father and six Secret Service agents are waiting for us to go jogging. I'm not going to be able to do that if I get any more aroused."

"Oops." Eyes twinkling, Cam lowered her head and kissed Blair's nipple. At her lover's swift gasp, she chuckled and stepped out of reach before Blair could do damage. "I'd better get dressed."

"You'd better, because I don't care if the Joint Chiefs of Staff are on the other side of that bedroom door. I'm not waiting much longer."

Cam grabbed for the shorts, T-shirt, and jog bra that lay on the counter and retreated to the other side of the bedroom, pulling on clothes as she moved. Since their arrival, they'd spent most of their time in the president's company. He still worked for part of each day, but they'd taken their meals with him, worked out with him in the mornings, and spent the evenings together relaxing in the entertainment center. Although she and Blair shared a bedroom and a bed, they hadn't made love in the two nights they'd been at Camp David. In truth, both of them had been emotionally and physically exhausted, and it had been enough just to hold each other safe while they slept.

"Tell me *you're* not ready," Blair said as she sat on the side of the bed to lace her running shoes.

There were some things that Cam would not tease about. She knelt by Blair's side and rested her hand on Blair's bare thigh. Her expression completely serious, she said softly, "I missed you so much this week. Holding you at night has been so good."

"Cam—"

"*But,*" Cam interrupted gently, tracing her fingertips lightly up and down Blair's leg, "I'm about ready to burst."

Blair's brilliant smile flashed. "Oh, good. That's fine, then." She leaned down and kissed Cam swiftly on the mouth, then sidestepped her kneeling lover and rose agilely to her feet. "Come on, darling. Let's not keep the president waiting."

Laughing, Cam followed her lover from the guest room and down the hall toward the main living area. As she did automatically several times a day, she mentally reviewed Blair's upcoming itinerary. The president's daughter had no trips scheduled for two months, and the gallery showing was her only public outing for several weeks. That meant they were facing a relatively quiet period. *Thank God. We all need a bit of a break.*

"Good morning," the president called heartily. "You two ready to go?"

"Yes sir," Cam replied, falling into step beside the president on the sidewalk in front of the compound. Blair dropped back a pace to run beside Deborah Kling, the only female agent on her father's first team and an old friend of Blair's.

As the group moved off onto a dirt path that led into the woods surrounding the compound, the president asked, "What are your long-term plans, Cam?"

"Sir?"

"Are you a career agent, or are you considering moving into the private sector at some point in the future?"

"I haven't really given it much thought, sir," Cam replied, glancing swiftly over her shoulder in Blair's direction. Her lover's attention was on something the Secret Service agent beside her was saying. "For the duration, sir, I don't plan on making any changes."

"I take that to mean the duration of my tenure?"

Cam nodded.

"Very diplomatic of you not to stipulate a time frame on that."

"I have every confidence that you will be reelected—"

Laughing, Andrew Powell interrupted. "We'll worry about that when we need to. I don't imagine, however, that Blair will want you to continue any longer than necessary in this particular line of work."

His tone was entirely conversational, and Cam didn't get the impression that he was probing for anything personal regarding her lover. Nevertheless, she replied neutrally, "We haven't talked about it, but she's sacrificed enough for the public welfare. I won't ask her to do it indefinitely."

"You mean she's sacrificed for *my* career, don't you?"

"Sir." Cam flushed. "I certainly meant no disresp—"

"It's Andrew, remember? And I know you didn't, Cam. And you need never apologize to me for loving my daughter."

Cam turned her head and met the president's gaze steadily. "I never would, sir."

The president grinned, and for an instant, he looked much younger. "I'm very glad you came this weekend, Cam."

"Yes, sir. So am I."

1100 02Sep01

```
Report - Strike Team Three. Departure
confirmed:      Washington      Dulles
International     Airport.     American
Airlines   Flight   77.   Destination:
Los Angeles. Target: Washington, DC.
Tickets    purchased,   Internet  credit
card sale. Team en route by automobile
to Silver Spring, Maryland.
```


Back in their room, Blair stripped out of her T-shirt and shorts. She reached for her bra and winced.

Instantly by her side, Cam asked, "Did you pull something?"

"No, it's all right," Blair said gently. "I think that problem stitch just got snagged."

Carefully, Cam eased the garment away from Blair's breast and drew it up over her head. After dropping the garment onto the bed, she turned her attention back to the incision. "Seems okay."

"I don't know," Blair mused. "I think you might need to kiss it and make it better."

"How much time do we have?"

"Time enough."

Cam pushed down her running shorts and kicked them off, then pulled her T-shirt and bra off in one motion. "Shower?"

Blair stepped close to her, the tips of her breasts just brushing

Cam's. Her nipples hardened instantly but there was no pain, only the heavy ache of desire. "That sounds like a very good place to start."

The water, just barely warm, was cool against Blair's overheated skin. She rested her shoulders against the slick tile and looked down at Cam, who knelt between her spread thighs. Steadying herself with the palm of her left hand against the wall, Blair teased the wet black strands of her lover's hair through her fingers while anticipation coalesced like a clenched hand in the pit of her stomach. Lids nearly closed, she arched her neck, choking on a groan as Cam's teeth tugged at the gold ring piercing her navel. Cam's face swam before her eyes, her vision blurring with the rush of desire bursting inside her head.

"Put your lips on me," Blair whispered, but her words were lost in the rush of water beating down around them. She tensed as Cam's fingers spread wide on the inside of her legs, opening her. "Please...suck me." But the plea faded on a sob as her breath fled. She lifted her hips and tightened her grip in Cam's hair, sliding her sex urgently against her lover's cheek. "Oh God, I need your mouth." But Cam only turned her head away and licked the soft skin high on the inside of Blair's trembling thigh.

The ache inside verged on pain, and when the muscles in her stomach spasmed, jerking her forward, nearly bending her double, Blair gave a desperate cry. She drove both hands into Cam's hair and pulled Cam's face to her, forcing her lover's mouth against her clitoris. "Please...baby, please."

Cam wrapped one arm around Blair's thighs and took her the way she needed to be taken, using her tongue and her teeth and her lips to fire the blood and ignite the nerve endings that throbbed with wild desperation beneath her mouth. She felt Blair's legs tighten and her clitoris swell and knew she was coming. Only then did she push her fingers inside, driving her to a second climax before the first had peaked. When Blair moaned and began to sag down the wall, Cam rose, her hand still deep within, and pulled Blair against her body, preventing her from falling.

"Hold me, hold me," Blair sobbed into Cam's neck.

"I will never let you go," Cam whispered fiercely.

Believing, Blair surrendered to her lover's tender care.

CHAPTER TWENTY-SIX

0600 05Sep01

```
Report: Strike Team Four. Departure
confirmed: United Airlines Flight
93 from Newark. Destination: San
Francisco. Target: Washington, DC.
Tickets purchased at Baltimore/
Washington International Airport, cash
transaction.
```

0700 06Sep01

Alone in an austere office in his rustic mountain compound, General Matheson logged on to the Internet and brought up a site featuring classic cars. He scrolled through the menus to a page displaying a '57 Mercury Cruiser and moved his cursor over the image until he found an html link, which he clicked to open.

```
Final communiqué. Four teams assembled
and dispatched: East Coast targets 1-
4 only. Teams five and six currently
deactivated. Date confirmed: 0900
11Sept2001. Glory to the righteous.
```

Matheson grunted and shrugged away a flicker of apprehension. There was no turning back now, even had he wanted to. These men were zealots and would not be deterred. They *would* strike, and he and his compatriots would take advantage of the shock and chaos to make their own voices heard. There had never been a better time for the Patriot mission than the present. With certain determination, he reached for his cell phone and punched in a familiar number. The call was answered at once.

"Hello, Agent," Matheson said quietly. "You are green-lighted. Your team will assemble tomorrow."

"Operation confirmed?"

"0900. 9-11."

"Very well." A few seconds of silence ensued. "I will assume command of the strike team. It's best if we terminate further communications."

Matheson hesitated, considering his options and the likelihood of repercussions if any part of the mission failed. It was imperative that he protect his organization to ensure the future of the freedom movement. "Agreed. Good luck and Godspeed."

0515 7 September 2001

Cam jerked fully awake at the first ring of the phone. She pulled her cell off the bedside table and sat up, opening the phone with one hand and flipping the covers back with the other. Her feet touched the floor and she stood, saying succinctly, "Roberts."

A second later, she sat back down on the edge of the bed. "No problem, Tom. What can I do for you?...Jesus, you're kidding...No, I understand...What do you want from my end?"

Listening intently, she made a mental list of things she needed to do. "Right. I'll take care of it." She laughed. "No, they certainly don't make it easy."

Terminating the call, she checked the clock. She had enough time to get in a run before the morning briefing. She was tired; she never slept well when she didn't sleep with Blair. And Blair had a busy weekend coming up, which meant more work for the team and more worry for her. She thought about the surprise call she'd just received from Washington and shook her head. More complications she didn't need.

"Christ. What a job."

0700 7 September 2001

"Good morning, everyone," Cam said briskly as she walked to the head of the table. "The itinerary for the weekend remains unchanged. Tonight at 2000 hours, Egret has the private opening at the Bleeker Gallery. Tomorrow evening at 2100 hours, the general showing. There will, however, be a change in the shift assignments for this evening. Please see Mac at 0900 hours for further details."

Mac straightened nearly imperceptibly, but his expression remained neutral. He hadn't been advised of any changes.

"In addition to the personal guest list, Egret has agreed to Ms. Bleeker's request that a small number of art dealers also attend the pre-show this evening." It wasn't unusual for dealers who represented wealthy clients or large consortiums to be allowed to preview the works before the gallery opened a show for general viewing. She looked at Mac. "Do you have those background checks completed?"

"I ran those," Cynthia Parker responded. She passed out information packets to each agent. "Bios and photos. Nothing tipped a flag."

"Good," Cam replied, flipping the folder open. She'd seen the list of names and had recognized two whom she'd met at her mother's shows over the years. "Just make certain you are all familiar with the—" she paused, staring at one image, "uh...the photographs of the dealers." *Jesus Christ.* The name below the photo read *Valerie Ross*. Carefully, she pressed her fingertips to the desktop to still the faint trembling. "Everyone else on the guest list should already be familiar to you."

Cam completed the rest of the briefing on autopilot and, when she'd finished, said quietly to Mac, "Wait a minute, will you, Mac?"

"Certainly, Commander."

Once they were alone, Cam pulled out the chair at the head of the table and settled into it, working not to allow her weariness to show. "I need you to rearrange the shift assignments for this evening. We need the entire team deployed."

"The *whole* team, Commander?"

"Yes." She rubbed at the headache beginning to form between

her eyes. "Bring up the schematics of the area for a two-block radius, would you."

Without another word, Mac plugged a video cable into his laptop and clicked an icon on the desktop. A detailed street map appeared on the wall screen at the opposite end of the conference room. Cam got up and walked to it, pulling a slim laser pointer from her inside breast pocket. "Call Captain Landers and inform her that we'll need vehicular and foot patrols here, here, and...here."

"Got it," he replied, although he didn't actually understand the order at all. Captain Stacy Landers was the NYPD security liaison with Egret's team, but local law enforcement was usually only deployed for large-scale public outings.

"Now let me see the gallery building, street level."

A second passed, and then a blueprint of the building that housed the Bleeker Gallery appeared. Front, rear, and side entrances were denoted by red semicircles with the distance in feet to the nearest street or alleyway marked in bright yellow numerals. On the interior of the structure, the rooms and hallways, as well as the heating ducts and gas, water, and electrical conduits, were all marked in distinguishing colors. "Put two people each here, here, and here," Cam instructed, again pinpointing the areas with the tiny bright red laser dot.

"That will leave us thin on Egret herself," Mac noted neutrally.

"Thinner than I'd like," Cam agreed. "Put Stark inside the gallery with me. You take the main entrance. That should be fine."

"Commander? Is there a problem I should be aware of regarding tonight's itinerary?"

"No, Mac. No problem." *At least I hope not—and nothing that I can tell you about now.*

Mac nodded, keeping his questions to himself. He trusted her implicitly, and even if he hadn't, he would have followed orders. Still, at times like this, it helped immeasurably that she had the total confidence of every one of her agents. "I'll see to it."

"Thank you." Cam breathed in slowly and let the air out on a sigh. Then she walked back to the head of the table. "There's one more thing."

Her second in command regarded her steadily.

"One of the art dealers," Cam said as she reached for the file Cynthia Parker had prepared, "Valerie Ross. I need everything there is on her, and I need it this morning."

"The background check is in there, Commander." Mac regarded Cam quizzically. "It's extensive."

Familiar with the standard checks, Cam nodded. "I want a deep-level check."

"Finances, database scans, photo runs?"

"Yes," Cam said quietly, opening the file and sliding it across the table to Mac. "Everything."

Mac looked down at the file. "Jesus," he said with uncharacteristic lack of restraint. "What's going on?"

"I don't know." Cam stared at the photo. "But we have to find out."

"Hi," Blair said, smiling, as she opened the door to her lover.

Cam smiled back, but her eyes were solemn. "You're all ready," she remarked, taking in the gym bag by the door and Blair's outfit, which consisted of a T-shirt, sweatpants, and gym shoes.

"And you're not. Aren't you coming?" Blair kept her tone light, but inwardly she was already preparing herself for disappointment. Cam was her lover, but this weekend, she was much more her security chief. After more than a decade of living with close security, Blair knew how much planning needed to be done in preparation for a public event like the gathering that evening. And she knew that Cam would oversee every detail personally.

"I'm definitely coming," Cam said reassuringly. "I left my gear downstairs in the locker room. But something's come up that I need to talk to you about first."

"All right." Blair took Cam's hand and led her to the breakfast bar. She eased a hip up onto one of the tall stools and waited for Cam to take a seat facing her. "What's going on, darling?"

"I'm not even sure I should be bringing this up now—hell, or at *all.*" Cam shook her head, disgusted at her own indecisiveness. "I've just spent the last forty minutes trying to make up my mind. Then it finally occurred to me that if I didn't discuss it with you, you might be pissed."

"Cameron," Blair said firmly. "Just tell me."

"One of the art dealers who Diane invited to the pre-opening show tonight is Claire."

"Claire." Blair's brows furrowed, the name meaning nothing to her. But she couldn't ever remember seeing Cam so uncomfortable. Angry, worried—even, on rare occasions, frightened. But never quite like this. Suddenly Blair stiffened, knowing with the sixth sense of a lioness whose territory was about to be invaded precisely to whom her lover referred. In a dangerously calm tone, Blair repeated, "Claire. Your Claire—of the beautiful face and the elegant body and the oh-so-sophisticated demeanor. That Claire."

"She's not *my* Claire," Cam pointed out. "And—"

"I notice that you didn't disagree with the rest of my assessment," Blair interjected conversationally, but her eyes glinted like shards of glass in the sunlight.

For a moment, Cam couldn't follow the direction of the discussion, and then she laughed. Not the wisest thing to do, but she couldn't help herself. "You're kidding! You can't actually think I'd look at any other woman in the world when I have you."

"You've done a hell of a lot more than *look* at her." Blair couldn't even think about Cam being with another woman, let alone acknowledge that she'd been with someone so obviously beautiful and undoubtedly accomplished. *In everything.* It made her want to hurl breakable objects.

"That was before you," Cam said gently. "Now, there's only you, and there will only ever *be* you."

Blair blinked. "I hate it when you do that."

"What?"

"Make me forget why I'm mad at you."

Cam stood and stepped between Blair's legs, resting both hands on her lover's waist. She kissed her lightly on the mouth and grinned. "I love you."

Blair bumped her head against Cam's chest. "You'd better, because I swear to God, I won't be accountable for my actions otherwise."

Laughing quietly, Cam eased an arm around Blair's shoulder and leaned against the counter with Blair resting along the curve of her body. "Believe me, you have nothing to worry about."

"So what's going on?" Blair regarded Cam curiously. "With Claire?"

"Apparently, she's not Claire. Well, she is, or at least *was,* but she's also Valerie Ross."

"An alias?"

"Nope." Cam gently massaged the muscles in Blair's shoulders. "According to our records check, she *really* is Valerie Ross."

"And is she really an art dealer?"

Cam nodded. "Apparently so."

"Well. She is quite the mystery woman." Blair hooked her fingers over Cam's belt and beneath the waistband of her trousers, rubbing the back of her hand over Cam's stomach. "High-class Washington call girl, high-rolling art dealer, and drop-dead gorgeous femme fatale. I'm going to have to hurt her."

"We can't find anything to suggest she's a threat," Cam replied quietly, "but I can have Diane try to reach her and rescind the invitation. Or I can have Mac stop her at the door."

"Why?" Blair's tone was curious. Unconsciously, she pulled the tail of Cam's shirt loose so she could touch her palm to skin.

"Because this is a special night for you, and I don't want anything to spoil it."

Blair leaned away far enough so that she could meet her lover's eyes. "You'd do that?"

A look of confusion crossed Cam's face. "Of course."

"I don't mind if she comes." Blair thought of the few brief moments late one night standing beneath a streetlight with Cam's lover, if that's what Claire—Valerie—truly had been. She remembered a beautiful woman with deep sadness in her eyes. She'd recognized the sadness born of loneliness because she'd felt it so often herself. "She probably doesn't even realize we'll be there. Often, when the gallery has a private showing for a few select dealers before the opening, the artist isn't present. Besides, if she's got a client who's interested, she couldn't turn down the invitation. It's bad for business."

Surprised, Cam shrugged. "I'm not interested in her reasons. I'm only interested in what's best for you."

"It's fine, darling." Blair stood and put her free arm around

Cam's neck while smoothing her palm up and down Cam's abdomen. She leaned hard into Cam with her thighs and pelvis, rolling her hips subtly. "Now, are you coming to the gym with me to spar?"

"Blair," Cam whispered, her voice husky. "It will hardly be a fair match if I'm too swollen to walk."

Blair chuckled. "All's fair in love and war, Commander."

1445 07Sep01

Five men crowded around a glass-topped dining-room table in a four-room condominium overlooking Central Park. None of them noticed the view. A blueprint was spread out in the center of the table, and several of the men held down the corners with their hands.

"The layout is simple," the brown-haired strike team leader said, punctuating his words with a finger tapping on the surface of the diagram. "Front and rear entrances, here and here."

"Guarded?" a gravelly voiced, heavyset man asked.

With an irritated flicker of his eyes at the interruption, the leader replied, "Not the rear, no. Routinely, there is a man posted only in the front lobby. The second elevator to the penthouse"—he pointed—"is keyed, but the common one to the rest of the building is not. The penthouse elevator can be called from the lobby, the command center—here, or from the penthouse floor."

"So," a sandy-haired, fresh-faced younger man commented, "we have two possible routes of access: from the lobby with a frontal assault, or, if that fails, from a flanking maneuver on the upper floors."

"Exactly." The team leader pointed to the rear entrance. "And this is the only exit other than through the lobby. It's easy to secure, and with all the rest of the confusion, if we move quickly, we should be out before anyone knows what's happened."

"Let's run through it then," the heavyset man suggested impatiently. "We've only got three days."

CHAPTER TWENTY-SEVEN

1523 7 September 2001

"Let me see that in the light," Blair said, reaching for Cam's chin.

"It's nothing," Cam said quickly, drawing her head away. The movement sent a hot stabbing pain into the base of her skull. She barely managed not to wince.

"Damn it, Cameron, it's *not* nothing. I can see the bruise from here." Blair stepped between Cam and the single bench in the center of the room, effectively preventing her from moving anywhere in the tiny women's changing area—too small to be called a locker room—in the far corner of the hard-core gym where she had kickboxed for almost two years. "What happened? You completely missed the block."

"Timing was off."

"Your timing is *never* off."

Cam worked her jaw back and forth experimentally. It hurt, but her teeth came together normally and everything seemed stable. "It's not broken. It'll be okay after a little ice."

Blair regarded Cam with a mixture of anger and concern. "And you've never missed that block before. Are you still upset about Claire?"

Cam's brows rose. "No. I wasn't even thinking about her."

"Then what *were* you *thinking* about?" Blair snapped. "Because it sure wasn't sparring. All you had to do to counter that kick was step into my body and take me..." Her eyes widened. *Step into my body and take me down. Into my body. Into my* breast.

Blair thumped her palm into the center of Cam's chest and backed her against the three rickety metal lockers, her face an inch from her lover's, her voice low, controlled, and filled with fury. "God damn it, I could've broken your *neck,* not just your jaw. If you didn't want to spar with me because you were worried about *hurting* me, you should've told me."

"It wasn't intentional," Cam said quietly. "I just hesitated when I realized where you'd take the hit."

"So you let me kick you in the face instead." Blair touched her fingers gently to the swelling on Cam's jaw. "God."

Cam settled her arms around Blair's waist and kissed her forehead, taking care not to move her head too much. The pain had actually subsided to a dull throb. She'd been hit before, and she knew no serious damage had been done. "It was just an accident. Next time I'll be sure to toss you on your ass. Hard, if that will make you happy."

Blair laughed in spite of herself, nestling her face against Cam's chest. "I hate for you to be hurt."

"I know." Cam untied the rolled red bandanna that Blair wore around her forehead when she sparred. She tossed it onto the bench behind them and combed her fingers through the damp tresses at her lover's neck. "Is everything okay with you?"

"I've got a sports bra on that's tight enough to cut off my circulation. My breast is fine." Blair tilted her head back and kissed the darkening smudge at the angle of the left side of Cam's jaw. "More than I can say for that."

"Mmm. I think that might have made it all better." Cam rested her head back against the flaking, green-painted locker, enjoying the sensation of Blair in her arms. Sparring with Blair always got her blood up, because Blair was the most beautiful when she was at her strongest. In the ring, with her muscled arms exposed, a cut-off T-shirt baring her stomach, and her toned legs dancing over the canvas, she was magnificent.

"What are you thinking about?" Blair murmured, kissing the pulse that beat at the base of Cam's neck. "Your heart just started hammering like crazy."

"You," Cam whispered. "I was thinking about what an incredible woman you are and how much you excite me."

The unexpected answer and the absolute seriousness in Cam's voice turned Blair's insides to liquid heat. "Don't move." She licked a tiny dab of sweat that had pooled in the hollow between Cam's collarbones with the tip of her tongue. Nearly purring, she stretched languidly against Cam's body. "You taste good."

Cam sighed, closing her eyes. "You feel good."

"Yeah, I do." Blair leaned back, her legs braced against Cam's, and pulled off her T-shirt.

"Blair," Cam warned.

"We're the only two women in the gym, Cam." Blair spoke quietly as she reached behind her and unhooked her bra. "Take this off for me."

Cam slipped her fingers beneath the shoulder straps and slid the bra down Blair's arms, exposing her breasts. She looked down, drawing a quick breath as she watched the sweat-glistening nipples harden in the air. "Oh, Christ."

Following Cam's gaze, Blair smiled lazily. "Now, put your hands on them." When Cam cupped her breasts, thumbs and forefingers automatically encircling her nipples, Blair closed her eyes and arched her back. "Oh, yes."

"You have such beautiful breasts," Cam murmured hoarsely.

"Just keep touching me." Blair shifted a few inches until her legs straddled Cam's thigh and then, in one swift motion, insinuated her fingers beneath the waistband of Cam's gym shorts and pushed her hand down between her legs.

Cam jerked, groaning in surprise.

"Shh," Blair soothed as she caught Cam's clitoris between her fingers. "Quietly, now."

"I can't," Cam said desperately. "Jesus, Blair."

"Squeeze my nipples." As she spoke, Blair stroked Cam's length, pulling the blood into the tense tissues beneath her fingers, teasing the nerve endings that already pulsed and quivered on the brink of explosion. As she worked Cam toward orgasm, Cam's fingers tugged spasmodically at her breasts, and the sharp points of pain became sweet pleasure in her depths. "That's it. That's it, darling...hold my breasts in your hands while I make you come."

Shivering, Cam closed her eyes tightly and braced herself for the orgasm that was fast climbing along her spine. She couldn't think, couldn't be sure *what* she was doing with her hands, didn't *want* to do anything except feel the weight and heat and wonder of

Blair's breasts against her skin as she came. Her knees buckled and only Blair's body straddling hers kept her upright. She groaned and choked back a cry and came hard in Blair's hand.

Blair watched Cam's face as the orgasm consumed her. *I will never be able to paint anything as beautiful as you are in this moment.* Feeling her breasts cradled in Cam's tender hands, Cam's passion flooding hers, she fought sudden tears and failed. Despite the moisture dampening her cheeks, as she rested her head against Cam's shoulder, Blair knew nothing but joy.

1930 7 September 2001

Cam knocked on Blair's door and checked her watch. Five minutes earlier, Mac had confirmed that the vehicles were waiting streetside, Captain Landers had verified that her people were in position on the perimeter, and the advance team at the gallery had radioed an all clear. Everything was set. Everything was as secure as she could make it.

The door opened, and Cam allowed herself a minute to be no one other than Blair's lover. She found Blair attractive in anything she wore, whether faded jeans and paint-splattered T-shirt or an elegant evening gown and diamonds. This evening, Blair had chosen a sleeveless black dress, so simple in design that it appeared to have no design at all. The shimmering silk sheath was scoop-necked, cut just low enough to reveal the barest hint of cleavage before it fell away in a gentle sweep that accentuated the sensual strength of Blair's body. Sapphires, the same deep blue as her eyes, glinted at her ears and throat, and tonight, in distinct contrast to her usual style at official functions, she had left her hair loose. The golden curls teased along her neck and shoulders, and it was all Cam could do not to drag her fingers through them. "Christ, you look beautiful."

"Thank you," Blair replied quietly. A smile flickered and was quickly gone. "Can you believe I'm nervous?"

"I can imagine." Cam leaned forward and gently kissed her, running the tip of her index finger along the edge of Blair's jaw. "But you're a wonderful artist, and your work is very special. Just enjoy tonight—you deserve it."

"I'll try." Blair hooked her arm through Cam's as they walked toward the elevator. Her lover wore a slate gray suit and open-collared charcoal silk shirt that lent her long, lean form a sharp, edgy look. "Your jaw looks better. And you look hot."

"I'm not supposed to look hot. I'm your escort, and I'm also working." Frowning, Cam keyed the elevator. "What I'm *supposed* to look like tonight is background."

"It's not working," Blair stated, her tension easing as they rode down to the lobby. "Well, it's *working,* but probably not the way you planned."

Just as the doors opened to reveal Stark, waiting to escort Blair to the Suburban, Cam muttered, "Don't start. I have to concentrate."

Blair laughed and forgot entirely why she had been nervous.

2043 7 September 2001

Blair stood with Marcea before one of her oils, their arms linked. "I'm still not certain that the texture of the paint is right for the tone of the work."

"Oh, I think it is." Marcea tilted her head, sweeping the canvas again. "If it were any thinner, you'd lose some of the impact of the color."

"It was so nice of you to come all the way East for this," Blair said. "I know how busy you are."

Marcea gave her a fond smile. "I wouldn't have missed it. First of all, I love your work. And," she slid her arm around Blair's waist in a gentle hug, "I wanted to be here for you. I know how difficult it can be with your heart up there on the walls for anyone to see. Not that you have anything to worry about."

"I've had paintings in galleries before, but never a solo showing." Blair glanced around the room and saw so many pieces of herself on display. For the most part, the people who strolled about were friends whom she trusted, but even so, she rarely exposed so much of her soul to anyone. *Only Cam has seen it all.* "It will almost be easier tomorrow night at the open house, with strangers. Somehow, their reactions don't seem as critical."

"I'd like to tell you that you'll get used to it, but you probably never will. Every time you let one go, you'll wonder if *anyone* will understand what you saw when you painted it, what you felt in your heart that compelled you to create it." Marcea shrugged, her expression distant. "But you'll keep doing it, because that's who you are."

Strangely, Blair was comforted by the sentiment, because coming from Marcea, an artist whom she revered, her own uncertainties seemed far less momentous. "It's a wonderful feeling in the moment, though, isn't it? When in the midst of painting you begin to see those indefinable emotions coming to life on the canvas."

Marcea's eyes brightened and she laughed. "I won't say it's the *best* thing I've ever experienced, but it comes close."

"Yes." Unconsciously, Blair's eyes drifted to Cam, who stood a few feet away, her attention seemingly focused entirely on the room. Despite the remote expression on her lover's face, Blair was certain that Cam knew precisely where she was. *It comes close— but it can't compare to her.*

"Everything is all right, I take it?" Marcea questioned gently, following Blair's gaze. "The press has left you alone about your relationship?"

Blair shrugged. "We're still getting the questions every time I'm out in public, but there isn't much more to say than what we've already said. For the time being, the newshounds are content with their usual speculations."

"Well, I suppose that's the best you could hope for then."

"Apparently." Blair gave a start as she spied Diane talking with another woman on the far side of the room. "Would you excuse me for a few minutes?"

"Of course. I want to have some time alone with these wonderful paintings."

Blair kissed Marcea on the cheek and headed across the room to where Diane stood with Valerie Ross. Singly, either woman would have been considered striking. Both were blond, fair skinned, fine boned and classically beautiful, and both radiated sensuality and confidence. Standing side by side, however, they were breathtaking.

Diane radiated the golden heat of sunlight. Her body language and sultry voice always reminded Blair of a young Lauren Bacall. In contrast, Valerie—Claire—was Bergman. Deceptively cool and remote on the surface, but ice was capable of burning, too. Under other circumstances, Blair would have enjoyed watching the two of them together, would have enjoyed speculating how one, or both, might have responded to her in an intimate setting. Now, she registered their individual magnetism and how together their allure was magnified, but she felt no compulsion, no desire, to experience any part of it herself.

The two women were so deep in conversation that they did not notice Blair until she stood beside them. "Good evening."

"Blair!" Diane kissed her cheek, then indicated her companion. "This is Valerie Ross, one of the art dealers here for the preview. This is her first time with us."

Blair looked into Valerie's eyes as she extended her hand, noticing as she hadn't that night in DC under the dim glow of the streetlights how piercingly intelligent those blue eyes were. "Blair Powell, Ms. Ross."

"Hello."

"I'm happy that you could join us this evening," Blair said smoothly as she released Valerie's hand. The other woman's grip had been firm, her palm warm and dry. She didn't appear nervous, but she was watching Blair intently.

"I have a client who saw one of your works in San Francisco not long ago and was very interested in what you're showing here."

Blair frowned. "San Francisco? I didn't show anything..." She laughed. "The sketch that Marcea Casells included in her recent show?"

Valerie nodded. "Yes. Apparently my client was quite captivated by it and was finally able to cajole Ms. Casells into revealing your name. I hope I haven't gotten her into any trouble."

"Not at all. Have you had a chance to look around this evening?"

"I've only just arrived." Valerie gave Diane a slow smile. "Ms. Bleeker and I were getting acquainted."

Blair was astounded to see Diane blush. She didn't think she'd ever witnessed that particular reaction from her friend before. "Is there anything in particular you're interested in?"

"My *client*," Valerie responded with the slightest emphasis on the word, "has rather eclectic tastes. I thought I'd just wander around for a few minutes. If you don't mind?"

"Absolutely," Diane interjected, resuming her role as Blair's agent. "Take your time. If you have any questions, I'd be more than happy to answer them, or, I'm certain, Ms. Powell would." She looked at Blair questioningly.

"Of course. I'd be happy to." Blair gestured to the small bar on the far side of the room. "I was just about to get a glass of wine. Would you like one?"

"Yes, that would be lovely."

"I'll see you later, then, Diane," Blair said as she and Valerie turned away.

As they moved through the crowd, Valerie said in a low tone, "I'm sorry. This is awkward. The invitation said it was a private pre-opening showing. Would you like me to leave?"

They had reached the bar, and Blair merely replied, "White wine?"

When Valerie nodded, Blair asked the tuxedoed woman managing the drinks for two glasses and handed one to her companion. She led Valerie to an out-of-the-way spot before speaking again. "*Is* there a client?"

Valerie's sculpted eyebrows rose. "Yes. A rather wealthy one who I'm quite sure will be making a purchase."

"Cam is here."

"Yes, I saw her."

"Is she any part of the reason that you're here?"

Valerie held Blair's gaze steadily. "No."

Blair sipped her wine and nodded. "I'm an artist, Valerie, and you're an art dealer. If Diane invited you, then she believes it's important for you to be here. So I'm pleased that you're here as well."

"Thank you, Ms. Powell." Valerie tasted the wine. It was a very good white burgundy, much better than the average fare at such gatherings. "Would you prefer that I not speak to Cameron?"

Cameron. Blair took a long slow breath, the corner of her

mouth finally lifting in a faint smile. "I doubt there's a lesbian on the planet immune to your charms, but I trust Cam to resist."

Valerie laughed, her alto voice rich and full. "Should I ask if those legions include you?"

"You can ask," Blair replied.

"No, I don't need to." Briefly, Valerie looked past Blair, finding Cam in the crowd. "I already know the answer. I do want to see your work, and I have work of my own to do. At some point, I'd like to say hello to...an old friend."

"I understand." Blair extended her hand. "Please let me know if there's anything you'd like to know about the paintings."

"I will. Thank you. It was nice meeting you, Ms. Powell."

Blair nodded. "And you, Ms. Ross."

2125 7 September 2001

Cam watched the encounter, her expression impassive. Blair and *Valerie* appeared intensely engaged, but there didn't appear to be any sign of imminent bloodshed. She hadn't really expected there to be. If Blair had not wanted Valerie to attend, she would have said so. And Valerie was much too savvy and sophisticated to be anything other than totally decorous. And, most importantly, Valerie knew that Cam loved Blair, and that whatever they might have shared belonged to the past. In fact, their relationship belonged to a completely different lifetime.

Cam checked her watch. One minute. She keyed her mic to the open channel for all of her agents. "All teams—no one enters the building from this point on, regardless of invitation. Copy?"

A chorus of affirmatives sounded as Cam made her way through the crowd to Blair's side. "Everything all right?"

"Mmm." Blair curled her fingers around the inside of Cam's forearm. "Yes. Fine. You?"

"Sure." At that moment, Cam heard the commotion that she had been expecting and reached for Blair's hand. "I'm so proud of you."

Confused, Blair looked at Cam and then toward the rear of the gallery where a tall, thin African American man entered, followed closely by two more Secret Service agents, Lucinda Washburn, and her father. "Oh my God. Dad!"

The president spied Blair and, grinning broadly, crossed the room with his customary purposeful stride, Lucinda at his side. He kissed a still-stunned Blair. "Hi, honey."

"Dad? Luce?" Blair stared at Cam. "Did you know about this?"

"Only since this morning. And I was sworn to secrecy," she hastily added.

"Don't blame Cam. I wanted to surprise you," the president said, "and you know that I can't go anywhere without someone announcing it. We didn't even let her tell her own team."

"This is so..." Blair put her arms around her father's neck and hugged him. Voice choked, she murmured, "Thank you so much."

"Don't thank me, honey," Andrew Powell whispered. "I love you."

Blair hugged him once more and then stepped back, her smile brilliant. "So, do you two want to look around?"

"How about a guided tour?"

Blair, flanked by her father and Lucinda, turned and headed toward the front of the gallery. Tom Turner, the president's security chief, fell into step with them along with the other agents.

"This has got to be the most exciting gallery showing *I've* ever been to," Valerie remarked as she stepped up to Cam's side.

Cam looked into the familiar blue eyes, her own impenetrable. "Have you been to many?"

"Quite a few, over the years."

"Are things going well?" Cam followed Blair with her eyes even as she spoke to the woman with whom she had once shared a part of herself, perhaps even a part of her heart.

"Yes. There don't seem to be any repercussions from the situation in DC."

"Good." Cam glanced at Valerie. "I'm glad."

"Well, I only wanted to say hello. And to wish you happiness, Cameron."

"Thank you." Cam smiled. "You, too. Valerie."

As Valerie moved off into the crowd, Cam's gaze had already returned to Blair.

CHAPTER TWENTY-EIGHT

1000 09Sep01

Report: Team One's pilot and six other
men checked out of the Panther Hotel in
Deerfield Beach, Florida. Destination:
Boston.

1005 9 September 2001

At the sound of footsteps, Diane looked up from where she sat reading the morning paper on her tiny balcony overlooking Central Park. "Good morning! I can't believe you're up before Cam."

"Neither can I," Blair said as she sat in the tan canvas director's chair opposite her friend and balanced a full cup of coffee on her knee. "She has to be totally exhausted not to wake up before this."

"Well, the reception last night *did* go on until almost four. And the two of you *have* been running around like maniacs for a month straight."

Blair, wearing only a borrowed T-shirt and her briefs, stretched out her legs and sipped her coffee. "I know. And she's not only had to worry about my security, she's had to worry about...my health."

"I'm sure she can handle it, but these few extra hours of sleep will probably help." Out of habit, Diane lowered her voice unnecessarily. "Where are the rest of your spookies?"

"Probably down on the street with the vehicle. They usually hang around in case I decide to go out wandering."

"You haven't done much of that in the last six months," Diane commented dryly.

"No." Blair smiled softly, thinking that the restless urge to escape her own life had abated since she'd fallen in love with Cam. "I'm getting downright boring."

"Oh, right." Diane snorted. "I wouldn't stray too far from home either if I had that woman of yours waiting for me."

Blair grinned, then sighed and leaned her head back, squinting into the sun. "God, what a weekend."

"Yes," Diane said fervently. "An *excellent* weekend. Between the Friday and Saturday shows, we sold a total of six paintings, and I anticipate at least four more will go before the end of the week. You, my love, are a great success."

"Maybe." Blair turned her head to regard Diane, her expression pensive. "Or maybe they just want to own something painted by the president's daughter."

"Darling, people do not spend thousands of dollars for souvenirs. Trust me, I know these buyers. And *they* know art."

Blair blushed. "You think?"

"God, I *know*." Diane's voice was a combination of fond exasperation and mild irritation. "Just because I'm your friend doesn't mean that I don't know my business. Because I do, and I wouldn't represent you if you weren't going to make me rich."

"I know, I know." Laughing, Blair propped a bare foot up on the railing.

With forced casualness, Diane asked, "So, what do you think of Valerie Ross?"

"Uh...well, I only spoke with her for a few minutes."

Diane arched her brow. "As I recall, it was closer to ten minutes. And did it really take you more than *one* to form an impression?"

"No, actually, it took about thirty seconds—maybe less. She's gorgeous, sophisticated, intelligent, and...well, I guess, sexy."

"You *guess?*"

"Okay, she's sexy." Blair pushed upright and regarded Diane intently. "Is this simply an academic discussion or does it have a point?"

"I really don't know." Diane sighed. "Her name first came to my attention about six months ago in conjunction with a large sale at another gallery. And she's currently representing a client whom

I know to be a generous buyer. That's why I extended an early invitation to her."

"Uh-huh. That's business. What about the rest?" For the second time in two days, Blair was surprised to see Diane blush. "Ooh, there *is* something going on."

"No," Diane said with a swift shake of her head. "There really isn't. She gave me her card along with an invitation to call her. She's in town for a few more days."

Carefully, Blair asked, "And are you going to?"

Diane turned in her chair, curling one silk-pajama-clad leg beneath her, and met Blair's probing gaze. "I don't know."

"Why? Did something about her bother you?"

"No." Diane toyed with the corner of the newspaper lying in her lap. "Well, yes."

Blair waited.

"Everything about her attracted me."

"Ahh, I see."

"No, I don't think you do." Diane considered how intense the connection with Valerie—a woman whom she barely knew—had seemed from the beginning. She'd not felt that kind of instant synergy with anyone in more years than she could remember. "I'm not sure that even *I* see."

Blair thought of what she knew, and did not know, about Valerie Ross. The only thing she was certain of was that Valerie had meant something to Cam, and Cam would not have trusted a woman who was not worthy of it. In her own brief conversations with Valerie, she had sensed both honor and integrity. *Is there anything else that really matters?*

"I think," Blair said gently, reaching out a hand to her best friend, "that if she affected you that much, then you should make that phone call."

"You don't think I'm being...rash?" Diane asked softly.

Blair laughed. "And if you are?"

Diane smiled ruefully. "Yes, I suppose there are far worse things than losing at love."

"Yes," Blair murmured. "And if you don't try, you can't win."

1115 9 September 2001

Cam walked out of the bathroom naked, toweling her hair. Blair sat on the edge of the bed with a cup of coffee. Another sat beside her on the nightstand.

"Hey," Cam said. "You abandoned me this morning."

"I didn't have the heart to wake you." Blair swung her legs up onto the bed and leaned back against the pillows, watching her lover with an appreciative smile. "You were really out."

"I always seem to sleep like the dead after we make love." Cam leaned down and kissed Blair's mouth. "I had a great time last night."

"At the gallery?" Blair's tone was teasing.

"Yes," Cam replied seriously as she straightened up. "And back here afterward, too. I especially liked the part where you begged me to—" She ducked as a pillow sailed toward her head.

"Be careful, Commander," Blair threatened. "I have ways of making your life hell."

Cam grinned. "Where's Diane?"

"She went out. A brunch date."

"Ah, sorry I missed her." Cam reached for her trousers, which she'd left across a chair the night before. "I guess it's time for me to check in with the team."

"Diane's having brunch with Valerie," Blair added quietly.

Cam picked up her pants, stepped into them, and, her expression unchanged, zipped the fly. "Really."

"Yes. A spur-of-the-moment thing." Blair's tone was neutral, but she watched her lover's face carefully. "Does that bother you?"

"Not for the reasons you might be thinking," Cam said gently. Still shirtless, she sat on the side of the bed and reached for the coffee Blair had brought for her. "I don't have any romantic feelings for...Valerie. I like her. I also like Diane." She sipped the coffee, her eyes on Blair. "But I love you, and Diane's your best friend. You're the one I care about."

"What do I have to do with it?"

"How are you going to feel if they start seeing one another seriously?"

Blair shrugged. "I honestly don't know. It's been a long time since Diane has had a real relationship. That can change things in a friendship, and I suppose it would take some adjusting on my part."

"Has our being together changed things for you and Diane?"

"I don't think so, but then most of the time we still see each other alone."

Cam nodded. "Diane doesn't know anything about Valerie's past, does she?"

"I don't see how she could, they just met." Blair sighed. "Do you think Valerie will tell her?"

"I don't know. But if she does, she won't mention me." Cam set the cup aside and covered Blair's hand where it lay on the bed with her own. "But *you* know. And if they're seeing each other, Diane would probably want the four of us to spend some time together. That would only be natural."

"Yes, I've thought of that." Blair gazed past Cam, her eyes distant, an image of Valerie in her mind. "I actually rather like Valerie myself." She looked back at Cam. "But she's beautiful and accomplished and sexy, and I'm not entirely certain that I could be trusted to behave rationally if she were anywhere near you."

"Jesus. Well. That could be dicey, then." Cam rubbed her forehead. "I guess we'll have to wait and see what happens between them."

"I suppose it would be good impulse-control training," Blair mused.

"I need you to believe me when I say that I'm not attracted to Valerie. And *she* knows that I love you and will respect that." Cam shifted onto the bed and put her arm around Blair's shoulders, relieved when Blair turned into her and wrapped an arm around her waist. "You're the only woman in my life, in my heart. You're the only woman for me, forever."

"I do believe you," Blair said quietly. She rubbed her cheek against Cam's breast, more for comfort than anything else. "I'm just so *crazy* about you. Sometimes it still makes *me* a little crazy."

"That's okay." Cam kissed the top of Blair's head. "I love you a little crazy, I just don't want you ever to doubt what we have."

"I don't doubt it. Sometimes I just worry I'll lose it."

"You won't." Cam turned swiftly and moved on top of Blair, fitting her thigh between Blair's legs. With one hand, she reached down and pulled Blair's T-shirt up, exposing her breasts and abdomen. As she kissed her, she stroked her fingers along Blair's side and down her thigh. When she felt Blair's breath quicken and her body rise to meet hers, Cam lowered her head and kissed Blair's breast. She ran her tongue lightly around Blair's nipple, then flicked it until it stiffened against her lips. "Do you have anywhere to be for the next hour or so?"

"No." Blair's voice was already thick with need.

Cam slipped her fingers beneath Blair's briefs and pushed them down, lifting her hips so that Blair could free herself of the garment. Then she slid down on the bed until her bare breasts nestled between Blair's legs. Looking up, she met Blair's hazy blue gaze. "Good."

0900 10Sep2001

> Report: Strike Team One pilots have departed for Portland, Maine. Remaining members of Teams One and Two have secured accommodations at Boston area hotels.

1230 10 September 2001

"There's something particularly sinful about leaving the office in the middle of the day," Renee Savard remarked as she leaned back into Stark's arms. They sat on the grass atop a knoll that overlooked the Pond in Central Park. Although the walking path was only fifteen yards behind them, they were secluded from casual view by the trees and shrubs that bordered one of the most idyllic spots in the park.

"Oh, I don't know." Stark clasped her arms loosely around Renee's waist, settled her chest against Renee's back, and nuzzled her lips behind her lover's ear. "Everybody's entitled to a lunch hour, even important FBI agents."

"Yes," Renee laughed and tilted her head back, turning her

face to kiss Stark's neck, "but I don't think they're supposed to sneak off to meet their lovers in Central Park."

"Well, we could've gone with my idea."

"Oh, sure," Renee scoffed. "I'd *really* be able to go back to the office and pore through a hundred field reports about potential subversive activity after having a nooner with you."

"Do you think it will be any easier going back to work thinking about it?" Stark nibbled on Renee's earlobe. "But not having *done* anything?"

"If I didn't know better, I'd think you were trying to tease me." Renee snugged her hips a little tighter into the space between Stark's legs and wrapped her arm around the outside of Stark's thigh. She smoothed her palm up and down the undersurface of her lover's leg.

"Oh, right," Stark said, her voice husky. "And you're *not* teasing?"

"Nope. I'm just appreciating you."

"Could you appreciate me a little further north?"

"Not unless you want to risk getting arrested."

Stark sighed. "Actually, I'd almost take the chance. You make me feel so good, I can barely think of anything else."

Head cushioned on Stark's shoulder, Renee regarded her tenderly. "Do you know that I spend 90 percent of my waking hours thinking about making love with you?"

"I still can't believe you...want me."

"Oh, sweetie," Renee breathed, "I am certifiably crazy over you."

"I keep expecting to wake up and find out this was all some fabulous dream." Stark kissed the corner of Renee's mouth and held her more tightly. "I didn't have any idea how good it could be."

"Neither did I." *I'd even stopped dreaming.*

"You know," Stark said softly, rocking Renee gently in her embrace, "tomorrow will be three weeks since you came to stay with me."

"It seems so much longer sometimes, as if I'd always been there with you." Renee's tone was quiet, uncharacteristically subdued. Contemplatively, she ran her fingertips up and down the trouser seam on the inside of Stark's leg. "But you're right.

Tomorrow our trial living-together period will be over."

"Uh-huh." Cautiously, Stark asked, "So, where do we go from here?"

"I guess we need to talk about that."

"I have the split shift tonight—I won't be home until late."

"Mmm, and we'll both have to be up and out again early in the morning." Renee kissed Stark's neck. "I think we should go out to dinner tomorrow night, some place secluded and romantic."

"That sounds kind of positive." Stark's heart was suddenly racing. *Say you'll stay.* "Are you going to give me a hint?"

"Oh, I don't think so." Renee curved her arm back and spread her fingers into Stark's hair, drawing her head down. Against Stark's mouth, she whispered, "Just remember how good it is when I make you wait."

Closing her eyes, Stark groaned softly just before Renee's kiss claimed her.

2330 10Sep01

The phone rang in a back room in a dingy apartment in Chelsea.

"Yeah," the Patriot leader rasped.

"Our target has returned to the nest. We have a green light."

"How many opposition forces can we anticipate?" The heavyset man gave a thumbs-up sign to his three comrades, who sat around a low table cleaning their rifles and readying for the morning assault.

"The routine briefing will be over by 0830, and only the day team will be on-site. Three, maybe four people in the command center, and one in the lobby." In a flat, emotionless tone, the Secret Service agent went on, "I'll handle things upstairs while you eliminate the person on the door and secure the exits."

"What about Roberts?"

"I'll make certain she doesn't get in the way."

"Tomorrow is the dawn of a new era in this country," the large man in the khaki fatigues said fervently. "And may God bless us all."

CHAPTER TWENTY-NINE

0430 11Sep01
Patriot encampment, Tennessee

General Matheson, in a crisp, starched khaki uniform with his rank insignia gleaming on his collar, sat down behind his desk and with a steady hand opened a predetermined satellite channel to monitor the real-time events that were about to reshape history and define his destiny. He pictured a heavily bearded man in coarse, dirty robes, crouched in the caves of his mountain stronghold half a world away, doing the same. They were not compatriots, merely temporary allies forged by necessity, and though their motivations differed, their goal was the same—to demonstrate to the world the weakness and decay at the heart of the greatest superpower history had ever known.

Whatever success their parallel battle plans achieved, life as they knew it was about to change forever.

0500 11 September 2001

Cam awakened without the benefit of the alarm, slipped quickly from bed, and pulled a T-shirt and gym shorts from her bureau. She dressed quickly and walked to the window that faced Gramercy Park. Across the square, above the trees, she could see the windows of Blair's loft. They were dark now, but the lights had still been burning at 2:00 a.m. when she'd finally gone to bed. She imagined that Blair had been painting, or perhaps reading, and when she herself had been unable to fall asleep, she'd briefly contemplated calling her. She had resisted the impulse, however, because sometimes hearing Blair's voice and knowing that she was so close was harder to bear than the simple pain of missing her.

With a sigh, Cam pushed the nonproductive thoughts away and buckled on a small pack containing her beeper, cell phone, weapon, and credentials.

After the briefing, I'll surprise Blair and take her out to breakfast. For once, her schedule is clear.

As she started her run, Cam thought fleetingly of how pleasant it would be to have a few unhurried hours with her lover.

0545 11Sep01

```
Report: Confirmed - Team One pilots
have passed through security check in
Portland, Maine. Departure as scheduled
for Logan Airport, Boston.
```

0550 11 September 2001

With her arm around Renee's waist and her breasts against Renee's back, Stark nuzzled her face in the sweet, warm skin of Renee's neck. "What kind of disciplinary action do you think we'd get if we skipped work today?"

Lazily, Renee turned onto her back and threaded both arms around Stark's neck, guiding her lover down on top of her. Lids heavy with the remnants of sleep and the first stirrings of desire, she murmured, "Do you have something besides duty in mind?"

"Oh, yeah," Stark said with a grin, settling her hips between Renee's thighs. "First I thought I'd start with this." She dipped her head and nipped the tip of Renee's chin, then licked the spot as Renee arched beneath her with a gasp of surprised pleasure. "And then," she ran her tongue slowly over Renee's lower lip, "I thou—"

"Sweetie," Renee interrupted, her voice pitched low and husky, "I have to leave in thirty-five minutes."

"Uh-huh." Stark lifted her head, a perplexed expression on

her face. "And your point is?"

Laughing, Renee reached up and brushed the hair from Stark's forehead. "You're going to wear me out."

"Is that even possible? Is there like some magic orgasm quota, and once you hit that number, you can't have any more?"

In a swift movement, Renee lifted her hips and rolled Stark over onto her back, following in one fluid motion until she straddled her. With her palm in the center of Stark's chest, she leaned forward, her breasts swaying in silent invitation. "If there is, I'm going to get there pretty fast, especially if you keep after me the way you have been."

"Jeez, you look so sexy when you sit on me like this." Stark lifted both hands and cupped Renee's breasts, brushing the tight pink nipples with her thumbs.

Surprised yet again, Renee arched into Stark's hands with a groan. "I love the way you touch me."

"That's good," Stark said, her throat dry and her stomach already simmering with need. "Because I can't seem to stop."

Renee dropped forward, catching herself with her palms on either side of Stark's shoulders, her breasts pressed into Stark's hands, her face inches above her lover's. She rocked her hips over Stark's stomach, slicking the soft skin with the warm, silken evidence of her desire. The tantalizing friction teased her already stiff clitoris, and her thighs trembled. Her eyes, glazed with urgent pleasure, found Stark's. "I don't want you to ever stop."

Before Stark could reply, Renee raised her hips and slid higher on the bed until she knelt just above Stark's face. Curling her fingers into Stark's hair, she held her head down while she lowered herself carefully to Stark's mouth. "One kiss."

With a groan, Stark wrapped her arms around Renee's hips as she took her into her mouth, thirsting for her passion. The wild heat and sweet scent overwhelmed her, and she closed her eyes to immerse herself in the wonder of her lover's desire.

Renee's stomach tightened at the first soft touch of Stark's tongue, and when the sharp pull of Stark's lips around her clitoris sent fire streaking along her spine, she pushed herself away and collapsed onto the bed, panting. "Okay. That will have to do until tonight."

"Oh my God," Stark exclaimed, rolling onto her side toward Renee and sliding one hand down Renee's abdomen, seeking entrance between her thighs. "I'll die. I mean it. I can't wait until tonight."

"You have a fabulous mouth," Renee gasped. "And I'm going to be thinking about it the entire day."

Stark stared in shock as Renee jumped from the bed and hurried naked toward the bathroom. Half a second later, she catapulted up in pursuit, shouting, "I'm going to make you pay for this!"

Outraged, delighted, and indescribably in love, Stark followed the beautiful sounds of her lover's laughter.

0800 11Sep01

> Report: Team One aboard American Airlines flight 11 has departed Logan Airport en route to Los Angeles. 81 passengers and 11 crew members.

0805 11 September 2001

"That's it, then," Cam finished. "Egret has no public appearances on the docket for the rest of the week, and her personal calendar is flexible. Standard shifts the rest of the week. She has a luncheon scheduled with the board members of the American Teacher's Association in DC on Saturday. Mac will go over those assignments tomorrow."

When she and Mac left the conference room to review reports and intelligence updates, the remaining agents began to gather their notes. The conversation was desultory as the night shift prepared to go off duty and the day shift sorted out their assignments.

Stark, the day-shift leader, looked toward Cynthia Parker. "You've got the lobby this morning, Cyn."

"Sure," Cynthia Parker replied. "I'll head down to relieve Foster as soon as I grab a cup of coffee."

Glancing at Felicia, Stark said, "You feel like joining me in the gym for a workout?"

"You go ahead. I'll join you as soon as I check my e-mail messages."

"No problem. See you there." Stark's nerves still jangled with an undercurrent of excitement and lingering arousal. An hour or so pumping iron sounded like just the antidote she required to clear her head.

0814 11Sep01

> Report: Confirmed - Team Two aboard United Airlines flight 175 has departed Logan Airport en route to Los Angeles. 56 passengers and 9 crew members.

0815 11 September 2001

"Everything looks to be routine, Mac," Cam said after a swift survey of the printouts that had come in from the various intelligence agencies. "I'm going to check in with Egret. We may be going out—I'll let you know."

"Sure, Commander." Mac rose as Cam left the room and crossed to the desk where Felicia sat studying her computer monitor.

"We haven't had much of a chance to talk lately," Mac said. When Felicia glanced up, a curious question in her eyes, he shrugged. "I know you're not interested in anything serious between us, but how about a friendly lunch sometime?"

"Do you really think that men and women can do anything that's *just* friendly?"

"I don't know," Mac answered honestly. "I'm not sure that I even *want* to where you're concerned. Maybe I'm hoping you'll change your mind when you discover what a nice guy I am."

Felicia couldn't help but smile. "Mac, I already know that." She studied his clear blue eyes, his handsome face, his gentle mouth. "Lunch would be nice."

0821 11Sep01

Report: Confirmed - Team Three aboard American Airlines flight 77 has departed Washington Dulles International Airport en route to Los Angeles. 58 passengers and 6 crew members.

0822 11 September 2001

"Hey," Blair exclaimed with pleasure, reaching out for Cam's hand and drawing her into the loft. She pushed the door closed and curled an arm around Cam's neck, pressing close to kiss her. "Mmm. This is a nice surprise."

Cam tightened her arms around Blair's waist and buried her face in her soft, fragrant hair. Silently, she just held on, filling the empty places inside with the comforting sense of her lover. Blair smelled of sunshine and sweet wildflowers.

"Cam?" Blair stroked Cam's neck and shoulders. "Darling? What's wrong?"

"Nothing," Cam replied, straightening. She kissed Blair once more, allowing the gentle heat of Blair's mouth to soothe the last sharp edges of her longing. "Just missed you."

"Then come to me, Cameron," Blair urged. "It's all right."

Cam smiled, the shadows in her eyes lifting. "I know, and I will. I'm still trying to judge how best to balance everything, that's all."

Her arms around Cam's waist now, Blair nodded. "I understand. But I miss you, too, every night when I close my eyes. Sometimes the only thing that keeps me from calling you is knowing that it will make things harder for you if I do."

"I love you." Cam kissed Blair once more. "So, if you're not already scheduled, how do you feel about joining me for a walk and breakfast somewhere?"

Delighted, Blair nodded. "Sounds perfect." She indicated her T-shirt and cotton pajama bottoms. "Let me grab a fast shower and change."

"Go ahead. I'll read the paper and wait."

0835 11 September 2001: Federal Aviation Administration has alerted the North American Aerospace Defense Command (NORAD) that American Airlines flight 11 has been hijacked.

0837 11 September 2001

The radio on Cam's belt crackled as Mac's voice sounded in the quiet loft.

"Commander, I think you should come downstairs."

Tossing the newspaper aside, Cam stood swiftly, alert to the concern in Mac's voice. "What is it?"

"I'm not sure, but I just received word that a commercial airliner has been hijacked in the Northeast corridor."

"I'll be right down." Cam crossed swiftly to the bathroom, opened the door, and called inside, "I need to check something with Mac. I'll be back."

"All right," Blair answered from the shower. "I'll see you in a few minutes."

0842 11Sep01

Report: Confirmed - Team Four aboard United Airlines flight 93 en route to San Francisco has departed from Newark Airport. 38 passengers and 7 crew members.

0843 11 September 2001

The instant Cam walked into the command center, she knew

from the expression on Mac's face that there was a serious problem. "Report."

"Look at this." Mac indicated the computer screen where he was monitoring encrypted messages transmitted from the Department of Defense to a select group of high-level recipients.

0843 11 September 2001: The FAA has notified NORAD that United Airlines flight 175 from Boston to LAX has been hijacked.

"That's the second plane." Mac's voice was flat, devoid of emotion. His body, however, was rigid with tension.

Two of them at once. Cam felt an instant unease and glanced at the bank of monitors that showed the building's exterior, the lobby, and the stairwells. Nothing seemed amiss—Foster and Parker were visible talking at the desk in the lobby. The street outside was clear. She turned her attention back to the computer as another message appeared.

0844 11 September 2001: NORAD has scrambled two F-15 fighters from Otis Air National Guard Base in Falmouth, Massachusetts on intercept course to New York City.

"Whatever's going on, someone thinks it's headed this way." Mac's hands were clenched on the desktop.

"Call Captain Landry and see if you can get a local update from the NYPD." Cam's voice was tight, her mind sorting possibilities and struggling to make sense of something that could not be rationalized by a sane mind.

"Roger that," Mac responded grimly. As he reached for the phone, Cam gripped his shoulder hard.

"Wait."

Mac swiveled back to his console, and as he read, his blood ran cold.

0847 11 September 2001: American
Airlines flight 11 has crashed into
the North Tower of the World Trade
Center.

It had begun.

"Oh my God," Mac uttered in a hushed, stunned voice.

It made no sense. It was inconceivable. It was too monumental to be absorbed.

Cam narrowed her eyes and focused on her duty, which was all that she could do in the face of such horror. "We're evacuating. *Now.* Advise Stark to get the cars."

Out of habit, Mac swept the bank of monitors to his right.

"Commander!"

Cam followed his gaze, a tight fist closing around her heart. On the monitor, four shadowy figures burst through the lobby door, automatic weapons raised. Cynthia Parker came out from behind the counter, her extended arms jerking slightly as she discharged her service weapon. The first man through the door fell. The one immediately behind him leveled his weapon and the muzzle flashed. In the eerie silence of the black-and-white tableau, Parker's body lifted from the floor and flew backward, disappearing out of range of the cameras.

"Signal red alert and lock us down," Cam snapped, drawing her automatic. "Evacuate through the rear. Use the stairs."

As Cam ran toward the stairwell to reach the penthouse and her lover, Foster stepped from the elevator into the foyer outside Blair's door.

CHAPTER THIRTY

0900 11 September 2001 (Sarasota, Florida): The president of the United States has been informed by the White House chief of staff that a plane has crashed into the World Trade Center.

Stark heard her radio sound a red alert at the same instant Mac burst through the doors of the gym. *Red alert—a direct assault on Egret.* She didn't need to know anything else; she was already on her feet and reaching for her weapon. Across the room, Felicia did the same.

"Stark, back up the commander in the Aerie," Mac gasped, his pale face streaked with sweat despite the cool, air-conditioned atmosphere in the command center. "Felicia, we need to get the cars."

There was no time for questions or explanations. There was no conversation at all as Felicia immediately disappeared with Mac. Stark raced down the narrow corridor outside the gym toward the stairwell at its end, her heart thundering with the adrenaline rush, but her mind completely clear. She had trained for this moment for years. She darted into the equipment room and grabbed a bulletproof vest. One was all she could carry, but one was all she needed. Less than thirty seconds after Mac's orders, she was in the stairwell. As she pounded up the stairs, taking two at a time, a brief shaft of light streaked across her line of vision, and she knew that someone had just gone through the door above into the penthouse foyer.

0901 11 September 2001

When the knock sounded at her door, Blair settled a navy blue New York Yankees baseball cap over her hair, tucked her wallet into the back pocket of her jeans, and crossed the loft with a rush of anticipation. She and Cam so rarely had unscheduled time together that this unexpected outing felt like a gift.

Maybe after breakfast, I can talk Cam into going off-radio for a few hours. Diane won't mind if we make an unplanned visit. God, only two days and it feels like forever since we've been alone together.

Her mind preoccupied with sweet remembrances of her last moments in Cam's arms and the promise of pleasures to come, she pulled open the door.

0902 11 September 2001: United Airlines flight 75 has crashed into the South Tower of the World Trade Center, demolishing floors 78 through 87.

0903 11 September 2001

Cam shouldered through the heavy metal stairwell door twenty feet from where Foster stood in front of Blair's apartment. In a fraction of a second, time slowed and her vision tunneled until all she saw was the man, the weapon raised in his hand, and the door to her lover's loft swinging open.

There was no time for analysis. No time for reason. The rules had been altered forever at 8:45 a.m., September 11, 2001.

"Foster," she shouted, leveling her automatic, "drop the weapon!"

When he heard his name, Foster hesitated in the act of centering his weapon on Blair Powell's chest. Swiftly, he swung to his left in the direction from which the command had come, preparing to fire.

Cam didn't hesitate. She knew only one thing, the only thing that mattered. Secret Service Agent Foster's automatic had been pointed at the most important person in her world.

She shot him through the forehead, and he dropped without a sound.

Then she was running, Blair's scream replacing the silence that had filled her mind since she'd seen the assault team come through the lobby door and kill her agent.

"Oh my God, Cam!" Blair stood in the doorway, staring at Foster's inert form, the blood pooling beneath his head and soaking into the Oriental carpet beneath his body. Her eyes wide with shock, she stared at her lover's grim face. Cam's eyes were hard, darker than Blair had ever seen them. "What's happening?"

"We're under attack. Let's go."

At that moment, Cam heard the stairwell door opening behind her. She shouldered Blair back into her apartment and pivoted toward the stairs, crouching into a firing stance.

"Commander, all clear," Stark shouted as she ran up, breathing hard but her voice steady.

Swiftly, Cam took the Kevlar vest from her and extended it to Blair. "Put this on." Then she bent down, picked up Foster's service automatic from where it lay by his lifeless right hand, and held it out to her lover. "Can you use this?"

"Yes," Blair replied, the faintest tremor in her voice. She shrugged into the vest, knowing there was no time to argue and knowing that she couldn't. Whatever had happened, Cam was in charge. Had to be in charge. There could only be one leader in moments like this.

"Good," Cam said. "Don't hesitate to fire, even on one of us. Let's go."

Blair gripped the gun tightly, swallowed back the bile that rose in her throat, and nodded. "All right."

With Stark in the lead, Cam took Blair's arm and kept her close as they rushed to the stairwell and started down. Their footsteps clattered eerily, amplified by the utter stillness in the stairwell after the thundering sound of the gunshot in the foyer. As they approached each landing, Stark trained her weapon on the door until Cam and Blair had passed, then skirted around them to lead the way down to the next floor.

The journey seemed endless, but it was only minutes before they reached the basement level that opened into a small service area at the rear of the building.

"Stay inside against the wall," Cam said curtly as she swept her arm across Blair's chest and pressed her lover against the concrete. "Do *not* come out unless you hear the order from me or Stark. If you don't get an all clear, go back upstairs and lock yourself in the command center." Cam held Blair's gaze for one fierce moment, then turned to Stark, who had taken a position on the opposite side of the door. "On three."

Stark two-fisted her weapon, raised it to chest level, and nodded.

Blair knew what the two women were going to do. They were going to go through that door, not knowing what was on the other side, prepared to fire or be fired upon. Neither woman was wearing body armor. In a matter of seconds, they could both be dead. She knew it, but she couldn't fathom it. Life couldn't be that precarious, could it? But of course, she knew that it could. "I love you."

Blair thought she'd spoken the words aloud, but she wasn't certain as she heard Cam begin the count in a strong, steady voice.

"One...two...three."

Cam and Stark pushed through the door together, Stark swinging her arms in an arc to the left as Cam swung right. The small turnaround was empty. Just as two black Suburbans careened up the alley, Cam heard a muted blast from somewhere inside the building and felt a faint tremor. She turned back into the basement, grasped Blair's arm and pulled her outside, handing her over to Stark.

"They just blew the stairwell doors from the lobby. Get her into the vehicle. Move. Move!"

The vehicles screeched to a halt, and Mac and Felicia jumped out. Stark herded Blair toward the open rear doors of the nearest vehicle. Blair looked over her shoulder for Cam, who covered their retreat, and caught the hint of movement in the doorway.

"Cam!" Blair screamed in warning.

Moving as one, Cam and Stark closed ranks, shoulder to shoulder, putting themselves between the building and Blair, while

Felicia grabbed the president's daughter around the waist and threw her bodily into the rear of the vehicle. Then the air erupted with the sound of gunfire and the acrid smell of cordite.

The first man to exit the building, automatic rifle blasting, went down amidst a fusillade of bullets. Out of the corner of her eye, Cam saw Mac drop his weapon and fly backward against the other Suburban before sliding to the ground. She fired in the direction of the building while backing toward the vehicle that held the president's daughter. Beside her, Stark did the same. They'd almost reached the cover of the open Suburban doors when Stark uttered a sharp cry, staggered a few steps, and then regained her footing.

Cam emptied her weapon in the direction of the last man standing and, reaching for the extra clip on her belt, blinked sweat from her eyes. No one returned fire. Her vision was blurry and the air in her lungs burned with every breath. She turned, afraid of what she might see. Stark leaned against the vehicle, partially shielding the interior with her body, a red stain high on the right arm of her T-shirt. The tension in Cam's chest eased when she saw Blair, kneeling on the backseat of the Suburban, Foster's automatic trained on the rear of the building.

Oh, Jesus, she's all right. Panting, Cam rasped hoarsely, "Davis, you hit?"

"No, I'm okay," Felicia shouted, already running toward Mac. He lay on his back, both hands clamped to his side. Blood ran in rivulets between his fingers, soaking his shirt and pants, and dripped into a spreading pool beneath his body. His face was white, his eyes glazed. "Oh my God, Mac."

"Davis," Cam commanded, stopping Felicia in her tracks. "Get in the car. You're driving."

Evacuating Egret had to be her priority. Everything and everyone else was secondary. Felicia looked up from Mac's body, eyes wide with shock, as Cam appeared beside her.

"*Now,* Davis," Cam snapped. Then she leaned down next to Mac and put her reloaded automatic into his hand. "Mac. Can you hear me?"

"Yes." His voice was hollow, but he focused on her face.

"I'll radio your location. You just have to hold on."

"Yes, ma'am." He closed his fingers weakly around the automatic. "Go."

"Stay awake, Mac." Cam gripped his shoulder for a second, then ran back toward the Suburban, which Felicia was edging around the second vehicle that Mac had been driving. Cam threw herself into the backseat, pulled the door closed, and shouted, "Get us out of here, Davis."

"Where?" Davis's voice was steady, her hands clenched on the wheel.

Cam focused on her lover. "Blair. Are you hurt?"

"No." Blair felt calm. Far too calm. "You are. So is Stark. You're both bleeding."

"Commander, extraction plan?" Davis inquired again from the front seat. She was driving north on First Avenue. The air reverberated with the wail of sirens. It sounded as if every emergency vehicle in the city was in motion.

"Just keep going—we have to get out of the city." As she spoke, Cam fumbled for her cell phone and took Foster's gun from Blair. "And Davis, raise emergency services. Get someone down there for Mac—Priority One."

"I'll do that, Commander," Stark said hoarsely. Her right arm shook and burned, but she had feeling in her fingers, and the pain wasn't much worse than the ache in her legs after a ten-mile run. She cradled the phone in the palm of her right hand and punched in numbers with her left. Every agent on Blair's team was familiar with the priority numbers in the event of an emergency involving the first daughter.

"Good," Cam responded. Thinking of the devastation at the World Trade Center, she could only imagine the chaos that must be overtaking not just the city, but the entire nation. "I'll try to raise Landers and secure an NYPD escort, but we may be on our own."

0912 11 September 2001: The Port Authority of New York and New Jersey has ordered that all bridges and tunnels in the metropolitan area be closed.

0918 11 September 2001

"Cam, let me look at you." Blair put her fingers beneath Cam's chin and turned her lover's head toward her. Her stomach lurched at the sight of blood running down the right side of her face. "You need medical attention."

"I'm all right." Cam clenched her teeth as she held the phone to her left ear. The dispatcher who had picked up the priority line at Captain Stacy Landers's extension had sounded breathless and close to panic. She'd put Cam on hold. "Davis, turn on the scanner."

"Darling," Blair insisted quietly. "I think you've been shot."

"Ricochet probably. See to Stark, would you?"

Across from them, Stark enunciated Blair's address in clear, sharp tones. "Rear of the building, federal agent down. Repeat, federal agent down. ETA?" Her face lost all remaining color. "*What?...* Yes. Yes. Copy."

Stark closed the phone and stared, stunned, at Cam. "He said that both towers of the World Trade Center have been hit by hijacked airliners."

"Yes. Right before the assault on the command center."

"All those people," Blair gasped. "Cam, what's happening?"

"How bad is it?" Stark asked, her voice wavering for the first time since the assault had begun. *Renee. Renee is there somewhere.* She felt something that she hadn't felt even when she'd been standing in the midst of a hail of bullets. Agonizing, gut-wrenching fear. "Do we know anything about casualties?"

"I don't have any details. The only thing I know for sure is that we're under attack, and the city is not secure." Cam straightened as a voice finally sounded in her phone. "This is Trailblazer One. We need immediate coordinates for evacuation." She gave their current location, then listened. "Understood. Yes." She glanced at her watch. "ETA ten minutes. Clear the way for us." Cam closed the phone and leaned forward to speak to Davis. At the sudden movement, a wave of dizziness took her by surprise, and she was forced to close her eyes against the unexpected vertigo. She sucked in a sharp breath and braced her arm against the seat to steady herself.

"Cam?" Blair touched her lover's shoulder with concern. The bleeding had slowed to a trickle, but Cam's face was ashen. Suddenly, Blair's heart seized. There'd been so many shots, so many. Maybe Cam was hurt somewhere else. "Darling, please. Lean back. Let me look at you."

Blair's voice floated to her from far away, a lilting sound that made Cam want to drift on the sweetness of it and just sleep. Blinking several times, Cam shook her head vigorously, the movement causing the pounding behind her eyes to escalate and her mind to clear behind the surge of pain. Hoarsely, she instructed, "Davis. Evacuation route Bravo. No escort, but they'll clear the bridge for us."

"Yes, Commander." Felicia stared straight ahead, deftly maneuvering the Suburban through the ever-increasing traffic. She knew her job. She knew her duty. She functioned as the well-trained professional she was, but all she could think about was Mac. He might be dying, and he was alone. *How can this be happening?*

CHAPTER THIRTY-ONE

0926 11 September 2001: The FAA has ordered all nonmilitary planes grounded and has canceled all flights in the United States.

0930 11 September 2001

"Davis, I'm patching NYPD traffic control through to you," Cam said. "They'll plot a route out of here for us."

Silently, Felicia adjusted the earphone from the NavCom, struggling to keep the image of Mac lying helpless and bleeding at bay while focusing on the directions relayed to her by an adrenaline-charged NYPD officer.

While Cam watched the street for signs of further attack, Foster's confiscated weapon in one hand and her cell phone in the other, Blair fought to clear her head of the kaleidoscope of nightmarish sounds and images that followed fast one upon the other. She could still hear the gunfire, smell the metallic odor of the bullets, see the neat round hole blossoming red in the center of Foster's forehead and Mac's body bouncing off the Suburban and crumpling to the ground. If all that weren't horror enough, she had visions of the tens of thousands of people in the World Trade Center who might be trapped, injured, or dying as a result of the plane crashes. It was more than she could absorb. Then a cold hand clamped around her heart. *If we're under this kind of attack* here, *what else might be happening?* "Cam! My fath—"

Shaking her head, Cam signaled with a tilt of her chin that she had an incoming call. "Roberts." She spared Blair a glance, her heart twisting at the panic she saw in her lover's eyes. She wanted to offer comfort, but she simply didn't have time. They weren't safe yet. "Egret is secure, but we've taken fire. I have casualties." She listened intently, narrowing her eyes against the throbbing pain at the base of her skull. "Negative...we've been internally compromised...Not in my opinion, no." She shook her head, and then regretted it as her stomach heaved. "No sign of pursuit. Negative...I am *not* relaying my position. I will advise when I've determined that we are secure." She shook her head again, the pain eclipsed by anger and frustration. "On *my* authority."

Abruptly, Cam terminated the call, rested her head against the seat, and closed her eyes for a second. Mercifully, the nausea subsided. She opened her eyes and met Blair's. "That was the White House security chief. The president is safe. He's in the air, location and destination unknown."

"Thank God." Blair studied Cam intently, noting the fine mist of sweat on her forehead. "You don't look well."

"I'm all right."

"Cam—"

Cam set the phone aside and rested her fingers on the top of Blair's hand. "My head took a glancing hit and it's stirred up the headache. Not too bad."

Blair bit back another question. There was nothing to be done—Cam had to do what she was doing. "What were you arguing about with the White House?"

"The Armageddon protocol has been set in motion, and the idiots don't understand our situation here."

"What do you mean?" Blair asked quietly. She'd never heard Cam say anything quite so critical of her superiors. The Armageddon protocol, she knew, was a response plan initially orchestrated by the Reagan administration in preparation for a nuclear attack or some other massive strike aimed at eliminating the president and other high-ranking federal officials. A shadow government consisting of a predetermined list of appointees would be sequestered in undisclosed, secure locations until the threat was contained. Such action would ensure that the government would continue to function even if the president, his staff, and his cabinet were destroyed.

"Ordinarily, we would proceed to a safe house, but with Foster..." A muscle in Cam's jaw bunched tightly and her fingers turned white as she gripped the dead agent's gun—the one he had trained on Blair's heart. "With one of my agents involved in the assault, I have to assume we are completely compromised. I can't trust the safe house locations or *any* evacuation plan to be secure." *We're out here alone.*

"Commander," Stark interrupted urgently. "I have Reynolds calling from command central."

Instantly, Cam held out her hand for the other phone. "Reynolds," she said sharply, "Mac Phillips has been wounded. He's in the...yes...yes. Status?...What about Parker?" She let out a breath, her eyes emptying of all emotion. "Evacuate and secure the building. Notify the FBI...wait...hold a minute." She passed the phone back to Stark. "I've got another priority call coming in. You work through securing the scene with him. See if he can get someone from the local FBI office. We need to keep this out of the news."

"Yes, ma'am." White faced, shivering in the sweat-soaked T-shirts and shorts she had been working out in, Stark extended her left hand. Her throbbing right arm was stiffening, and she cradled it against her abdomen to help contain the pain. She forced herself to think about the myriad details that needed to be addressed—most importantly, determining the identity of the unknown assailants. But what she desperately wanted to do was to ask for information about the situation at the World Trade Center. Her lover was there somewhere. But Blair was still in danger, and her duty came first. "All right, Reynolds. Listen up."

0941 11 September 2001: American Airlines flight 77 has crashed into the west side of the Pentagon.

"Jesus Christ," Cam breathed as she heard the words she could not believe. Phone to her ear, she glanced at Blair. "They're evacuating the White House. A hijacked airliner just hit the Pentagon."

"Oh my dear Lord." Blair's eyes grew huge, brimming with

agony and despair. "This can't be happening. Oh, Cam."

"We're leaving the city, Commander. Your orders?" Felicia's voice through the open partition that separated the rear compartment from the driver's area was hollow, eerily devoid of inflection.

Blair wasn't certain that Cam had heard the question, but it was clear to her that no previously determined official destination was secure. Suddenly, she leaned toward the front and spoke to Felicia in a low voice. "Drive to the Mass Turnpike and head east. And I need to use your phone."

Briefly, Felicia flicked her eyes to Blair's in the rearview mirror, then back to the road as she removed her cell phone from the pocket of her sweats. Handing it through to Blair, she murmured, "Yes, ma'am."

While what was left of her security team attempted to coordinate their safe passage, the president's daughter decided to make arrangements for a temporary sanctuary on her own. She'd spent half her life disappearing, and she'd been very good at it. Praying that she could get an open line in the midst of a panic that must be overburdening the telephone systems, she pushed 411. Sighing in relief when an operator finally answered, she gave a name and address and waited for a connection. *Answer. Please answer.*

Expelling a pent-up breath at the sound of a voice on the line, Blair said urgently, "Tanner? It's Blair. I've got a problem."

Blair closed the phone just as Stark and Cam finished their calls. She looked from her lover to Paula Stark. Both were hurt. Both at the very minimum needed first aid for their wounds, if not professional medical attention. Felicia was holding up, but she looked shell-shocked. What she was about to say was only going to add immeasurably to everyone's pain, but there was nothing she could do. In a voice dry as tinder, she repeated what she'd just been told. "The South Tower of the World Trade Center just collapsed."

"No!" Stark jerked forward on her seat, her eyes wild. "That's impossible. There are 50,000 people in that building." *Renee! Renee is there!*

"Paula," Blair said softly.

"Listen," Felicia said abruptly from the front seat. "I've got something coming over the scanner here."

The vehicle grew eerily quiet as the sound of a disembodied voice filled the silence.

United Airlines flight 93 has crashed in Shanksville, Pennsylvania, presumably en route to a target in Washington, DC.

"Is that number four?" Blair's voice was tight with disbelief. "This can't be. This just can't be."

Cam reached for Blair's hand as Stark slumped in her seat, her face ashen. "It's imperative now that we maintain radio silence. No one makes any calls except me."

"Renee is in the South Tower," Stark said, her voice trembling. "Can I call her?"

"I'm sorry, no." Cam's tone revealed none of her regret. "We have no idea who is behind these attacks, or how much they know, or where the next target might be. We can't risk broadcasting our location."

"Cam," Blair said quietly, her heart aching. "One more call couldn't hurt, could it?"

"I don't know *what* might hurt at this point. I can't risk it." The disappointment in Blair's face stung, and Cam's question came out more abruptly than she intended. "Who were you just talking to?"

Taken aback, Blair stared, and caught the flicker of pain in Cam's eyes before they went flat. That brief glimpse of her lover's anguish dispelled her own mounting anger. Cam's leg was rigid beneath their joined hands. The only visible sign of the terrible strain she was under was the low, tight tone of her voice. The depths of her charcoal eyes, however, were nothing more than opaque obsidian reflections, more impenetrable than Blair had ever seen. *Oh, darling, I can't imagine what it's costing you to do this.*

Gently, Blair replied, "An old friend of mine from prep school. We can go there—it's as secure as any place right now. Probably more."

Cam narrowed her eyes. "Were you lovers?"

Blair blinked. "I hardly think that matters now."

Impatiently, Cam shook her head and bit back a grunt of pain. "No, if you *were,* it's probably a matter of record. Somewhere, someone put it in a file, and we don't know what intelligence has been compromised."

"God, do you really think something from so long ago—"

"I don't *know,* Blair. Jesus, I've got one dead agent—"

"Mac?" Felicia cried.

"No," Cam replied swiftly. "Parker. Reynolds said Mac was unconscious but alive when he reached him. He managed to commandeer a NYPD cruiser off the street to transport Mac to NYU hospital." In a gentler tone, she added, "That's all I know, except that Mac is tough."

Blair stroked her hand absently along Cam's thigh. "Tanner was never my lover. And she lives in a fairly remote area. I told her we were coming."

Cam sorted through options, ranking them in order of possible security risks. Until she had more information about the nature and extent of the attacks, she couldn't be certain that any federal or military installation was secure. In all likelihood, Foster had passed along the details of their internal evac routes to whoever was behind the assault. She had to admit they'd be better off lying low in a civilian location. "All right. Where are we going?"

"Whitley Island."

1005 11 September 2001: The skies over America are empty.

For almost a minute, there was complete silence in the vehicle. Felicia drove east toward the Mass Turnpike at a steady sixty-five miles per hour. Stark leaned against the door, her face turned to the window, her eyes glazed. She was shivering uncontrollably.

"Cam," Blair said quietly, nodding in Stark's direction. "She needs medical attention. And so do you."

"I don't want to stop yet." Cam kept her voice low out of habit, although in actuality, the only people she could absolutely trust were in the car with her. Other than Mac, and she missed him tremendously now. "I don't think we're being pursued, but I don't know if there's another assault team looking for us or already on an intercept course. The last thing I want to do is go to a hospital and televise to the world where you are."

"Can't we drop *her* off at a hospital somewhere, then?"

A brief, sad smile crossed Cam's face. "You don't really think she'd go, do you? Plus, I can't afford to lose another agent. I need her on the job."

"You can assemble the rest of the team in a few hours once we reach Tanner's."

"No, I can't." Cam rubbed her eyes. "Foster was part of the attack, Blair. I can't trust any of the agents now. Every one of them is a suspect."

"All right," Blair conceded. Carefully, she moved to the opposite seat, knelt facing the rear, and leaned over the back of the seat into the storage compartment behind it. She rummaged around until she found the emergency medical kit, which she lifted back over the seat and set on the floor. Then she resumed her search and, a few minutes later, swiveled around with a bundle of clothing in her arms. "The Suburbans may be ugly as hell, but they're very well equipped. I've got the ever-present blue polo shirts and one-size-fits-all khaki pants. Felicia and Paula can at least get out of their damp clothes."

"Davis," Cam said. "Pull into the first drive-off you see. Park well away from any other vehicles."

"Yes, ma'am."

Ten minutes later, Davis pulled the Suburban into a rest stop, drove to the far end of the narrow parking lot, and stopped. Blair slid over next to Stark.

"Paula," she said gently, putting her hand lightly on Stark's arm. "Let's get your T-shirt off so I can take a look at your shoulder. I've got a dry shirt for you, too."

Stark, her gaze slightly unfocused, searched Blair's face. She blinked. "Thank you. You don't need to do that. I can take care of it. You should see to the commander."

"Yes, I will. But you first." Patiently, Blair waited.

After another few seconds' hesitation, Stark lifted her T-shirt with her left hand, but couldn't mange to raise her right.

"Let me help you with that," Blair said, carefully manipulating the garment and working it slowly over Stark's injured right arm. The sports bra she wore beneath was wet with sweat and blood. "Take off the bra, too."

Stark flushed.

"It's okay, Paula."

Stark glanced across the compartment to Cam, who sat quietly with her eyes trained out the rear window, scanning the incoming vehicles, her weapon still at the ready. The sight of the commander, so steady, so focused, infused Stark with purpose. *I need to get myself together. The commander needs backup.* Quietly, she said to Blair, "Can you help me, please."

"Of course."

After helping Stark out of her underwear, Blair cleansed the jagged bullet wound in Stark's deltoid area with peroxide, applied an antibiotic ointment, and bandaged it. Throughout the process, Stark remained still and silent. "Let me help you get a dry shirt on."

As Stark carefully pulled on the shirt, another bulletin came over the scanner.

1028 11 September 2001: The North Tower of the World Trade Center has collapsed.

With an agonized moan, Stark pushed open the door and bolted from the car.

When Blair moved to follow, Cam said quietly, "Let her go."

Blair's patience snapped. "For God's sake, Cam. There's no danger here, and she's suffering. I don't want her to be alone with this."

"She *needs* to be alone with it." Cam's voice revealed no hint of anger, only sadness. "She needs to put it away for now, and she will. Just give her a minute."

"Is that what they teach you?" Blair demanded wildly. "To bury your pain, even when it's killing you?"

"We don't bury it, Blair. We just save it."

The grief in Cam's face brought tears to Blair's eyes. "Oh, Cam. I'm sorry." Quickly, she crossed the space between them and curled up against Cam's side, threading an arm around her lover's waist and resting her head against her shoulder. "I'm so sorry. None of this is your fault, and everything you're doing is to protect me. I know that, and still I resent what this job does to you."

Cam pressed her lips to Blair's hair and closed her eyes. "I would do anything not to lose you."

"I know." Blair lifted her face and kissed Cam's neck. "I love you." She held Cam a moment longer, then pushed away. "It's time for you to get cleaned up, Commander."

By the time Blair had tended to Cam's scalp wound, Stark, hollow eyed and beyond pale, had returned.

"All right, Stark?" Cam asked.

"Yes, ma'am." Stark's voice was raspy and sore from choking back the bile that had threatened to erupt when she'd heard the bulletin. She had to believe that Renee was still alive. She simply had no other choice. Any other possibility was more than she could bear. "I'm ready."

"Davis," Cam said, "Ms. Powell will give you directions to Whitley Island. Get us there as quickly as you can."

CHAPTER THIRTY-TWO

1344 11 September 2001: The aircraft carriers USS *George Washington* and USS *John F. Kennedy* along with five warships have been deployed from the US Naval Station in Norfolk, Virginia to New York.

"Turn here," Blair said, peering out the side window at the open ten-foot-high wrought iron gates that stretched between high stone walls that were almost completely hidden by the dense native foliage.

"Is this the end of the island?" Cam asked. She'd been taking careful note of the topography and population distribution ever since they'd crossed the causeway from the mainland onto Whitley Island. There seemed to be very few residences on the island itself, although she'd caught sight of a marina at the southern tip that appeared to be fairly populated. The isolated locale was both an advantage and a strategic problem. They would be difficult to find, but if detected by unfriendly forces, it would be almost impossible for them to escape.

"Yes, the Whitley estate occupies the entire north half of the island." Wearily, Blair pushed a hand through her hair and glanced across the confines of the rear compartment to Stark. The young agent's eyes were open but so blank that Blair thought she might be asleep. She leaned close to Cam. "We need to have her looked at."

"I know." Cam brushed her fingers over the top of Blair's hand. "It may be twelve to twenty-four hours until I can establish secure links with Washington and get an accurate assessment of our security situation. Until then, we're going to be in a communication blackout. So no hospitals yet."

"What if Tanner could bring a doctor out here?" Blair pushed, because both Stark and Cam needed medical attention. She'd cleaned their wounds, but Stark gave every sign of being in shock, and it was clear that Cam was fighting a headache and possibly worse.

"Give me a few hours to assess the situation, and then I'll let you know my decision."

"All right." Blair squeezed Cam's hand. "Thank you."

As the car slowed, a large stone edifice fronted by terraced gardens, fountains, and flagstone walks came into view. Davis stopped the Suburban in a circular turnaround just opposite the wide steps that led up to a spacious veranda.

Cam gave Blair a raised eyebrow. Blair shrugged.

"This is Whitley Island, and *that's* Whitley Manor."

At that moment, the reigning Whitley came through the front door. Tanner Whitley was Blair's age, but dark and muscular where Blair was blond and lithe. Not quite as tall as Cam, she nevertheless exuded a similar aura of confidence and command, even in sun-bleached khaki deck pants and a short-sleeved cotton work shirt. She stopped by the side of the vehicle, her dark eyes beneath heavy, nearly straight brows and a slash of dark hair giving her a brooding, James Dean look.

Per protocol, Cam opened the rear door as Felicia came around the front. Blair stepped out between them with Stark exiting close behind.

"Blair," Tanner Whitley said with obvious affection as she stepped forward and kissed Blair on the cheek. "How are you?"

For the first time since the entire nightmare had burst upon her six hours earlier, Blair felt the full weight of the horror—not just her own personal fear and trauma, but what the innocent people in New York City and Pennsylvania and Washington and the rest of the country must be suffering. She reached for Cam, linked arms, and pressed close to her lover for comfort and support. "We're a little banged up, but basically okay. Tanner, this is my lover, Commander Cameron Roberts. My security staff, Felicia Davis and Paula Stark."

Tanner nodded to the agents and extended her hand to Cam.

"Commander."

Their dark eyes were equally appraising as they studied each other.

"Ms. Whitley. I'd like to get Blair inside, if you don't mind," Cam said. "Also, is there somewhere we can put the Suburban where it would not be visible to air surveillance?"

Tanner's gaze did not waver, but her expression registered immediate respect. "Certainly. Please go inside. The kitchen is through to the rear, and our housekeeper, May, will be happy to fix you something for lunch. I'll move the vehicle to the garage myself. My mother is..." Tanner swallowed. "My mother just returned to DC this past weekend, so her car is not here."

"Thank you." Cam nodded to Stark and Davis. "Let's go."

Once inside, the group gravitated toward the sound of a television in a large living room that faced the ocean. No one, however, spared the breathtaking view an instant's attention. The wall-mounted HDTV was tuned to CNN, and within seconds, the tape and voice-over had looped through the devastation in Manhattan, Washington, DC, and a field not far from Pittsburgh, Pennsylvania. A well-known anchorman repeated the message that had been playing all afternoon.

"Mayor Giuliani has promised that rescue teams will work around the clock until all survivors have been found. At the present time, the number of police, firefighters, emergency personnel, and civilians potentially trapped in the rubble of the twin towers is unknown."

There was no mention of any attempt on Blair's life.

As the litany of destruction and devastation continued, the air in the room reverberated with the sound of Stark's uneven breathing and Davis's muffled moans of disbelief. Speechless with shock and horror, Blair stared at the screen while Cam's mind rebelled at the thought that such a huge-scale, coordinated attack could have been planned and executed within their own borders. *Why didn't we know this was coming?*

Finally, Cam broke the silence that had overtaken the group. "Blair, I think perhaps Davis and Stark could do with some food. You, too."

"What about you?" Blair didn't see any purpose in pointing

out that Cam was white as a sheet and that smudges of pain and fatigue rimmed her eyes. She was certain that her lover felt every bit as bad as she looked. She just wouldn't acknowledge it, even to herself.

"I need to establish a secure connection, if I can, to DC."

"You won't be any use to me in a crisis situation if you're too weak or ill to think, let alone fight." Blair moved closer, out of earshot of Felicia and Stark, both of whom still sat on the sofa, their attention riveted to the news broadcast. "You look like hell. We don't know how long we might be here. We don't know how long it might be until we get a relief team. We *all* need a meal, showers, and fresh clothes. Plus, I want Tanner to get a doctor out here." When Cam started to protest, Blair shook her head sharply. "I'm sure she can handle it discreetly. I'm not backing down on this, Cameron."

"I..." Cam's brows furrowed as her phone vibrated. She glanced down, but didn't recognize the number on the readout. She flicked it open and said curtly, "Roberts. Yes, *sir.*" She held out the phone to Blair. "Your father. Two minutes, sweetheart. That's all we can risk."

"Daddy?" Blair said quickly. "Are you okay?...No, I'm fine. No, really. Are you sure *you're* all right?" Blair glanced at Cam, who checked her watch and nodded to go ahead. "I'm perfectly safe, but I think you should talk to her. Be careful. I love you."

"Sir," Cam said sharply. "I believe we are secure. At the present time, it's my opinion that no one should be advised of our location. I prefer to brief you myself, sir, as soon as the situation is contained." She listened intently, then nodded. "Yes sir, that should be fine. Thank you."

Cam severed the connection, then said quietly, "We're here for twenty-four hours. That should give the CIA, the NSC, and the FBI time to construct an initial ongoing threat assessment. Until then, we're safer here than anywhere else. Are you okay with that?"

"Yes. I'd like to be with my father, but I suppose that's not possible right now." Blair struggled to keep the fear from her voice. "You really think he's all right?"

"Yes," Cam replied, sliding her arm around Blair's waist and kissing her temple. "If they'd been able to bring off an attempt on him, they would have. They tried for you instead."

Blair heard the bitterness and saw the anguish in Cam's eyes. "You can't possibly think that any part of that was your fault."

Cam looked away.

"Cam," Blair said, resting her palm against Cam's chest. "No."

"Foster was my man," Cam said. *And he came within seconds of killing you today.*

Before Blair could protest further, Tanner walked into the room.

"I'll show you to your rooms, and then when you're settled, May has set out a buffet in the dining room. Just help yourselves." She balled her fists into the pockets of her khakis and rocked slightly on the balls of her feet. She looked from Blair to Cam. "Do you have any idea what's going on?"

"No," Cam said quietly. "No more than what's on the television."

Tanner sighed. "I got a ten-second call this morning from Adrienne..." She looked at Cam. "My lover—Adrienne Pierce. She's a navy captain stationed nearby, and she said they'd been ordered to lockdown and that she didn't know when she might call again. That's the last I heard."

Cam saw the distress in the other woman's eyes and sympathized. The same story, she was sure, was being repeated across the country, and nowhere more so than up and down the Northeast corridor. The lines of communication were in chaos, and no one could be certain that the attacks were over. Although her main priority remained Blair's safety, she could appreciate the anxiety and frustration of not knowing the status of friends and loved ones and having no way to reach them. "When and if I know anything that I can disclose, I'll tell you."

As she straightened, Tanner's expression became one of resolve. "Of course. Please, let me get you all settled."

Blair watched silently as the doctor examined Cam. "She had a serious head injury not more than six weeks ago. She was unconscious then and probably shouldn't even have returned to duty as quickly as she did."

"Did you have a CAT scan performed?" the slender, blond man inquired as he studied Cam's retina with an ophthalmoscope.

"Yes. It was normal."

"No evidence of cerebral edema or bleeding?"

Blair's stomach tightened and her mouth went dry. "What? Why? Did you find something wrong?"

Dr. Anthony Wade turned with an apologetic smile. "I'm sorry. Just routine questions. Everything seems fine thus far."

"Oh." Blair couldn't keep the relief from her voice. "What about the...bullet wound?"

"You did a good job with the first aid. Most of it is within the scalp, and although I could suture it, at this point there's a lower risk of infection if I don't." He gave Cam a reproachful look. "As long as you take it easy and don't get banged around any more, you should be fine."

"Thank you," Cam replied dryly. "What about my agent, Paula Stark?" Over Blair's objections, she'd insisted that he examine Stark before looking at her.

"I wanted her to immobilize her right arm, just to reduce the pain. The wound itself penetrated just to the fascial level but didn't violate the muscular compartment. I Steri-Stripped it closed, but it won't hold if she gets into any kind of physical altercation."

"Hopefully, that won't be necessary."

The doctor grimaced. "She also informed me that she couldn't immobilize her weapon arm, so she very politely declined to follow my instructions."

A smile quirked the corner of Cam's mouth as Blair made a disgusted sound. "I'll see that she gets as much rest as possible."

With a sigh, the doctor packed up his equipment. He glanced from Cam to the president's daughter. "Unfortunately, I don't think that's going to be possible for anyone for a while, is it?"

Cam said nothing. There was nothing she could say that would make the truth any more bearable.

1854 11 September 2001: The president has returned on board helicopter Marine One to the White House.

"Stark," Cam said quietly. "I'll need you on the first shift in the morning. Go get some sleep."

"I'm fine, Commander. You don't have enough people for perimeter patrol without me."

"Our perimeter is secure on three sides unless there is an ocean approach, and we'll hear that coming in plenty of time. Davis and I will cover the front."

Stark looked as if she was about to protest further, but Cam turned and walked into the other room where Davis waited, giving her no opportunity to object.

"Paula," Blair said gently, "you *do* need to get some rest."

Stark sat forward on the sofa, her elbows on her knees, and cradled her head in her hands. She stared at the floor, and when she spoke, her voice was thick with pain. "I'm afraid Renee is dead." She raised anguished eyes to Blair's. "God. All those people."

"You can't think that." Swiftly, Blair rose from the chair where she had been pretending to read the newspaper and crossed to the sofa. Without conscious thought, she slipped her arm around Stark's waist. "She's an FBI agent stationed at the epicenter of a terrorist attack. You know her—she's going to be working nonstop for *days*. Plus, it's got to be chaos there, and who knows what the communication situation is like. There's no way she would have been able to call you, even if she *could* find a free minute to do it."

"Her office was in the South Tower." Stark shuddered. At the news of the towers' collapse, she hadn't been able to think of anything except that she had lost the woman she loved. Voice breaking, she whispered, "I don't think I can take it."

Blair knew exactly what she was feeling. She'd almost lost Cam, and she was never going to get over the terror of those few days when Cam had lain in the hospital on life support. She pulled Stark into her arms and kissed her forehead. "You can't give up, okay? You just have to keep on going. Okay? Promise?"

Stark was silent, because she couldn't bring herself to lie. She wasn't certain where she would find the strength to carry on. She closed her eyes and allowed herself to be comforted. For that isolated moment, the steady strength of Blair's heart beating close to hers was enough.

Chapter Thirty-Three

Blair leaned on the railing of the upper deck, listening to the surf and watching the moonlight dance across the waves. The water was nearly as dark as the midnight sky overhead. She turned at the sound of the sliding glass doors opening behind her and recognized Tanner's form backlit by the few lights burning in the house. "Hi. I thought you'd turned in."

"No, I'm too wired to sleep."

"Me, too," Blair sighed.

"Mind a little company?" Tanner asked quietly.

"No." Blair regarded Tanner in the moonlight. "I haven't had much of a chance to talk to you. Sorry."

Tanner shook her head. "It's not a great time for catching up."

Blair studied Tanner's bold profile, silvered by moonlight. "You know, you look...older."

"I'm not sure how to take that," Tanner remarked with a short laugh.

Blair laughed as well. "Actually, you don't look *older* as much as you look...calmer. Even in the midst of everything that's going on, you look settled somehow."

"My life here is pretty much just what I want it to be, that's true."

"You managed to escape the clutches of the dreaded Whitley Corporation?"

"I still go into the offices on the mainland a few days a month, but I spend most of my time running the marina. Adrienne's stationed nearby, and the island is our home."

"You sound as if that agrees with you."

Tanner smiled, thinking about the new direction her life had taken in the last few years. "I can't even begin to tell you how good it is...my life now...working here on the island, living with Adrienne. All of it."

Considering the way her own life had changed in less than a year, thinking of Cam, Blair said, "Believe it or not, I *can* imagine it." She shrugged and gave a small laugh. "I never thought I'd be able to say that, but being with Cam...it's the best thing that's ever happened to me."

"Well. I think I'm speechless."

"Yes. I am sometimes, still, too." Blair sighed. It seemed a very long time ago that she and Tanner had been young and wild and, for all their youthful pain, blissfully naïve. "Have you heard from Adrienne?"

"No." Tanner rolled her shoulders and distractedly ran a hand through her thick dark hair. "I'm sure that doesn't mean anything, but I'd feel a hell of a lot better if I could just hear her voice."

Blair reached over and covered Tanner's hand where it curled over the railing. She tapped the thin gold band on Tanner's ring finger. "I noticed this earlier. Congratulations."

"Thanks." Tanner lifted her face to the sky and closed her eyes briefly, wondering if life would ever be the same again. "You know, I can't reach my mother in DC, either. Her husband is a navy captain. He's got an office in the Pentagon."

"Oh, Tanner. God. You must be so worried, and I never even asked. I'm sorry. You've been a lifesaver today and—"

"Don't apologize." Tanner bumped Blair's shoulder with hers. "I don't know what happened to you this morning in New York, but considering that two of your security team showed up here with gunshot wounds, I figure you had other things on your mind."

"It almost feels like a dream." Blair shivered, more from memory than the chill gust of ocean air. "A terrible, horrible dream."

"I know." Tanner took a deep breath and fought back the melancholy and fear. "I've tried calling my mother, but I can't get through. From what I can gather from the television reports, it might be hours or even days before the phone systems get sorted out."

"At the moment," Blair said with regret, "there isn't even any way that *I* can contact someone in DC to try to find out for you. I'm sorry."

"I understand, and I wouldn't expect you to anyhow." Tanner turned her back to the water, leaned her hips against the railing, and looked into the house. Through the glass doors, she saw a shadow move across the swath of light that angled out from the living room. "Are Cam and Felicia going to stay up all night standing guard?"

"I'm sure that's what they have planned," Blair said grimly. "But that's not going to happen. We've all been through a lot, and Cam has been shot. She's going to get some sleep tonight, no matter how much she protests."

"I think I might be able to help out there," Tanner said, pushing resolutely away from the railing. "Let me make some calls."

Cam stood by the leaded-glass windows that looked out onto the curving approach road to Whitley Manor. In the moonlight, the landscape appeared untamed, almost otherworldly. It was hard to believe that beyond the confines of that isolated, protected place, the world was in chaos.

Blair hooked her arms around Cam's waist from behind and rested her cheek against Cam's back. "What are you thinking about?"

Cam laced her fingers through Blair's and absently drew Blair's hand beneath her jacket and pressed it to her stomach. The warmth of Blair's palm against her body eased the ache in her heart. "Just wondering what's happening out there tonight. Trying to get a grip on what happened today."

"Come to bed, Cam."

"Tanner has called in her corporate security team," Cam said, ignoring Blair's request. "She assures me they'll ask no questions and do the job as efficiently and effectively as military police. In fact, some of them used to *be* military police."

"And you don't believe her?" Blair slowly rubbed her hand up and down the center of Cam's abdomen and pressed more closely against her back, needing the contact more than she had realized.

"No, I *do* believe her. I'm absolutely certain that she knows exactly what her people are capable of." Cam sighed. "Unlike me."

"Cam..."

Cam turned, keeping her hand in Blair's. Her smile was rueful. "I should apologize. I don't ordinarily indulge in self-pity."

"Darling, don't." Blair lifted a hand and caressed Cam's cheek. "At least wait until we understand what happened with Foster. If there's blame to be assigned, I know that you will accept responsibility for whatever part might be yours. But until then, don't torture yourself. Please."

"How is it that you know me so well?" Cam rested her forehead against Blair's. *God, I'm so tired.*

"Because I love you so much." Blair gave Cam's hand a tug and, to her enormous relief, Cam followed her as she led the way through the house and upstairs to the bedroom they would share. "Just sleep with me for a few hours and then, if you have to, you can go back downstairs. But I need you now."

"I need you, too." Nearly stumbling with fatigue, Cam stripped off her clothes and left them in a heap by the bed. She kept her weapon holstered on a table by the bedside. She and Blair slid into bed at the same time and moved into each other's embrace.

Blair curled into the curve of Cam's side, her head on Cam's shoulder and one leg and an arm thrown over her body. "How's your headache?"

Cam gently kissed Blair's mouth before closing her eyes. "Better."

"When we get home," Blair's voice hitched, but she continued after drawing a steadying breath, "I want you to move in with me. I don't want to wait. I love you, and I want you in my life. Full-time, all the time."

"Is this because of today?"

"Partly, yes. But ever since we got back from Europe, I've been struggling to feel okay about being without you. Today made me realize that there are no certainties in life, and that the most important thing in mine is you."

"Oh, Christ, I love you." Cam turned on her side and gathered Blair into her arms, their bodies joining along their lengths. She cupped the back of Blair's neck in the palm of her hand as she kissed her, still gently, but deep and long. When she drew her mouth away, she whispered, "If I lost you, it would kill me."

Blair gave a small cry and tightened her hold on her lover. She pressed her face to Cam's neck and stroked her hand up and down Cam's back, over her shoulders, until finally she laced her fingers into Cam's hair. "We'll take care of each other. We'll be together—do you hear me? We're going to be together. I promise."

Finally, safe in the comfort of her lover's arms, Cam slept.

The first thing she saw was Parker, lying on her back, her arms stretched out to her sides. Her eyes were open, empty, glazed with that peculiar blankness that only death can bestow. The crimson starburst in the center of her chest seemed nothing more than an afterthought once she'd looked into those eyes.

Turning, she ran, the breath burning in her chest, the muscles in her legs trembling, threatening to abandon her before she could reach...She almost tripped on the leg extending out into the stairwell from the landing just above. Grasping the metal railing with her free hand, clutching her weapon in the other, she looked down. Stark lay still, a perfect maroon circle punched between her thick, dark brows. A river of red snaked down from that tiny crater and pooled in the corner of her eye before overflowing onto her cheek like tears.

Oh Jesus. I'm going to lose them all.

Heart pounding, stomach heaving, she stared up the final flight of stairs to the solid gray metal door at the top. Beyond that door lay everything that mattered in her life. She couldn't move her legs. She couldn't climb the stairs. She couldn't reach—would never reach—the top in time. She crumpled to her knees, her weapon dropping unnoticed from her limp fingers. Hands clutching at cold stone, she dragged herself upward, one agonizingly slow step at a time.

When she finally reached the door, there was no handle.

It's so heavy. I can't open it. Please. Please. I have to get through.

By the time she'd pried her fingers into the narrow crevice around the edges and inched the door open, her hands were torn and bleeding. Still on her knees, she fell through to the other side and saw, down the long tunnel of the hallway, the body outside the open door. Every laborious inch cost her blood, every breath clawed at her screaming lungs, and the terror in her belly eviscerated her with razor-sharp talons.

A lifetime later, her vision dim with sweat and tears, she touched a trembling hand to the pale, cold cheek. A single drop of blood, dew on the rose, lay like a forgotten kiss upon her lover's lips.

Blair. Oh God, Blair.

With a silent scream, Cam jolted awake, rolled from the bed, and stumbled hurriedly to the bathroom. She'd barely managed to get the door closed behind her, automatically thumbing the lock, before her legs gave out and she was on her knees, vomiting. It hurt, in her body, in her heart, as the images seared into her brain one after the other. Her stomach rolled, and she continued to retch long after there was nothing left inside her but grief.

In the distance, she heard a muted shout and felt the faint vibration of the bathroom door shaking. Some part of her brain registered that if she didn't get to her feet, get the door open, Blair would break it down. Pale and dizzy, she pulled herself up with one hand on the sink and turned on the cold water. She cupped her hands under the tap and splashed her face until her head stopped spinning.

"Cam! Cam, open the door!"

The words were clear now, and the pounding incessant.

Blinking to clear her vision, Cam opened the cabinet above the sink and fumbled out the small bottle of mouthwash. She rinsed, gagging again, but finally managing to hold everything in at last.

"Just a minute," she called hoarsely. She took a breath, steadied herself, and unlocked the door.

Blair's eyes were wild as she came flying in. Her voice vibrated with fear and fury. "Don't you *ever* lock me out again when you need help."

"Blair," Cam said weakly, "I—"

"Oh God, what is it?" Blair cried, her trembling hands framing Cam's face. "Are you sick? Cam...oh, Cam." Tears overflowed her lashes and she pulled Cam against her, running hands over her shoulders, her back, wanting desperately to shield her, heal her.

"Dream," Cam gasped, wrapping her arms around Blair's

waist and holding on. "Just give me another minute."

"All right, darling. It's all right." Blair found Cam's hand, clasped it tightly, and gently drew her back into the bedroom and into bed. Her heart was pounding, her own stomach tight with dread and the lingering panic she'd felt upon awakening to the terrifying sound of Cam moaning. She'd never, never known Cam to break. The very thought of how much pain her lover must be in for that to happen tore her heart to shreds.

Working hard to keep her voice steady and calm, she settled Cam against her side and stroked her face gently. "Sweetheart, can you tell me?"

"It was just a dream. A very bad dream," Cam replied, her voice stronger as the night terror left her. "I saw Parker...she was dead. Then Stark...her, too." Cam pressed her forehead hard to Blair's shoulder and closed her eyes tightly. "Oh God, then...you."

"No," Blair soothed, brushing her fingers through Cam's hair, her free arm holding her close. "No, darling. Not me. Not Stark. We're here. We're both all right."

Cam shivered. "I couldn't reach you. I couldn't save you." She lifted her face, her dark eyes bleeding with loss. "I couldn't save Parker, and that's no dream."

Blair held her lover's gaze. "I know. I'm so sorry." She kissed Cam's forehead, then her mouth, tenderly. "If there was any way you could have stopped what happened today, I know that you would have." When she felt Cam stiffen, she said quickly, "No. It's *true*. Tragic, horrible things happened to so many people today. Things probably no one could have stopped. Perhaps someday we'll know who or why or how, but of one thing I'm certain. If you hadn't been there, I'd be dead."

"I was so fucking scared that I couldn't keep you safe." The words burned in Cam's throat.

"But you did." Blair brushed her lips over Cam's again. *I forget—we all forget—what that costs you.* As she guided Cam's head down to her breast, wanting never to let her go, she murmured, "We're together now, and I'm not going to let anything change that. Ever."

The sound of Cam's phone woke them just after five. Cam's head pounded, but it was a clean, sharp headache with none of the sickness she'd felt the night before. Blair was beside her, naked and warm and alive. She felt her world right itself as she rolled over and picked up her phone.

"Roberts." She stretched out an arm as Blair moved closer to curl against her and wrap an arm around her waist. Automatically, Cam rested her chin against the top of Blair's head. "Yes sir, we're secure. No problems, and I don't anticipate any. Yes, sir."

Cam extended the phone to Blair. "Your father again."

"Hi," Blair said. "You're at the residence? Is everything okay?...Yes, all right, if Cam thinks we should." Blair laughed quietly, rubbing her palm over Cam's chest. "Yes, Dad, I understand that you're the president. But she's my security chief."

"Blair," Cam whispered urgently.

Blair looked at Cam. "Well, you are."

"And I'd like it to stay that way. Tell him *yes.*"

"Dad? You can go ahead and send a helicopter."

CHAPTER THIRTY-FOUR

When Cam walked into the living room to inform Felicia Davis of their departure plans, she was surprised to find Paula Stark standing guard at the wide front windows. "Where's Davis?"

Stark turned from her survey of the grounds and the distant front gate, her expression somber. "I relieved her at 0400."

Cam nodded, thinking that if she hadn't fallen asleep after the nightmare and its aftermath, she would have relieved Davis herself. She couldn't fault Stark for being responsible, even if she had been ordered to get some sleep. "Very well." As Stark turned back to her silent vigil, Cam walked up beside her. "We're evacuating—ETD 0730. Once Egret is secure, you can call Renee."

"I'm sure she's up to her eyeballs in fieldwork right now," Stark said flatly. "I imagine, being right there..." Her voice wavered, and she drew a long breath. "Being right there, she's got to be one of the lead agents. She probably won't even answer her phone."

"No," Cam agreed, because the assessment was technically accurate and any other alternative scenario was unacceptable. There would be time to think the unthinkable if Savard failed to respond after a reasonable wait. *And who knows what's reasonable any longer?* "She probably won't see any downtime for another twenty-four hours at least."

Stark nodded, still at rigid attention, her jaw set and her eyes bleak. "Yes. That's what I figure, too."

In a rare gesture, Cam squeezed Stark's shoulder briefly. "I'll advise Davis to relieve you."

"It's not necessary, Commander. I'm fine."

"Yes, I know you are." They stood side by side in silence, watching the sea breeze blow the last edges of the night clouds from the sky. Eventually, without touching her again, Cam said,

"There's coffee in the kitchen. Get some, then grab a shower. We're headed to DC."

Stark jerked in surprise. *But Renee's in New York!* With effort, she forced herself to reply quietly. "Yes, ma'am."

Cam wanted to add some word of reassurance, but she thought too much of Stark to lie. They both knew the chances of hearing from Renee—or not. Before she turned away, she said quietly, "You did a fine job yesterday, Agent Stark."

"It was an honor, Commander."

Their eyes met, steady and strong. Then Cam nodded and left Stark to her duty. A few minutes later, she stood with Blair in the kitchen, drinking coffee. Felicia entered, looking worn but in control. "A car was just cleared through the front gate by the private security team."

"Thank you," Cam said, setting her cup on the breakfast bar. "Do we have identification?"

"No, without a comm link, I have no way of receiving that information." Felicia didn't look or sound pleased. After the ambush the day before, none of the team was likely to take anything at face value ever again. "I assume it's someone known to them, but..."

Foster was known to us, too, and he *orchestrated an assassination attempt that very nearly succeeded.* Cam headed for the front of the house. "Let's just see for ourselves."

Tanner waited on the verge of the circular drive. A black sedan pulled to a stop just in front of her, and a tall thin blond in a rumpled navy uniform stepped out and hurried around the front of the vehicle.

Meeting her halfway, Tanner immediately slipped both arms around her waist. "Are you all right?"

"Just tired," Adrienne Pierce replied. She kissed Tanner softly, then stroked her cheek while searching her eyes. "How about you?"

"Much better now." Tanner brushed her fingers down Adrienne's arm and clasped her hand. "I am so glad you're home."

"Have you heard anything from Constance and Tom?"

"She just called," Tanner replied, her relief at having heard from her mother clear. "They're fine."

"Good." Adrienne slid her arm around Tanner's waist. "Why is there a guard at our gate?"

"We've got unexpected visitors."

At the sound of footsteps on the veranda, Adrienne shifted her gaze from her lover to take a close look at the women who gathered at the top of the stairs. "I see." She recognized Blair Powell although they had met only a few times. The others were easily identifiable as Secret Service agents just by the way they carried themselves and observed her with polite but intent attention. "*Special* visitors. Why are they here?"

"I don't know. Blair called yesterday shortly after the...attacks. She said that she needed a secure place to stay."

The president's daughter needs a safe house? Adrienne's heart hammered as she glanced quickly around. "My God, are they here alone?"

"There's just Blair and three agents." Tanner lowered her voice, although no one could hear them. "They're all a little beat up."

That information, coupled with the level of wartime preparedness she had just been part of at the base, made Adrienne wish she had brought a security team with her. Blair Powell was in *her* home in the midst of a national crisis, and surprisingly undefended. It didn't make sense. But then, absolutely nothing about the last twenty-two hours made sense. "You called in your own security?"

"I was a bit nervous."

Adrienne laughed thinly. "I can see why. I wonder if I can get some MPs out here—"

"I don't think that's necessary," Tanner informed Adrienne as they crossed the driveway and started up the steps. "Blair told me just a little while ago that they would be leaving shortly."

"And *I* only have two hours before I have to head back to the base. I'm sorry I can't stay with you longer."

Tanner gripped her arm more tightly. "You don't have to apologize. I miss you, and I'm worried about you. But I understand."

With a sigh, Adrienne slid her arm around Tanner, allowing herself the comfort of leaning into her lover's solid body. "God, it's good to be home."

Tanner, in turn, hooked an arm around Adrienne's waist and together, they ascended the stairs to where Blair stood with Cam and Felicia. Stark came through the front door just as they reached the deck, and the six women met in a small circle. Stark and Felicia stood slightly behind and on either side of Blair, who stepped forward with Cam and extended her hand to Adrienne.

"Hello, Adrienne. I'm sorry about the welcoming committee—I'm sure you didn't count on us."

Adrienne smiled and took Blair's hand. "I'm happy to see you. I wish it were under different circumstances."

"Yes, we all do." Blair indicated Cam. "Adrienne Pierce, my partner and security chief, Cameron Roberts."

Cam shook Adrienne's hand as well. "Captain."

"How do you do." Adrienne smiled wearily. "Have you all had breakfast?"

"Yes, Tanner and May have taken wonderful care of us—" Blair broke off at the sound of a distant reverberation growing louder.

Cam stepped away from the small group and looked up into the sky, then back at Blair. "It appears that our ride is here."

Everyone turned and watched as Marine One, the presidential helicopter, settled down on the far side of the lawn. Four marines emerged, heads down to escape the buffeting of the rapidly spinning rotors, and hurried toward the house.

"I'm afraid we're going to have to be rude," Blair said, glancing from Adrienne to Tanner. "I wish it hadn't taken this to get us together again. I've missed you both."

Tanner took Blair's hand and squeezed it. "Me, too. When things...settle down, come back. You and Cameron, come back and spend some time with us."

"I'd like that very much." Blair leaned forward and kissed first Tanner's cheek, then Adrienne's. By then, Cam, Felicia, and Stark, along with the military escort, stood waiting to take her to the helicopter. For one moment, she considered telling Cam that she wanted to stay. Whitley Island was an oasis in a world gone mad, and she knew that as soon as she returned to Washington, she might be safe, but she might not be free. She looked to Cam, who was observing her intently. *Stay here with me. Let the world take care of itself.*

But she was the daughter of the president of the United States, and in the midst of a national crisis, her place was with him. With one last look at her old friends, she turned, walked down the stairs, and was quickly surrounded by her guards.

Once they were in the air, Cam signaled to the marine captain beside her for a secure communication line. Blair sat on her other side with Stark and Davis across the aisle in facing seats. The noise of the rotors made conversation almost impossible. With the headphones pressed to her ears, Cam requested a patch-through to the command center in Manhattan. She wasn't particularly surprised when John Fielding answered, knowing that in the absence of specific orders, her team would assemble there.

"This is Roberts. What's the word on Mac?" she shouted. Hunched forward, she listened intently. "Okay...right...you're in charge of the local field investigation. Have the FBI been on scene?...say again?" Unable to make out his response, she shook her head in frustration and checked her watch. "Stand by for another call at 1130. Full briefing then."

As soon as she terminated the call, Blair grasped Cam's forearm and leaned close. "What about Mac?"

"Last update he's in the ICU, but stable."

One of many fears lifted from Blair's heart. At least *one* of her absent friends was going to be all right. Now, if only they'd hear from Renee. As Cam leaned forward to relay the news to Stark and Felicia, Blair closed her eyes, her right hand resting on Cam's knee. Once they landed, they would both be immersed in official duties, and she wanted these final few moments of connection.

Lucinda Washburn met them just inside the West Wing. The first thing she did was kiss Blair's cheek. "Your father's going to be very happy to see you. He's in a security meeting right now, but he asked that you wait for him at the residence."

"All right." Blair glanced at Cam. "Can you come with me?"

"I need to report in. Stewart needs to be briefed about the events of yesterday." She touched Blair's hand fleetingly. "I'll make it as fast as I can. You should try to get some sleep."

Blair tilted her head, smiling faintly. "And you, Commander, should take your own advice."

"Point taken, Ms. Powell." Cam leaned close enough for a kiss, but merely whispered, "Please don't leave the residence without me."

"No," Blair murmured, her eyes on Cam's. "I won't go anywhere without you. Don't worry."

Lucinda cleared her throat. "We should go, Blair. Everyone's schedule is very tight."

Blair moved back from Cam and regarded the chief of staff with a cool, calm expression. "Yes, of course." She nodded once to Cam. "I'll see you later, Commander."

"Ms. Powell," Cam said quietly as she watched her lover walk away. Then she turned to Stark and Davis. "You're both relieved...temporarily. Until I know Egret's plans, I need you both to remain available. Get rooms at the usual hotel so I can reach you on short notice." She hesitated, then added, "I'm sorry. I realize that both of you might prefer to return to Manhattan. As soon as I can reassemble a secure team, I'll give you some downtime."

"Is it all right if we disclose our location now?" Stark asked. She felt like she'd been clinging to the side of a cliff in high winds and rain for over twenty-four hours. Her hands were numb, her grip was slipping, and she was about to plummet. She needed so desperately to hear Renee's voice.

"Yes, go ahead." Cam regarded Felicia. "Fielding is running the command center. He should have an update on Mac's situation."

"Thank you. I'll speak to him, then, with your permission."

"Fine. Then both of you, get some sleep. You're first team until further notice."

Both women nodded wearily and then left together for the crosstown cab ride. Cam walked out of the West Wing and started toward the Treasury Building. She needed to advise her superiors that the president's daughter's security team was seriously compromised, and that she couldn't be sure that all of her remaining agents were trustworthy. She had lost one agent, she had another who was critically injured, and the president's daughter had barely escaped a kidnapping or assassination attempt. At the moment she wasn't certain which. Given the degree of penetration by the perpetrators, it was entirely likely that by the end of the day, she would no longer *be* the president's daughter's security chief.

In some respects, that would make her life much easier—her personal and professional lives would no longer be in direct conflict. It would probably make Blair happier, and that was no small consideration in Cam's mind. But her duty was not done, and *would* not be done, until she had brought to justice the men and women behind the attack on Blair. Whether she retained her position with Blair's team or not, officially or unofficially, she intended to find them. Someone had tried to murder the president's daughter; someone had tried to murder her lover. She wanted retribution, and she wanted to make it very clear to whoever might be planning the next assault that Blair Powell was not a target for terrorism.

Stark called Renee's number for the seventh time. She got the same recorded message. Out of service. *All the news reports said the cellular carriers are either overloaded or down. It doesn't mean anything.*

She checked her personal voice mail. There was nothing from Renee. She hung up, then redialed her home number.

"Honey? Renee, if you check the answering machine and get this message, call me on my cell or at the usual place in DC. Okay? I love you, honey."

She ended the call and sat motionless on the side of the bed, staring at her hands. They were shaking. She was shaking. Everything inside of her felt like it was coming apart. She didn't know what to do, so she lay down on the bed fully clothed and curled on her side. She closed her eyes, knowing she wouldn't sleep, and waited for the phone to ring.

CHAPTER THIRTY-FIVE

Stewart Carlisle, a deputy director of the Secret Service and Cam's immediate supervisor, shot up from behind his desk the instant Cam walked into his office. "Christ Almighty, there are bodies lying all over Egret's apartment building. There was a dead agent right outside her goddamned door! *Tell me* that someone didn't almost shoot her."

Cam had a ferocious headache that wasn't helped by the lack of sleep or the need for a decent meal or the immediate interrogation. However, considering what had happened to the nation the day before, she understood that no one in law enforcement was going to be getting regular sleep or food or much in the way of a break for months to come. So, steadfastly ignoring the throbbing pain behind her eyes, she took her customary chair across from Carlisle's desk and waited for him to sit back down.

"The dead agent is David Foster, and—"

"I *know* who he is," Carlisle snapped. "What I *don't* know is what happened to him."

"He's also one of the people who tried to assassinate Blair Powell."

"Oh fuck. Jesus. Are you sure?"

The muscles on either side of Cam's neck tightened, but her voice was steady. "Positive."

"And he ended up dead—how?"

"I shot him myself."

Carlisle pushed back in his chair and expelled a long breath. "Well, we have a very big problem."

Grimly, Cam smiled. "That would be my assessment as well."

The first thing Blair did when Lucinda left her in her father's private study was to call Diane. "Hey. It's me."

"Oh thank God! I've been calling you nonstop for twenty-four hours." Diane's voice was tight with strain and sharp with accusation. "When I didn't get an answer, I walked down to your place. There was an FBI agent—"

"Renee? Was it Renee Savard? You remember her, the really nice—"

"Uh-uh. No. It was a guy, some stone-faced suit who didn't care who I was or what I had to say. God—are you all right? All I could think was that you'd been whisked away to some missile silo in Montana or someplace."

"I'm sorry," Blair said quietly.

"Where *are* you?"

"I'm in DC. I'll be here a while—I don't know how long."

Her uncharacteristically subdued tone must have registered with her friend, because Diane's next words were gentle. "But you're okay?"

"Yes. How about you?"

"It's—unreal here. But I'm...managing." Diane sighed. "I'm glad that Cam's mother left Monday for California."

"I have to call her next. The weekend, the show at the gallery— it all seems like another lifetime, not just a few days ago."

"I know."

"I'd better go, Di," Blair said, suddenly weary in body and soul. "I'll call you again soon. I love you."

"Oh God." Diane's voice wavered. "I love you. Take care of yourself—and Cam."

"Yes. I'll do that."

After speaking with Marcea and assuring her that both she and Cam were unharmed, Blair leaned her head back against the sofa and closed her eyes.

"Blair," a quiet voice murmured.

Blair jerked upright, her eyes darting open at the gentle touch upon her shoulder. Blinking in confusion, she stared at her father.

"Dad?"

"I'm sorry, honey," the president said softly. "I didn't mean to startle you."

Blair shook her head, pushing her hair back with one hand. "No, you didn't. I just...What time is it?"

He glanced at his watch. "Three in the afternoon."

"I thought Cam would be back by now."

"Every available agent in every branch of federal law enforcement is up to their eyeballs right now trying to get a handle on what happened yesterday." The president sat beside Blair and tentatively placed his arm around her shoulder. "I'm sure she's no different, and considering what happened at your apartment building yesterday," his grip on her tightened as he kissed her cheek, "she's going to be very busy."

Despite her surprise at his unusual physical display, Blair nevertheless leaned her head against his shoulder. "After all the hijackings...all the terrible things in the last twenty-four hours... what happened to me seems so minor."

"No," President Powell murmured. "What happened to you could easily have been the worst thing I've ever experienced. I'm just so grateful that you're all right."

"And *I'm* grateful that *you* weren't in DC yesterday."

The president gave Blair one last hug and then stood. "I'd like you to stay here for a while, until we have a better understanding of the ongoing threat level."

"How long?" Blair asked cautiously.

"A week." He met her eyes. "At least."

"I can't live here, Dad." Blair held his gaze. "I have a life. I have a lover who needs me, and we can't be together here."

"Cam is welcome to stay in the residence with you," he suggested quickly.

Blair laughed and shook her head. "Dad. Please. We really don't want to waste resources managing the press just now—and I doubt that Cam would agree anyhow. She's a...stickler...for protocol."

The president smiled. "That must drive you crazy."

"More than you can imagine." But Blair's tone was gentle, her eyes soft.

"The Security Council and the Secret Service, and now probably the CIA and FBI as well, are going to want to know what happened at your apartment yesterday, Blair."

"Is Cam in trouble?" At his silence, Blair stiffened. "How could she be? She saved my *life*."

"I don't know if she's in trouble. At this point, I don't even have a good idea where the investigations will focus—we don't even know where to start looking. But Cam will be asked some hard questions."

"You'll protect her, won't you, Dad?"

"If I can." His voice was steady and his tone unwavering. He never lied to his daughter.

Blair nodded silently. *She* would protect her lover, no matter what was coming.

Stark rolled onto her back and opened her eyes, disoriented and confused. There was very little light in the room. *Nighttime? Yes, it must be after eight o'clock.* She was in a strange room— the hotel. She was alone; she felt so empty inside. Finally, she registered what had awakened her.

She stared at the door. Someone was knocking. Someone was calling her name.

"Oh, Jesus!"

Stark bolted from the bed, nearly falling. Her legs were shaking, whether from hunger or fatigue or hope she didn't know, but she managed to propel herself across the unfamiliar room, only knocking into one footstool in the midst of her mad dash. The swift pain in her shin didn't even register. She'd been so distracted earlier, she hadn't flipped the security latch, and all she needed to do was grab the handle and pull. She yanked the door open, heart pounding. The surge of pain in her injured shoulder never even registered as her gaze fell on the woman in the hall.

"Oh, thank you...God, thank you."

"Yes. Oh, sweetie, yes."

They fell on each other, unmindful of the partially open door bouncing against their backs, talking over each other as their hands roamed frantically, seeking reassurance and comfort.

"Everything was so crazy—the attacks—"

"I thought you were in the building—"

"We had no word on casualties."

"I couldn't reach you—the phones, the security blackout—oh, baby, I was so afraid."

"I don't know what I would have done—"

"All I could think was I'd lost you."

"I love you so much."

"I love you. God, I love you."

"Don't let go."

"No, I won't. Never. Never."

Finally, Stark was able to pull away enough to look into Renee's eyes. The wellspring of pain in their depths broke her heart. With trembling fingers she caressed her lover's cheek, then drew her into the room, letting the door swing closed behind them. "Tell me what to do. Tell me how to help you."

Shaking her head, Renee pressed her face to Stark's neck and held on. Her voice was a fragile whisper. "As soon as we got word that the tower had been hit, we started evacuation procedures. We literally dumped Priority One files into the shredders on our way out the door. Within half an hour, we were outside on the street, but we still had no idea what was happening. Our radio links were still working, but it was chaos. None of the messages we could pick up were making any sense. Then..." her voice wavered, "we got an emergency call from Stacy Landers about an armed assault on Egret." She lifted her head and searched Stark's face, her expression a mixture of disbelief and terror. "Landers said there were dead and injured at the command center. I thought...oh God...the first thing I thought was that I'd lost you. And everything inside of me just... stopped."

"And I thought...when I heard about the towers...and then I couldn't reach you..." As tears streaked Stark's face, she fell silent. Unable to stop caressing Renee's back, her arms, her face, afraid that she might disappear at any second, Stark pressed a cheek to her lover's. "I love you so *much*. I thought I might die without you."

With a small cry, Renee clasped Stark more tightly. "I'm sorry, baby. Oh God, I'm sorry. I couldn't call you—I'm not even supposed to be here now. But when I finally got your phone messages, I had to see you." She stroked Stark's face, her neck, her chest, keeping her abdomen and thighs melded to her. "I had to touch you—not just talk to you. Oh, Paula, I love you. I love you."

Falling back on routine, because trying to make sense of what had happened in the last thirty-six hours was beyond impossible, Stark asked shakily, "You're investigating the attack on Egret?"

Renee nodded. "We were the closest team initially, and now... every other available field agent is working Ground Zero." She took Stark's hand, loath to move away from her even that much, and drew her toward the bed. Once there, she clicked on the bedside light before drawing Stark down beside her on top of the covers. "There's not much to say right now about the attacks—any of them. We don't know much."

"That's all right," Stark said immediately, turning on her side and wrapping an arm around Renee's waist. "I don't want to talk about it right now. I just want to get used to you being here—you being all right." She drew back, her eyes suddenly intent. "You are, aren't you? You weren't hurt yesterday?"

"No," Renee said quickly. "We were gone before it...really got bad."

Relieved, and feeling guilty for it, Stark just nodded.

"What about you?" Renee questioned, running her fingers up and down Stark's arm. "When I saw one dead agent in the lobby and another outside Egret's apartment, and then Mac—God, baby. You're all right?"

"Yeah." Stark's throat suddenly felt tight, and she blinked away the images of Mac bleeding into the ground and the memory of bullets slicing the air around her. "Just a nick."

Renee jerked. "A nick? You were hit?"

The near panic in her voice cleared Stark's head of the cobwebs of fatigue and horror as nothing else could have. She gathered Renee close, and with her lips to Renee's forehead, murmured, "I'm okay. A round just grazed my shoulder. It's nothing."

"I want to see."

Ignoring her demand, Stark questioned gently, "How long can you stay?"

"I need to be back tonight. Everyone at headquarters—God, everyone *everywhere*—is screaming for information. I don't think anyone is going to be sleeping for the foreseeable future."

"I know. I can't leave here yet, either. I don't know how long it will be before I can get back home."

"That's okay. I'll be there." Renee slid her leg between Stark's thighs and kissed her, massaging her back with firm hands as her lips glided softly over Stark's mouth. After a moment, she drew back, breathless. "As long as we'll be together eventually, that's all that matters."

"That's everything," Stark whispered. Then she caressed her palm along the length of Renee's thigh and tugged the blouse free from the waistband of Renee's slacks when she reached it. With her fingers caressing the warm, smooth planes of Renee's abdomen she confessed, "I need you so much. Can you stay for another hour? Can you stay and let me touch you?"

"Yes. Oh, yes."

Slowly, careful of bruises in body and soul, they tenderly brushed lips and fingers over the flesh they bared as they helped each other to undress. When at last they came together, breast to breast and belly to belly, their soft cries spoke of longing and love and gratitude. Gently, they joined passion and promises, holding each other safe in the only unassailable place remaining to them— within the sanctuary of their own hearts.

Blair scooped up the bedside phone on the first ring. "Yes?"

"This is the duty officer, Ms. Powell. I'm sorry to disturb you, but Commander Roberts sai—"

"Is she there?" Blair sat up, brushing the hair from her face with one hand as she checked the clock. 2:20 a.m. Once again, she'd fallen asleep without meaning to. The shower she'd taken earlier had relaxed her, and she'd only intended to stretch out on the bed for a minute. That had been four hours ago. "Please show her up."

"Yes, ma'am."

By the time the knock sounded at her door, Blair had donned a T-shirt and soft cotton drawstring pants. She opened the door to allow her lover entrance, nodded her thanks to the officer, and closed the door once more. Turning to Cam, she put both arms around Cam's neck and kissed her for a long moment. Drawing back, she appraised her critically. "You look exhausted."

"Yeah. I'm a little beat."

The very fact that Cam admitted to being tired told Blair just how close to the edge she was. She took Cam's hand. "Come on. Let's get you into the shower and then into bed."

"I probably shouldn't stay. I just wanted—"

"You're *staying*."

Through a fog of fatigue, Cam heard the edge of steel in her lover's voice. She was too tired to argue, and she really didn't want to. What she wanted to do was lie down beside Blair, pillow her head on Blair's breast, and sleep. "All right. But if you don't mind a little sweat, I'd rather just go to bed."

Blair smiled. "I've always thought a little sweat was sexy, when it was yours. Come on, Commander." As she led Cam through the suite, she asked as casually as she could, "Did everything go all right with the debriefing?"

Cam grimaced as she shrugged out of her jacket. "There wasn't much to debrief. The formal investigative panel hasn't even been convened yet. I just gave Stewart a general rundown."

"So there's likely to be more questions?" With practiced moves, Blair unbuckled the leather straps around Cam's shoulders and slid off the weapon harness. As if by second nature, she put the holster and weapon on the night table next to Cam's usual side of the bed.

"A lot of them," Cam grunted as she unbuckled her belt and after toeing off her shoes let her pants fall at her feet. "Starting tomorrow, probably." She pushed off her underwear and sat on the side of the bed to unbutton her shirt.

Blair leaned over, pushed Cam's hands away, and deftly worked the buttons open. She lifted the shirt off and tossed it onto the floor. "How's your head?"

Cam dropped back onto the pillows with a groan. "It's been worse." Then she extended one arm toward Blair. "Come lie down. I've missed you."

"Mmm, me, too." Blair settled onto the bed and encircled Cam's shoulders, drawing her close. "I love you."

"Thank God." Cam nuzzled her face against Blair's breast.

With a weary sigh, she murmured, "Everything will be different now, baby. The whole world's going to change."

Blair's heart lurched, but she pushed aside the fear. Cam was here, in her arms, solid and real. Their love was real. "We'll be all right as long as we have each other."

"Yes," Cam said faintly as she surrendered to exhaustion within the protective circle of her lover's arms. "Together...I promise."

The End

About the Author

Radclyﬀe is a member of the Golden Crown Literary Society, Pink Ink, the Romance Writers of America, and a two-time recipient of the Alice B. award for lesbian fiction. She has written numerous best-selling lesbian romances (*Safe Harbor* and its sequel *Beyond the Breakwater, Innocent Hearts, Love's Melody Lost, Love's Tender Warriors, Tomorrow's Promise, Passion's Bright Fury, Love's Masquerade, shadowland,* and *Fated Love*), two romance/intrigue series: the Honor series *(Above All, Honor, Honor Bound, Love & Honor,* and *Honor Guards*) and the Justice series (*Shield of Justice,* the prequel *A Matter of Trust, In Pursuit of Justice,* and *Justice in the Shadows)*, as well as an erotica collection: *Change of Pace – Erotic Interludes*.

She lives with her partner, Lee, in Philadelphia, PA where she both writes and practices surgery full-time. She is also the president of Bold Strokes Books, a lesbian publishing company.

Her upcoming works include: *Justice Served* (June 2005); *Stolen Moments: Erotic Interludes 2*, ed. with Stacia Seaman (September 2005), and *Honor Reclaimed* (December 2005)

Look for information about these works at www.radfic.com and www.boldstrokesbooks.com.

Other Books Available From
Bold Strokes Books

Distant Shores, Silent Thunder by Radclyffe. Ex-lovers, would-be lovers, and old rivals find their paths unwillingly entwined when Doctors KT O'Bannon and Tory King- and the women who love them-are forced to examine the boundaries of love, friendship, and the ties that transcend time. (1-933110-08-2)

Hunter's Pursuit by Kim Baldwin. A raging blizzard, a remote mountain hideaway, and more than one killer-for hire set a scene for disaster-or desire-when reluctant assassin Katarzyna Demetrious rescues a stranger and unwittingly exposes her heart. (1-933110-09-0)

The Walls of Westernfort by Jane Fletcher. All Temple Guard Natasha Ionadis wants is to serve the Goddess, and she volunteers eagerly for a dangerous mission to infiltrate a band of rebels. But once away from the temple, the issues are no longer so simple, especially in light of her attraction to one of the rebels. Is it too late to work out what she really wants from life? (1-933110-24-4)

Change Of Pace: *Erotic Interludes* by Radclyffe. Twenty-five hot-wired encounters guaranteed to spark more than just your imagination. Erotica as you've always dreamed of it. (1-933110-07-4)

Fated Love by Radclyffe. Amidst the chaos and drama of a busy emergency room, two women must contend not only with the fragile nature of life, but also with the mysteries of the heart and the irresistible forces of fate. (1-933110-05-8)

Justice in the Shadows by Radclyffe. In a shadow world of secrets, lies, and hidden agendas, Detective Sergeant Rebecca Frye and her lover, Dr. Catherine Rawlings, join forces once again in the elusive search for justice. (1-933110-03-1)

shadowland by Radclyffe. In a world on the far edge of desire, two women are drawn together by power, passion, and dark pleasures. An erotic romance. (1-933110-11-2)

Love's Masquerade by Radclyffe. Plunged into the often indistinguishable realms of fiction, fantasy, and hidden desires, Auden Frost discovers a shifting landscape that will force her to question everything she has believed to be true about herself and the nature of love. (1-933110-14-7)

Beyond the Breakwater by Radclyffe. One Province-town summer three women learn the true meaning of love, friendship, and family. Second in the Provincetown Tales. (1-933110-06-6)

Tomorrow's Promise by Radclyffe. One timeless summer, two very different women discover the power of passion to heal and the promise of hope that only love can bestow. (1-933110-12-0)

Love's Tender Warriors by Radclyffe. Two women who have accepted loneliness as a way of life learn that love is worth fighting for and a battle they cannot afford to lose. (1-933110-02-3)

Love's Melody Lost by Radclyffe. A secretive artist with a haunted past and a young woman escaping a life that proved to be a lie find their destinies entwined. (1-933110-00-7)

Safe Harbor by Radclyffe. A mysterious newcomer, a reclusive doctor, and a troubled gay teenager learn about love, friendship, and trust during one tumultuous summer in Provincetown. First in the Provincetown Tales. (1-933110-13-9)

Above All, Honor by Radclyffe. The first in the Honor series introduces single-minded Secret Service Agent Cameron Roberts and the woman she is sworn to protect—Blair Powell, the daughter of the president of the United States. First in the Honor series. (1-933110-04-X)

Love & Honor by Radclyffe. The president's daughter and her security chief are faced with difficult choices as they battle a tangled web of Washington intrigue for...love and honor. Third in the Honor series. (1-933110-10-4)

Honor Guards by Radclyffe. In a journey that begins on the streets of Paris's Left Bank and culminates in a wild flight for their lives, the president's daughter and those who are sworn to protect her wage a desperate struggle for survival. Fourth in the Honor series. (1-933110-01-5)